CALYX
BOOKS

SWITCH

SWITCH

by carol guess

calyx books ■ corvallis oregon

The publication of this book was supported in part with grants from the Oregon Arts Commission and the Meyer Memorial Trust.

With grateful appreciation, CALYX acknowledges the following "Immortals" who provided substantial support for this book:

Beta Anderson

Melissa Beal, in memory of Dr. Paul B. Beal

Katheryne C. Howe

The Microsoft Foundation

Cover art and design by Cheryl McLean.

CALYX Books are distributed to the trade by Consortium Book Sales & Distribution, Inc., St. Paul, MN, 1-800-283-3572.
CALYX Books are also available through major library distributors, jobbers, and most small press distributors including: Airlift, Baker & Taylor, Banyan Tree, Bookpeople, Ingram, Koen, and Small Press Distribution. For personal orders or other information write: CALYX Books, PO Box B, Corvallis, OR 97339, 541-753-9384, FAX 541-753-0515

∞

The paper in this book meets the guidelines for permanence and durability of the Committee on Production Guidelines for Book Longevity of the Council on Library Resources and the minimum requirements of the American National Standard for the Permanence of Paper for Printed Library Materials Z38.48-1984.

Alternative Library of Congress Cataloging-in-Publication Data
Guess, Carol.
   Switch. Corvallis, OR: CALYX Books, copyright 1998.
   1. Lesbians—Indiana—Fiction. 2. Indiana—Fiction. 3. Working class—Indiana—Fiction. 4. Mormon missionaries—Indiana—Fiction. 5. Butch and femme (Lesbianism)—Fiction. 6. Waitresses—Indiana—Fiction. 7. Diners (Restaurants)—Indiana—Fiction. 8. Lesbian fiction. 9. Magic realist fiction. 10. Bisexuals—Indiana—Fiction. I. Title. II. CALYX Books.

Library of Congress Cataloging-in-Publication Data
Guess, Carol
   Switch / Carol Guess.
        p.   cm.
   ISBN 0-934971-61-7 (hardcover: alk. paper) : $28.95   —ISBN 0-934971-60-9 (pbk: alk. paper) : $14.95
   I. Title.
PS3557.U34 38S95 1998   98-13703
813'.54--dc21   CIP
Printed in the U.S.A.
9 8 7 6 5 4 3 2 1

Published by CALYX Books
PO Box B ■ Corvallis, OR 97339

This book is dedicated with love to Brandon Derfler.

■ ■ ■

ACKNOWLEDGEMENTS

Thanks to my colleagues at Nebraska Wesleyan University for their intellectual enthusiasm, and to Liz Ahl, Deb Archer, Chauna Craig, Tonia Matthew, Lizanne Minerva, Ladette Randolph, Julie Thompson, Nichola Torbett, and Eric Wendt for powerful coffee, companionship, and conversation.

Special thanks to my family, Alison, Gerry, and Harry Guess, and to Sandy Yannone.

I'm indebted to my editors at CALYX Books for attentive readings and creative revision suggestions.

Chapter One appears in a slightly different form in *Love Shook My Heart: New Lesbian Love Stories*, edited by Irene Zahava, Alyson Publications, 1998.

Grateful acknowledgement is made for permission from the publisher to reprint an excerpt from *Epistemology of the Closet* by Eve Kosofsky Sedgwick, copyright © 1990 The Regents of the University of California.

People are different from each other. It is astonishing how few respectable conceptual tools we have for dealing with this self-evident fact.

—Eve Kosofsky Sedgwick,
Epistemology of the Closet

CONTENTS

PROLOGUE: CADDIE
■ ■
■

Once upon a time, I had a brother named Patrick, four years younger. Sweet and chubby and good. Handsome for twelve. He had a pal named Kathy McGuire, and they'd sit out in the yard after dinner and imagine what it must feel like to fly an airplane. They'd shut their eyes, reach their hands out, and say aloud the words to summon clouds. Looked kind of funny from the outside, but I understood about dreams, how important they are, what happens when kids don't have them. And just sitting underneath a shade of trees, waving their arms about and humming wasn't anything compared to the kinds of dream-trouble some kids got themselves into. Me and Ma counted ourselves lucky. Figured Patrick would be an easy boy to raise.

We didn't count on someone else giving him driving lessons.

Patrick knew something about cars. Our daddy was killed in a wreck when Pat was five; some drunk drove through a red, hitting Dad's truck on the driver's side. Nothing the ambulance could do. And Dad himself dried out for almost seven months. That was the year I stopped believing. Seemed like somebody's joke up above, and I'm not interested in a God who twists pain back around. But it taught me a lesson early. When I hit fifteen and some of my pals started driving, doing crazy kid things behind the wheel, I stayed serious. Wouldn't let anyone drive me anywhere unless I knew it was for a purpose. Wouldn't get in with anyone breathing fumes, and wouldn't let anyone pass the limit.

Ma and I figured Patrick would be the same. He was small when Dad died, but he understood about leaving and not coming back. Since he'd loved Dad the best of all of us, he had serious thoughts in his head after the accident.

What got in the way was his dream of being a pilot.

Some kids shuffle their desires like a dealer's deck. But Patrick decided on flying around the same time he started talking. Stuck with it till it was a part of him, much as his blond hair and changeable eyes, something people thought of when they thought of Patrick Ruby. Inseparable from his name.

It was all about sky and the way clouds called him.

Some evenings after supper, Patrick and I would walk Elvira, our beagle, around the ridge of hill beyond the elementary school. When we got to where we could let her loose, we'd talk or not (Patrick and I both appreciated a good silence), sometimes examining grass, sometimes examining the way the school building looked at dusk. Mostly I looked down, and Pat looked up. He'd watch the sky shift, and drift off himself till I had to shake him alive to bring him home before dark.

One night, when he'd drifted specially far and I'd had to shake his shoulders for what felt like minutes, I told him jokingly that I thought I'd lost him. He looked back at me, his face serious, and said someday maybe I would.

All the symptoms were there. He'd spend hours dreaming of his beloved, watching and wanting and whispering. He wrote silly poems, missed meals, planned his life amidst the aching blue.

I had to ask.

Patrick said yes. Said there was something between them, that he'd spoken and she'd responded. Said it was mutual, that he'd made a promise to come to her someday, since she couldn't come to him.

Sky being sky.

He'd sit out in the yard with Kath (folks said they'd be sweethearts, but I knew where his true heart belonged), and they'd dream up ways to meet the curly clouds and imagine how blue would look up close and consider the significance of rain and droughts and snow. I knew someday he'd leave us, find a route up into another air, but I figured I'd be gone by then anyhow, and old, and wouldn't much care about the way things happened.

Ma and I both thought he was safe for the time at hand. How could we guess about a car named Nancy?

I was mending the night it happened. Maybe sweeping also, maybe dishes thrown in—I know mending, because it was a Tuesday evening. Tuesday meant I also took the trash out, though maybe that week it never happened, and the dried food curdled in the can, stinking up the house.

Neither one of us would've noticed.

Because by then the Rubys were down to two.

I was working on someone's pleated dress shirt, pleats that needed stitches specially small. I was mending and had the radio on for com-

pany—probably I was daydreaming also, not about men (I never dreamed of romance, though I expected to marry one day because it was what all girls did and I was no different), but about Melly, my best friend in sixth grade, and where she was now (she'd moved to Texas and wrote to say she sometimes wore boots) and if I'd ever see her again and if I did, how we'd walk by the river, shoes in our hands, skirts (because we both wore dresses in summer, liking the feel of a strong breeze between our legs) hitched just over our knees—when I heard the sound, not from the back lawn (because then I'd have ignored it, thinking it was Jessup or Caitlin Fry, making trouble for their poor mother), but from the kitchen, so I knew it was Ma's voice, though it echoed like an animal's: a cat, clawing a terrible fight. My mouth was full of pins, and for a second I couldn't think how to take them out, just sat, my lips studded silver, my hands full of the needle and yards of sheer white cloth, unable to run or even walk in the direction of that steady, streaming sound. I did an ugly thing then. I turned the radio higher, high as it would go. I turned it up, took the pins out, and hummed as loud as my throat would burr, like an airplane buzzing overhead.

The solid strand of sound coming from the kitchen was the same color and texture as the cord Ma unreeled when Dad died.

Ma took slow steps into the living room and tugged the cloth from my hands, using it to wipe her face, over and over, till her cheeks were raw from the rubbing, over and over, till her motion turned from cleaning tears to tearing, tearing at her skin with the pleated cloth, rubbing down like digging, so I grabbed her wrists and held them to try to calm her but she was stronger, Ma, and so she freed them up and hit me, half on the cheek, half on the throat.

Patrick had gone off with JayCee Mathia. Kath had gone with them to watch, so she saw it all. Seems JayCee noticed what I'd also seen—Patrick gazing on the sky like it was a woman. Seems he made fun of that, and it broke Patrick's concentration. Seems he invited Patrick to drive, saying if Patrick really wanted to be a pilot—and wasn't that the one thing we all knew about Pat?—he'd need to learn how to drive a car: fast, up and over all obstacles. Because flying and driving weren't so different (JayCee said), and if Patrick couldn't drive like a real racer, well, he was no pilot, sky or no sky. JayCee challenged him then and there to a race out past Clarry Street, where they were putting in the ritzy new subdivision. There was a long stretch of unnamed dirt road. At the start of it there were some houses under construction, but the road stretched on for some length till it hit an abrupt curve, then another stretch of blank road, straight like an arrow until dead stop—a full screen of trees, miles of forest to be uprooted later for two-story colonials with oval swimming pools out back.

Pat said no at first.

But JayCee wore him down. Volunteered his brother's car for Patrick ("The Nancy," after the ship he'd sailed in the Navy), said he'd take his daddy's car himself. I guess Pat was so tempted that he forgot our father. Only Kath said—eventually—that really he remembered. He thought winning the race would undo the bad luck (the Rubys owned nothing else) that got started when our father's truck crumpled and bled.

Only thing was, Pat couldn't drive for beans. Oh, I'd given him a few careful lessons. When the time came for him to get his license, I wanted him to have a head start on caution and good sense. But I guess he thought his hands knew more than they did. Maybe all those years of dreaming flying convinced him that he was ready for the real thing. Or maybe dreaming and real had stopped being different by then.

It was a race, but it was also chicken. The idea was for JayCee and Pat to ride the nameless road, starting where the last of the skeleton houses stopped. Only it wasn't that whoever got to the forest first won. It was that whoever stopped first, or swerved his car away, lost.

The driver whose hood kissed the tree line would win.

JayCee said it was the difference between making out and fucking. Pointed to the forest and said you can press, but you can't go in. Kath told us all this later, when she finally spoke. Words just spilled from her throat like vomit. She couldn't seem to stop telling the story of every-thing JayCee and Patrick had said and done. So it was drive hard, and whoever let his hands swerve the wheel first, lost. Kath was set for judge, to stand midway down the second stretch, where she could see but wouldn't get in the way of sudden motion.

I never learned why Pat loved sky and not earth or water.

Would it have worked?

Can a man mate with an element?

I think she called to him, first in his language, then in hers. I think they touched and promised something. But was it a promise he was able to keep?

His car skidded when he made the curve and headed too fast towards the forest, the angle odd, so that when he turned the wheel to swerve, his voice tearing "Chicken," the car spun, tearing anyway towards trees, red Nancy a rapid spiral, till its hood bore deep into the thigh of an oak, glass creaming glitter-froth across bough after bough, Pat's body also meeting wood, making sounds like the sounds of birds when the forest is afire and they panic for direction, leaving their nests behind for smoke to brighten, then blanch.

Ma's hair bleached silver overnight.

Two years later she fell in love again.

Death was a sweet slow spouse. I lined her coffin with peach silk and pinned a note inside.

My eyes began changing colors after that.

When it storms now and clouds form circles, loosening rain that drizzles like falling glass, I sometimes allow myself to imagine that the sound of thunder is the sound my brother makes in his element.

CHAPTER ONE: CADDIE
■ ■
■

For several years I lived with a small, olive-skinned woman named Jo, who passed as a man at the brake factory where she worked. The factory was six blocks from our house; often, I'd walk with her in the mornings, carrying her lunch in a wide grey box, carrying an umbrella (for it rained more in those days), and stopping once or twice on the way to kiss. The men who worked Jo's shift knew my name, and when they saw us saying good-bye at the corner, they'd heckle Jo good-naturedly. It amazes me now to think it, but we were never found out, and after the first year or so we began to take the men's comments for granted, to believe in them ourselves, to believe that we were assured a place in their particular order.

We fought often, Jo and I, often and hard, but our fights were always contained within our walls. On the street, in the diner where I worked, and in front of the factory, we were unified, not because we felt the need to perform, but because our fights were always relative; outside, it was still us against them. And always, always, our fights ended with the same threat: Jo running her hands through my long hair, saying, "Don't you cut this, Caddie. Don't you change this." What there was between us—electricity and patience—traveled the bridge of my reddish-black hair. My feminine exterior made her invisible as a woman, even as it thrilled her. Wrapping her fingers around the nape of my skull, she'd say, "Don't you change this, Caddie. Caddie, don't you change."

She left me the night of our third winter's first real frost. She must've taken her things and burdened them on her shoulders. When I woke, the frost was settled in for four good months, and she was gone. I watched at the factory door for her small self, but she never appeared, and after a week I dared enter the office—the first time I'd ever been inside the factory. The narrow woman behind the battered desk put down the phone long enough to tell me Jo had quit, not on the day she'd left me, but two weeks before. I tried counting the ways we'd made love those fourteen days and felt sick and foreign inside myself, as if I was pregnant. The frost stayed and stayed, and each night I imagined her soft half smile, her harsh laugh, and the cold got beneath my skin and lodged, past the help of any fire.

With spring I grew restless and moved into an apartment. The two small rooms felt alternately cramped and vacant; the walls were cross-hatched with other people's scratches. I hung a photo of Jo on the wall of the second room, but her face loomed like some terrible Jesus and spoke to me like the Goose Girl's Falada, so I took it down. After that I played ugly, ordinary music so loudly and consistently that I was evicted. I moved across the street to a second-floor apartment whose sunny windows meant nothing to me. In between my shifts at the diner I slept, never dreaming but always wanting to, sometimes waking up with the taste of Jo's skin on my lips, as if my mouth had a memory.

Because Jo was the first person to say that she loved me, I did not know who I was now. I tried talking to other people, but all I wanted to discuss was passion, so I stayed quiet. I had nothing to help me decipher the world or understand what it meant that I wanted no part of it.

I did not know where to go.

I had met Jo by accident, known her for a woman and wondered. It had happened by chance, but now I couldn't rely on chance. I knew there were others like us because Jo had told stories. She'd been in love and had been loved before. So yes, there were others, and I knew in my blood that there were others. But where—I didn't know that. I kept my eyes open, that was all.

After Jo, for a while there was David. The first day he appeared in the diner I stood over him to take his order, and he hung his head like some shy horse. I liked the way his black hair lay ragged just above his collar. Somehow I knew even before he showed his face that he would look like Jo; the surprise was that he looked more like Jo than himself. He courted me hard and might have taken me far away from Cartwheel, Indiana, to one of those warm southern states he talked about often. I could've had fat babies and a house with a garage. But kissing David wasn't like kissing Jo. He'd press me against his pickup, fumble with my shirt, grab my nipples with hands curled almost into fists. I liked the feel of his hips against mine, but my breasts hurt and his tongue moved too fast. Kissing David wasn't like kissing Jo. Let me say simply that he lacked some things and had an overabundance of others. Let me say simply that he moved on, taking a young girl with him, and that I stayed to serve coffee and the $1.75 special to the regulars, five days a week, 5:45 a.m. to 3:00.

Maybe eight months went by after David. Some things inside me closed. At first I worried that they'd never open back, but after a time I stopped worrying and began to accept the shut-down feeling. I looked neither at women nor men, neither left nor right as I walked to work. When I ate my lunch, I sat in a corner of the diner, reading magazines full of recipes and hints on how to please a husband once you had one. I sat alone, and the regulars knew me well enough to know I wanted it that way. I felt myself going gradually ice but couldn't stop it and wasn't sure I wanted to. It seemed necessary. Most folks knew about Jo, so I had sympathy—they'd say, "Her man left her." So I was safe and cold and well fed in Cartwheel, Indiana, and I did not imagine my life switching gears.

Marv and Helen, the owners of the diner, hired their girls carefully, knowing that a good waitress keeps customers better than good food. Selena was the pretty one: flirty and sassy, still single, serving up hope with each order. Bet was married-steady, calm and attentive; the regulars chose Bet's tables when they were tired or needed their food done quick. Picky eaters chose Bet. And me? I was the listener. I got the religious fanatics and the hard up and the angry young men who planned to leave someday for Indy. We balanced out, but Marv and Helen thought there was room for another. The diner was large, with more tables and floor space than Big Boy—we waitresses had it tough. We not only took orders and served, we also bused, took turns at the register, and filled take-out orders—big business, what with the factory and all. There were two cooks, Marv and Bobby. Helen managed the business end of things, and the three of us took care of customers up front. Service had gotten so frantic that Marv and Helen wanted another girl. "We'll float Bet," Helen explained. "She can work in back with Bobby and come up front with Caddie, Selena, and the new girl when the register and carryout get busy."

So Marv and Helen hung up a sign, and for over a week we had girls streaming in and out, a regular pageant, almost as good for business as the spring tractor pull.

Selena and Bet and I watched the parade skeptically. We wanted to be sure there was no duplication. She had to be different, not competition but complement, someone we could rely on but shove around a little at first, someone who wouldn't break, but not a tough girl. When Gwen walked in, Bet nudged me and Selena pointed; they knew, and when I saw her, I knew too. Gwen would be the sweet one, the one to giggle, nod shyly, and occasionally fumble, serving Marigold Spencer the blueberry-walnut instead of the pecan pie. We all three conferred, and I walked back to tell Marv we'd spotted her, that she was Gwen, and that she was to be the girleen among us.

Gwen started working that week. At twenty-one she was pretty in a childish way, round face pale and cheerful, gold hair to her waist, brown eyes set slightly too far apart for beauty. When she laughed, she covered her mouth with her right hand; she had buck teeth and hated her own smiles. Her dresses were handmade, pinks and blues, small flowers pulled around her waist in simple stitches. "Gwennie," the factory men called her, and the name stuck. She looked young and simple, but she wasn't stupid. She earned her tips, flirting in her own shy and awkward way, acting the part of someone slightly more naive and cheerful than she really was. She could've been a threat to all of us, but instead she deferred. Used to older sisters, she gave us the better tables, pressed her back against the counter when we needed to pass with trays of food, and waited to use the register.

Some weeks after Gwen first started working, there was a morning rush—suddenly a line to sit, everyone short-tempered and hurried. Even Arthur Parks, a calm, decent man who tipped well and never asked for refills, sounded impatient. Things didn't calm down until ten-thirty, when the place cleared out as suddenly as it had filled. As the last of the factory men filed through the back exit, the front door jangled and Cory Flint walked in, just off from the 2:00 a.m. to 10:00 shift at the bank where he worked as a watchman. As I served Cory his hash browns, he motioned towards Gwen.

"New girl?" he asked, and I nodded. "She looks too young to be feeding strangers."

"Better than feeding a strange man of her own," I sassed back, and he grinned, showing off his gold-capped tooth. Then he looked down at the blue-rimmed plate I'd set before him.

"She sure is a pretty one," as he unrolled his fork and spoon and knife from inside a paper napkin. "Sure has some pretty dress on, with flowers scattered all unusual like, up around her waist." I watched as he cut his fried ham into little triangles. "Sure has some pretty field of flowers on, that's right."

I turned his coffee cup upright and filled it silently, then walked behind the counter, where Gwen and Bobby were looking over a newspaper someone had left behind. "I'm going outside to catch a smoke," I said, to neither one of them in particular. "Call me if someone hits one of my tables."

Out back on the stoop, I held a cigarette between my fingers, wanting only the feel of it, not the taste or the heat. The sky was cloudy with factory smoke. I watched the blackish coils go grey, then fade into the dirty expanse of sky. To my right, a huge cross rose up from the Baptist church. To my left, cars lined up for the bank's drive-through window. I thought for a second about Jo, how she'd loved cars, her fascination with anything that meant easy motion. I stood up and dusted off my skirt, but as I pulled the belt straight around my waist, I felt something close over me. Without wanting to I shut my eyes and put my fingers to my lips, imagining that I was standing in our old yellow kitchen while Jo knelt down in front of me, her hands on my hips, my hands on her head, her eyes buried inside me.

When Gwen touched my shoulder I jumped. "You've got a man," she said. "Table five. Not a regular." I tossed my unlit cigarette into the grass and followed her inside.

That night I dreamed about Gwen. I woke long before my alarm and sat up in bed, my arms wrapped around my knees, listening to the clock as it toyed with its minutes. The sky outside was black, cut with stars that looked close but which I knew to be unreachable. Then I got up, slipped on my robe, and pulled a book from the nightstand. In the kitchen I cut myself a piece of pie and put on water for tea. Opening the book, I read, "In the beginning...." I read for two hours, until it was time to dress for work. I made myself read out loud, without stopping, because I felt dirty and dizzy with what I'd seen myself do. Gwen wasn't Jo, I knew that much. Gwen had long hair like me, wore dresses and heels, flirted with the men from the factory. Gwen had a beau. I'd seen them kiss in the parking lot before work. Gwen was a woman. I didn't know what wanting her would make me.

All day at work I broke things: plates empty and full, coffee cups, saucers grey with men's stubbed ash. At two Bobby came up behind me and tugged on the knot of my apron.

"Yo, honeypie. Marv's got a note out for ya," he said. I stomped into the kitchen, where Marv was flipping burgers on the grill.

"Caddie, seems like something might be bothering you. Seems like you probably aren't running up our china bill just because. You gonna tell me what that something is? Or you gonna tell me, maybe, that it's

none of Marv's business but that you'll handle those plates a ways better
next time, huh?" Marv watched the meat carefully while he spoke, tilt-
ing his head, scraping at the grill with a spatula.

I liked Marv. He'd been kind to me all five years I'd worked at the
diner. I knew he wanted me to tell him something he could understand
and fix. But what to say? "Marv," I imagined myself saying to the tiny
man bent over a row of frozen burgers, "Marv, my man Jo was really
someone's Josephine. And now this Gwen we've got, well, I've taken to
dreaming about kissing her. I think I'm in love with her. And I've been
saying my Bible to scare it out of me, but I'm afraid that hasn't done
anything but make me more curious about her little flowered dress."
Thinking this way I laughed, and even with Marv's surprised face turned
towards me I couldn't stop laughing. My mouth stayed open and sound
came out, sound like something tangled unwinding, sweet and jagged
at once, out of place, unstoppable.

CHAPTER TWO: JO
■ ■
■

Roy Birdy's a factory man. Works on the line like myself. We talk at lunch, mostly about fishing, wrist pain, and Jesus. We're in agreement on two out of three. On the line, that's enough to earn you a pal. So when Roy turned forty-five and his wife threw a party, I found myself invited. They wrote out cards and everything. Guess I should've known it'd be more than a couple of fellas sitting around on the Birdys' porch, spitting cig butts into the bushes, talking union, rolling their wrists the way linemen do. But I didn't think much about it, just showed up dressed ordinary, with a store-bought pie for a present. When I saw it was fancy, I almost turned around to go, but Roy's wife Bet saw me hesitate and touched my shoulder. Set a beer in my hand, told me I couldn't leave till I'd finished at least one.

I might've held to one if the Birdys' maybe-daughter hadn't spent the party serving. I was sitting on a spongy orange chair in their living room, wondering how much longer I had to listen to Sid Harkins talk about carpal tunnel syndrome, when Selena Martinez sashayed in with a plate full of nutcake, sliced like paper, and a bowl of butter pats wrapped in foil. That's when I realized it was a diner party. Bet works at the M&H, long hours in a five-day week just like Roy. Proud of what she does, so when she celebrates, she takes the diner home. When I saw the butter, folded up neat as hospital corners, I knew Marv and Helen were in charge of the kitchen. Figured Selena was our waitress for the day—not my choice, mind you, but tolerable.

I'd started in on my third slice when the door to the kitchen opened again, and it was time for another pass around. Cheese biscuits, buttery on top, with a little red pepper tucked away inside like teeth. Cream cheese to go with, a thick slab sliced like bread, still drizzled with ice water from being kept cold. On top of the biscuits, the cheese melted into cream, and it was hard to keep our plates full of anything but crumbs and drizzle. We kept eating, and the kitchen kept the biscuits coming, till Bet warned us to save space for cake because it was Roy's birthday, and we had to sing, after all.

Selena took our plates, and it really did feel like the diner then, with Bet nudging me and Selena winking. Lots of folks push me towards her and I let them, but only so far. Come too close and I get stubborn, stir my feet in the soil and stay. Bet and Selena know that now, both of them. Early on, Selena tried harder, but I made it clear that wasn't what I wanted. Now it's a game, and since it keeps folks from asking questions, I play along. And there I was playing, winking back at Selena, tapping my foot as if I'd found something to celebrate, when the door to the Birdys' kitchen swung open, their maybe-daughter's eyes looked through me, and I knew she'd seen my secret body.

We all sang "Happy Birthday."

Roy blew at the cake till his face turned damp.

Bet forked slices onto paper plates and Roy unwrapped his beer coasters, tie, and white cotton socks and Cory Flint spilled coffee and Arthur Parks asked if he could light one up and all the while I kept my eyes on their carpet—pale blue plush—and soon there were cake crumbs scattered in swirly designs and then white ribbon and green wrapping paper and then scuff marks from Tom Jensen's shoes when he got up to go home to walk the dog and Selena's pointy-toed brown shoes beside my work boots and then she was gone too and so was their maybe-daughter and I looked up and almost everyone was gone but me.

Bet smiled. I think she thought I'd fallen asleep. Gave me what was left of the biscuits to take home, even wrapped some cream cheese in wax paper and slipped it along. She was kind, Bet, but wrong also—I hadn't slept.

I'd been found out.

Caddie was the first woman who knew right away. No fogginess, no sham. She knew, for no past reason. It was a sign of her attention to the world around her. The whole time I knew her, she took in more things than most people. She saw me and wondered. I wanted to tell her I knew she saw but couldn't. So I hid my head and crammed in cake. Watched icing nuggets and sticky crumbs flutter to the carpet till it was safe to sit up, unfold my cap from my back pocket, and shake the Birdys' hands good-bye.

I spent the next few days on the line thinking about ways to ask Roy Birdy about his maybe-daughter. I couldn't remember him mentioning kids, but then factory men are quiet about personal things, and even though the two of us counted each other close, we never got nosy about bedroom business. Once in a harvest moon he'd tell me something about Bet, like when she had that operation and he was throwing up his food over it, or when they had a fight because she wanted him in church where he said eight years ago he'd never set foot again. But mostly we talked the usual, with sports, beer, or union business for variety. It didn't strike me funny that he might have a grown-up daughter, twenty-three, twenty-four or thereabouts, and just keep forgetting to mention her to me in the four years we'd worked the line. What I didn't know was how to ask after her without sounding like a scammer. Besides, I didn't want to lead into questions I couldn't answer. So I worked the topic of conversation back around to his birthday, which wasn't hard because Roy enjoys a party. I figured I'd start in on the cake, try to work up to the lady whose face was lit by tiny candles.

Roy beat me to it. He was talking about Bet, the hours she put into planning. Said she'd asked around at the diner for special help with serving and cooking. Said everyone was plenty happy to help, even Caddie. I tried to remember which one of the diner girls was called Caddie. My puzzlement must've shown on my face, because Roy swallowed his bite of sandwich and nodded.

"Caddie's new. She's the one made up the cake."

I laughed. Roy asked me what was funny, and I explained that I took her for his daughter.

"Naw. No kids. Don't much like the noise and Bet's always been afraid to carry."

I tried to get him to talk some more about Caddie, but he changed the subject back to birthdays, to how presents were always socks and such, how no one ever thought to give a man what he might really use. I just nodded, like I knew what he was talking about. Like I agreed. There are things I've told Roy and things I'll never tell. What a man might really use is one of the latter.

I became a man because the city of Cartwheel left me no choice.

After junior year in high school, I skipped out of Martinsville for Indy. It was the usual story. I worked the graveyard shift cleaning toilets in a second-rate hotel and shared a two-room place over a bowling alley. I still dressed like a girl back then—an ugly one, for sure, but still a girl. I had two denim skirts and one bra that I washed out once a week in the sink. The girls I lived with were always trying to poof me up, but even then I kept my hair short and didn't bother with the razor. When they tried fixing me up with so-and-so's brother I told them I was engaged to a Navy man whose ship never docked. I stayed there four years. My roommates changed periodically, and my job, but I couldn't tell the difference. Everything was one long blur. I kept myself going by reminding myself I was lucky to be alive.

When I turned twenty-one, everything happened. My roommates at that time were prissy ones, Eenie and Meenie I called them, really Fran and Sally. They insisted on dragging me out for a beer. We dropped into the slimy dungeon of some bar. The stairs seemed to fall forever into a basement where the walls were lined with kissing couples, men riding women's thighs, women smearing lipstick over men's stubbled cheeks. Even with the beer I was clawing to get out. I couldn't stand it. What had always been wrong with me was suddenly more so. I slipped into the bathroom, told them I was sick, and walked myself home, leaving Eenie and Meenie to find their own evening's entertainment.

It was on the way home that I got the idea.

Now, no matter who you are, no matter what your persuasion, by the time you hit seventeen you know what a queer is and where they meet. It's street knowledge, meant to keep you from saying "No" or "Yes" in the wrong tone of voice.

I knew that The Alley was a queer bar because Nadine and Monica, several roomies back, kept giggling over one of the men in their office. "Flaming!" Nadine would toss her ponytail, and Monica would jab me in the ribs. I'd giggle through bites of hamburger, since I knew I was supposed to find it funny. "Bet he hangs out at The Alley." Monica winked at me. I winked back, knowingly, I thought, though later she put her hand on my leg and massaged my thigh. "Are you OK, Josephine? You look sort of queasy."

The Alley. I found myself standing in front of a tiny sign marking an unlit doorway in an alley even I wasn't ordinarily brave enough to walk through at night. I knocked. No answer. I knocked again, then figured it might be open. It was. The man at the door, beefy and fierce-looking, took me in with one long glance, then snatched too many bills from my hand and let me pass.

As my eyes adjusted to the darkness, I saw that this bar was just like any other, and my stomach flip-flopped—disappointment. There were men and there were women. Then I began noticing that at some of the tables, men sat in pairs. Were they holding hands, that couple in the far left corner? Was that a kiss I glimpsed out of the corner of my eye? Luckily for me, as I stumbled to a stool by the bar, some sweet faggot, surely an Eagle Scout in a former life, took me by the elbow and smiled into my astonished face.

"You got the wrong bar, butchie," he said. "That'd be The Mermaid, over on Michigan. Lemme draw you directions." I still have that scrap of paper somewhere. It was the start of something and the end of something else. As I made my way out the door, he called after me, not unkindly, "One more thing, butchie—lose the dress!"

It took me two weeks to work up the nerve to visit The Mermaid. The rest is history—in Indy, anyway. I spent a blissful couple of months scamming, till one unfortunate day Eenie (or was it Meenie?) walked in on me with a femme spread open on my bed like a pearly oyster. My squeamish roomie squealed, and the next thing I knew, all my worldly goods were occupying sidewalk space, the femme's heels click-clacking away while I scrambled to pick up what I could and stuff it into a garbage bag.

"Dyke!"

I fled the street, all my possessions on my back. A pack rat. That was how, at 1:47 p.m. on a Tuesday afternoon, midsummer, I hopped a bus bound for nowhere, towns even smaller than Martinsville, the sorts of towns I'd vowed never to set foot in again.

It was a mistake, but I'm a stubborn one. Once I make a mistake, I keep going with it until my luck turns and sour tastes sweet again. I slept on the bus, my cheeks heavy with shame and fright. When I woke up, the bus was pulling into a tiny, grit-covered station with a faded sign overhead: "Cartwheel, Indiana, Welcomes YOU!"

It was smoke that lured me, even then. Smoke, barreling into the sky from factory stacks too big for the tiny town to contain. Smoke, and I remembered my granddad's saying—"Where there's smoke, there's jobs." Smoke, so without letting myself think things through, I hopped off the bus, careful not to let my things fall through the hole just starting in the plastic bag, and set off in the direction of what looked to be the town's main drag.

Dinnertime, and was I hungry. The first place I came to was a Big Boy. With a wad of money in my pocket (I'd been planning to pay next month's rent early—not my fault they lost an honest roomie), it felt safe to splurge, so I went ahead. "Please wait to be seated," the sign chided. So I waited.

And waited, wondering impatiently why the "Sir" the nice waitress kept calling wasn't budging.

It took awhile to realize "Sir" meant me.

Do all of us who pass come to the other sex by accident? Manhood found me, there in the Big Boy. I was so used to roomies who knew me as Josephine, so used to folks who took my gawkiness, my resistance to girlishness as simple tomboyishness, that it hadn't occurred to me someone might honestly confuse me with a man. But once it happened, it was like nicotine. No going back, no stopping, at least not without the kind of pain that tears you from yourself. I turned to face the waitress—"Maxine-May-I-Help-You," her name tag blurted—and accepted my destiny.

Chicken fried steak never tasted so fine.

When I asked after lodging, she said there was one motel, but too far down to walk. I could see in her eyes that she wanted to make me another kind of offer, but I wasn't ready yet for serious barter. Sex is low on my list when I'm in danger. So I smiled a wait-and-see smile, strolled back to the bus station, hid my bag under a bench, and waited till dark, when I curled beside my bag and snored away.

Come dawn, I sniffed the air for smoke and set off after. The factory looked close but receded like a mirage the closer I came. Finally I found myself standing before a scruffy woman in what passed for a front office. "Job," I heard myself say, and then my nickname, "Josie. Josie Waddell." When the nice, nearly deaf lady recited my name back to me—"Joseph," she called me, "Joseph Waddell"—I opened my mouth to correct her and then stopped, teeth scraping air.

I'm still thankful.

Joseph Waddell bought a pair of denim overalls, a pair of jeans, a packet of men's white undershirts, and three plaid shirts: one red, one blue, one green and purple (for Fridays). Joseph Waddell bought a pair of work boots and five pairs of thick cotton socks.

Joseph Waddell bought a razor and a packet of blades.

When Caddie's eyes met mine that first time in the Birdys' living room, over candles tufting a field of white sugar, she saw me and wondered. I wanted to tell her I knew she saw but couldn't. So I ducked my head and studied carpet but didn't forget. The day after my talk with Roy, I woke up a good hour early, picked my Friday plaid shirt, and tied my boot laces especially tight. Opened the diner door quick, so I'd look casual. Stood a minute, pretending to wind my watch, while I figured out which tables were hers. Then walked over to a booth, not looking at women or men, not looking left or right. Sat down, as if I was still sleepy. Didn't meet her eyes when she filled my cup with coffee.

I'd been hoping for brave. But brave didn't find me. Instead, I hid my head in the menu and called on breakfast like Caddie could bring me ordinary food and leave me satisfied. She wrote the order carefully in her little book. She had a name tag on, white to match her blue and white checkered apron, with her name cut into the plastic, C and A and two Ds, then I and E to top it off. It wasn't a name I'd heard before. It wasn't a name to roll easily off the tongue. Caddie—it reminded me of golf. I tried to think what I knew of golf: green lawns, moneyed folk traveling in little carts, wheels frisking beneath fringed tops. Was she from money, did her daddy play golf in those expensive knitted shirts like men on television? She didn't look like money. She smelled of hot water and salt and some kind of fruit—that part changed with the day's pie.

I started making time for breakfast, a meal I've never found much use for. I'm not a morning person. Ten till midnight are my best hours; I like to run my clock up sharp against the new. I'd rather leave soggy scrambleds and barley puffs to other folks, folks who maybe look forward to the beginning of things, instead of craving the winding down. So a couple of the factory men teased me when weekdays found me suddenly hungry for chilled tomato juice and toast. To keep them from teasing me to torture, I sat in someone else's section at least twice a week. Tried to make it look like picking Caddie's tables was pure coincidence, tried so hard, in fact, that Caddie told me later she had no idea I was interested in her.

"There I was flirting, and you acted all bored and sleepy."

We laughed about it later, but her words stung. I thought I'd been courteous and subtle. Were my courting manners so clumsy, so childish as to pass unnoticed? I wanted to think I'd been smooth and sleek, that a blind man could've mistaken me for a cat's belly.

It took three months of breakfasts before ordinary chatter turned to sweethearts' banter. She got me nervous when she filled my coffee. No surprise when one day I tipped my cup at the sight of her coming. She stopped, dead in the aisle, a pot of hot coffee in each hand, and laughed and laughed. Not a giggle—Caddie wasn't much for silliness—but deep, winding up from her belly, and very loud. All of Caddie's sounds startled people. Even her sighs shook still air. I felt my back break sweat, and I grabbed for a napkin to try to wipe away the hot black drip. Abruptly she stopped laughing, put the coffeepots back on their coils, and marched over to my table. Made me take my hands away, mopped at the spill with the cloth she kept tucked in the waistband of her apron. A green cloth with white ribbing, one of those handy cloths that soaks things up like a sponge, but stays thin and flexible.

"This here's a magic cloth," she said, laying it down lengthwise to catch the spill. "Makes any mistake vanish before your very eyes."

Around us, the diner had gone back to its ordinary chatter. No one was listening. It was the two of us, and I understood her meaning.

"I'm not one for vanishing."

The first lie I ever told her.

"What about mistakes?" She didn't glance away from where she was rubbing an old spot on the table, grit smudged and dried into a scratch.

"If you think you know something, you probably do."

Caddie's eyes were a different color. They were always changing. She looked through me instead of over, flicked the cloth one last time, took my dirty saucer, and stole a clean one from the table behind. "I'm old-fashioned. I like water and watching sky. I have Sundays and Mondays off. I go to the lake sometimes."

"Sunday's fine."

"You have to ask."

"Caddie, would you like to go to the lake with me this Sunday?"

She didn't answer, but wrote on the check, "3 p.m. is a fine time."

Trouble was, neither one of us owned transportation. I'd seen her walking about town, not only to work but carrying groceries and even laundry. The next day I stopped by the diner and sat in her section, shamefaced. But when I told her my dilemma, she just laughed.

"I'll borrow Selena's or Marv and Helen's. Give me your address, and I'll stop on by."

Three o'clock sharp, and she showed up on the stoop of my apartment with Marv and Helen's truck and a basket full of food she'd filched from the diner: ham sandwiches, pecan pie, applesauce in a round glass jar, coffee to start and finish things off. All the way south on 37 we were raucous, Caddie singing bits of popular songs, me whistling, making cracks about the advertisements, imitating the DJ's voice. But once we hit Bloomington, out towards the lake, we both got quiet. I don't know if it was the caffeine wearing off (we'd each had a cup for the road) or shyness taking over or the sight of all those trees to make us feel small and unimportant in the scheme of things. I don't know, but we both got quiet quick, and by the time we reached the lake, I had my window up, my face pressed against the glass.

Caddie had to drive twenty minutes or so to find a spot away from all the kids and campers. We found what looked to be a quiet shady circle, but the ground was wet and there was trash scattered about, broken glass and the like. So we were about to get back in the car when Caddie pointed past me to a clump of trees. Some folks were gathered there, but they were leaving. We hauled the basket in their direction. As they passed us, one of the little kids tugged on Caddie's skirt. She stopped and waved, one hand, while he waved back at her with two.

I set a towel on a patch of grass. The food was good. When I asked her if it was stolen, she laughed, that clear, winding laugh. If there were folks beyond the trees, they would've known it was Caddie. She said the food wasn't stolen, just borrowed. I don't remember what else we talked about. It wasn't raucous, but it wasn't serious either. After we'd eaten all we could, Caddie lay on her back (dirtying her dress but not caring), shaded her eyes, and spoke.

"Is Joseph your real name? Or is your real name longer?"

"Longer."

"Another question. What do you do with secrets?"

"Keep them."

"Do you ever tell?"

I scootched over to where she lay and touched her elbow. She took my hand and put it on her breast. We kissed and did date-like things, not too heavy. I didn't let her touch me anywhere that might tell stories. There was no saying the words out loud. Once said, if the risk was lost, we'd separate, and I'd leave town. The full length of my real name was that serious.

It was dark when we drove back to Cartwheel. She invited me into her house with a smile that made me think of fire. Was the cloth she used to swipe spills at the diner some witch's scrap, a newfangled crystal ball? I wanted to believe that when she wiped a table clean, her eyes went from green to blue on purpose. That the blue looked into the shiny surface and saw in the gleam somebody's future history. I wanted to believe she'd whisper "Josephine" once we'd settled into her kitchen and lit up.

Instead we sat silent, staining the air with cigarettes, admiring violets in a thick glass jar. We sat silent, too newly met to read each other's fear.

That was when I thought of Jackie's letter. Rummaging in my jacket pocket, I found the yellow envelope: slit at the top, daisies around all four sides, a stamp with a cowboy roping a steer. The return address was a small square sticker with her married name, Mrs. Clarence Robert Hadland, and a little string of flowers underneath the zip. My sister's big on flowers, especially the yellow kind.

I set the envelope face down on the table. Rubbing up against the sticky vinyl cloth was my given name—Josephine Sue Waddell. I tugged the letter out with my right hand, steadying the upside-down envelope with my left.

"Read it out loud." I handed Caddie the letter and listened while her voice echoed Jackie's words. How she hoped I'd found work in Cartwheel. How she missed me, how the cows didn't give as much now that I wasn't there to oversee the milking. How no one wanted to clean the snakes out from behind the tractors. She wished I'd write, send a picture. She and Clarence were trying again. The doctor said the miscarriage didn't mean it couldn't ever happen. One of Billy's dogs got caught in the combine. The Jackson's oldest had taken up drinking again. She prayed at night—for me and for the family dead and for conception, two minutes each.

"Does she use a timer?"

I thought of Jackie, kneeling beside her bed, palms touching. She always prayed with her hands stretched straight up above her; she claimed it was because it brought them nearer to God, but I think it was because the ache in her arms made her feel pious. She used to cut herself, not deep but skimmy like a paper cut, Christmas and Easter eves. Said she heard a voice tell her, "Do it." Same voice told her yellow flowers bring luck, that she looks good in blue but not orange, and to marry Clarence.

I told Caddie maybe. It wasn't out of the thinkable.

"What if one of us is wrong?" It was Caddie said it. She watched me as if waiting for something to show.

Our chairs were still touching, but our bodies were our own. She wanted me to speak, and I wanted her. It began to seem that nothing would ever happen. The violets would die and fall off, and the air would collect more ash. We'd go to work when morning came but never speak again because we'd come too close for friendship but not close enough for daily honey. I was mute with despair when she asked if she could tell me a story. Her eyes changed color as she told about her brother, who'd loved sky but lost at chicken because he waited too long.

I stayed listening even after Caddie finished speaking. Outside rain drizzled like falling glass. Our hands met on the envelope, together starting the slide towards the edge of the table, towards *yes*.

CHAPTER THREE: CADDIE
■ ■
■

If I had my Gwen, we'd circle each other's lips with red paint. We'd trade dresses, my waist snug against her fabric's smaller measure, her ankles nearly covered by my longer hems. We'd primp each other up, undoing it all come evening's dark and dropped curtains.

But not like dolls. Not ever dolls.

Beautiful animals.

It was because Gwen was so beautiful that breakfast was hell. She'd set each saucer down with sugar, and the men sassed back. Not brash like Selena, but not cautious like Bet either. Just this side of awkward, as if flirting was that day's lesson. You'd think the men would've caught on, realized no one stays innocent that long. But they fell for it, and it got to where men took Gwen's tables first. Even some of the regulars, like Arthur Parks and Cory Flint and Mitch Haskell, steady men Bet and Selena and I had served years running. One rainy Thursday Roy Birdy walked in, head buried in the paper, and sat in Gwen's section. Real casual, like it was an accident. Didn't meet my eyes when I brushed past him, but I saw him glance up at Gwen and smile like some busted star.

I waited for Selena and Bet to notice.

Some Saturday nights the three of us went to the Yellow Horse for drinks and pool. Jo taught me how to work a basic cue, and too much practice taught me wicked aim, so it was always Selena and Bet against Caddie Solo. Which was how I liked it—the two of them close, me on the edge of inside.

Maybe four months into Gwen's beginning at the diner, Selena nudged me while I was ringing up a takeout. "The Horse tonight?" When I nodded, she lifted her tray into the air and whispered, "Just three."

I didn't have to ask who'd be the odd girl out.

That night the first game was mine, the second Selena and Bet's. I was setting up for another when Selena put an arm around my waist.

"Tie's enough. Time for talking."

Bet ordered a pitcher and we settled into a booth behind the pool tables. While I fumbled in my bag for a loose cigarette, Selena cleared her throat.

"Seems like we've got a serious problem on our hands. Seems like some certain person wants to steal our men's attention. Tips and flirtations are flying in one direction and one direction only in today's wind. Am I alone, or do you two ladies see the situation the same?"

Bet nodded yes, yes, and patted our hands. I summoned Gwen's face to my memory's eye. What would it be like to take Gwen out for a night at the Yellow Horse? I wondered if she played pool, if she'd need me to teach her. I imagined standing behind her, angling her hips properly against the table, stretching my arm atop hers along the cue. Jo and I used to play for hours. If we lost the table, we'd climb upstairs to our favorite booth in the alcove and sequester ourselves, leaning across our mugs during slow songs to stroke each other's smiles.

"Caddie?"

If I took Gwen out on the town, I'd have to hide our purpose. I'd have to treat her like a best friend or a sister, not touching, nothing serious or romantic. We couldn't hold hands across the table and we couldn't kiss. We could only sit, tap our feet, maybe let our ankles lock if we were specially brave.

"Caddie, I know you've taken a liking to the girl. Bet and I can handle this ourselves. We don't need a third girl in."

I thought about Jo. How we'd been two. It was never three or one, even when we had friends along or came by ourselves. Even alone, I was part of something. If I had Gwen, I'd still be single in other folks' eyes. Worst of all? If I brought her to the Yellow Horse, it would be two to me, but not to her.

"Seems like you need to make a decision." Selena fiddled with her shirt, setting the sleeves off the shoulder. "Caddie. Are you in with us or wanting out?"

"What's in and what's out?" I thought of Gwen's habit of covering her mouth when she laughed. Jo used to say I laughed to start thunder. Were Gwen and I too different? Or too much the same? Selena took out a tiny jar of lip gloss and offered it around. Bet jabbed her pinky in, but I shook my head. Lipstick pleases me—Passion Fruit and Fire Door especially— but the waxy feel of gloss makes my words sticky. Gwen wore full-face makeup and always dresses: flowers, dots, fruit, small animals. Once or twice she'd worn a hat to work and Selena got green fast because the hat made Gwen's eyes look specially big. Even Arthur Parks looked up when Gwen wore her hat. It made her move differently too, not more delicately, like you'd think, but more confidently. And the way Gwen moved was important to me, because that was what told me she probably wouldn't want to be kissing me out back.

When I found Jo, I knew right off she was Josephine and not Joseph. I was learning how to refill ketchup bottles when she came up to the register. My back was turned when I heard her voice—a man's voice, only sort of fake. Like a man answering the phone and getting his boss. Selena flirted a little, used the name "Joseph." I had to turn my head. Thought I must've gone wrong in my first estimation.

I looked at Jo and saw right through her, to the self no one else wanted or dared to see. I've always been one to ask questions with my eyes, so figuring her out wasn't surprising. It was more surprising to me that other people hadn't. I recognized her secret as genuine—not a joke, common knowledge, or something people pretended not to know. I was surrounded by unknowing and the will to want things left unknown. The frustration of not being able to communicate to her that I stood with her in a circle at the center of all that ignorance weighed my shoulders down like a tray of greasy dishes. I stared, hoping her face would turn to meet my answers. But she uncreased three bills, put the change in her back pocket, and held the door open for a lady on her way out, so I tucked the knowing in my apron, as if she'd left me a tip. It made me want to come back the next morning, even though my calves ached and I had a blister on the back of my left heel.

"Caddie, come back." Bet put her hand on my thigh. I could feel the stickiness of Selena's lip gloss on her pinky.

"Daydreaming?" Selena blew smoke away from the table.

"Missing Jo."

"Thing is, Caddie, we haven't got a plan. That's why we came tonight. To plan things. What we need to know from you is whether you want to help." Selena didn't look anxious, just impatient. I bent down and unrolled the top of my knee high stocking. There was an itch just underneath the band. There was always an itch just underneath whatever band.

How could I say yes to a plan I didn't know anything about?

How could I say no, when it involved Gwen?

If the plan would bring me closer to her, with whatever kind of close-ness, then it would serve my purpose. Even if—and I caught myself at the thought, but it was already part of me—that meant doing something not so nice.

Was it worth cruelty to speak to her? To touch her, just on the shoulder or the hand?

"Yes."

We closed the bar and went home with pockets full of napkins, inky lists of strategies and schemes.

The next day at the diner was for watching, a job that suited me just fine. As I mopped a sticky table, I gazed at Gwen's back, the coil of hair at her nape, the edge of petticoat sticking out from the right side of her skirt (she favored her left hip when she stood so her skirts hung un-evenly). I remembered the way Jo stood: legs planted, feet sure of the ground beneath. Yet for all her sturdy uprightness, there was something secretive about Jo's motions. She walked as if she was using one kind of energy to propel herself, but had in reserve a whole different way to move. There was a tension about her that drew women to her, but it was unsettling too. More than once, she told me that my calm drew her to me. Jo loved quietude and softness and hated the kind of coy energy women like Selena gave off.

Gwen's gestures were different—nothing hidden. Everything was sur-face-close. She was the kind of girl who'd never had a secret and prob-ably couldn't keep one if she had. You could just tell that her beau liked her that way—simple. Their kisses were never passionate, but breezy, bodies barely touching, all four feet facing front. I tried to imagine whether Jo would've been stirred by Gwen. Were simplicity and calmness inter-changeable in her eyes?

What was it made me want her? Not her secrets but her lack of depth—the opposite of what had made me court my Josephine. When Jo had met me, I'd been like Gwen to her, my face still unlined. She'd liked teaching me pool, liked teaching me, and I'd liked learning. Wanting Jo was about wanting to know things; wanting Gwen was about wanting to share. When I dreamed her up, I dreamed her innocent. The thrill came in imagining how she'd change. If I held and kissed her she'd have a secret, all right. She wouldn't be a paper doll any longer. I wanted to make Gwen over, to complicate her. I wanted to watch her metamor-phose in the secret circle of my arms.

All morning I watched, and I watched all afternoon. Now that I had permission, watching was easy. The next day I got to the diner early, just to watch her beau peck her on the cheek and wave good-bye with his elbow. Did he fall asleep after, his crumbled sex sagging along her tingling thigh? I remembered the way David used to summon narcolepsy, nodding off while I stared, unfascinated, at whatever cracks or webs dotted that night's ceiling. Did she ever clamber on top, did he ever ask her for something she wouldn't give, did they take turns, did she want him to eat, did he grimace, did they talk of babies or emotions or was it mostly motion, sound, sweat, vertigo?

If I had my Gwen, what would we do? Jo never let me touch her; there were mysteries yet to unravel. Taste and scent. I'd gone so far, but no further. I could imagine pinning Gwen, rocking against her, rowing her further and further from the land men called love. I knew if she let me touch her once I'd be her future. It was that strong a thing. But just then all I could do was watch and take notes on her every move, which I did with pleasure.

We met again at the Horse the next Saturday, each of us carrying a notebook filled with Gwen observations. Selena's lists were precise and pragmatic, pages torn from a spy's almanac. Bet's pages were filled with copious (and to my mind insignificant) details about Gwen's work habits. When she finished reading and closed her book, I reached under my seat for my own.

I'd chosen a three-section spiral notepad, the kind I'd had in high school. The only covers available at the grocery were children's cartoon figures—plump teddy bears in tutus and tuxes picnicking around a toadstool, garish muscular robots armed and taking aim, or pouty model-princesses in gauzy garments, fixing each other's hair in front of a mirror made of a dewdrop resting on a giant rose. I picked the princesses—they seemed apropos for my love offerings. But I had a hard time keeping my words simple. I'd even torn out a page where my comments turned to dreamy poetry. As I began to read, Selena and Bet bent towards me, the better to hear over the busy music.

"Today Gwen punched the time clock two minutes late. She spent those extra two minutes having a kiss with her beau in the parking lot in front of his pickup, which is red and has a Confederate flag for a front license plate. After they kissed and she went inside, he wiped his mouth with his sleeve. I think this was because Gwen wears a lot of lipstick.

Her lipstick is always pink, which matches her cheeks, which are a pretty, sunny-day pink color also."

Selena interrupted me. "Less about her boyfriend. We're not interested in him."

But I am, I thought. It was hard, always keeping green jealousy to myself. As I read, Selena and Bet leaned closer still. Suddenly I had the funniest notion. What if I kissed one of them right then and there? Would they laugh, like I was a party girl gone clever? Would they look shocked and get their hair in a huff? It was so tempting that I had to stop reading and sit straight up in my chair, soothing my nerves with a sip of beer. I didn't feel much of anything for Selena or Bet, but it wasn't about feeling something. It was about knowing I shouldn't. That was why the temptation came on so strong.

"Good job, Caddie." Selena smiled so that her fillings showed. Bet made little clapping motions with her hands. "That last part was very useful." I'd described the way Cory Flint flirted with Gwen and the shy way Gwen flirted back.

"So what's next?" Bet looked at Selena.

"Cig and a light, anybody?"

"I thought you were quitting." Selena handed me a pack and a lighter: pink enamel, with her name painted in black across the front.

"Too much stress." I let smoke fill my lungs till the itching stopped. The old familiar warmth made my hands tingle. "What's next, Selena?"

"Depends on what you girls want."

Bet raised an eyebrow. I tried to respond but the skin around my eyes felt steam-bath tight.

"Let's start with the obvious. Do we want her fired, or do we just want to teach her a lesson?"

"Fired." "Lesson." Bet and I spoke at once.

"Gwen hasn't done anything wrong," I frowned at Bet. "She's young, that's all. She doesn't understand that she can't hog tables and tips."

"And men's attention."

"And men's attention." I seconded that motion. "But we can explain that easily. I can just take her aside, give her a little talking-to, make things clear so—"

"Would you?" Selena's tone startled me. For a second, I was afraid she could see my motives written on my forehead. Then I realized she was eager, not angry or suspicious. She didn't want to talk to Gwen. Why hadn't I understood? Both women's relationships to Gwen were so different from mine. She was their rival; younger and prettier, she stood to deprive them of something, or so they felt. It seemed so low, what they'd set out to do. To stop sweet humor in its tracks, to force another woman to play a game that only men won in the end.

"I'll talk to her. Let's see if it works."

That night four women slept, and one woman dreamed technicolor dreams. It was just Gwen I wanted. No god, no earthly treat could substitute for what was beating underneath her skirt. I wanted her. And I wanted to find a way to tell her alongside or through the telling I'd promised Selena and Bet. Was there some way to mix tips on waitressing etiquette with courtship's ardor?

I cornered her. It was hard to watch her tickle her cheek with the end of her braid, the edges frayed slightly, as if she hadn't trimmed it in too long. She was so blonde that her eyebrows disappeared with only freckles to border where colorless air began and translucent features ended. She nearly vanished on pale days when she stood with her back to white sky and kissed that stubborn beau. I cornered her against the coffeemaker on our break and watched her rub the edge of her braid around first her right fist, then her left, noticing for the first time that her blonde was closer to white than to the yellow of her skirt or the gold of her ring.

The ring on her left hand. The ring on her ring finger.

She giggled. She was always giggling. More like a child than a grown-up woman. For the first time since meeting Gwen I felt puzzled. Was this the same woman I'd wanted to press up against a wall? The very same. She put a finger in her mouth. I looked away. She was a child. I felt sick inside.

"You're marrying soon." That was what came out. I couldn't speak the pieces I'd rehearsed.

"Tim asked me two days past." Why hadn't I noticed her wealthy hand? Was her skin truly so gold to my eyes that no metal outshone it?

"When's the wedding?"

Said she was planning me and Selena and Bet for bridesmaids. Made me scrawl the date in ink across the back of my hand so I wouldn't forget.

Selena and Bet were satisfied. That took care of that.

I passed the lucky beau on my way home.

"Congratulations," I said, waving my dated fist in his face.

He looked surprised. My hand grazed his glasses. I wanted to rub it in.

Jo used to say that marriage is about controlling. A way to keep two people together no matter what. "What's wrong with that?" I'd say. I wanted Jo and only Jo in my bed till they buried her.

"You can't know," she'd say. It made her angry when I talked about always. "How can you say you want Jo always in your bed and still say you'd accept my changes? If I changed, I wouldn't be Jo any longer. You can't know what it would mean for me to be different. You love the person in front of you," and she'd put her hand on my belly, rub me like a cat, "but if the years alter me, that person might be different, inside and out."

It was strange philosophy to me, and I told her so. "Josephine Sue, you think too much," I said. "You think too much and make what's simple and ordinary, like love, into something only professors can understand. I love you. My love is about what's inside of you. That doesn't change. That stays the same."

"What if I were a woman to the rest of the world?"

So impossible it made me smirk. She only said it once, and I laughed so hard and teasing that she let fall her philosopher's face and hugged me, two short hugs, like diamonds. But if it had happened, I'd have stuck by her. Now I regret not speaking that promise aloud. I worry that all her strange philosophy was just insecurity, fear that I'd leave her if she came to hose and skirts, took up drinking, fell ill, wanted kids or pets or separate beds, found God, or went to college. Even with a death's-head face or a brain full of books, I'd have loved Jo with best certainty. But she left me—no reason to think she'd ever be back. For a time I had Gwen as a distraction, but now she was leaving also, wooed silly by some man's gold circle.

That Saturday night, Selena and Bet and I played pool—three games. I won all three. It was easy. I'd gone ice again so my hands were steady. Nothing to distract me from pressing my hips against the table, bending my head to the cue's angle, drawing my arm back like a bow and fixing the ball with my gaze like an animal. For a moment its number was the only clear thing in the room, which quickly became my universe. Smoke, stale tunes, the hot breath of gossip on my cheek, my own history wadded about my ankles like a dropped dress.

Monday morning Gwen sashayed in, pockets full of silk swatches she shoved underneath our noses. Selena and Bet were pleased. My cheeks curdled. Cory Flint was back at my table—no fun watching Gwen serve hash if she was wearing Bubba's ring.

"Of course I'm tired," I snapped when he asked, and poured his coffee so fast it splashed the saucer. Tired of almost-maybe. Tired of coming and going, going and gone. I wanted someone to stay with me, someone who'd spin to a stop in my arms and cease circling. Once or twice I caught myself watching Selena, but it made me laugh to think of Selena loving anyone for real. She was so skittish. She could flirt for hours without coming up for air.

And I didn't love Selena. I missed Jo and wished Gwen and had come to hate my own company. Once I realized that, I knew what I needed— to get back to who I'd been before. Not someone's companion or complement, but Caddie Solo. I went back to sitting by myself at work and started skipping out of Saturday nights with Selena and Bet. When they asked why, I told them I was low on cash. Mostly they didn't ask. All caught up in Gwen's wedding plans, they seemed to have forgotten that only a few weeks back they'd wanted her fired. The shift was about a man—having one gave Gwen access to closeness with the women around her. When Gwen touched women, her embraces loosened, deepened, and relaxed. The ring served as veil and barrier both. She could touch and be touched freely by women, though not, any longer, by men. Was there passion in her affection for women? I watched and tried to gauge. What was the difference between what I felt for Gwen and what Gwen felt for the gaggle of women surrounding her?

She must have noticed that I hung back from the celebration and thought it was jealousy, wishing I had a beau of my own to woo me. One afternoon on my lunch break, as I sat in a corner booth with my free lunch and *The Cartwheel Chronicle*, Gwen slid into the seat across from me, her dress making an *S* sound, slick fabric on vinyl.

"Caddie." When I didn't look up from the front page, she jostled the paper. "Caddie, I have a question to ask you."

It was I who had questions. I stared at her bow-shaped lips, outlined in a darker shade than the plush pink she'd used to fill them in. I stared at the oval locket she wore, its cheap silver flaking at the clasp. I stared at the crescent neckline of her peach and white striped dress, its center plunge revealing a faint crease. Did her beau reach in, did he burrow, did he trace his name?

I remembered the way Jo and I had fought, the aphrodisiacal quality of our arguments, the frenetic lovemaking that followed anger. Jo's laugh was harsh, and her very bones were dense as shields. Times, my kindnesses and sweet words fell like ill-sent arrows. She'd turn away or cross her arms over her unbound chest, sulking like a hay-sick horse.

Gwen tapped a red fingernail on my empty plate. "I wanted to ask you, not Bet or Selena, because seems to me you'd know the answer best."

I tried to remember the question. I'd been so absorbed in thoughts of Jo that I'd missed it.

Gwen didn't seem to notice and began listing all the possible answers herself. The question concerned her dress. Whether it should be white or off or cream, whether it should drop straight or pucker, whether there should be flowers or lace at the neck and hem, and what shape waistline in between.

It was the in-between that mattered.

"I don't want folks to notice." She smiled, mistaking my gape-mouthed goggle for a grin good luck. Did he fuck her in his truck, night spotting the windows with miscellaneous stars, engine purring, radio tuned low to his favorite station? Did the lyrics ever specially strike her: "Baby baby" or "Oh baby" or "Oh oh oh baby"?

"Red's fine." I bused my own dishes, wiped my own drips, wished I'd thought to drop myself a tip. Her turn to stare. "You want to lie and wear white, Gwen, that's your choice. But just see if God strikes you."

I bought wine on my way home and drank alone that night. The next day Gwen tiptoed around, avoiding me, till I stopped her during a lull.

"I'm sorry." I'd thought my words through, intent on honesty. "I'm just jealous, that's all. I wish it was me. The marriage would last forever, we'd be perfectly contented, and the baby would be named Josephine and grow up to be a famous actress."

"Oh, Caddie." She hugged me, the first time I'd let her. I couldn't feel the bulge, but as I buried my face in her neck, I smelled baby oil and talc. I shouldn't have, but I let my tongue touch the ridge of lace around her neck.

No one was looking. No one knows but Cat, to this day.

Two months later, when her father gave her away, I didn't even cry. I still have the bridesmaid's dress: pale green, pumps dyed to match. The color of an Indiana sky when a storm sports a funnel. When I got home, I sat up stargazing, trying to remember why Jo and I had ever fought.

Jo's secret of secrets was that she both craved and disliked change.

So much depended on it. She needed to transform herself in small ways on a daily basis in order to keep her job at the factory—binding her breasts, clipping hair that threatened to curl, choosing shirts and trousers that hid her hips. Equally important was my steadiness. She'd muss my long hair—"Caddie, don't you change this"—threatening me if I threatened to alter the difference between us by becoming more the same.

Thinking back, my face took longer to paint than it took her to dress; my lingerie and hose bound no less tightly than her thick cloth swatches and leather belts. Who had changed and who had stayed the same? To what effect and for what purpose? But at the time I accepted her vision that Jo metamorphosed while Caddie stagnated.

Was falling for Gwen about wanting sameness? If I had my Gwen, we'd circle each other's waists with scarlet fingers. We'd scan shops together, looking for bargains on dresses or hose. Or was it about wanting difference? If I had my Gwen, would I become a taller, plumper Jo, shaky in heels, tugging at the lacy sleeves of my blouse like a straitjacket?

Who was I now?

Caddie Solo.

But was *solo* part of my name or a present term of endearment? I shut my door tighter. I turned down the temperature. I stopped the polite smiles and hellos and how-are-yous altogether.

Back to the freezer.

For all her motherly solicitude, it wasn't Bet tried to pull me out of my blue funk, nor Gwen, in whom my admission of jealousy (though how she misrecognized it!) sparked a condescending if well-intentioned warmth, culminating some months after the wedding in the offer of a "Cartwheel cut-up"—a double blind date, me and Selena with two of Gwen's husband's "close" friends. (Turned out he hardly knew them; they played b-ball the odd Saturday. Turned out Selena and I walked back to my apartment past midnight, after refusing to knock over a per- fectly serene sleeping bovine.) No, it wasn't Bet, and it wasn't Gwen, but Selena who finally set about giving me a talking-to. I was slicing pie for the dessert window, irritable because the knife I'd been given was dull. When I asked her if she had any better, she frowned.

"Caddie, who'd trust you with anything sharp these mornings?" She had her apron hitched up underneath her armpits but a splotch of some sauce or other had lodged on the collar. When I pried it off with my fingernail, she thanked me with a slap on the back and a carving knife.

"Be careful." She headed for the kitchen, then hesitated. "Wait a minute. I want to watch."

Did she think I was that far gone?

Was I?

Hard for me to say, since I was half absent even from myself, but I didn't think it was death I wanted. I liked life well enough when I wasn't feeling anything. Selena's words were hard for me to gauge. I replayed them in my mind days after, listening for condescension or frustration, finding none but remaining wary. Why did she care?

Several days later, I was cleaning the countertop after the noontime rush when one of Selena's skirts rustled behind me. Selena wore skirts with a capital *S*: they hitched or plunged, billowed or torqued, flowed or clung like a second pair of skivvies. She sewed her own; although each fabric was a different pattern and texture, they had noise in common. "I appreciate attention when I enter a room," she'd say, but I suspected she did it for her own pleasure. I'd walked in on her any number of times in the empty kitchen, alone on the stoop, or in a closed-off corner of the diner and seen her smoothing a ruffled pleat, fingering a hem, or running one barely exposed calf along the other. Selena loved music and her skirts sang. When something whistled or stirred or clicked in the diner, it was always Selena, save for the time a sparrow fluttered its way in, fooling us with its Selena-sounds.

But that morning it was Selena and no sparrow who spoke my name. I greeted her without turning from my task. My name again, another rustle, and she began working beside me, sponging up as I dusted crumbs.

"How was Monsieur Flint?" I'd noticed her working Cory's table midmorning. Now that Gwen was engaged, he often picked one of Selena's tables and they bantered back and forth about the weather, diner antics, whatever sounds and shadows he'd seen on his watchman's shift. Gwen whispered about the two of them, wanting me to paint love pictures with her. But I refused. Cory and Selena were both back-fence flirts— beyond the friendly banter and inviting smiles was a hunter's nightmare of wire mesh, thick and prickly and permanent.

"Said he heard something around four-thirty. Turned out to be another raccoon in the garbage cans." Folks joked that Cory was the bank's worst enemy because he prayed for a holdup every night. He and Selena had that craving in common. She liked to stir things up, busying herself with other people's passions. When I first began working at the diner, I'd hoped for a friendship with Selena—courted her in fact, sitting with her at lunch, asking her to bars and movies, confiding bits and pieces of my history. What I really wanted was someone to share with me the burden of Jo's secret body, but as time passed and she took and took and never gave back, I began to pull away. I couldn't stomach a friendship that wasn't also an exchange. Selena wouldn't confess or confide. Though we never spoke of it, I think we both understood the reason for my retreat.

I finished the counter and lined sugar jars on a plastic tray.

Selena sucked in her breath.

"Caddie, look."

Inside one clear, faceted glass jar was a bee, its dense wings folded into a brittle fan. Crouched atop the hill of sugar, it might've been queen of some ghost landscape, but its drunken sway suggested instead the shock of a mourner.

"Pretty." I set the jar beside another, just like it but bee-less.

Selena snatched it away. "Aren't you going to take it outside?"

"It's dying anyway." I think I wanted her angry so she'd leave me alone. Instead she grabbed my elbow with one hand and pulled me towards the door.

There was something unsettling for me in Selena's urgency. She had within her the seeds of fanaticism. When something intrigued her, she abandoned whatever she was doing to follow without first investing any sort of care. But I agreed about the bee. Why watch something meant for motion sit stilled by the grainy nothingness of sugar? She made me stand on the stoop while she stepped into the ragged bushes. Holding the jar as far from her face as her arms would allow, she unscrewed the lid, scrunched up her eyes, and dumped the contents upside down. The bee plummeted with the sugar. Selena opened her eyes and scrambled beside me on the stoop. The bee didn't stir. We watched while it didn't stir some more, and didn't; finally Selena prodded its crusted body with a stick.

"Caddie, what's wrong?"

"I think it's dead."

"Of course it's dead." The bee no longer mattered to Selena. "I mean with you. You're acting funny again, like you did after Jo left. I thought you were over him."

Her, I thought. *Over her.* When Jo and I first began dating, I was afraid I'd slip and use the wrong pronoun. I had to train my tongue and mind till my lips made Jo a man, while my heart translated her back into a woman. After a time, the act of translation began to feel automatic. I found myself inadvertently translating other people's words, as well. Gwen's boyfriend became her girlfriend, Roy's woman became his man, and so forth. I no longer worried that my lips would give me away. Caution had permeated my bloodstream. I sometimes even fancied that my lip color had changed, deepening from mauve to scarlet, because more blood was needed there to weigh down my pout and ward off spontaneity.

"Are you?" Her skirt made a sound like someone brushing their hair.

I stepped into the bushes and picked up the bee, thinking one of its wings had fluttered a little. But it was just the wind.

"Tell me it's dead."

"Of course it's dead."

I covered my left hand with my apron like a kitchen mitt, placed the bee inside, and crushed it. Then I stepped out of the bushes, took my apron off, and wiped the sugar from my shoes with the checkered cloth. When my soles were clean, I held the door open for Selena and Tom Jensen, whose car had pulled up while I was cleaning my shoes. They hesitated, both waiting to see what I'd do next, so I stepped inside and shut the door on their watching eyes, letting the AC dry the sweat on my left palm, which had just started to sting.

Selena left me alone the rest of the day, but the next morning she tapped me on the shoulder while I was chatting with Tiffany, Bobby's fifteen-year-old sister. It was an unwritten rule that we never interrupted each other when we were talking to customers, so I figured she wanted something serious. I left Tiffany to her fries, forgetting the ketchup I'd promised—the bottle on her table was jammed, its throat glogged with thick red paste.

Selena was mixing a milk shake for a little kid who came in once a week with her allowance for a shake and a slice of apple pie. I watched as Selena spritzed whipped cream on top of frothy chocolate, then sprinkled jimmies lasciviously over that. She put ice cream on the pie too, but I caught a glimpse of Beth's ticket and Selena didn't charge her for any of the extras.

"One Beth Taylor special, coming up." She winked and slid Beth her pie, then grabbed my sleeve. Selena always approached things—buildings, people, questions—from odd angles.

"We're going on break," she called to Bobby through the cook's window. He signaled five minutes with a greasy palm. Out back, Selena lit up and I lit off her tip. As she took a drag, she pointed to the sky and asked, "What do you think of that?" Factory smoke hung in shards below the clouds, dirty twins. But when I made some comment about pollution, she shook her head. "Over there," pointing to the cross that split the front of the Baptist church into two dull brick rectangles. "Do you believe in it?"

"I used to know what I believed."

Selena exhaled over her shoulder. "Me too."

I moved to go back inside, but she put one foot in front of mine, blocking the door, our legs an *X*, like kids playing Twister.

"Caddie, I want to ask you something."

"We need to get back to tables."

Without a word she opened the door and motioned me inside. But as I entered the overripe air of the kitchen, she murmured, "How about tonight at the Yellow Horse?"

When I stopped by Tiffany's table, she had a knife down the sullen ketchup's throat. I told her I'd bring another bottle, but she'd gone sulky in my absence, determined to do it herself. I watched from behind the counter as she doused her fries in gooey red syrup. Bobby applauded from the cook's window.

That night I was late to the Horse. While I was in my robe braiding my hair, I heard a voice outside the door calling my name. At first I thought it was Selena, but when I glanced out the peephole, no one was there. Five minutes later, again, "Caddie." Still the peephole revealed an empty landing. Fright started, a low rumbling like hunger in my stomach. When it startled me again, I picked up the telephone. After a yowl to scar anyone's ears I understood.

Up two flights to pause and scratch at number six. How she got smart enough to make my name come first, I'll never know. But it opened my door for her, and she stayed on. So orange she was almost red, with bits of black and grey speckled in, Cat found me, the way cats will. She strutted over to my sofa, coiled, and fell instantly asleep. I set out saucers of water and milk, dressed, and left to meet Selena. I decided to worry about the creature when I got back from the Horse.

The bar was crowded. I found Selena beneath the clock in the booth Jo and I had always favored. She'd already ordered two beers and handed me a bottle as I slid into the booth.

We started off gossiping about Marv and Helen. They were so close, it was uncanny. Everyone who knew the couple envied their bond.

Selena finished peeling the label off her bottle. "I don't think anyone understands someone else's ways with a lover."

Certainly it was true that I could never explain to another person how I'd moved in Jo's presence, or that with Jo it was every day different. Selena had always been warm to Jo, flirting and teasing. When I began working the diner, I'd thought at first that they were coupled up. But Jo chose me instead. Selena never stopped her flirting, but somehow it was always clear to the three of us that she meant nothing by it. Her interest in Jo was something to push the workday along. Truth be told, that interest came as a relief to Jo and me, because it assured us that she took Jo for a man. We played along, even allowing Selena to think I was jealous and watchful. Looking back, the tension triangle seems a cruel game.

"What was it like, Caddie?"

Selena's face looked the way it had on a forgotten day just before Marv and Helen took Gwen on board. Back then Bet and Selena and I were even worse overworked, always flying too fast and too long, till sometimes one of us would snap and come to crying back in the kitchen or even behind the register. One day I'd gone into the kitchen to prod Bobby on a hurry-up take-out order. He winked and told me to wait a second while he finished the burgers. I'd just leaned against the counter and closed my eyes for the day's first moment of rest when I heard a scraping noise coming from the storage closet. I figured the sound for a mouse and opened the door cautiously. But instead of a critter, I found Selena, her back against the far wall, shoes off, legs in a V, her hands on her thighs. The expression on her face was all wrong for storage, and her shoes belonged on her stockinged feet. I felt as if I'd walked in on someone in the ladies'.

Just then Bobby handed me the take-out order in its crisp white bag with "M&H Diner" printed in red letters across a marquee. I ran out front to hand the order to Mr. and Mrs. Out-of-Town-Impatient. Selena

acted as if nothing had happened. When I thought it over later, I realized nothing had.

"What was it like, Caddie?"

Were there words to tell about being with a woman without letting on
that she was one? Could I talk truly about Jo without using her sex? For
so long I'd convinced myself that when I said "Jo loved me" or "Jo left
me," my meaning came clear enough for empathy. But now I felt the
inadequacy of my tongue and looked at Selena helplessly. We sat not
speaking, maybe not even blinking. I thought, *What was it like, what
was it like,* unable even to think through a secret answer, to summon a
single photograph except for a stark shot of Selena flirting with Jo at a
party, Jo whispering to me behind cupped hands to fake jealousy. Why
had Selena asked? What did she know about my Jo-Jo-Josephine's stolen territory? I saw again her face in the closet and felt once more the
wrongness of it. I didn't understand what she wanted to know.

"Jo was good to me." All I could come up with, not quite the truth.

Curiosity spread across Selena's face like a sunburn. She began asking
questions about the house Jo and I had shared. Did I ever think back to
it, recreating the inside? Did I ever walk by to see who lived there now,
what color the wooden door (red in our time), how faded the brick,
what pattern the garden, with its rocks and rectangles of flowers?

Selena's talk of inside and outside made me suspicious. I thought she'd
asked me to the Horse because she was worried I was charming knives
and drinking straight from the bottle. But it seemed that what she wanted
was talk about Jo. I felt tricked. She was getting too close, once again
revealing nothing of her own. So I moved from flower beds to Gwen's
bouquet. Decided I'd press for a little information of my own.

So much of Selena was about taking in and holding on. She didn't give
back—even her teasing ways had a selfishness about them. Yet there was
an intensity about her that made me suspect she wanted something from
someone. I sometimes wondered if Selena's mixed-up wanting signals
had to do with women. Was she doing her courting from the wrong side
of the fence? I was tempted to ask her or to give advice. But something
told me not to, and it wasn't the same fear that kept me from touching
Gwen. Lodged inside my soul was the certainty that Gwen would never
touch me back. Something else shook me away from Selena. It was the
way she looked at me, burrowing—something she did with men also.

Her eyes went through you, not in order to understand or to seek sympathy, but to take you apart. It was as if she couldn't bear to see surfaces, as if there was something ugly for her about the very shape of a human body. Most of the time she kept that stare a secret. She'd flirt with anyone, joshing to let you know she knew what you wanted most to hear. It was pleasant to let Selena play with you till she started really looking. Then you wanted to push your chair back and change the subject quick.

What puzzled me was connecting the two Selenas: the barfly flirt and the quiet woman with razor-blade eyes. Was flirtatiousness a way of avoiding what she saw when she stopped to really look? I wondered why burrowing. I wondered what it was about surfaces that fascinated and repulsed her. In the course of my wondering I stopped feeling afraid.

Selena was talking about Gwen's wedding, though not about Gwen, her bewhiskered beau, or the dimpled flower girl. She was word-painting the church: its cavernous ceiling, ornate moldings, burgundy and cerulean stained glass, vast wooden cross. She described the way the thick walnut pews must've felt to all those watchers, women with stockinged legs (how rough the wood, how numerous the snags), men with creased pants and knitted socks (how dry the air for legs encased in wool). I had to remind myself that she hadn't been sitting but standing beside me in a green tornado dress, watching the giveaway, pretending not to see Gwen's stomach or her beau's restless eyes. Selena's words were poetry. They built the church for me, till I forgot where we were and what I was sipping. I was standing again, looking on, listening for the march, smelling the dying flowers and the hot breath of the priest as he pronounced words to bind two people together for life, words I'd wanted for my own, words I still believed might have kept Jo by my side at least a little longer. I was watching and crying, not for growing Gwen or that nervous groom, but for what Jo and I couldn't have, the chance to say "till death" and be a part of each other our whole lives long, one of us in white or maybe both in black, color only in our kiss, our lips parting instantly to let our tongues meet, and her hands unable to stay but roaming down the sides of my body, what she called the slide that made her hungry, then turning to accept recognition before driving off, scattering cans and streamers, startling other drivers with the sound of our future tumbling behind us. As I imagined the kiss, I wanted to tell Selena my dreaming for the first time. Since fear was gone and she'd transported us both to the same stone church, I leaned across the booth and cupped her chin in my hands (I'd stopped thinking) and said, "This is what it was like," kissing the dart at the center of her coral lips.

When I try to separate out what it was that drew me further into Jo's mouth, till sometimes I worried I'd choke her with my lust, I can't get specific. The buds of her tongue felt like the smell of her neck, which tasted like the sound of her voice when she worked my name into something holy. But with Selena, the smell of her perfume (musk), the taste of her lipstick (wax), and the beer on her tongue (malt) stayed separate from the taste of her skin and mouth itself. None of it unpleasant and yet something was off, and not just because Selena wasn't Jo, or even David.

What was wrong was that there was too much body in it.

When a lamp comes on in a pitch-dark room, you're made aware of light, how it can startle, even wound. Selena's skin against mine felt so much like flesh that I couldn't stop thinking of it as flaky skin and hair, quick blood and sleeping bone pressing against my own body, suddenly aware of its own tingling liveness, not in an excited way (the way a sunset or black coffee makes a body come alive), but as if in preparation for flight, resistance, or the slow falling-to-pieces our bodies instinctively follow to death.

When we left off, I looked down, not ready to meet Selena's eyes. I hadn't been afraid till then. I kept my glance on the table, playing with the napkin underneath my beer, tearing the edges off, until it fit the round bottom of the bottle perfectly. When I finally looked up, her eyes were burrowing, picking through surface to what quivered beneath. But it wasn't my surface or my interior that she was seeing.

She was somewhere else.

"Wood," she said, holding up her left palm. "Slick, but at the joint, the varnish was worn so thin the edges pricked."

My kiss—she'd missed it. She was still in that church. She'd never left it. All the while we were lipping, she was stroking the wooden cross. Now she was describing the narrow splinter that pierced her left hand at the very moment Gwen promised to obey.

"Oak, wasn't it?"

But she didn't hear me. She was describing the way her skin ridged after, a subtle scar at the joint where her ring finger met her palm. The wood stayed underneath her skin, visible for several days till it became one with her flesh and only the off-white of the scar's lip and the faint pain when something pressed against it were left to remind her of where the two had met.

"Walnut. Maple. Chestnut." I searched my mind for others. "Cedar." Her eyes were on her creamy scar, raised like a seam, ridged round like a ring. "Mahogany. Pine."

Selena looked at me—me, Caddie, a tall, plump girl reciting the names of trees—and snapped out of it. Selena said oak, yes, she believed it was oak, and then she drove me home. I watched her hands on the wheel, spelling *steady* silently to myself, forward and back. When she dropped me off, I waited until she backed out before poking my key in the lock, then watched from the window as her car braked at the stop. Only after it vanished did I draw the curtains.

By then there was something wound twice around my ankles, entangling me in its warmth.

In the morning, after I'd had my coffee, I named her Cat, because it was the one name that could never be a mistake, no matter what her other people had tagged her: Milo or Angel, Tabitha or Sug. A cat is always anyway Cat to its owners. Funny that humans are different, sticking to proper names, rarely acknowledging what animals we are. I named her Cat because I recognized exactly who and what she was. When she wrapped herself, that first night, around my throat like a golden chain, I parted the fur on her belly like a locket and slipped my picture in.

In case she'd forgotten.

I wanted her to remember. So when we were alone, around ten, after the first rush of the day, I slipped my arm around her narrow shoulders (looking first left, then right, then left again to be sure there weren't any customers; Bet was in back and Gwen, home sick) and squeezed and rubbed my cheek against hers for one split second before busying my hands with cleaning (as if it had never happened). I wanted her to remember my kiss or at least the church. I wanted her to remember the way it was in that far back booth, but she stayed casual, flirting the usual, and when Cory Flint came in she stopped the chat she was making with me to lope over to the seat he'd chosen and bat eyes and smirk and write out an order.

I broke a plate. Not right then but later that afternoon. I wanted Selena to remember. It seemed logical that the sound of china splintering would remind her of the wooden splinter in her left palm. But the plate hit the floor with plunk instead of shatter and simply halved. Folks said it was magic that I could drop a thing and have it break exactly in two. I knew it wasn't magic at all, but luckless Caddie's ordinary music—what happened when I tried to make something come true for the second time.

That night Cat warmed me, and the next.

I gave up on reminding Selena of our kiss.

And maybe she did remember, and maybe it scared her, because suddenly she was deeper into conversations and glances and games with Cory than ever. Gwen was back to trying to snap a heart-shaped photo, but I wanted to wait, to watch and see what would happen when two flirts tried to take off from the same runway. One afternoon Cory didn't come and didn't come, and we noticed but didn't think too much about it. But when two days and then three and a week and then two passed without a sign of Mr. Flint, Gwen rolled her eyes and I rolled mine and sure enough, on Tuesday after work, Gwen happened to pass the Big Boy and there he was in the window.

Gwen told me the next morning and we spent some time speculating, but pretty soon the sky took our attention away. It was raining hard, thunder and flashes thrown in. Around noon there was a creaking and then a shudder as the sole tree in sight splintered and sliced through some wire or other. A few minutes later the diner went black as the sky in the window. Bobby scurried into the kitchen quick to check the refrigerator doors and take the meat off the grill so it wouldn't smolder when the energy started up again. Meanwhile, Marv called electric and found out it wasn't our tree that did it, but a tangle of trees and wire a few blocks up. They said two hours, maybe three. When he hung up, Marv marched over to the door of the diner, flipped "Open" to "Closed," and told the remaining customers that their meals were on the house. One or two folks left anyway, but for the rest it was like a party. Selena, Gwen, Bet, and I counted it a break. We offered up water but not much else. Once the last customer left, the four of us took a booth and helped ourselves to pie (Dutch apple), Marv egging us on, saying "It'll only go bad," though Bobby wouldn't let Gwen open the freezer for ice cream. ("If you keep it shut, the cold lasts up to twelve hours.") When Gwen sulked, Bet tore open one of those little coffee creamers and poured it over Gwen's piece. Gwen said later that she liked it better, and that was how her creamy habit got started.

While this was going on, Selena and I were joshing, saying Bet should give Gwen cooking lessons because Gwen couldn't boil water. Silly stuff. Then somehow talk turned to flirting, the subtle ways we each had of making tips slide easier off the sticky fingers of worn-down factory workers. By then even Gwen knew all the other girls' secrets. We worked too closely together, bumping and sliding and bustling about, not to know each other's tricks. It was an easy leap from there to romance. Pretty soon Cory's name came up. I was sitting beside Selena and felt her thighs tense against vinyl. In the dim light of the stormed-in, shut-down diner, her face collected shadows. The sky outside had gone green. I caught Bet worrying her brows over the tornado color. Then Gwen asked Selena a question, and we all lost track of the weather.

She started off with a giggle. Even in the near dark, her hand flew to cover her mouth. "What happened between you and Cory?"

There was a flurry outside—a garbage can gone helicopter or a broken branch become a giant pencil. We scrambled to the door, all but Selena. When Bet, Gwen, and I eased back into the booth, Selena had taken the tops off the salt and pepper shakers and begun pouring both out onto the table—a grainy grey mountain. Gwen's face did puzzle-wrinkles, and Bet bit her lower lip, but I understood.

She was burying something. While we watched, she finished pouring, then flattened the miniature mountain with one manicured hand. The table became a sandy beach. Who can resist the tide, who can resist summer seasons? We all dug in. Bet and Gwen reached round to the tables front and back and spilled more salt, more pepper. We rolled our cuffs and let our fingers wiggle, etching initials and tiny faces, teardrops, trees, cat's whiskers in the grainy slather that entertained us even after the storm died down, the lights went up, and we woke from dreaming to find Marv and Helen standing side by side, watching us in silence, their mouths oddly similar in the newly garish glow.

After we'd cleaned up the messes scattered round the diner, Marv let us go and closed shop. My feet made sluggish squishes as I waded home. Maybe it was watching Selena bury her secret like a treasure or maybe it was watching Marv and Helen together, so much the Marrieds. Maybe it was letting my palm brush Gwen's roly-poly thumb as we swabbed at seasonings or maybe it was just the weather that made me want to speak my heart to anyone who'd listen. It was a desire like any other, but so strong that I almost believed someone would be waiting inside my apartment, someone with the sharpest of ears, the easiest of patience, and the most compassionate of hearts. I even called out a name, tentatively at first, then louder—her name of course, the name of the woman who'd wrecked me for any other kind of loving.

"Jo," I called and called, scalding my throat with my own hot breath, but only Cat came, with her easy cat swagger, to curl beside me on the sofa and prod my tears, hurrying them down my cheeks so she could taste salt before they met my lips.

It felt strange at first, but I went ahead. Bent my mouth to her prickle-ears and spun out my story. About loving Jo and her leave-taking. About dour David, Gwennie, and Selena's strange sympathy. I told Cat about lonely, how it felt to have a heart bigger than a haystack or a house, so big it beat and beat until I couldn't sleep or concentrate on anything but passion.

"I hate my big fat human heart," I told her, and she shivered, bristling with understanding, or maybe thirsting for cream.

Chapter Four: Jo
■ ■
■

There are things you can teach a person. How to fix a faucet. How to bake a pie. Love can be taught, but passion? Passion's something you can't instruct. It has to be there or it won't happen. Some people are born with it. If your sight is good you can see the color riding just beneath the skin, a faint red-gold where blue should be by rights. Caddie's eyes gave her away. They were always shifting, and when I touched her it was every day different. I'd stroke and stroke but the direction shifted like wind and yet somehow her body always told me she loved me. I never had doubts. She was born to sex and I was it for her and her eyes were always the signal. If I could've licked those eyes I would've, if I could've taken her face inside me, then I would've let her touch me. But her hands, her hands were blue beneath the skin, not red-gold; it was her face I wanted inside of me. Her face I could never have and so I cupped my fists over my sex when she pushed and prodded, I pushed her away, I laughed at her efforts to disrobe me and told her "no, no, you still yourself girl, you femme, you Caddie-golden-eyes," and she'd shake, angry, till I opened her body like an orphan's only gift and saw colors, her cunt the tint of dried blood, smelling of wood and steam, its folds coarse as red pepper.

We waited to tell folks we were together.

It wasn't because of how we did our loving. I wasn't afraid someone would learn the spelling of my proper name. Most folks see only what they want to see, meaning they wake up and hit the pillow blind, knowing exactly what they knew the day before. Most folks see only what they expect to see, meaning they cross with the light, turning their heads once for each direction, never looking up to see what might be falling, or down to see what might be snaked. So I felt safe, hidden inside my two short letters. I knew I'd never be Josephine unless someone wanted or expected to find her.

"Did I want or expect?" Caddie asked me once. I'll admit it was hard to answer. By the time she saw Jackie's envelope, she already expected Josephine. She'd seen through me long before that day. Yet I was new for Caddie, the first she'd even heard of, so her wanting seemed the more mysterious.

It was desire without knowledge.

Maybe that was why her eyes seared me. They showed her need but also her whole soul's ignorance. It was as if her eyes knew before the rest of her, body and spirit both, what it was she wanted. They sought, and the rest of her followed, obedient, unquestioning. I've never met anyone so willing to be led by her eyes alone. There was never any fear or shyness behind them, though Caddie herself was often frightened, easily shy. But her eyes had their own ways. I was never certain whether they revealed her truest self or whether they belied what was truly Caddie.

The other women, the femmes I'd taken during my time in Indy— shyness cloaked them, even in bed. It astonishes me now, but Caddie was the first woman I'd ever loved who looked me in the eye when I did that touching. Then she grimaced, and her eyes closed. When she opened them, they were a different color.

It wasn't fear of being found out that worried me. What threatened me and Caddie was other folks' jealousy. It ran both ways. Men at the diner had gotten used to Caddie single. Her tips came thicker because she flirted lively. My job didn't depend on winks like Caddie's, but Selena and Bet enjoyed teasing me, and the men on the line liked to paint me Don Juan. I told them stories about women, fantastic but true. They filled their ears, empty bellies at a banquet, never stopping to ask me my secret or suspect I had a secret life. They seemed to think I knew things only from scamming. They didn't understand the difference between felt and found knowledge. What I knew, I knew first because of how my very body worked. To be with a woman using the wrong map, the map of a man's body, is to travel to the city and see only the tourist spots.

I had the map the natives use.

I knew the language, not from books but from gossip. There's grammar, and then there's slang.

If they saw me with a steady, would I become another dull pair of hands? Would I lose my spot at the lunch table, spotlit, surrounded by hungry faces? I gave them hints, and they pleased their wives. I kept their mouths open and their eyes interested. If I had a steady, I couldn't speak about capers. That was a rule, unspoken but policed. Steady men didn't tell stories. Stories were for single. Steady men listened in.

What I didn't understand was that steady is a country.

The first man I told was Roy Birdy. It was lunchtime. We were outside on the steps overlooking the parking lot. The asphalt gleamed like black sugar. Roy was picking his sandwich apart, taking out the tired lettuce.

"What's that?"

"Sprouts." Every now and again Bet got fancy. He wrapped them in a leaf of soggy lettuce and dropped the bundle into one of the potted azaleas.

I figured invoking Bet was a way to break the news. "Roy, remember how I thought Caddie was your daughter?"

He nodded, busy picking raisins out of a chocolate chip cookie.

"Well, it's a good thing she isn't, because there's a rumor going around about the two of us."

"I've heard it." He wiped his hands on his jeans. "You trying to tell me it's a true story?"

Seems folks had guessed because of the way Caddie laughed when I did something clumsy. Seems folks had guessed because of the way my eyes followed her as she raced around the diner. "Like at a tennis match," Roy grinned, "your eyes following the whites of her socks every which way." When the whistle blew and we headed back to the line, Roy stopped at the door to slap me on the back.

"Congratulations, Jo." He smiled, wide, so that the gap between his bottom teeth showed clear as gin.

Letting me know they were about to take me in.

They took me in, those married men—*me* meaning the two of us, Caddie and me both, till we weren't Caddie and I but Joandcaddie (Caddieandjo with the waitresses). They pulled me towards them, and it was a different kind of closeness from their listening to my stories. I wasn't outside entertainment, I was part of something. Before Caddie, my tales were money. Men lent me attention in exchange for learning or laughing or a little excitement. After Caddie, I didn't have to spend. They didn't ask anything of me, just accepted that I was one of them, now that I played by their rules.

Steady.

They believed in Settling Down. They believed in Sacrifice. They wanted things neat, every man to his woman. The only way they knew how to deal with single was to make it a laugh and a wonder, like a made-for-TV movie, something they knew was real to someone somewhere else but felt artificial enough not to threaten the real they'd chosen.

I started getting invited to dinner parties, never just me, but Joandcaddie. And it was like the ark, all twos, each two pretending they were of the same species. Pretending also that they were intended to be together, as if Roy couldn't just as easily have married Glenda, as if Bet couldn't just as easily have married Arthur. They strung fences around their marriages, posted "Keep Out" signs every few yards. The fear in the air at those parties was tangible. They kept it contained by talking Steady like it was the True Religion; they blended in, safely indistinguishable, bold colors mixed together to a flat dull puce.

I remember the first diner party Caddie brought me to. Roy was there, and we were holed up in the corner, making bets on who Selena would nick on next, when suddenly a blur of a face whizzed by.

"Who was that?"

Roy laughed. "They never stay put for long, those two. Have to be working even when rest comes around. But that's how the diner took off. Ambition, Marv calls it. Or maybe Helen said it first. They're the *M* and the *H* in M&H, and as straight a couple as you'll ever find."

But they have one face, I wanted to say. It took awhile for me to see that Helen and Marv were so leaf-rakingly normal that you almost never saw their faces. They were worse even than Mitzie and Lester, and they could get pretty cuddlelumps sometimes. Helen and Marv blended in, till I got to worrying that someday I'd call Marv "Helen" or the other way round. Don't get me wrong, I liked them well enough. They treated their girls mostly with respect. They did a little parading and had a reputation for picking pretty ones, but once a girl got in, she was paid fair with plenty of breaks, snacks, and "How was your day?" Caddie had good things to say, and so did Bet and Selena. Every so often they'd loan some poor kid money, they always had a shoulder to cry on if someone's tears needed airing, and they let Bobby and the waitresses in on most big decisions. So I liked Helen and Marv just fine, what I knew of them.

It was Helenandmarv I couldn't stand.

I didn't want to blend into Caddie, till when people described one of us, our features and words became a sloppy mix. But pretty soon worrying over Joandcaddie turned into worrying over something else, and I almost wished for a time when all I'd had to fret for was my love's face layered over mine.

A little over one year into Joandcaddie, the question came for the first time. Caddie and I lived six blocks from the factory. We'd moved into a tiny house, and I'd changed my work shift start so she could walk me to the factory on her way to the diner. We were kissing on the corner opposite the M&H when Cory Flint stopped at the red just a few feet behind us. We could hear the squeak of a window rolling down.

"When's the wedding?"

I've never wanted marriage. Why sign papers telling some god or government you promise your heart will only hold one person's picture? How anyone can promise to love one person forever is beyond me. Why they'd want to say such a promise in front of anyone beside that one person is a big puzzle. Shouldn't promises be private? But for the steady men, marriage was the fence that kept them keen neighbors. Beyond marriage was chaos. So the pressure started, first subtle as the squeak of a rolled-down window, finally loud as some rock band's sweaty drummer.

I don't like much popular music because it seems the refrain is all there is to the song. Just a couple lines to the story, then "Ohhh baby," ten hundred times over. That's how our lives felt that whole second year—like a popular song, barely any story, only "When's the wedding?" and even "When are the kids coming?" till "When's the wedding?" started to sound like its own word, "Whensaweddik?" Some fancy disease or the capital of a foreign country.

It was Caddie finally figured out how to make folks quiet down. She made up some excuse, something about religious differences. I don't remember what kind of belief she said we each had. Maybe she never needed to get that specific. Around Cartwheel, folks stop asking questions when God's name comes up. Caddie took care of appearances so that our shacking up unmarried made some sense. Things got easy again, at least on the outside.

But things at home stayed tense. To begin, it made us angry that we didn't have a choice. The way the law worked, there was no way we could have ourselves a real wedding. But angry as I got at the principle of the thing, at the way men and women together could take everything for granted, still, Caddie was even angrier. I'd never wanted to get married. I only hated the law that said I couldn't. Caddie saw things differently. She didn't hate the law, just wanted to be inside it.

Caddie wanted a wedding.

At least, that was what she said she wanted. But I think she confused the empty air at the center of a ring with the clouds swirling around the center of a fortune-teller's crystal ball. No wedding ring can predict the future; no words, spoken or written, can make what's yet to come stay safe. Caddie wanted promises. She wanted to know we'd stay together no matter what. What she didn't understand was how deep into the dictionary the definition of *what* can go.

"You can't know," I'd tell her. "How can you say you want Jo always in your bed and still say you'd accept my changes? If I changed, I wouldn't be Jo any longer. You can't know what it would mean for me to be different."

She'd shake her head. Say she loved what was inside of me. Say what was inside wouldn't change. Say marriage was about seeing through someone deep enough to know for sure you liked what they kept hidden, enough to want to keep it by you always, for as much of forever as you had the luck to win.

A nice idea, that. But who's to guarantee our insides stay the same when our outsides do their shifting? We fought often, till it got to where Caddie was torn up most of the time with wanting something I couldn't give her. Those fights stayed on, even after folks stopped asking about marriage and kids, because at the bottom of the marriage question was a deeper one. Something about travel, something about holding on. Caddie wanted to know if I was going to stick around. Asking about a wedding was one way of asking how long I planned to stay.

At first I pretended I didn't understand the question.

Then she broke something. A china clock, the only thing I had left of my mother to remind me of her hands. The clock's hands were sudden and gentle both, like Ma's, and china white, the color she'd protected with hats and lotions all her life. I'd thought they were unstoppable, stubborn the way only time or a mother can be. But Caddie broke those hands, dropped the clock on its face and watched it shatter. Since it was the only clock we had that worked, she stopped time too.

"How will I know to get to work on schedule?" My voice shook. She was on her knees, picking pieces off the speckled carpet. "Caddie? How will I know?"

"How do you think it feels for me, never knowing? How do you think it feels for me, Josephine Sue?"

She sat back on her knees and looked up at me, only it felt like she was looking down. Usually it seemed between us like I was taller. But really Caddie was bigger by a good six inches—broader too, big-boned and plump, all curves and flesh to my sharp angles. In her angry looking up she seemed suddenly full-size. It made me wonder why she'd always looked small to me. I didn't answer her question. She stood, cradling cracked china in her palm. Then she dropped the shards in the wastebasket and put her hands on my shoulders and things felt backwards, because there was power and roughness in her palms. This time the way she asked the question made me think I'd better answer.

"I need to know what kind of calendar you're keeping. Goddamn, Jo, you know perfectly well what it is I'm asking." She walked over to the sofa and plunked down, letting her hands fall between her legs into the lap of her skirt, where they plucked yellow roses.

"You want to know how long I'm going to stick around."

"I want to know when you're going to leave me."

She looked like dough waiting for a cookie cutter's imprint, pale fleshy body curved in on itself, breasts loose under the buttoned front of her flower-garden dress. I watched as her hands tried to sever the roses from their stems. She bit her lower lip, clenched her teeth, bit her lower lip again. Caddie reminded me of a clock, always moving in one direction. I placed my hands underneath the fall of her heavy hair, that black that veered, along the crown and around her nape, towards red. Sometimes I imagined I could make it stand on its own, but as I lifted her hair, it slid through my hands like river water.

Her hair. Her hair and her dresses and the way she moved, not cautious, even a little brash, but delicate still, the way girls grow to be delicate if they believe the lies their mothers tell them. Caddie was a believer. Her faith in her girlhood shone so clear through her thick hourglass figure that, standing beside her, I looked like a believer too. She wiped away all traces of blasphemy from my face. She made me a man. If she changed, my name would change with her.

"Don't you cut this, Caddie. Don't you change."

"Is that a promise?"

I let her hair slide through my hands. As she spoke, I watched her mouth open and close, open and close, till it blurred and something took its place—a box, hinged, with a burgundy lid. My old traveling case. I saw the things I'd take with me, loosely arranged, as if I'd left in no small hurry. I saw my hands folding and arranging, and I saw that outside it was winter.

But I didn't tell her. She never did believe in magic. Instead I wrapped my arms around her body and pressed her back, back, till she gave in and I kneaded her belly and worked my way under her skirt. Soon her breathing told me she'd forgotten her question.

We stayed together fourteen more months.

Her questions never stopped. I'd talk about love and change and the way the two felt separate in my heart. I'd say love changes, change changes love, and so the circle's set. What Caddie didn't understand was that her own insistence in her faithfulness just made me insecure. How could I possibly stay with someone who could promise, in advance, that she'd love anyone I became? What kind of person could love anyone I might be? But she was Caddie, and so she promised, and so I never could, and it went on, months of it, until it began to interfere with our passion as well as our quiet times. Our kisses began to taste hollow at the center, like a chocolate heart you bite in half. When she parted her lips to let my tongue inside, I never felt welcome, only hostage. We began to frighten each other, and to take fright. The skin around our wrists thickened, as if our bodies were preparing to survive new scars.

Yet I never stopped loving Caddie. And I never stopped seeing her the way she first appeared to me, her mouth a song waiting to happen, her eyes full of mirrored fire. But the song was all about someone else's days, and the fire was waiting to be blown out. Caddie's face was never its own story. She simply took on the features of the plots around her. I didn't trust her to stay loving steady, through winter weather or colder, through summer's grassy slivers. I didn't trust her talk or the colors her eyes showed when she said "forever." Nothing's steady except change; even its steadiness ebbs and stalls.

So I stopped believing Caddie's sugar, even at night when I rode her sleepy body. But I never stopped loving, and in my dreams, Caddie wrapped her arms around me like shiny paper around some valuable present.

Mornings, I'd drink my coffee quick and get on with business. Working the line. Plucking grass and sometimes an old guitar. Loving Caddie. Splitting her open, my fingers peeling back the soft, rosy skin, pressing my eyes against her hairy inner thighs, running my tongue around and around in narrowing circles. She'd pull my head into her cunt so tight I couldn't see to breathe, couldn't breathe to smell. The scent of water, salt. The scent of pressure. She'd grip my ears like she'd tug them off, and only then (with the feel of moving forward, as if I could work my whole face in, a backwards baby) could I believe I knew her, inside and out. That was when I'd say I loved her, a whisper that shivered, my breath warm and wet, so close my words became part of her inner ocean.

I let Caddie think I was coming when part of me was already gone.

My first good-bye was to the factory—two weeks notice. I'm a work-horse and do right by those that take me on. But Caddie. I struggled with whether to tell, whether it would hurt her more to wake and find me gone or to count the days, me whispering in her ears all along, telling her how much I loved her chubby waist, her wetness. I couldn't decide and let decision-making slide and slide and slide the way rain falls, till I was soaked in it. Then my two weeks were up and I stumbled over the threshold. It was Caddie's home by then. I didn't trust her. There was no way to test her. I stumbled into winter's zero with only dreams to predict in what disguise I'd be back.

CHAPTER FIVE: CADDIE
■ ■
■

Gwen's baby was curdled. Milk-sour, its face too small, and blue. It was so skanky, that baby. But Gwen tended to it the way she tended to all male things. When she first brought it to the diner for a visit, dazed husband in tow, she dressed Sean up in a little knitted chef's outfit with a tiny hood embroidered to look like one of Bobby's bandannas. "Thank god it's a boy," her husband said, handing around Marlboros like they were fat cigars. Gwen lit up and the smoke seemed to seep from between her teeth, circling and then vanishing over the little one's hooded head.

When Gwen came back to work, she was changed. Everyone noticed it, not just me. She acted older, now that she was a mother and all, even if the tiny person she'd birthed was a veritable eyesore. What was also different was the way she moved, and the way her eyes met other people's. Always before, there'd been such shyness to Gwen. It held her back, her shyness. There was a childishness to it that looked charming till you got too close and saw it for an eagerness to please that was self-destructive. Because of the work involved—carrying, staying up late, nursing, and so forth—we were all watching for her to come back dog-worn-down, but instead there was something more solid about her. Maybe because of the change, or maybe because birthing was something only women understood, I hoped Gwen's baby would bring us closer. I figured the way to her heart was loving this thing she'd made and that if I showed interest in something that had once been a part of her, she'd finally see me: me, Caddie.

But it was so ugly, that baby.

"Something wrong around the eyes," Bet said, after Gwen and her man and the small blanket bundle had come and gone. "Something shifty. Too far apart."

"I think they're too close together." Selena passed us with a tray balanced on her shoulder. A moment later she passed us again. This time she stopped and set the tray down by the register.

"Doc says it's perfectly healthy." Bet shrugged. "But there's something off, that's for certain."

"Sean looks exactly like his father."

Bet and Selena stared at me. It was so true none of us could think of another thing to say. The baby had all of Tim's features and none of Gwen's, as if adultery could be imprinted on a child wrong-parent round.

"Why didn't I see that right off?" Selena murmured. I thought about it while I walked home. Tim's face was so different from Gwen's. His eyes and chin were rock-steady, harsh but not earnest, simple but not warm. What was special about his face was its hint of brutality, shadowy like stubble. On the baby it stood out like a third eye, lending it an inhuman air.

Gwen took a whole month off. That caused some stir. Maybe in fancy cities, girls took time off to have babies, staying propped up in bed reading movie star magazines, eating M&Ms, and sewing booties. But in Cartwheel folks worked in spite of their bodies. I remembered stories Jo had told me about factory men mangled by machinery who came to work the next day simply because it never occurred to them not to. Bet and Selena used Gwen's long stay to talk her down. I stood up for her like always, but it was starting to worry me. I was so tired of having to bury what I felt for Gwen from everyone. If she'd been a man, no matter how nasty, Selena and Bet would've giggled and teased and sent me to his table even when he took their stations. But Gwen. It wore me down, and I resolved not to think so much about her, to focus on making my tips heavier, and on the weather. Spring was nearing, and spring always felt a friend to me.

But when Gwen came back, plumper, still ripe looking, I had to suck in my breath. There was still the thing about her that drew me, indescribable. She was so different from Jo, yet the tug was the same. I wanted to name it, to distill it so I could understand. They were opposites, those two, but the air around them swirled for me and I always thought of the same smell: sugar doughnuts, the way the air in Cartwheel smelled Tuesday and Thursday mornings because of Bobby's baking.

Gwen and Tim couldn't afford a sitter, so once Gwen went back to work, they had to struggle to patch things together. When Gwen started walking to work in the morning, Selena asked after her husband's truck. Gwen explained that Tim had gone back to the graveyard shift so he could watch the baby till she got off at three. We were all impressed with Tim's sacrifice, especially Bet. Roy once worked nights. He still talked about how hard it was—the isolation, the creepiness of the factory when the windows looked blank, the absence of camaraderie since so many of the night shift workers hated the job, were on the lam or hiding from wives and kids they didn't specially want to see. Gwen said Tim didn't mind, but I was curious. One night into morning when I couldn't sleep, I decided to walk to Foodville, where Tim worked. It was several blocks away, but although the streets weren't well lit, night didn't scare me.

My apartment was on Addison. I ambled along till it met Third, and then kept on towards the intersection of Third and Old Station. Old Station was what the diner was on. The two streets intersected at what was, many years ago, the town's only traffic light.

Foodville's parking lot was empty but for three or four cars and a pickup in the far left corner, its windows steamy. I remembered making out in a parking lot with Kathy McGuire's brother Bix when I was a freshman and he was a junior. He drove a VW, and my breasts alone took up half the front seat. What seemed funny now was that I had no idea back then what girls could do, myself included.

Tim's truck was parked close to the entrance. I could see Gwen's garter hanging from the rearview mirror. The automatic doors slid open. I picked up a basket from a stack as tall as my head. Then I ambled towards the ice cream aisle, trying to look casual.

The grocery at night was like the surprise of snow when you think autumn will last forever. Usually groceries are full of people bustling, each with their own little food story: a fancy holiday dinner, breakfast for the family, a week's worth of meals for one. But Foodville was mostly deserted. I kept expecting to see shoppers as I rounded each aisle, but there were only a few isolated carts. I passed an army man, his cart piled high with SpaghettiOs and frozen burritos. A frazzled-looking woman in heels clattered past, hugging a carton of milk to her chest. In the cookie aisle I passed a fat woman who jumped when she saw me and looked down at the Fudge Nutsos she was holding as if she had no idea how they'd gotten there. I tried to imagine how it must feel to be hungry all the time, to eat and eat and yet still want more, but it felt plausible, even familiar, and that depressed me, so I moved on to another aisle. The next was empty, and the next, but in Toiletries and Feminine Hygiene, a man in black jeans and a grey T-shirt stood staring at rows of tampons, picking boxes off the shelves. I wondered if his girlfriend had sent him, or if he'd always been curious about what women's bodies did and thought this was his chance to find out. That was the feel of the place. Secrets were revealed under fluorescent lighting, then safely bagged in brown paper, hidden from everyone but the graveyard shift checker. That was when I realized a checker had power—the knowledge of how people put their lives together when they thought no one was looking.

I strolled around the store, putting things in my basket and taking them out, acting as if I was serious about wanting something to snack on. I finally decided on three cans of cat food and some toilet paper—things I couldn't sneak or beg home from the diner. Then I walked towards the register very slowly, because the Fudge Nutsos woman was in Tim's line already, but the other checker was open. I stopped to kill time at the magazine rack, and read the cover of *Cosmo* with great enthusiasm. When the woman was safely headed towards the door, I stepped casually up to Tim's station.

The black belt slid forward silently. Tim didn't look up, just watched each can of cat food stutter towards him. I toyed with my purse, smiling violently, waiting for him to notice me and remember how we'd met. "One-twenty-seven," he said without looking away from the register. I handed him two soiled bills (tips, crumpled and smudged from hours in my apron) and watched while he smoothed them against the register. He pushed a button, handed me a receipt without looking me in the eyes, and then simply walked away. I stared at his back, thinking to ask for my seventy-three cents back, when I heard a clink and a jingle and a puddle of coins appeared at the bottom of a metal dish.

That morning Cat feasted on liver niblets while I thought about animals, their beauty and restless loyalty. When I met Gwen and Selena on the stoop of the M&H at 5:45, I smiled harder at Gwen than I ever had before, because I understood about not seeing because you weren't used to being seen.

A few weeks after I visited Foodville, Gwen showed up at the M&H with Sean in tow. Before we opened, she pulled Marv aside for a whispered conference. Tim had taken a day job, she explained to us all later. Without money for a sitter and with her sisters too busy to help on a daily basis, she needed to bring Sean along while she put in her hours. Marv liked Gwen quite a bit, so he didn't hesitate his yes, and after that Gwen brought the baby to work. She even stored his baby seat in the kitchen—"Too heavy for me to carry every day," she explained. When Bobby hoisted it over his shoulder, he had to agree.

At first the rest of us were ticked—a busy kitchen's no place for an infant—but pretty soon Bobby and Bet warmed up to Sean. We all took turns watching while Gwen ran her orders, though mostly Sean stayed in back with the cooks. Propped on the counter in his baby seat, safely distant from the grill, he'd pedal his feet ceaselessly while his eyes followed the flames. He loved fire, Sean. We'd joke with Gwen that she'd birthed an arsonist. Bet would pop in back and feed him smooshed pie filling and ice cream. The attention lit Gwen's face like a Christmas pine. But I held back, and Selena too, till one day I caught Selena bending over the baby seat, running her hands along the molded white plastic. She had the same expression she'd worn the day I found her in the storage room, and I felt ashamed. There had to be something odd about me because I couldn't find it in me to love that child.

Still, I put on a show for Gwen's sake, and because I felt sorry for the baby, with his beady mouth and shifty eyes. It must've worked, because one Thursday when Gwen and I clocked out at the same time, she called my name before I disappeared around the corner.

"Caddie!" Her back was burdened with a huge blue and peach striped diaper bag decorated with clown faces, her left shoulder with a dirty beige cotton purse, and her chest with Sean, his baby carrier slung so that his face was snuggled between her breasts. "Would you like to walk partway together?"

The puzzled expression on my face must've shown Gwen what I was thinking.

"Didn't I tell you?" She shifted her purse to her right shoulder. "I just moved closer to the diner. Tim and I—we decided our old place was too far away from town. Now that we have the baby and all."

"Let me carry your bag," I said, by way of yes. She handed Sean over while she shrugged out of the diaper bag's straps. Holding him pressed against my chest, I could feel his tiny baby heart beating and his tiny baby feet kicking against my belly. But I still didn't feel what I thought I should. The intensity. Right then I wondered whether Gwen felt it. I'd always just assumed she loved her son the way they say mothers must love their children. But where did that love come from? It wasn't in my body, I'd always known that. The space where a child could've been was empty or too small or filled with some other hunger.

We walked awhile without speaking. When we turned onto Third, Gwen pointed out her apartment complex: four rows of flimsy one-story wooden buildings, barracks with windows like Swiss cheese holes. Lake Glossy, it was called, though there wasn't any lake and the only glossy thing about the place was the crushed glass littering the sidewalk. My apartment building was two blocks down and one block over, a squat brick square without a name.

"Do you want to come in?"

The apartment was three tiny rooms—a combination kitchen/living room, narrow bath, and bedroom. The thick air smelled of formula, diapers, and talc. When we entered, Sean started to cry as if on cue. Gwen shushed him hard, her voice grittier than I'd ever heard it. "Shut UP, Sean, do you HEAR?" Turning to me, her tone flat and apologetic, "Caddie, I need to feed him." I examined the movie star photos pasted to the refrigerator while she sat down at the rickety card table and unbuttoned her blouse.

The narrow window in the kitchen looked out onto the street; the bedroom bordered a parking lot. Traffic noises crackled like AM radio, but I could hear Sean suckling over the skids and horns. When my brother was born, I'd watched my mother breast-feed. I remember sensing her pleasure, loving his small slurps and coos. The sounds Sean made were different. As he drank, I edged away from Gwen's chair towards the window. It was wrong, the noise. There was more tearing in it than hunger.

When he'd finished, Gwen slipped away to put Sean to sleep. Unasked, I set about making coffee and cut us both slices of raisin bread, buttered as I do, both sides. The coffee smelled strong. I'd slipped cinnamon in, special, so the room would smell like care instead of babies. When Gwen emerged from the bedroom, I was sitting at the card table with coffee, milk, sugar, and buttery bread spread out neatly, newspapers and bills shoved under the table.

"Oh," she said. That was all, but it was enough. She sat down and I noticed that she was heavier, heavier even than when she'd been carrying Sean. It suited her, that roundness. Her breasts looked comfortable on her body, and her chin's extra weight made her look less afraid. But under her eyes the flesh was too thin. It was as if she'd lost ounces of herself in places, ounces that had floated to someplace else.

"Oh." Gwen's mouth was still open in surprise. I wanted that mouth to have coffee in it, bread, and sugar: tiny grains, each carrying a spurt of sweetness. I fixed a cup, remembering from the diner that she took her coffee mostly milk and dense with sugar—gritty, even. I held it out to her and she did drink. The cars were quiet for once, and we just sat. I ate a slice of bread, holding it carefully by the crusts, showing Gwen how to hold it so she wouldn't smear her hands. We finished the things I'd set out, and then I thanked her, and she thanked me, and I went home. It was seven when I got to my place. I'd spent four hours waiting for Gwen to open. Forgiving her when she couldn't. Forgiving myself.

We spent time together after that. We'd walk home, me carrying her diaper bag, Gwen coddling Sean. Always she'd feed him, change him, set him to sleep; always we'd sit silently, eating things I'd set out. Pretty soon I started sneaking things into my bag, treats to surprise her. Oatmeal cookies, muffins, banana bread I'd baked at home. Gwen never said anything, but she ate hungrily and never suggested we save anything for Tim. Once I tried asking in a roundabout way whether Tim brought food home for their supper.

"No," she said. "He doesn't do that. No." She didn't seem to like to talk about Tim, so I put my questions away.

Because of the baby, Gwen cut back on her shifts, working four days instead of her usual five. She had Wednesdays off, and the day dragged for me. I had no reason to dress up or act spunky, and no one to walk me home. Still, there was some pleasure in walking alone, things I noticed only in solitude—the way grass changed color in patches, the sounds of cars when they stopped on a dime. Thinking of cars reminded me of Jo's hands and the brakes she'd made at the factory, all day among so many metals, making magic stop signs only cars could read. How many cars in town or even far away, Utah or Alaska, had parts that girl had touched, parts she'd shaped the way she'd shaped my pulse? It seemed right somehow to know she'd made travel possible, but sad to think she made *stop* happen, never *go*.

I was thinking about Jo one Wednesday as I walked home from the diner. The air was too warm and my feet were too tired, so I decided to cut through Gwen's complex to shorten the trip. I walked through the parking lot behind Gwen's building, glancing in the windows as I passed: curtains, cats, a dying cactus. Two doors down from Gwen's, I paused to watch a dog shove its nose between two grey blinds. "Good boy," I called, and it barked back.

The barking must've woken the baby, because just then I recognized Sean's shrill cry. His yowls were distinctive, astonishingly off-key, as if he was missing the part of his brain that taught him to cry properly. It stung to listen. I imagined neighbors everywhere peering out their windows to scold Gwen into action. As his cries bled on and on, I walked over to Gwen's bedroom window, where flimsy checkered curtains sagged on the sill.

Sean's cries hadn't stopped. I pressed my face against the glass. The curtains were parted just a sliver at the center. Sure enough, he lay sprawled in his crib, mouth open to the ceiling, howling cruel vowels. But no grey-haired friend or angelic sister entered to chasten or comfort him. He howled on and on, till it hurt to watch, till a thought began to rouse itself within me, ugly but feasible.

I glanced around. The parking lot appeared deserted. The window stuck at first, but it wasn't locked and slid open without much effort on my second try. It was low to the floor, and I stepped down easily onto carpet from my awkward perch on the sill.

It never occurred to me that I might get caught or to think that Tim might be sprawled on the sofa, dozing, and wake with a start. It never occurred to me that I might interrupt some gawky high school girl's late afternoon rendezvous with her beau on Gwen's couch. My head was so filled with Sean's cries that I would've done anything to stop them. The sounds he made were musty, rancid even. I just wanted them to stop and didn't think about the consequences. That's what I tell myself, though sometimes now I wonder if the reason I didn't worry more about breaking in was because I already knew what I'd find. I felt no remorse as I approached Gwen's ugly baby, tugged him from his crib, and pressed him to my chest, cries and all.

His sounds kept on but no longer bothered me because a daunting smell had taken over. Through the slick plastic of his tiny diaper I could feel liquidy warmth. Breathing through my mouth, I carried him over to the ironing board Gwen used as a changing table. I undid the diaper gingerly and dropped it into the foot-pedal wastebasket beneath the board. Then I set out with baby wipes to undo the damage, which was extensive. I wiped and tossed and wiped and tossed. Then I powdered, finally slipping Sean into a new diaper.

By then his cries had changed to a sound I'd never heard him make before.

"Say that again, boy," I whispered, and he did. "Gurgle." It was almost pretty, that sound. "Say again," and he did, and then another new one, "Gaaaaa." There was lace in it. The vowels strung together properly. His back felt warm and silky, and his breath was a little breeze. "Gaaaaa," his mouth made. "Say again," and I walked him into the kitchen.

There was no Gwen; there was no sitter. As I paced around the apartment, Sean pressed against one shoulder, I saw only a single cereal bowl in the sink and a large Styrofoam box on the table. Sandwich crusts and a few soggy fries were littered inside, the remnants of the lunch Gwen had taken home with her the day before.

Not only was there no sitter, there was no Tim.

Why hadn't I noticed before? Not once, not once in all my visits had I seen one thing to make me think Gwen's husband actually lived here. She never mentioned him anymore. I stepped into the bathroom and searched the cabinets—one toothbrush, one hairbrush, a lady's pink plastic razor, cosmetics in a basket over the toilet, but that was all. She'd been waiting for me to ask, the question lined her silence, but I'd been too something—desirous?—to notice.

I heard noises: steps, the rattle of keys. With no time to think, I took the coward's route, ran into the bedroom and set Sean back in his crib. To the sound of a lock clicking, I climbed back out the window the way I'd come. My instinct was to run, but curiosity won out. From a safe distance I watched Gwen enter the room.

Cries escaped the window, shrill and desolate. Not Sean's.

■ ■ ■

I held onto Gwen's secret life simply because I did not know who to tell.

The secret bound us, circular, a wedding ring too loose for one woman's finger. But I wore it and she didn't. I saw through her, but she didn't know it, and so she didn't know we shared a secret.

The day after my break-in, I arrived at work a little early and watched her snail-shape's slow approach, baby cupped against her chest, diaper bag arched on her back like a shell. There looked to be love in her labor, love, and that made it hard to imagine this woman leaving her child to the mercy of air. It was her mystery, the way she let go of her baby. The way she wouldn't turn to us for help.

An ugly mystery. After all, a baby. I wondered if a child understood loneliness, if it could sense abandonment, if there was a difference between Gwen going into the kitchen for a glass of water and Gwen leaving Sean for hours while she did her shopping. I imagined Sean gazing around the crib, trying to comprehend bars and stuffed bears, listening to trucks in the lot out back. Did every shape, every sound mean some strange baby thing, something he'd soon forget, never to be remembered? Maybe after the death that I imagined birth to be—the tearing away—a child was so full of sadness it couldn't speak. Maybe he knew everything, but grief glazed his eyes and stopped his tongue.

Did Sean know his father was gone?

I still wanted Gwen.

But this animal gesture, this abandonment. What mother would leave her child to straddle its own filth? It was why I never wanted children, what I'd seen in Gwen—the potential to abuse them, not out of cruelty, but sheer disinterest or desperation. It was neglect, pure and simple, neglect, but how to explain how I knew what I did? I rehearsed words in my head. *Gwen, the other day I climbed through your window and changed your kid's diaper.* But the lines never came out and the secret grew, bulky as Gwen's packhorse shape.

We continued walking home together. As always she asked me to come in and pass the time. Once I'd jumped at the chance, but now it was *no no no* and soon she noticed.

"Caddie, is something wrong? You're always too busy to see me, nowadays. Seems like you might be sick and tired of sitting in my smelly old place, listening to Sean snore and waiting for him to poop. Why don't we go out on the town some Saturday night, just us two? We'll leave the boys at home," she tugged on Sean's hood, "have a few beers and a heart-to-heart."

"Grand." It would be the perfect time to tell her. "But Gwen, promise me you'll find a sitter so Tim doesn't resent us for sticking him with the baby."

Gwen's face stayed smooth. I began just then to realize she was skilled. "That might be hard."

"Why don't you call Selena?" Gwen's eyes lit as I spoke. Why hadn't we thought of it before? She was single and reliable, she had a truck, and she needed money. "Her TV is busted. She can watch her dramas while we paint the town."

Starry. I felt starry. All week long I counted the days till Saturday. We could stay out all night if it pleased us. The thing was settled when Gwen asked Selena to sit, and Selena said yes. She seemed to like the little fellow. Certainly she spent enough time admiring his baby seat. We went giddy over it, even telling Helen, who just smiled her Mona Lisa smile. I got so gleeful I nearly forgot the weight of my knowing.

But before Saturday came round, Bobby took the burden off my hands. It was the stroller that caught his eye. On Thursday around ten-thirty, Gwen ambled out front with Sean for a quick smoke, then stole a corner booth to gulp some breakfast. Bobby was rotating the pie dishes in the dessert case when he saw the thing. I heard his shock before I saw it; the door jangled and he was gone, returning a few seconds later with Sean in his arms.

Cory Flint set his toast butter-side down on the counter and I poured his coffee into his saucer while we watched Bobby march over to Gwen. He meant business; his boots jangled. Gwen looked glazed, her eyes glued to Sean's crocheted booties. When Bobby reached the table, he set the baby down on the counter and tossed a handful of sugar packets at Sean's feet for him to play with.

"What were you thinking?"

Gwen shrugged. "I'm eating breakfast. Is that a problem?"

"You can't just leave a child by its lonesome. He could've swung his stroller off into the parking lot or choked on his hat or been kidnapped by any old monster driving by."

"It only takes me seven minutes to eat."

"In thirty seconds Sean could swallow a button off his sweater."

Gwen pushed her dishes aside, picked up her baby, and headed for the kitchen. A few minutes later she appeared with Sean's baby carrier turned wrong-way round, his fuzzy head poking out from her back like a camel's hump. She worked that way all shift, only sitting down once or twice to rest. Towards the end of the day Marv came up to her, his face open, but she whipped out her order pad and began adding up tabs with ferocious intensity. At exactly three o'clock she clocked out. I followed five minutes later and caught up with her as she left the diner.

"Gwen, wait up."

"What do you want?"

"Just walking company."

She started to say no; I saw her lips shape that syllable. But she stopped herself before N became O became No Caddie company. Instead she handed me her baby. "My back hurts. You hold him, please?" We walked together down the driveway.

When we reached her apartment, she unlocked the door and took Sean from my arms but didn't invite me in. I'd turned around, my face set towards home, when she called out, "Stay?"

Inside she fed Sean. When she put him to sleep, she beckoned me into her bedroom with one finger. We both stood over him as he spit bubbles and kicked restlessly. His face was bright pink and his bald head had bluish veins zigzagging towards his temples. "Sometimes I wake up in the middle of the night and I don't know who he is." Gwen began humming softly and Sean's kicking slowed. As she bent to kiss him and tighten his diaper around his poky belly, I glanced over at her bed—one pillow, tossed on a diagonal at the head of the mattress.

We sat as always—sipping coffee, eating Oreos, and watching the road through the center part in her blue and white checkered curtains. My dress felt sticky underneath the arms and at my back. For a long while no cars passed and I got bored staring at the same wilty tree, waiting for someone else to make something happen.

"I don't always know how." Gwen's forehead wrinkled. "Sometimes I just have to make it all up. And sometimes I get it wrong."

"I know about making it up as you go along."

"I hate rules." She glanced away, but I could see water edging her eyes like translucent mascara. "Caddie, has it ever been like this for you? You have something. Someone. And it's what you thought you wanted, but then it isn't anymore. Only you can't go back. You're in a new country, and the old country is underwater. I didn't ask to have Sean. Tim said he couldn't have children. Then he laughed when I stopped bleeding and started puking. He said, 'A baby is a life.' He said it was mine now and here's money to keep it. He said 'I do' but he really didn't. Now I'm stuck with Sean twenty-four, seven and he doesn't understand what I tell him. You can't make a baby do anything. I thought if I left him alone for little pieces of time—"

"It doesn't work that way with babies."

"Oh, Caddie." Gwen's face filled with water. "He looks exactly like his father."

It felt strange to hear my name with tears in it. Pushing my chair back, I stood up and walked around the table, then put my hands on Gwen's shoulders. We stayed still for a while, touching. The neighbors to the left of Gwen's apartment opened and shut their door. "Grover!" Through the window, a dog appeared in the road, skittering to safety as a car slipped past. Even if we never moved from this room, we'd still be witnesses to live things giving themselves away.

"Some people, when they see babies, they think of time in a good way. Time going forward, being the future. Not just today. But when I look at Sean," she reached up and put her palm on my hand. I could feel her ring. "I think of dying. How one day he'll be nothing again, the way he was." She'd worn her diamond. She didn't usually. Mostly it was the plain gold band. But Gwen had her diamond on, and it had somehow turned around so that the stone pressed into my knuckle. Later, when I looked it over, I could see the indentation and a scratch the size of a needle's eye. "Caddie, if I could push him back inside me, I would." Gwen's dress was flowers, pink and white blooms against faint yellow stripes. The stripes didn't match up around the arms. I wondered why she hadn't chosen a simpler pattern. While I was thinking this, while she was speaking, she grasped my hand. I felt the moment give itself up to me and understood how Jo must've felt, wanting me, not sure I was offering what she wished. I felt Gwen's hand collect around mine and I almost took it and squeezed and bent over her head to kiss the raggedy part in her hair.

Instead I let go of her hand and stepped away from her chair. "It'll do us good to go out on Saturday. You'll cheer up." I made my face chipper. "What are you cooking Tim for dinner?"

In other words, I failed her.

That night I took out my Bible again, thinking Ruth's story might comfort me. But all those commandments, all those orders, all those ways to be with no room for the world I saw and struggled in just made me tired. So I put the book away and dredged up a pen and a scrap of paper.

My list was headed "Safe Distance." I wrote up eight ways to stop myself from getting too close. Like, "Don't touch her." Like, "Think how she left her son." But for every wrong there was a right waiting to be written in my silent list, the list I kept in my head. *She wants something. She's just like you, only she doesn't know it. You be her teacher.*

All the next day at work I read my lists over to myself in my head. It's a wonder I didn't write them down on my pad; instead of "turkey club," I might've scrawled *Tim's gone;* instead of "two eggs over easy," I might've jotted *Gwen could please me.*

Little love letters, but also little warnings—she's a girl, like me. She's not Jo. She'll never throw me over, tumble on top, pin me down. And she'll taste of girlish things, perfume and powder between her legs. It's a wonder I didn't give myself away when I asked her, right there in front of a customer, "Are we still on for tomorrow?" Gwen just nodded, her whole body moving a little with the gesture, so that Sean's pom-pom hat bobbed into his sleepy eyes.

It was sad to see Gwen carrying Sean all shift. Her back hurt her—anyone could see it. Even Marv commented quietly to me. Around eleven Bobby slipped out from the kitchen and walked over to where Gwen was wiping up a spill. "Why don't you set Sean in back like you used to? He can watch me cook. His baby seat's all ready."

Selena and I were kneeling on opposite seats of the same booth, cleaning the windows' dusty blinds. I paused to watch as Selena wiped each individual slat twice, once with a cloth drenched in window cleaner, once with a clean cloth, softer. Her hands were so gentle. Everything Selena did seemed so thorough. But as Bobby spoke, her hands stuttered clumsily so that the blinds shook, chattering against the glass like teeth.

For a long moment Gwen was silent. Then she swung Sean's carrier around so that his head bristled her chin. Stroking his forehead, tucking his cap more securely over his tiny head, she smiled at her son. It was the first real smile I'd seen her give Sean, though it might've been for Bobby's benefit. When she looked up at Bobby, her face went plain. She swung Sean's carrier around till he rested on her back again and returned to her scrubbing.

Watching Gwen, a sort of dizziness set in. I felt that I was on the edge of knowing something very important. She set the sponge going in circles; there was something I almost knew, something I could almost understand. But then it was gone and Selena was murmuring, her elbow lightly brushing mine. "You have to love it," she was saying, and I knew she meant Sean, but her voice was too low for Gwen to hear, almost too low for me to listen. She seemed to be speaking to the blinds with her low, low voice and her fluttering hands, like sign language, the way they made something of air, fingers, and nothingness.

Bobby was back in the kitchen. The lunch crowd was starting to trickle in. Selena and I left the blinds half tended, took out our pads, and began taking orders. The rush lasted till one-thirty, when I slipped into the kitchen to let Bobby know his sister wanted to talk to him.

"Tiffany's in booth seven. Said to stop by when you have a clean grill and a spot of time." He didn't seem to hear me. "Everything OK?"

Bobby handed me a note scrawled on a receipt, in Gwen's curlicue hand and all caps. "IM' A GOOD MOTHER DONT' SAY IM' NOT." He leaned over the grill and let the paper catch flame. "I just told her the truth."

I could smell the note, smell the ink. I could smell the word *mother*, smoldering.

"What'd I do? Can't a grown-up teach a kid a lesson?"

"Give Gwen some time. You miss tending Sean yourself, that's all. Maybe if you said it that way, she'd forgive you for chiding her."

He must've said something because the next morning Gwen walked matter-of-factly into the kitchen and set Sean in his baby seat, within sight but out of reach of the grill's flames. Sean gurgled as Gwen strapped him in, safe enough for any journey. It made me imagine the diner a train, swaying side to side, elephantine, Sean safely seat belted while we large folk rattled restlessly. After that morning Gwen almost always parked him grillside. He'd pedal his booties frantically and spout glee-ful bubbles while Marv and Bobby showed off their prowess. Some-times for a change of scenery Helen took him into her office, where she'd set up a miniature crib made of old vegetable crates. Sometimes Bet or Selena carried him into the front room, propping him on the table of a booth like a zoo exhibit. With so much attention, the baby started looking human. It made me wonder if the thing that kept him ugly for so long was loneliness.

Sean's newfound happiness was one of the things on my mind as I scootched into a booth to wait for Gwen at the Yellow Horse. She came running into the bar as if from a rainstorm. For Gwen, this was an es-cape. It made me sure, more than ever, that I could never be a mother. Watching her running, taking the stairs two at a time, her girlishness thrown off like a cloak, I recognized how precious my freedom to come and go and cry and sleep on my own clock's inner hours. When she slid across from me, it was like Jo sliding into home through a cloud of red dust. Her brash clumsiness made me want her, and then there I was again, heavy with desire at the Yellow Horse, gazing into a foamy head of beer as if drinking could ever ease not fitting in.

"Being here reminds me of being with Jo." It seemed safe enough to say. Gwen didn't need to know why.

In the dim light of the bar, her lips glowed neon. "You've never told me much about him. You split up right before I started working at the diner, right?" There was more curiosity in those words than in all the phrases Gwen had ever spoken in my direction. I'd forgotten that she hadn't known Jo and didn't know our history. It felt odd to talk about Jo with Gwen—odd, but sexy also. Gwen leaned forward across the table and my descriptions began shifting till what I was describing wasn't Jo's face, her job, or our small house, but the sensuousness of our everyday life together.

Gwen played with her glass, picking it up, putting it down again. It was so tempting to tell her I knew or to ask some pointed question. But instead I waited for the word *Tim* to form on her lips, wondering if his departure was as mysterious as Jo's.

"Men are jerks. Sometimes I think I should just go queer. Next time I see Tim, I'll tell him, 'Go fetch,'" and she dropped her ring into her glass, gold on gold, the outline of the circle barely visible. Gwen's elbows shook the table. I'd never seen her loose like this. Snorting a little, she kept on. "Yeah, maybe those queer girls have it right. But they're so ugly. Have you ever seen a queer girl, Caddie? They look like mules."

"I hate seeing you upset, Gwennie. Maybe we shouldn't talk about love mysteries."

"But I want to hear more about Jo!" Petulant. "I'm not leaving till you tell me about your fine romance. Why aren't you still together?"

"Jo took off." I pushed my chair back. The radio was set to some diva, crooning. "It ended about a year before you came to work. I woke up one morning alone—no Jo. Coldest winter on record. All I remember is trying to get warm, my fingers white at the tips. Even the simplest sentences iced over the second they hit the air. It was cold outside, and it was cold of Jo to leave without warning. But the worst thing? It was all planned out. Jo decided at least two weeks in advance that she was going to leave me."

Gwen tipped her glass, fumbling till she found her ring. Beer trickled onto the table, staining the lacy cuffs of her blouse. "No way, Caddie. I can't believe it." She stood up, untangling her purse, put on her sweater wrong arm in, took it off, stumblingly put it on again. I rushed to keep up with her. The slip felt heavy on my tongue. Now what? She'd never speak to me again. I dropped a few crumpled bills onto the table, hoping it was enough. Outside she walked quickly towards Selena's truck. Her stride was steady for a drunk, but I didn't want her to drive.

"Hand me the keys."

"I'm so disgusted I can hardly *see.*" She unlocked the driver's seat and slid inside.

"Gwen, I'm sorry. I should've told you. I knew you'd be angry. Look, you shouldn't drive."

"Bastard!" Gwen slammed her fist against the steering wheel. The horn blurted an accompaniment. She slid out of the front seat, handed me the keys, and walked around, wobbling, to the passenger's side. "I'm so disgusted I can hardly *see.* Caddie, I *swear.*"

"I knew you'd be mad. Try to understand, please, Gwen. Try to—"

"I just can't believe both our lovers left us the same way. Except when my man left, I had a baby to think about. At least Jo didn't leave you with one crying and one on the way."

Somehow she hadn't heard. I'd slipped, but nothing had come of it. I started the ignition and breathed out. The car's stirrings echoed my sigh. Then it sunk in—"one on the way"—and I remembered I wasn't supposed to know Tim was gone. Act surprised, Caddie. "Your husband left you?"

She pressed her face against the window. "When I started bringing Sean to work was when Tim left."

"And now you're pregnant again?"

"Was." She turned from the window to look at me, but my eyes were on the road: narrow, one lane over Tompkins Bridge. When we paused for a red light at Murphysville Road, I fiddled with the radio. "Busted," Gwen tapped the dial with one finger. "But I can sing." Her voice came towards me as if from far away, surprisingly deep, even husky, as if all the things she knew she kept hidden in her throat.

When we arrived at her apartment, I parked Selena's truck in the lot. Gwen wanted to drive me home, but I refused.

"I'd rather walk."

"Caddie, don't. I'd feel terrible if some bastard jumped you." Bastard got her started on Tim again. She rambled while I leaned against the hood. I didn't want to be rude, so I stayed till the ranting stopped and she remembered who I was. "Caddie." Her face was simple again. Placid. "Caddie," and I liked the way she said my name, coming down hard on the first syllable. "Why don't you stay over?"

Selena was only too happy not to have to drive me home. Sean had cried for hours, she said, and only just gone to sleep. The TV was on, its light blue and chilly. Voices breezed from the screen like stray diner gossip. I switched off the set as Selena collected her things. "Sleep tight," she said. Then the door was shut, the apartment quiet, and Gwen and I alone, preparing to spend the night.

I borrowed a washcloth to scrub my face and teeth. Inside the tiny bathroom, the sound of the faucet blocked everything out. I held my hands under the water while I filled the sink. Steam floated, glossy. When the water was near to overflowing, I sunk my face into it like an anchor, letting my hair float, weedy, around my eyes. When I came up I gulped air, then scrubbed at my head with a towel. Everything was quiet except for a gurgling I couldn't place—the drain? But the sink had run dry. I opened the door a crack. It was coming from Gwen's room. Someone talking, someone answering—Tim? Had Tim come back, had I nearly slept beside him, my hands full of his girl in gaudy dreams, committing adultery on his sofa even as he snored his night away, forgiven too easily, cozy beside our Gwen? There was a glass on the sink. I took Gwen's green toothbrush out and set it against the wall.

"I'm sorry, I'm sorry," over and over again. She was *sorry sorry sorry, sorry* for leaving him, *sorry* for not watching out. Sean answered with short gurgles, then coos, a lilt in his breath I hadn't heard before. "Not your fault you look like your father."

I slept on Gwen's sofa, chilly beneath a flimsy sheet printed with Raggedy Anns and Andys. Before I went to sleep, I looked down at the sheet, row after row of raggedy girls tied to raggedy boys. "Good night, Gwen."

"Good night, Caddie." Then she vanished behind the battered brown door. I was cold and coiled into a ball to keep from shivering. Huddled like that, my limbs curved against each other for warmth, I thought of Gwen and Tim, sharing space. Or not sharing. In an odd way Gwen's pregnancies made sense to me. I remembered sleeping with David, how sex happened. When I signaled my desires, he'd shut down, but when he let on that he wanted something, an unstoppable clock was set in motion. Sex with David was only ever an interlude, a spot of time disconnected from the rest of the day's emotions and events. With Jo, sex was everything and everywhere. It was all time, and time was sex, so that once I realized she would probably leave me, I broke her mother's china clock.

Maybe Gwen's mistake was an excess of passion. But she'd said it was Tim's doing, Tim's lie. How many lies had David told me? I remembered him pushing my face between his legs. The taste was bitter, not sweet. His sweat too was bitter, almost rancid. I remembered the smell Jo gave off when she pleased me, the scent of her orgasm, the feel of her body coiling in sync with mine. But time moved differently, not just bodies. David was quick. Everything happened in one brown paper package. With Jo, touch lingered. There was no start or stop. But I'd never given back what she'd given to me. What if I took a woman and found the experience wanting, what if I didn't know how?

I'd always thought that if Jo came back, I'd take her in without question. That night, remembering David, remembering how Jo had pleased me but stopped my hand when I tried to touch, I began to doubt. If she came back, I'd want more from her than she'd given before. Give and take, push and pull; I'd want to try my turn at holding her down, watching her shiver as I took her with one hand.

She'd have to give something up, if she came back.

Then that thought passed, and I was lonely again.

I dreamed of Gwen. In my dream her bedroom was decorated with live things: plants and flowers, everything wild, a blossom field in a fairy tale. No Sean, but small animals everywhere. She was lying like a princess on a great bed, her hair all golden and spread out on the pillow, not straggly like it was mostly. Below her closed eyelids her skin was smooth. The shadows and bags of sleepless nights were gone.

Gwen sat up, very prissy and dainty. When she saw me, her face squinched, like she'd eaten a lemon. "I thought I told you to clean the bathroom," she said. Looking down, I realized I held a bucket in my left hand, full of toilet cleaner and Comet and whatnot. In my right hand was a huge scrub brush. I scurried away, but not fast enough. Ivy grew around my feet as I ran, covering Gwen instantly, tripping me up.

I woke before it swallowed me whole, shook off Ann and Andy, splashed water on my face in her bathroom, scrawled "Thanks" in eyebrow pencil on a paper towel by the sink, and tiptoed out, shutting the door quietly behind me.

On Tuesday I lingered on my walk to work, so I missed the usual huddle on the front steps of the diner. All shift I was clumsy. Plates spoke to me, asking me to free them from human bondage and I obliged, splattering strawberry topping all over my tennies.

I no longer wanted to kiss her. She was just a girl, a little cruel sometimes, a little stupid. I felt love fly up, as much a mystery as when love flew down. Was desire simply lost, like an odd earring or stray sock, something to be searched for and found again? If I called its name, would it fly back to me? Around ten-thirty I stepped out back to smoke and Gwen joined me, lighting her cigarette off mine. The nicotine sparked tingles in my blood, but Gwen bored me. I was back to Caddie Solo, cold in spite of stern tobacco.

"C'mon," I said, "we'll be late for the second half of our shift."

She exhaled one last long breath, a beautiful, sheer white stream that covered her like a gown. As the lacy white veil disappeared, we turned and went inside.

■■■

It was Cat came to comfort me when I gave Gwen up.

First inching towards bed, then curling, whip-smart, at the foot of the blanket. One morning I woke up ticklish, something twitching, all atangle—Cat resting on my forehead like a cap, tail a matching scarf across my throat. Without Jo or an imaginary Gwen to warm my nights, I needed something to ease heat in. Cat's supple body seemed to say the soothing, silly things a lover might say after sex and before sleep. Sometimes her purr sounded like the blurred words Jo spoke as she drifted off to sleep, the "mergalan" she used to mumble into my throat, telling me (I liked to think) that there was no one else, telling me she loved me so much more than the ones who'd come before. Telling me she'd never leave me. Sweet, though we both knew she was lying. Without a lover to mumble, sleep came slow. Cat restored slumber, and for that I was grateful.

But there were other things.

I've never been one to crush animals to my bosom. Meat's money. That's how I was raised and how the heartland thinks. Cat softened me, got me to where Marv's burgers sickened my belly if I thought too long about where they came from. I started eating more pie, more cottage cheese with pineapple, more German potato salad and vegetable soup. I avoided BLTs, Bobby's fried ham, and Marv's lemon chicken till Selena asked after my fickle ways with food.

When I explained that Cat got me thinking about animals as animals, not so much as meat, Selena sort of smirked and I thought she'd tease. But her smirk was friendly. We were sitting on stools in front of the counter and all of a sudden she spun around, the way little kids do. Her crinkly skirt flew as she twirled.

"You love her," Selena said, matter-of-factly. I'd never thought it that way before, but there it was. I'd pressed her slick fur to my face, I'd run my hands across her slinky back, I'd fed her little kibbles and warmed her in quilts and nubby blankets. She cared for me, even licking at tears when I cried. I hadn't thought Selena would understand, but she did. She surprised me with opening herself up to knowing how it might be to care for a four-legged beastie. "You're different when you want to be," Selena added, and her words were warm.

It wasn't just food things that changed after Cat came. Time moved differently too. So I wasn't surprised when Selena found the deer, her body unnaturally supple, as if trying to remember motion. Somehow Cat had prepared me for that and all that happened after.

It was a tree that housed her.

Behind the diner, a stretch of woods. Not forest, nothing quite so grand, only clumps of moss and oaks and walnuts. When snow came to Cartwheel, the spare woods went elegant and glossy—trees flung with lace, glass shivering the creek, slivers of stars fallen across the footpath. Sometimes a few of us would save Sunday to rendezvous in the diner, special. Helen and Marv called it a snow day. We'd meet in the shut-down place, its darkness and emptiness mysterious, fix cocoa and sugar cookies and maple snow, and take short walks through the burdened trees.

Spring changed everything. All the weight of the snow became noise, the sound of ice speeding to meet the earth, the creek breaking free of its frozen cover. Snow fell in lumpy chunks to the ground. I swear it made me hungry to see it, it looked so much like bread. "Manna," Bet called it, because spring was manna to us working girls. Winter was hard in Cartwheel. When folks from Indy complained about their seasons, we just laughed. Indy was nothing like our windswept home, where even light snow danced so lustily that driving was tense. Winter in Cartwheel meant people stocked their basements with canned peaches and beans and flour. Winter in Cartwheel meant people ate at home.

Spring signaled the beginning of making money again. We were all in debt from winter's bills and boots, so we needed tips and our smiles widened. We didn't have time for making cookies or taking walks in the woods out back. But that year we all had cabin fever. Our hands were rubbed raw from shoveling, our lips chapped till we wore them white instead of rose. We needed to know the sun was coming, to feel its breath on our shoulders, to walk ground that was damp instead of crisp. There were new sensations to be had, now that spring was come, so when Selena suggested a Sunday trip to see the trees showing off their buds, Gwen and I agreed.

"I've got church," Bet said, so she was out. We decided not to tell Bobby, Helen, or Marv. We'd pack a lunch and walk awhile, till we found a clearing good for gobbling sandwiches and soda.

It felt sweet to stride after winter's small steps. It felt snug to touch live things again: the ragged bark of trees, cupped blossoms, a fallen bird's nest. Mostly it felt strong to walk without boots and layers of woolsies, and to breathe deeply without feeling the sting of cold air coat our lungs.

We hiked to our usual spot, a clearing within sight of the diner, but before we could unpack our lunches, Selena suggested we keep on. "I've never been this way," pointing towards where the woods met Quarry Road, "and I want to see if it's any different." So we headed towards the road, guided by faint traffic sounds and Selena's sense of direction, taking our time, touching things that begged touching, listening for birds, watching for sun.

There was a clump of bushes, a split-open stump, a patch of moss, a straggle of oaks, and then we saw and didn't see. We'd gone past the stump a few paces before Selena stopped, her face drained of color.

"What was that?"

The minute she said it, Gwen and I spied, in our past vision, the deer in her coffin. We all three rushed back and skidded to a pause in front of her impossible pose. She was young, a fawn almost, and gawky-skinny. Her fur was a sunset, her legs spare and elegant, her ears useless now for any task but beauty. Her hooves made me ashamed of my silly, stubby nails with their chipped pink paint. They were feet and hands both, a deep glossy brown. They'd ridden over yesterday's earth like boats, her tail a downed sail, or maybe a target.

We were listening for live things. Why should we hear the dead, and why should we see, when we were watching for sunlight, legs folded in on themselves like shadows, a broken neck drooping like a useless prayer? Once a man died of a heart attack in Dairy Queen while I was eating a sundae. I didn't see but heard the gasp and thud of it. It's not what people say, death. It isn't slow and soft. Always there's the ragged grasping. How can you help but reach for someone or something to pull you back towards the roll and swag of the living? There's something wrong with folding the dead into their caskets. Death should look like itself, to remind us of the difference between sleeping and letting go.

"Shot," Selena said. It was a hunter's work, a fresh kill. Her body was warm, you could see that, and Gwen touched it, so we knew for sure. Someone had taken her because he wanted to prove that he could balance her body in the sight of his gun for the seconds it took to pull the trigger. Her way of probing the earth and nibbling at greeny things attracted him, the way a girl's breasts high in a halter top and a girl's butt rounded out in a fringed mini attracted the men down at The Depot, where I worked for three months years ago, in another town.

He'd made her a sculpture. But not a sculpture of a deer.

"She looks human," Gwen gasped.

It was in the way he'd folded her forelegs into her chest, crossing her arms, like a girl when she hides her breasts from the boys at school. Her hind legs were crossed like a fancy lady's, sitting and sipping tea, careful not to let her lacy slip show at the spot where her skirt hem hit her knees. He'd crisscrossed her, till she looked like the kind of girl who stares in the mirror at nineteen, touching the scar hidden by thick, reddish-black hair, running her palms down the skimpy length of a halter, feeling the nub of sequins against her raw hands, knowing her reflection is the only home she has.

We fled.

I wished I'd taken running seriously in junior high. I wished I could've made it through that stretch of trees in two seconds, but the route dragged on, forever, Gwen at my heels (she had flimsy shoes), Selena far ahead (perky and athletic go together, I guess), the sun beaming now that we had no desire for it, our breathing and stumbling all mixed together, our ankles protesting against scratches and snarls till finally the diner glowed silver in our sight. For some reason Selena had the key, and without asking whether it was right—what was right, now that we'd seen this thing?—we let ourselves in and collected our breath in the quiet, shutdown kitchen. After a time of panting, Gwen set about silently making coffee, I rummaged for cream, and Selena slipped into the front room for sugar. What was funny was how we all three took our coffee the same, heavy with cream, loaded down with sugar, till black was fawn-colored. There had to be sweetness in our mouths, there had to be something heavy to taste, not the watery, slight tang of black coffee, but a drink so rich that we could concentrate, for one moment, on taste.

When we'd finished drinking all we could, I washed the cups while Gwen wiped the table and Selena rinsed out the coffeemaker. "What should we name her?" Selena asked.

That was when I got the idea for the funeral.

Oh, we talked some later about how horrible and how could anyone do such a thing and what a sadist ("What's a sadist?" Gwen asked). But mostly we took anger for granted and let it stay a cloud, a scent, a shiver.

What we focused on was the caring-for.

I can't remember what name we gave her. Mostly she was doe. Soon Doe became her name. We brought Bet in on it, then told Helen and Marv and Bobby. It was Bobby volunteered to carve a box for her. It was

Bobby too who agreed to go out to the woods and tug her from the tree. "Three shots in the back, and a sloppy job of it." He started to say more, but I stopped him.

He took her body and rested it in the shed. "It's going fast, of course, so I'll build this box tonight and we'll do the burial tomorrow." We had to plan it overnight, Gwen, Selena, Bet, and I. Bobby tried to be in on the planning, but Selena spoke for us when she told him no.

"The ceremony has to be ladies only."

The next night we four gathered behind the diner around the raggedy pine box Bobby had built. We'd dug a grave earlier that day in the softest spot we could find. I'd wanted us to do that ourselves too, but Gwen and Bet pooped out and asked Marv and Bobby for help. That made me mad. Selena too. "We could've built the box ourselves, if we'd tried," I said.

We all dressed in dark colors for the ceremony. Selena didn't own but one black thing, and that was a prom gown slit straight up the back, sleeves off the shoulder. Bet and I looked pretty much the same in navy skirt and blouse sets, but Bet's grey hair was hidden under a spiffy black beret. "Got it for Christmas some years back. When me and Roy were going to see the Eiffel Tower. Then we heard about the plane crash, you know, the big one out at O'Hare, and that was the end of wanting to fly over some ocean just to find romance we could get cheaper at home."

Selena, Gwen, and I exchanged glances. Bet was clueless sometimes. "Who'd want to sleep with Roy, anyway?" Gwen giggled into my ear, but I didn't nod. Roy had been good to Jo. They'd been best buds at the factory. Roy was who Jo first talked to about asking me out.

Gwen's outfit was another doozie. Like all of her dresses, it was hand-made, "a few years back for my grandfather's funeral." And like every-thing she ever wore, it had flowers on it, this time embroidered onto the cloth.

You know how something you see wrong can haunt you? When Gwen first showed up at our meeting place, all I could see of her in the dim light was the scrawled outline of bushy flowers floating everywhere, out of control. That red thread ("on sale at Odd Lots, they never said why") was glow in the dark—not the usual neon candy color kind of glow, but a Halloween crimson, the kind of red your own body makes when the skin first splits around a cut. Gwen's dress and shoes disappeared against the night sky, but those red flowers pulsed, and her blonde hair floated like a hand hovering over a screaming mouth. Then she went back to being Gwen, so ordinary.

We started the procession. All at once our jokes fled like balloons. We stepped stern. We took walking seriously. Selena, Gwen, and I carried her on our shoulders while Bet walked in front with a flashlight, a Bible, and a black cotton cloth. After a slow stretch of walking, I felt a finger on my arm. "Caddie," Selena's voice was slight as her touch, "look round, but don't do it fast." I turned my head. At first dusk was everything, but then another shape came clear—a fifth mourner, also in black, wobbly heels crunching the dirt.

We'd forgotten her, forgotten that she was a lady too. I couldn't remember the last time Helen had joined us for gossip or to share a cigarette when things slowed down. She usually stayed in her office, doing the numbers and daily things. She ran the place, but it was easy to forget her. Marv was always there, flipping burgers or spicing soups. When Helen appeared, it was with him. The couple had a way of blending together. Yet somehow none of us were shocked to see her or shocked that she was alone. It wasn't something the men could do. The deer was a doe. The hunter had raped her. Up to us to mourn, up to us to remember.

When we reached the dirt clearing we'd spread near the stump, we tried to set her down in unison, but I slipped a little and there was a thump before Gwen and Selena could ease their parts to earth. "That's the Lord clapping his hands for our labor," Bet said. Selena rolled her eyes, but at least it glossed over my Caddie-clumsiness.

We pushed the coffin to the edge of the hole. Bet draped the black cloth over the lid and set the flashlight on top. We three faced her, our hands joined, while she read stretches from the Bible, weird bits. There was the Good Shepherd and his lambs, which I pretty much expected, but also some from Noah, which was clever, and Genesis, about the snake. Then Selena said a prayer, which sounded mostly like we were getting ready to eat dinner, and Gwen sang in that husky voice I loved. While she sang we closed our eyes because the song worked more on our hearts than the Bible ever could. It wasn't about deer but about loving someone who slipped away like water. The way she sang made me wish she'd never stop. When we opened our eyes, something had changed. At first I thought it was just darkness, falling this new way through the skimpy tree cover, dappling everything with polka dots. Then I realized that Helen had moved over to the pile of sticks and dried leaves.

"It's time to light this," she said, nudging a twig with her toe. We all jumped at the sound of her voice. Gwen fumbled in her pocket for matches, and even though we'd agreed beforehand that I would light the fire, there was no question now that Helen would toss the match. She held it up to her lips before the throw. Her face looked older in the glow of the burn. Then the wood was on fire, and the sweet smell of earth mingled with the sour smell of smoke and burning moss. We stood silent and still. When the last ash had eaten itself and red had burned to glimmer, Selena and I walked back to the diner for water to douse it out.

When we returned to the site, the fire was mostly done. "The moss and wood on the bottom were damp," Bet explained. Helen was kneeling by the circle and Gwen looked sleepy. When Selena and I poured blue water on the dying orange of all that rotting wood, the fire let out a sound halfway between a squeak and a sigh. All five of us prodded at it with sticks just to be sure it was out. When the last ember was gone, we walked back to the diner.

Dinner was spaghetti with meatballs and spaghetti with mushrooms. I was flattered that Helen made a whole pan of mushroom sauce for me, so I ate a lot to show I was thankful. What was odd about the dinner was how regular it was. It might've been any meal at the diner, except that we were all eating together, not in shifts, and we were all eating the same thing. Also unusual was the music of the meal. The diner made noises we'd never paid attention to before, because there were usually so many human voices to cover over.

"The building's speaking," I said to Selena. She looked back at me with a shocked expression, so maybe the noises didn't seem significant to her, but to me they took on a soothing tone. No one spoke of what we'd just done. Even weeks and months later we didn't speak of it among ourselves, and Bobby and Marv never mentioned it in our hearing. Still, like most happenings in Cartwheel, word got out. A few days after, Billy Simms made a joke about our ceremony while Selena was pouring his coffee. Somehow her practiced wrist slipped and a puddle of black liquid dribbled over the table, staining his pants before he could jump out of the booth. After that the funeral was something folks mentioned with respect. Once when I went out to visit, I found fresh flowers on the grave.

A few weeks later I went back to eating meat. I don't know why, but I wish I did, because then maybe I'd know why changes don't always stay the same.

Doe's death got me thinking about how things leave, sometimes without anything new to fill the gap. Gwen had Sean to remind her of Tim, to take her places she'd never gone before in her heart. But Jo left me nothing. I'd wanted Gwen to fill that space but now I'd left off desiring her, my love dissolved like a grain of salt in a vat of Bobby's stew.

It was Helen I turned to, surprising us both.

Helen was so normal that I knew she couldn't truly understand what I was feeling. Mostly I was curious about what she had with Marv. What was it like to live in an ordinary way, to be one of the Marrieds? I wondered if she felt him a flower beneath her, or if love gradually faded, like color from old clothes. I wasn't sure how to ask her what I wanted to know, since I had to hedge about who I was. Finally I decided to say that I envied what she had with Marv—so smooth, so simple. They never fought but touched each other's shoulders at times, as if to say, "I remember our wedding." I'd never seen them kiss—none of us had—but there was passion in their glances, or so Selena and I liked to speculate. They worked and lived and clung together. I worried I'd never have that again, so I wanted to think over what was missing. How to go on, knowing it was lost.

Helen's office was tucked away in an alcove beside the storage room.

"Who is it?" she called anxiously, as if I'd knocked on the door of a lonely cabin in lumber woods. I felt sad for her. Grappling with money all day long must bring a tension to the soul that doesn't erase easily. To work with numbers means to be on edge, aware of distrust, temptation, laziness. It was better to work with my hands, I long ago decided, even though I was good enough at math as a girl.

Helen was surrounded by numbers.

Charts climbing the walls, graphs dripping from the ceiling, scraps littering the floor. There weren't any pictures, except for the sunset on the Cartwheel Brake and Tire calendar. No photos either. No paintings, cups, or plastic figurines. None of the things bank tellers keep in their cubicles and teachers keep on their desks. Nothing but numbers. It seemed cold somehow, all those numbers adding and subtracting themselves while Helen's fingers watched, especially since I'd come to talk about what no numbers could measure—love and its quirky rumbles.

"What's on your mind, Caddie Ruby?" The lilt in her voice matched Marv's. That alikeness in difference was what I could fathom of the Marrieds. With Jo the thing that drew me was how she could've been like me but wasn't and then beneath it all was anyhow. With Gwen, the thing that drew me was that she could've been like me but wasn't and then beneath it all really wasn't. With both of them there was a circle to it, a following of this till it turned into that, and the curves where we fit together made together feel inevitable, even when it wasn't.

David had been only what he was, no surprises. When he was body, his body was exactly what was there. I wanted him to take something off and have surprises beneath. I wanted him to twist away from who he seemed, the way in bed Jo could all of a sudden become a woman, wanting me, and then flip back again to where she loomed over me, shadow, not wanting anything but to give, pushing me into taking, making me quiet until I couldn't stand it and silence turned me into some other thing—motion maybe, maybe an animal. I'd wanted Gwen under the sheets so much because I'd imagined she might dolphin that way too, her girlishness vanishing once I'd showed what I could do. I'd imagined she might've watched sometimes, not taking any longer but only awed, playing with gifts, giving and giving, surprised because giving was the same as taking.

David had only folded into himself. He wanted things the same in the dark as they were in the day. He fucked the way he ate. Once you'd spent five minutes with him, there was nothing left to explore. In that cramped, sweaty bed in his trailer out in the middle of nowhere, I'd hoped for something to make privacy worthwhile. But instead he pushed me down so I was lying on my back, just lying there, not even shifting to touch any part of him, so I had no view of anything like sky or carpet or walls, only the dead light bulb, bare, and while I lay there he undid his pants. I got a little excited then, thinking, this is where things change and become passion. I'd never been with a man before, not willingly that is, and though I'd never felt I was missing anything when I was with Jo, I saw it in the magazines and on TV and on the streets and in the air, so I thought there was a thing I could feel that I had never known.

I shouldn't have bled, the insides of my body having broken long ago one early, early morning behind the dumpster in the parking lot of The Depot. But maybe it didn't count, because I did. Did bleed. I thought of Jo's fingers, how they could be inside and still be gentle. While David was busy, I wondered why he'd gone so far away. It wasn't only pain, but how he could seek his pleasure inside me without ever greeting mine. His pleasure seemed a separate activity, a sort of sport, like baseball or hockey. With Jo no matter what she did or didn't do, she was always with me. David went away, so I went away too.

How had it happened? One minute I was stewing over how to speak with numbers spying, the next minute I was crying, little girl cries, "Uh, uh, uh."

I'd said the story aloud. Helen was stroking my wrists, calling me Caddie Ruby, telling me really I was too sad to be true, and to have a chocolate. She slid open a desk drawer full of candies: little hard ones, thick velvety dark bars, red and black strings of licorice like a great braid of my hair. I don't know why but I was feeling grabby and took one of each kind, just to have.

I'd never spoken to anyone about David. Folks had known; they'd seen us argue in the lot. That feather of a girl he'd taken with him had always watched me, her eyes like pepper, from the window of the booth where she sat to eat her English. But I'd never taken all the things that David did and set them out. I'd served Helen without meaning to. I'd gone away, like I used to, and while I was gone I was still a waitress. Thinking that made me laugh, and Helen smiled her beautiful prairie smile and laughed too. I popped a hard candy but right off I spit it out into my hand because I'd suddenly choked on a great fat terror.

"Are you OK?" She thwacked me on the back. "Caddie, don't choke, we need you."

I just sat, a great lump. What else had I told her?

Had I said aloud about Jo and Gwen?

Surely she wouldn't be laughing, wouldn't be touching me if I had. I needed to know fast what I'd said, since I couldn't be sure I'd stay in my body. I wanted to ask, "What did I just say?" but it felt too weird.

"You never talk, Ruby." Helen had a chocolate in her hands and was unwrapping the foil, using her fingernails to peel the edges away from the bar. When she was finished, the sheet lay in her hand, star-silver, specks of chocolate like rust on its surface. "After Jo left, you just shut down. We wanted you to talk about him. We tried, do you remember? It's hard to admit your man's left you, but you shouldn't feel ashamed."

With cocoa dissolving on my tongue, I felt bravery creep into my mouth, lush and sweet. *Jo had a secret body.* Why was it our story never slept? It was always on the waking edge, waiting between blinks, ready to escape through some sense or other. I'd never imagined, before I met Jo, that a secret could have such a metabolism. "It wasn't shame." I watched Helen smooth the foil out with the side of her hand, over and over, rowing through shiny water. "There were just things that happened between us I can't describe." She'd finished flattening it. The silver looked like a sheet of paper. She set the chocolate in my lap, tugged open the deepest drawer, and placed the foil inside on top of a great stack of sheets, too many for me to count.

I handed her a chunk of chocolate, but she shook her head. "Allergic." Then she got up, her chair turning slowly after she stood. "That's the way with most. Couples, I mean. There are always secrets. It's what binds two together." I'd never thought that way, but it was true. "You have to have a private language, names you call each other that no one else knows. You have to carve out a tiny world for yourself. That's how you make a marriage stay."

"We weren't married."

"You wanted to be different."

"It wasn't that."

"You didn't want to be a wife."

"More that." And true—wife, no. There wasn't wife or husband with Jo and me. There were names: Josephine, Caddie. We were never Marrieds whose TV set was always on. We had passion to bind us, not calm, though back then I wanted marriage very intensely, my wanting matched only by her not willing. What was the word we'd fought over? The first letter matched my name. I could feel it, slippery and cool along my tongue. I could taste it, bitter as baking chocolate: change. How had those fights sounded, how had they looked?

We were always in the kitchen, the warmest room in the house. I liked it because it meant food was ready at hand. Jo liked it because of the colors—yellow and orange walls, dense like sun, and a blue refrigerator, magnetic like sky. Together we'd painted the rickety table a grassy shade of green, so sitting in the room was like sitting outside, only no bugs, and the air smelled of cookies or bacon instead of earth. That was one of the places she'd take me, first thing when I walked in the door, tugging my skirt up or down around my feet. But it was where we'd done our fighting too.

I've lied in my life, but not often to Jo. And I wasn't lying when I told her I'd love her no matter who she became. That was why I wanted to join the Marrieds. I wanted to know we'd always have each other, but it seemed the more I told her my love was unconditional, the less she believed me, and maybe the less she liked me. She seemed to think I must have demons in me to know I could love her no matter what.

Or maybe the demons were Jo's all along.

It felt like a test sometimes, Jo claiming I'd prove myself a liar, me wondering what she'd do if I changed too. She'd hold my hair and tell me to stay the same pretty Caddie, and that was fine at the time, because my body wasn't altering its girlish ways. But later I wondered if I wasn't lucky she left when she did. The scars are starting, and the grey. My breasts hang from my body a different way today than yesterday. I could promise her forever-fever, but I couldn't promise a museum. Nothing seemed to satisfy Jo but that. The Caddie Museum—imagine it. My body stuffed, propped against a glass case full of dresses and mascara wands, my apron hanging special at the center. It got ugly sometimes, running in place to try to stay the same. Long after, following the first deep grief and bitter hardship, I came to believe in luck, knowing her vanishing was what brought newness into my life.

I didn't think too much about where she'd gone. When a lover leaves, it's no matter where or what for. She'll take another, your heart knows it—another girl, but also another sunny kitchen and another fistful of hair, the same words clamped round it like a tortoiseshell barrette. *Don't you change.* Would she ever find her? Someone who could stagnate, a still pond?

I hoped I'd never have to see it because it sounded sad.

There are secrets and then there are secrets. But I didn't speak aloud. Instead I watched Helen's body do nervous dances. Usually she was steady, a graceful grey rock.

"Caddie, maybe I'm misunderstanding. Are you trying to tell me something different? Not about lover's secrets but something ugly?" Helen paced the narrow room and I saw again how she fit Marv: their stride was the same.

"Not violence. Jo was good to me. Our secrets were more like—"

"Let me guess."

"Go on." I held my breath.

"Bed things. And you had no one to tell or ask how it really should be."

I didn't intend to cry again but my eyes just got started. Helen tugged me into her and we stood twined together. Though I didn't want to press close, she pulled tighter until I could feel her whole body. The buttons on her shirt clung like tiny hands. She held me till the shakiness died down, and then we both pulled away at once and looked down at our shoes.

I knew I should keep quiet. She'd come too close. But I couldn't let her go about her business thinking Jo and I had been ugly with each other.

"Not bad things. Good, very good."

"But puzzling."

"Puzzling." *Let's leave it at that.*

She seemed to read my thoughts. "I'll keep it for you." The sticky calendar sunset gleamed on flimsy paper.

"Keep what?"

"Your secret. I'll hold it. I'll be your bank."

While I was thinking about "bank," Marv poked his head in. "Caddie, you're wanted up front." His eyes lit fire. "Selena's juggling seven. Can you finish your heart-to-heart some other minute?" He walked over to Helen's chair and sat down. I stuffed my candy in my apron pocket and started out.

"Ruby. Remember what I said."

"What'd you say?" Marv's face flattened like Helen's foil.

"I came to gripe about not sleeping and having sniffs, and she told me I could take tomorrow off."

Helen nodded. "I don't want her staying sick. It costs more in the long run."

"You need a day off, you got it. Caddie, you haven't been out in over a year. Perfect attendance, that's right, like how at Foodville they wear the little flowers. Just ask us anytime."

"You two are the greatest." I meant it, but not for what they thought. I liked how they looked together, Helen behind him, resting her hands on his shoulders, making the number one, not two. I shut the door behind me. The ugly thing was that for a moment I held still and listened. I wanted a piece of their secret, how they'd made together happen steady for so long. But there was nothing except the sound of foil crumpling, and shame covered me for listening.

Maybe it was all those numbers—their detail and precision—that made me pay enough attention to the world around me to see something so small. As I walked past the storage room door, I noticed long scratches, as if someone had run a nail down the length of the wood.

I ducked inside, just to check that nothing was out of place. Glancing around, I reassured myself that everything was as I'd left it that morning when I'd pulled ketchup and jelly for the breakfast tables. The bottom shelf furthest from the door was dusty, so I knelt to wipe it off with my candy-heavy apron. I found the thing by accident. Pocketed the ring because it seemed right to ask the others who had lost it. But two steps and I turned back. It had been placed there. Somehow I knew that. Probably it was Gwen's—her ceremony. She'd set it down so she could forget Tim, but know that when she needed it back, she could find it.

I left it there—a narrow circle, gold as Gwen's hair—in its circle of dust. Then I moved a jar of mint jelly in front of it. No one ever ate mint jelly; it was on the menu, but we never served lamb, and besides, everyone agreed that it was nasty. The jar would stay, and the ring, till Gwen was ready to pawn it or pass it along.

Jo had given me a ring. I would always wear it. She'd circled my breasts with her tongue, two rings really, a great figure eight I could sometimes still feel. When I loved Josephine, there was proof, every day, of who I was. If the Marrieds around us couldn't see it, they could still see who I was with Jo. All they didn't know was that we were totally different from who we appeared to be.

Now I was Caddie Solo. That was who I was and how I looked, so for once I matched, except my old secret hadn't disappeared. I still had it in me to have loved her and to love another Jo or crush my heart out on another Gwen. That part of me was still inside, but without a girl to make me open, my secret festered, silent and invisible. If I hadn't had to join Selena in serving, I would've turned on my heels and blabbed my whole self to Marv and Helen. I felt the fire of my secret like bleach in my mouth. I needed to spit it out or burn myself to death from inside.

Coming into the dining room from the kitchen was like driving out of a tunnel and onto a curve. Selena's breakneck smirk reminded me right away that I was riding a pass. Usually she was good at juggling, but the place had filled up unexpectedly. I felt sorry for letting my troubles turn hers. After a quick apology and a gift of hard candy from my dusty apron, I set to work, even taking over altogether for a few so she could rest her soles. "They feel like chimneys." I knew exactly what she meant.

While Selena went out back to smoke, I scuttled. I needed to apologize to Gwen too, but we were both too busy for talk. Finally, when she sighed a long breath beside the register, I ambled up and held out a chocolate.

"This sweet says sorry."

She tore off the foil, letting bits fall to the floor. "Did you know," she said, covering her lips with her hand as she spoke, "chocolate is fatal to dogs?"

"Cats too?"

"I'm not sure. Don't feed them any."

Gwen's words stung. I didn't want to think of Cat as different. It scared me to know there were ordinary things I could give her—love in the form of rich, dark sugar—that would hurt her, even take her away. There shouldn't have been any lines; love should've looked the same, but it didn't. There were lines, only I didn't know them. They were secret and subtle, and I would have to be careful.

I went home that night and cried into her fur.

Sometimes when I cried the way I did that night or when I was full of the unexpected joy girls, weather, and music brought me, I heard again the voice that called my name on the landing. I heard again, in the buzz of her purr, my name, and truer things about me. She connected herself to me with sound, sound and the kneading motion she made on my lap, kneading and the game she'd play of vanishing—into a closet, behind a box, on a shelf—and reappearing, as if to remind me of what I'd missed. I was coming to understand why people went off, all weighted down with binoculars and water, into the jungle to study apes. For a few weeks I thought about trying to contact someone—maybe at the Indy zoo?—who'd know how I could get that kind of job. Better than waitressing, though probably similar, what with smooshing bananas and cleaning up after careless creatures with opposable thumbs. But the more I thought it out, the less I figured I could do it. Probably I'd get sick of peeing in bushes and sleeping on moss. Probably I'd get sick of eating peanut butter and raisins. Probably you needed more school than I could ever stomach, college at least. And me without a high school finish.

No jungle, then. But speech. I'd seen films on Wild Kingdom where scientists used treats to get gorillas to talk. The idea was always to teach them language—not love, which they already knew, or religion, which they were too smart to need in the first place. The scientists wanted to know what gorillas would say if they could say something. Intriguing, but dangerous too, like looking for life on another planet. What if you found it? And what if it wasn't what you'd hoped for? It made me ponder, but the drive was there. That night, crying into Cat's ruffly layers, I decided to start teaching her to speak.

I made a list: "Words Cat Ought to Know." The first word on the list was "Cat." The second was "Caddie." The third was "love." Maybe *cheese* and *mouse* would've been easier, but I figured there was no point in talking to someone who didn't know who I was.

I picked her up from a cushion. When you pick up a cat, it goes limp on you; it's like holding butter. I draped her across my chest and she reeled out a purr like a banner. It still sounded like *Caddie* to me, her gruff voice. The whole time, it sounded like *Caddie*. I've never met an animal since that could say my name. Cat fell asleep but I sat up awhile, my tears dried into salty itchy patches, my face tight from crying, but my heart soft. Maybe I could teach her to know. It was so intimate, how we were in the apartment together. I told her things I'd told no one, not even Jo, and she always listened, her great gold eyes drenching me with what had to be understanding.

But what if I was wrong? What if the gold beneath the clear glass of her beautiful eyes was a color, not an emotion? What if she cared for me the way some people believed animals cared, because I fed her and stroked her and let her sleep on my lap? What if love wasn't something animals could fathom? I bent to stroke her head and her low purr flickered. I touched one finger lightly to the lump in her throat. It had to be love. She vibrated the way I'd vibrated beneath Jo's touch once—my skin flushed, my breathing heavy. Cat's purr was no different.

The next day I decided to ask folks what method they thought I might take in my teaching. First thing in the morning, before we were even open for business, Bobby asked me to help him mix the filling for a Boston cream pie. "The cream needs to pour in smooth while I'm beating the batter. Just pour, very steady, not all at once. That's good, Caddie. See, then it comes out silky, no lumps. Now the melted butter. Just like that, slow and smooth."

Cream reminded me of Cat. "Bobby, if you wanted to teach a cat to speak, how would you train her?"

"See this batter?" It was a pale mocha color, mottled with gold-white streaks. "If I offered you a spoonful, wouldn't you say just about anything?"

"So cheese bits, maybe?"

"Fish or bits of chicken. Anything small to whet your pal's appetite. Now watch. I'm going to pour this in, but slowly, stirring all the while."

All morning the rich scent of pies baking lured customers to order sweets. Selena was mixing a shake for a tourist type who'd parked his motorcycle across two spaces in the lot when I asked her my Cat question.

"Don't cats like cozy spaces? I'd fix her a little house, a box maybe, and let her hide."

I shouldered the tray of food for table nine. Both thoughts made sense. I might have to go down to Cartwheel Public, see if they had any books on apes. While I was thinking this and remembering that Laddie Farris had asked for extra napkins, Marv ambled over to the register with the bank deposit envelope and the key to the drawer.

He squinted at me. "Caddie, I thought you were sick and needed a day at home."

I'd never meant to take a day away from the diner. It was just an excuse to cover how Helen and I had talked. Taking a day off would be a broken promise. I couldn't say to customers, "See you in the morning." Besides, what would I do with myself—sit at home, read *Cosmo*, and eat away at the stash of candy bars beneath the sink? Days off were to hoard, not spend. Once I'd spent my day, if I ever fell sick I'd have to slog myself to work with wobbly feet and misty vision. I'd already done that many times before, but I made it through by reminding myself that I'd never taken a sick day so if I had to, I could.

Jo was the same about working; she pushed herself more than most. One thing I could count on was that wherever Jo had got to, she was working hard at being the thing she needed most to be. When she'd worked the factory, she'd put her all into the line, but also into what went with: her change of name, body, being. It was as much her job to bind her breasts as it was to keep the brake parts moving on the conveyor.

Had it been my job to tend my hair and line my eyelids? I'd never thought it quite that way. Maybe I'd gotten sloppy; maybe that was why she left me. The *why* question was a harsh one. It was too easy to turn it back on myself. That was the one thing folks had wanted to talk about, though: *what happened, did you fight, did he take another girl, did you ask for a ring, were you a greedy girl, Caddie?* Right then I wanted to know, in a way I never had before. It was far enough off, that first cold winter.

"Caddie, this fried ham needs something tart. Yellow mustard or that horseradish sauce Bobby used to make. Be a good one, and scurry. I'm working the line at one."

Jim O'Donnell's voice broke the thread between us. If Marv wanted me home, he'd have to say. I never could read minds and never claimed to. Up the tray again, on to table nine—a rowdy family, three kids named Buster. Then I brought Laddie Farris extra napkins, bustled into the kitchen to borrow a jar of Bobby's famous sauce, and left Jim's ticket by his plate. When I scrawled that check, I wrote myself a note on the page that followed: "box tonight." I thought I might forget, my mind was so busy with details.

Mostly I was trying to make sense of Marv's squint. Possibly it had nothing to do with me, but it was also possible that he really did want me to stay home. Had they taken on one salary too many when they hired Gwen? Money was a mystery to me, and Marv and Helen rarely shared diner business. It seemed to me (though I felt guilty thinking it, and blue) that if anyone should go, it was Gwen. But decisions get made by coin toss sometimes. Maybe my name was the president's profile.

It scared me less than it might've. Every month or two, on a Sunday, I took myself out to breakfast at the Big Boy and sat in Maxine Pickle's section so we could chat awhile about the profession. We'd talk about the best shoes to waitress in, how much we hated drunks, tricks for serving that saved our backs. We'd break confidence and share trade secrets: their biscuit recipe for Bobby's hash, how each spot made money off the daily special. Maxine I counted for a friend, although we never did anything outside of visit each other. Her day off was Wednesday, so every month or two, on a Wednesday, she'd stop by the M&H for breakfast and we'd chatter, me having to watch, the way she did when I stopped by, to be sure I didn't get lost in our conversation.

Big Boy was different from the diner. It was a chain and had a huge staff turnover. Once after a long talk about money worries and bad jobs we'd had before we'd started serving, Maxine winked as she wrote out my check. "Caddie, you're a good one. Not flighty like those little girlies. You ever need tables, you come by and ask for Maxie. I'll get you in. Might be washing for a couple weeks, but you'll have tables soon enough."

I wanted to touch her hand. It was always a burden, feeling more than other girls. That had been the relief with Jo—finally letting out all that emotion. Knowing she wouldn't skimp or scooch away.

"Thanks, Maxine." I made my smile small so my heart wouldn't spill. Maxine's body was very round. I always wanted to feel how her breasts led into her belly. There weren't separate parts to her, like models in magazines or *Playboy* spreads. Everything flowed together and moved when she did. I wanted to tell her she was beautiful, but that would never happen because Maxine was like Gwen.

I was starting to be able to tell.

It was a skill, like balancing a tray or memorizing who ordered what. Sometimes you didn't know you were learning till you'd done the thing right a couple times. At first it took a lot out of you. It was embarrassing when you made mistakes. But the knowledge had layers to it, and they added up. Even on girls like me you could tell by the eyes.

So I had a place at Big Boy if I needed one. I didn't have to crawl down to the Blue Tango and hike my skirts to keep Cat in chow. Besides, I knew too many folks in this town to strip. If I had to, I'd leave town for someplace no one knew me, so the shame would be general, not a personal thing.

At 3:06 I made my way into the kitchen to punch out. Marv was waiting by the time clock, holding my time card like a bouquet of posies.

My card's familiar kathunk wasn't soothing. "Marv, are you trying to tell me something? There's a lot of salary going around right now."

Marv took my wrist. "Caddie, we need you here. We'd be lost if you ever let go."

"I won't let go." His words reminded me of tug-of-war with Pat. We'd pull till one tumbled and then tumble both. We were boys together, and later, sewing or talking, girls too. I missed him—not often, because I'd made myself forget. But sometimes words ghosted him up, and I'd look at the sky and wonder.

Marv let go of my wrist and reached to pat me on the shoulder. All of his touches were awkward, like the first time someone holds a child. But I grinned at him and it was OK again. Still, on my walk home I was dizzy with recollections—Marv's face, Maxine's body, Pat's sky. When Cat met me at the door, I had to hold her to wind down.

I decided not to glance over my bills or scrub the coffee-stained cup I'd left to soak. Instead I cradled Cat in my lap as I sank onto the sofa. There was gravel in her purr, stones shifting. When they settled, words: "Come let me comfort." Then she was buzz and scritch again, not words but noise, and I felt silly for believing in the voice I'd dreamed up. But holding her close, tossing mousy toys, and feeding kibbly bits were so delightful that my heart eased. I set water for tea, took two candy bars from beneath the sink, and turned back the covers on my bed. While I was waiting for the tea to steep, I cut Cat a tiny cube of cheese. She mewled. I had to cut her two more before she was satisfied.

I curled up in bed with my cup. Cat pounced, and a little peppermint spilled onto the blanket. Sleepy, she was soft and spongy; moving, she was arrow-taut. She nibbled my toes and then climbed onto my thighs, kneading me, till the prickle of claws became pain and I had to distract her with a blanket cave. I dozed off after that. The next thing I knew it was 9:17. I turned over and tried to sleep some more, but my mind was heavy with thoughts of Jo. Jo—I'd already forgotten the note I'd written: "box tonight." Cat ran into the kitchen as if she knew exactly what I was thinking.

Beneath the sink, behind the candy bars and extra paper towels, I found a rusty grey metal box with a lock on the side and a black handle on top. When Jo left me, she took all her things. I'd hoped to find some stray sock, cigarette, or scrap of paper in the laundry basket or a cob-webbed corner of the house. But she'd wiped away all traces of her time with me as neatly as Bobby cleaned his grill. Only when I was packing to move out of our old house did I find proof I hadn't invented her. The box was hidden in the attic crawl space, behind a cardboard carton full of old bills. I remembered the day she'd bought it. "Better than a bank," she'd said. She didn't trust people holding her money for her. But after a time she'd put her money in a bank like everybody else, so she could write checks and collect interest and stop worrying she'd be robbed of all she had.

I sat on the floor, opened a candy bar, and examined the box's rusty edges. What I liked was how it changed. I kept it under the leaky sink on purpose, so it would rust slowly and seem alive. She'd long ago lost the key. The lock was too rusty to use it now, anyway, and it was empty inside. I kept it empty because I had nothing else of hers to hold. There had been photographs—four of them. Only four because we worried that photos might show her secret. There had been hair, culled from my brush, which she borrowed, and a stack of junk mail that came to the house addressed to "Mr. Joseph Waddell." She also left behind the things she'd given me: a wicker basket to hold my makeup and a photograph of myself in a wooden frame.

"Why me? Shouldn't the frame have you in it?"

"You know what we decided—photos are dangerous. Besides, you're pretty and I'm not."

"You don't try to be pretty, Jo. If you wanted to be Josephine, you could."

"I know." She was smoking and exhaled too close to my face, so that my eyes stung. "I didn't say I wanted to be, I just said I wasn't."

For a while, to please her, I propped the frame beside our bed—on her side, till I came home one day and she'd moved it to mine. I reminded myself that it was a gift, that whether I liked it or not didn't matter. The spirit of the thing, I said to myself. Keep to that. But late nights and early mornings I dozed and woke to my own image, peering out at me as if to say, *You're trapped.* There was no leaping out from it; no way for that Caddie to change position.

Jo loved me—me Caddie, and Caddie's body. She wanted something David would ask for later, something the men at The Depot had tried to steal. She wanted a photograph, not of my face, not of me sipping coffee at the kitchen table, but of me spread out, my breasts winking, the space between my legs changed from a *V* into a hole. For a long time I said "No," then I started saying "Never." Then I started saying "Don't even ask." One day she stopped asking and never asked again. I thought, *She's listening,* and found calm until she bought the frame.

After I unwrapped the picture, I had to wash my hands. I hadn't just torn away paper, but clothing. The me beneath the wrapping was bare, my body open like a family Bible. She'd taken the shot while I lay sleeping. My face was gone, gone, gone; you could see that by my expression, which wasn't hungry so much as dreamy. All I could feel was anger. Anger, but with wonder layered over—what did it mean that she'd not only taken the photo, but wrapped it as a gift for me? The look on her face said it wasn't a joke. We fought so often, Jo and I. I was tired of fighting, but especially of what came after: the fear of being found out burdened alone, twenty-four, seven. We couldn't afford to disagree. So I bit my lip, bruising it, and said, "Where should we put it?"

After she left me, I put the frame inside the wicker basket, along with her photographs and bits of hair. When I was sure she was gone forever, I took all those things to a field and set them alight. When it came to the sleepy picture of me, I tore it to pieces before I lit the match, in case raccoons scattered the ash pile, and my breasts wound up trash scraps on someone's yard. When I'd finished everything I doused the pile, left it to soak overnight, and dumped it in the trash the next morning.

The box came later, when I was ready to remember. Ready to hang onto something that changed before my eyes. Every so often, I checked on the progress of the rust, admiring its swirly designs. The reddish-black color reminded me of my hair, which also grew uncontrollably, and which Jo had admired, or at least needed to pass. Holding the box, remembering her quirky ways, how passionate we'd been together and how ill-matched, I remembered something I'd forgotten. "How can I be sure," she was fond of saying, "that you aren't just with me because I'm the only one you know?" Sure I'd leave her or be unfaithful. Sure I'd start sleeping with men or secret myself up to Indy and find another girl. Her worries were always the same, and she was always inconsolable. At first her jealousy fueled our passion, but after a time we both grew tired.

I'd long ago stopped believing she might come back. But what if she entered my life from another angle? Would I recognize her if she changed? Cat purred up and I pressed her to me, stroking her fur in our common language. What if one day Jo showed up at the diner, all decked out in curls and heels? It was the sort of thing she'd do, all right—she liked disguises, secret knowing. But, oh, I'd liked it too. Hadn't I, though. Watching (never touching) as she peeled off her man's costume, revealing the softness beneath the binding—that body, that woman's body, more beautiful for the way she hid it, more elegant and round and edible for the wrapper of dirty flannel and ripped denim and the stony face she wore to let the world know she didn't believe in soft, round, warm, wet things.

When really she was all of those.

Only for me.

No wonder she worried about me giving myself away. I was Caddie to the world—the body everyone saw was the body she unraveled. If Mike, Matt, and Ron could have me with their eyes, how could I be hers, special? She wanted some secret vision of me no one else could have. She wanted to unwrap me the way she unbound her breasts at night. Try as I might to explain that I did have a secret body—that loving her was my secret, that who I was with her wasn't the girl Mike, Matt, and Ron imagined me to be—she never believed me. It bothered me, but when we touched, I forgot. Forgot and forgave.

She tried though. There was the business with the tattoo. "I want you to get a tattoo," she said one morning over breakfast. It made me laugh, the thought, me being such a girl and all.

"Little rosebuds and teddy bears?"

"A name."

"Jo?"

"Josephine."

I looked down at my eggs (it was Sunday and she'd cooked omelettes; I remember the taste of cheese and butter). "Too risky," I said finally. To my surprise, she let it go.

A few weeks later she gave me the sleepy photo.

Why hadn't I seen her departure coming? The signs were there—jealousy, taking control, holding on as if I was a roller coaster. But I'd believed that if I could bear the tension, so could Jo.

I tucked the box back underneath the sink. Then I set my alarm, brushed my teeth, and fell asleep.

My dreams that night were strange.

I dreamed Jo called to me, her voice echoing through the apartment. Something was wrong, she needed help, but I wasn't sure where to find her, or if I would still recognize her when I did.

I woke at ten till five, just before my alarm blared its trumpet. Stumbling into the kitchen, I was startled by a faint knocking. I reached for the bread knife in the top cabinet drawer, but it was only Cat, trapped beneath the sink. I must've shut her in by accident when I put the box back. When I let her out, she mewed pitifully for several minutes until I stroked her belly and opened a can of Fish Fancies.

"I wish I could teach you to speak." It didn't occur to me till much later, after I'd lost her, that perhaps *she* could've taught *me* to speak her language. I should've tried, at least. Maybe I was the one missing the understanding.

CHAPTER SIX: SELENA

■ ■
■

Saturday night they cruise the strip. Their cars flare purple beneath, and inside they pulse and tremble red. It's a thirty-minute drive from Martinsville to Bloomington. They take 37 cautiously, but once they reach College Avenue, they hit the pedal, neon lemmings, and congregate in the parking lot across from the Bloomington police. From there they make a steady circle—past the courthouse, down Kirkwood, a left into the alley behind the Von Lee Cinema, and up Kirkwood to the lot again for another sip, another toke. Their radios are tuned to the same station. The songs rise and collect, lyrics vapid as steam above the cooling asphalt. They memorize the words, each secretly believing love is the thing that will take them far from Indiana.

I was a cruiser's chick once. I rode the strip too, but then I stopped believing. Saw through the hypocrisy of sugar words and beer-soaked kisses. It wasn't me my boyfriend loved, not my body he could lose himself in probing. No, the real sex on the strip made a grinding sound and then a screech—tires meeting pavement, rolling past, leaving skids behind.

I don't believe the things other people believe about love. Maybe there are folks like me somewhere else, but in Cartwheel I stand out peculiar. So I keep my thoughts to myself and hide behind the rustle of my skirts. To everyone around me, I'm just Selena—Selena the pretty one, Selena-sure-serve at the M&H, Selena the one single men can always count on. Because nobody knows why.

Bet and I take breaks together. I'm a cigarette believer, and Bet sometimes sneaks a smoke, even though she says aspiring cooks shouldn't. One October morning we were out back of the diner, warming our lungs, freezing our toes, talking about nothing in particular.

"Selena." Her question came out of grey air. It wasn't something she'd tried on me before. "Do you ever get tired of sleeping alone?"

But I don't, I thought. *I have my bed for company.* I concentrated on exhaling a perfect circle. "I don't need a man," I said, and had my mouth open to continue that train of thought when Bet grabbed my arm and dragged me, cigarette and all, through the diner. We skidded past the dish room and into the little bathroom off the grill. She dragged me in and shut the door behind us. There was barely room for two. My nose was almost pressed against the mirror lining the back of the door.

"Look." She pointed to the face in the mirror—my face—and stretched her hand out, as if to say, *See yourself*. And I did. I looked Selena head-on. A thick bob of brown curls, tight, absolutely natural. Green eyes, bright as a stoplight. Cocoa-colored skin. Strong shoulders, lots of curves, long legs, a narrow waist.

"She's pretty," I said to Bet. "So what's your point?"

She crossed her arms and leaned against the sink. "Why don't you let some nice factory boy take you home once in a while? Is it because of Jo? Are you still hoping?"

Jo was a sweet-faced farm boy who sat in my section of the diner till Caddie caught his eye. Something different about him, though I never figured out what. Different's what I like. Still, the morning he switched tables, sitting patiently behind a paper till Caddie ambled past and took his order, I felt relief more than anything. I didn't want Jo asking questions I couldn't answer. What Bet didn't understand, what no one knew, was that I was already taken. I had my love and my love loved me. Right under everyone's nose.

But of course I couldn't tell her, much as I trusted Bet to keep a secret. There are secrets and then there are mysteries. My love was a mystery, even to me. So I took advantage of the rumors about me and Jo and told Bet I was stuck on Jo, couldn't get him out of my head. I told her I was jealous and hurt he'd chosen Caddie over me. Bet nodded like she understood and maybe she did—there's the keen thing about lying. It can create bonds between two people, bonds that stay, even if they're first built on something sheer from the imagination. Real things aren't always born of what's true. Sometimes lies come first, and truth comes after.

I don't believe the things other people believe about love.

When I was a cruiser's girl, kissing boys just never felt right. Every mouth cupped mine like a mask to stop my breathing. I'd come home and scrub all the places his hands had strayed, but by then it was too late. I'd lost my body. I could feel it bloating, belly and thighs and breasts like balloons. I could feel my skin itching and shedding in flakes like tears. I could feel my stomach eating itself and my heart thudding slower, wishing and waiting simply to stop.

It wasn't because they were boys, I know, because I've given it some thought. I'm not the kind of person to shy away from questions, even hard ones. So yes, I've thought about girls, but I know what was wrong with boys would be wrong still. It wasn't anatomy in particular, but anatomy in general. It was because they were human. Too much body.

When you kiss people, you smell and taste and feel their day—the bitter dregs of morning coffee, fried onions at noon, and the soft scum of cucumber seeds from some stale dinner salad. You taste the stress along the backside of their teeth and feel in the rhythm of their lips the games their mama played when she jounced them on her scabby knees, skirt twitching high tide, *up-sa-daisy* and *rock-a-bye*. The twang and blubber of baby music rises laughter in your throat, laughter you stifle while you simulate passion.

Objects are better.

With people, you can never be sure they love you for who you really are. Tricks and dodges. Veils and hustles. With objects, it's never any other way. Nothing is hidden. Straight lines and stillness. Joints and surfaces.

Take furniture, for instance. One hot summer when I was nearly seventeen and a recent West High dropout, I worked at the mall in Martinsville, where Mama and I lived then. I slogged nine to five at Klein's Shoes, selling sandals and pom-pom socks, smelling sweaty toes all day and dreaming of feet at night—flat arches, bulbous corns, bunions and callouses, shoe-strap blisters. I didn't mind the hours, and the AC made the mall one of the better places to spend a southern Indiana summer. But the customers. I had to unroll linty socks, tug leather and canvas over greasy heels. I had to twinkle my lashes at jowls and bald spots, saggy breasts, and crinkly bellies. Too much body in the job to suit me, too much touch and breath-to-cheek. I wished for wood then, though I didn't know why.

Across from Klein's was Martinsville Chair and Sofa, MACS for short. Sometimes on break I'd visit the Barcoloungers and LA-Z-BOYs, take a short trip with the kickstand loose and my eyes closed, dreaming of sleep and the luxury of Sundays. One chair in particular caught my eye—black vinyl, sleek and cool to the touch, cushions with just enough give, generous arms ribbed to swelling. I'd sit in that roguish chair, lean back, let my feet rest on the stool that slid out slick as a baby's head from between its mama's legs. I'd sit, nodding off to the Muzak. I'd sit and travel somewhere else.

It was real for me, that chair, more real than Jimmy's tonsil-swabbing kisses, more real than Fred's Day-Glo condoms, sky-blue to light the dim of his father's Chrysler. That black vinyl chair was a special one. We had a connection, the chair and I. When I touched it, I could feel consent and hear in the give of its springs a lullaby turned love song.

It didn't sell all summer. Its gleamy glints dimmed when other voices approached, and its slippery skin slicked clammy beneath each stranger's weight. It didn't sell, and I burned big hopes MACS would drop the price till even Selena could shovel over enough quarters. But the tag never slimmed enough, and so my last day on the job I settled in and whispered a talking-to. It was a plush good-bye—such shifting of springs as I sat taking leave of my beautiful creature. Good-bye is never simply said, especially not in a mall with so many passersby. But they stumbled past, oblivious, missing Klein's Selena as she rubbed her back up and down, taking a cat's leave of her first true love. I'd thought my creature would understand. But instead its headrest snagged my hair, its rectangular armrests tightened till my ribs crunched, and I had to extract myself, tough as pulling teeth.

It was my first experience with the rage of objects.

It took some getting over. My shattered soul needed mending. To ease heartbreak I began haunting the cinema, sitting through flicks time and again. I'd watch love and power played out on the big screen, count heads, nibble greasy corn, and try to forget the feel of soft springs and softer vinyl. One night, as some couple's kisses chimed the hour in the middle of a teen-slasher double feature, my gaze swerved and my heart stopped running. Around me and above, beneath, beside, breathed the building itself, its glassy front windows and brash marquee, curvaceous ceiling and sturdy walls, its sticky, tilted floor, a floor that knew the soles of so many citizens. It was the building I belonged to, not the fleeting images on screen or the shabby, spectacled crowds, Aunt Abbys and Uncle Joes come to cuddle away from the kids, draggy from days of dull jobs, glassy-eyed with the thrill of escape and a bloated, insistent anxiety about the possibility of human intelligence. It was the building I loved. When the theater closed for the night, in the early morning hours, I drove restlessly, hoping speed and danger would clarify this new self-knowledge.

I spent my adolescence and early twenties falling in and out of love with buildings. I loved the way all young people do, fast and too hard, each new beau a savior. I was no different from the restless youth scratching the strip except that while they raced through spontaneous couplings to stall in shotgun or debtor's marriages, I held back, thrilled with the chase and the glint of the new.

The first real, lasting love I found took me by surprise. There I was, searching for thrills in the cinema, the public library, the post office, when all along my love was underneath my very toes. By then Mama and I had moved to Cartwheel. She'd rented a tiny house and I'd found a job cleaning rooms at the Sleepy Stay. Maybe I came home sated, because I didn't think much about our house until after Mama's death.

Mama was the only person I've ever trusted. She was pure good, through and through. She made everyone else look like bruised fruit. After she was gone, I stopped going to the cinema, the public library, the post office. After work I'd come right home to tend to our house, gently, as if it still held her body. I filled that house with glints and rustles to distract me from the vacuum her coffin left behind.

Mama bought the house with her body. The man who owned it owned my mama. Maybe he made her my mama—who knows? Mr. Bradley, his name was. She picked corn and strawberries on his farm midway between Cartwheel and Martinsville, and did God knows what else for him on her off-hours. She died in a field accident. A combine. He came by the house to tell me himself. I think he thought he was being gracious. I was lying on the couch, still in my maid's uniform, exhausted from a long day's work. He didn't knock, just walked right in.

"Your mother." His voice trailed off and I knew, not only that she'd died, but that he'd fucked or loved her, one or the other. I don't know what I expected from him. A hug? A fancy funeral? Instead he handed me the deed to the house and left.

I never saw him again. No use. I can't prove anything.

Mama was full-blooded Mexican, and for a long while I let myself believe that I was too. But she wanted me to be ordinary, which in her eyes meant Anglo. She tried to get me to pick up white bread ways, like cruising and dances and greasy burgers. I did too. But only to please her. After her death I stopped trying. Spent my time indulging my true passion—fixing up the house till it was worthy of adoration.

For several years that house was where my heart stretched taut. Then Sleepy Stay cut back. After I got "reassigned," I was tempted to take any old job to fill the gap, but luckily I waited. When the spot at the M&H opened up, I knew it was for me. The apron made noise when I walked, and the other waitresses had secrets too. I could tell.

I had no idea it was the beginning of another love.

My first year or so, I thought of the diner only as what won me dinner, never giving structure a second thought. Then one Thursday, with
Marv and Helen on their first vacation in years, I had to lock up all by
myself. I parked my truck right out front, meaning to head home in an
hour or two.

But I never left the M&H. When Bobby came to open and set up
baking at four-thirty the next morning, I tried to look as if I'd just arrived,
mistakenly thinking it was an hour later than it was. We laughed over
that one, me and Bobby, laughed over Selena's silly mistake, laughed
and laughed, his loud guffaws trailing me long after work was over.
Only by then it was my own laughter, loud and raucous because I knew
what no one else did—what came between night shift and morning,
closing and opening.

Love comes slow to Indiana. It takes its dismal pace from grey skies
and fickle weather. I often wonder how hearts pulse in Alaska or Missis-
sippi. How do folks there take their sweethearts—with a grasp or a sizzle,
scrambling or stepping high? When I found what I'd been seeking, everything seemed to slip into slow motion. I wanted the world to turn
faster, but it seemed I hadn't used up my share of waiting.

The first trick was letting myself in.

Diner was calling to me, no doubts there. But I couldn't break a shiny
window, slice through chrome or torch iron to enter what I hoped to
hold. No, I couldn't wreck the thing I loved, not even for the chance to
love it harder. I'm different from many that way. Most people chop and
sliver, thinking they'll have a better chance to hang onto something that's
been damaged by their own two hands.

I prefer keys.

Metal's a favorite of mine. Slick and shiny, the sheen reflecting the
depth of its desire. Hold a key in your hand and you hold a wild thing,
a thing that owns what some folks only dream about—the potential for
secrecy. Keys make secrets. We all carry an invisible set with us, scrape
them on other folks' locks from time to time. But the set I finagled out of
Marv and Helen was visible. What happened was so simple it almost
bored me. One morning, while we were slitting the blinds and setting
up, Marv mentioned to all of us that he was on the lookout for cleanup
help. They needed someone to come in while the place was sleeping to
do big-scale stuff, like the refrigerator and freezer, coffee machines, and
dessert case.

"All those doilies," sighed Bet, but I jumped at the chance. It would
mean a little extra cash, but that wasn't why.

Keys.

My own set.

That was when I started courting.

I'm not much of a girly one. I look the part, but when it comes to loving, I move first and take things quick. Pretty soon I was visiting the diner every evening. I'd stay till one, drive home for a catnap, then drive back in time to work at 5:45. Sometimes I'd start nodding off, but I worried I'd get caught if I stayed over. Sooner or later Marv would forget his jacket or Helen her ulcer medicine, and they would slip back into the diner, startling me awake. If they heard the sigh of my snores or the papery rustle of my skirts, they might mistake me for a criminal and sneak up on me. What then? I couldn't imagine Marv with a gun, but Helen maybe. She'd certainly have precise aim. So I had to find some way to sleep within my beloved that would still be safe if someone entered the diner.

I thought about the shelf under the counter and the space beneath the booths. But it was the storage room that finally caught my attention. Long, narrow, and dark, it was perfect for hiding out. I fixed myself a pallet out of flour sacks and found a rice bag for a pillow. When I tested it out, it was actually comfortable, once I got used to the feel of wooden boards beneath my back. It was comfortable, and it was mine. Things were certain, but I waited to move in. I wanted a ceremony to make sleeping over matter because this passion was different.

I'd loved and been in love with buildings before, but I didn't want to spend the night the way I had with the others—casually, not caring if the timing was perfect or only halfway. I wanted the diner to be ready, same as me, and I wanted the thing to stick, holy. I wanted approval too, the way the other married couples had their true loves blessed. I knew I could make it happen, I just wasn't sure how much I'd have to hide.

I like buildings but I like words too. Lying isn't such a sin as people make it out to be. If you take words and make them mean something else, you're just being creative. That's all I ever am. Creative. I didn't want to hurt anyone. I didn't want anyone to question their own delights. So there shouldn't have been any problems. Everything should've slipped smooth as Bobby's Boston cream pie. But of course a human had to come along and spoil it all with competition. I'd waited on Cory Flint for several years but never guessed he had the same inclinations. I think I first sensed the layers beneath his friendly banter shortly after Gwen came to wait tables. He seemed to be scoping her out, but I knew better. One morning he ordered pancakes instead of fried ham. I acted surprised, and he chattered casually with me about Gwen.

"Thought I'd order something different this time, since Gwennie suggested cakes might be good."

"Gwen would know." I grinned. "She eats 'em every morning." It was true, and I thought nothing of it, till I came back after he'd left and noticed spots of syrup on the table.

Most factory boys eat sloppy. They grew up without mamas or ran away from home at seventeen. They could care less for manners. It's the same for new young mothers and high schoolers, but factory boys are the worst. It didn't surprise me that Cory left spots of syrup at his table and it didn't irk me to wipe them up. That's my job, same as working watchman is his.

What bothered me were the letters: *CF.*

I remember going on a date with some guy, I think his name was Mike, and he took me to a pub, sat me at a dimly lit back booth, and carved our initials into the table: *M&S.* While he carved, I tried not to wince, but all I could think about was the prick of that knife meeting wood and what the table must be feeling. Wood's tender. No one knows because it hides its scars inside itself, circle on circle, roundness that looks as if it always forgives. But the raw truth is that wood holds grudges. I knew that booth would forever remember me as an accomplice to a rape.

When I saw Cory's spilt syrup, shaped like a *C,* shaped like an *F,* I knew then and there that I'd found someone else who loved things enough not to want to violate their surfaces with knives, pens, or nails. Syrup's easy. It feels warm and sticky. I wished I'd thought of syrup myself.

At first I was happy for Cory. I thought, *He knows what I know. We're kin, we've found our pleasure.* Some never do. Anyone can wall herself off from the space her soul feels most at home. I have a sort of radar, enough to spot someone whose deepest desires are hidden from her very self. I know about closets. Funny thing is, for me it's a closet that most satisfies my desires. *Irony,* as Mrs. Meechum would've said in eleventh grade. Who says I missed out, skipping senior year?

Cory Flint, closet case. Even I would never have guessed it. He seemed so *Playboy*-boring in his dense desire. Prior to his pancake breakfast I'd have bet money that he had nothing to hide, not because he was so honest (he didn't tip well enough to think highly of him), but because he didn't seem creative enough to think up lusciousness. When I saw that syrup, I knew I'd underestimated him. What I didn't realize was that he would become a first-rate rival.

I began noticing the care he took with everything he touched inside the diner. When he opened the door to the M&H, he slid his hand along its inner knob, closing it gently so the bell barely shook. Then he'd cross the room slowly, choosing an out-of-the-way booth. Before, I'd thought his sluggish pace and hide-away habits were simple tiredness. He worked night shift and claimed his body had never gotten used to sleeping during the day. But soon I realized tiredness was all a big fraud. Cory crossed the room slowly so his feet could enjoy every tiled step. When he slid into a booth, he eased across the vinyl gingerly so he could savor the feel of its slippery surface. Sometimes after he'd ordered and before we brought his food, he'd rest his head against the table like it was a pillow. "Poor Cory," Gwen would murmur. She'd amble over to talk to him, even rub his neck above the collar. I wanted to alert her that it was all a hoax, but why bother? She was so simple, Gwen. She'd never understand funky desire.

It didn't worry me at first. I loved the diner, and the diner loved me. It was only when a series of accidents happened that I started fretting. First, right in front of the breakfast crowd, I slipped on a puddle of coffee that sprang up like a mirage. A few days later I chipped a plate when I set it down on a fork I'd have sworn appeared by magic on the counter. Then I jammed the blinds while I was cleaning them. "Are you OK?" Caddie asked me, thinking I was tired or overworked.

But I knew the diner was trying to tell me something.

I don't take vows lightly. Up to me to ward off danger, up to me to shoo Cory off my turf. Slowly, subtly, I let him know he wasn't wanted. For a few weeks it was simple things like mangling his order, charging too high for too little. But he just moved over to Gwen's section, pretending to flirt with her. I knew it was a ruse, so when Gwen's tables were full and he once more found himself in one of mine, I went for the jugular.

Gwen stopped by with coffee as I was taking Cory's order. "Refill?" she asked. He beamed. I waited till she'd poured and passed by. Then out with it.

"She's mine," I said. "I was here first. I've worked the diner for going on seven years now. You've only been breakfasting for three. I think it's time you found another diner."

"What's that you're saying, Selena?"

I set my order pad down on the table. "We're neither one of us stupid. I see where your eyes go. I read the set of your lips." I watched as the meaning of the words hit home.

"Jesus." He spit a mouthful of coffee into his cup. "I can't believe it. I never knew you were...like that."

"No shame in it." I smiled my best church smile. "Besides, it takes one to know one."

Was the battle too easy? To do Cory credit, he didn't hang on. All he asked for was one meal good-bye. I told him to take it in Gwen's section and he thanked me for that. Said it showed I hadn't lost all self-respect.

I told him my mama taught me one or two things right.

I can't help wishing I'd been up close to see it, that last supper. What did he order? Did he steal a sugar packet to remember the diner? All I know is that once Gwen spotted Cory down at the Big Boy, rumors spread fast. I overheard all sorts of stories. There was truth to all of them—most every drama is made of the same ingredients. Naturally folks thought Cory and I were the couple that said the sad good-byes.

They had no idea it was a triangle.

I felt a little bit sorry for Cory. So one morning, on my day off, I stopped by the Big Boy for a quick Danish (store bought, possibly frozen) and a cup of black coffee (same brand we used, but burned). I read the paper, tried to look casual. Just before ten, I went into the kitchen, courtesy of Maria, an old friend of mine from the Sleepy Stay.

I didn't tell the whole story, just enough to let her think something was up between me and Cory. She let me hang out in back, behind the grill. From there I could catch glimpses of where he sat and where his eyes went. Sure enough, he took a booth in the back and slid in like the vinyl loved his frumpy butt more than a calf loves a teat. It was funny to watch, and heartening. He'd found a new love. Now I could better enjoy my own.

Safe. I was safe again.

Once I'd recovered, I started noticing things I'd missed while the war and worry were upon me—like Caddie and what she'd found to fill her time. Caddie intrigues me. I've long suspected her desires are quirky,

like mine. I've even tried to ask her, poking and probing, pushing romance questions her way. She never bites, but I haven't given up. If I
knew for sure that she was different I might tell her my history. A love
story isn't finished until someone other than the lovers knows the tale.

After Jo, Caddie's romantic life went downhill. If it's true you can judge
a man's lovemaking by the size of his tips, David was no doozie. Sometimes he'd leave ten pennies in the bottom of a milk glass. The other
girls would scorn to search, so I'd fish them out, rinse them off, and
count them while Caddie tallied up his bill at the register. I'd make sure
he heard each penny clank as I dropped it in my apron pocket. But he
had no shame, David—no shame and no dignity. When Caddie dumped
him, the whole diner cheered silently. Helen and Marv let us hand round
free day-old Danish to celebrate, and everyone was chipper, though we
kept quiet about it for Caddie's sweet sake.

David bounced back so fast you couldn't see the springs. Pity for the
poor scrawny one who went with him. She was your average good girl,
all freckles and skinny ankles with the plaid Catholic school skirts and
cheap gold cross. The kind of toothy one you run into ten years later
and don't recognize because she's buying stacks of pot pies and diapers
at the Foodville. But she goofed, she believed his rancid words, she
went with him. Bet and I saw it coming and tried to think up ways to
warn her, but it happened too fast.

There should be nets for girls who try to fly and fall.

After that, Caddie just settled. Single became her, and maybe she recognized it, because she stopped trying for men. Not that they let her
alone, mind you. Her skirts were silent, but her eyes were hungry. All
kinds of men and boys tried to fill her up.

For a time I believed she liked her lonely life.

Then one day she invited me back to her place. It was a first and a last.
We don't have much to say to each other, Caddie and I. My secrets
weigh me down, and she has lots of her own. We're neither one of us
much for small talk. So we sat at her kitchen table and ate pie and
watched her cat roll a catnip ball, getting high and cooing like a crazy
bird, all sparks and orange hair, eyes flashing.

I tried to pick it up but it skittered under the sofa. "Boy or girl?"

"Both," she said, "or neither. I don't know."

"I could tell," I offered, but she shook her head. Her bangs flip-flopped
in her eyes. They were new, the bangs, and didn't suit her.

"I don't want to know. Cat has its mysteries, and I let it be."

Much as I've always figured Caddie for an honest one, I didn't believe her. Something told me she knew perfectly well what the cat's sex was, and maybe more besides. But I don't believe in pushing people, so we just sat, eating pie (sort of apple, sort of pecan—even her food was a mystery), watching this maybe girl, maybe boy cat lope around after its ball, watching it go round itself and roll, and then when we were done with sweetness and the cat was done with its drug, suddenly it was on Caddie's lap, cooing again (it never sounded like a cat, but sometimes like a bird, sometimes human), and Caddie was fingering it like a piano.

I watched those fingers fly.

Hers were fingers that could balance trays full of food and brimming pots of coffee, fingers that could snap up an order on the register in two seconds flat. She had nice hands, Caddie, but even nicer fingers. That was probably what drove Jo away. A woman with fingers that agile is a woman too good for a man. While I watched, the cat arched its back and chuckled—I swear it chuckled like a man. That was when the idea washed over me, salty, stinging a little like ocean breakers.

Caddie was like me.

She didn't love the right way or what she was supposed to.

I could see it in the way she fingered the cat. All touch was sensual for Caddie. There was love in her touch, and a kind of satisfaction. She rubbed her index and middle fingers in a line along the cat's back, then let her whole hand rest on its belly, tickling the fine hairs lightly, blowing gently on its crown, scratching behind its ears (soft, like grass after rain) while she whispered something I couldn't catch—a name, instructions, or a hiding place. Tomorrow's promise. I understood then that Caddie loved her cat.

She *loved* her cat.

Why not? Me, I'm into things that don't move, only shift or sway. They're easiest to hold onto, easiest to trust. It seems if you wanted something that bled red, you'd pick another human. At least the language barrier wouldn't be so stern. I wouldn't want to love a little beastie. There's that musky animal smell, same as humans but stronger, clots and gnarls of hair, the stealth and yowls and disappearances. Anything that moves can flee. Why set yourself up to be abandoned? The diner would never leave me. I had it to myself for as long as I wanted its walls wrapped around me. But we make our own choices. If Caddie loved creatures, who was I to tell her what was wrong or right? It was good to see her deep into her loving like that, letting the cat rub all over her lap, leaving pools of fur on her thighs and sometimes spittle, cooing the way it did, and giggling, pawing at air and then scrambling to get up and joust with sunlight.

"You sure love your cat." I wanted her to know I understood.

Caddie grinned. She was so intense she sometimes scared me with her gazes—straight to the heart of a girl, like a gun. But when she grinned, the glint in her eyes became a candle. Smiling, there was no more rapid fire. I was glad.

"We're good for each other," was all she said.

When Caddie and Gwen first started hanging round, I didn't understand it. I thought Caddie was done with humans for good and had moved, like me, into another realm. But the two got tight and then stuck. One day they were edgy with each other, two girls too much alike to share space with men and not think *rival*. The next day they were all chitter-chatter and Saturday-night-on-the-town-dontcha-think?

I wasn't the only one who noticed the trajectory of the thing.

Helen said something to me once. "They've gotten close, yes?" pointing towards Caddie and Gwen hunched over a pot of coffee behind the counter, giggling. "Close as sisters. What do you think of that?"

"Not like sisters. Sisters yank hair and tattle. Sisters struggle." There wasn't any struggle here, just empathy and warmth. But living things fade, flowers; temperatures change, rise or sink away. One day Caddie showed up too late to chat with Gwen on the stoop before work. Then there was a cloud over Caddie's head and she looked at Gwen sidewards. Soon it was over.

Everyone called it a lover's quarrel.

Some man wanted Caddie first, then found Gwen's favor, was the way the rumor spread. Wildfire. Folks started whispering about Gwen's ring, saying she'd cheated on Tim with Caddie's secret beau. I did my best to squelch the rumor, me and Bet both, but it was no use. The talk didn't stifle till the truth got out that Tim had left Gwen. Then the rumors did a 180, and folks got to wondering if Caddie had won Tim away.

Talk calmed down after a time, with Caddie and Gwen none the wiser. Folks gossip in Cartwheel, but it rarely comes round to meanness. More like storytelling Saturdays in the children's room at the library, only for grown-ups and without the puppets. I never bought the story about the beau or Caddie charming Tim away. If they'd fought over a man, I would've smelled it. The invisible thread that bound them snapped, and they spoke to each other the way they spoke to the rest of us, sometimes chipper, sometimes surly, depending on weather, moodiness, and time of day. They weren't enemies (which was how some folks painted it), but they weren't best friends either. Just ordinary, though the ordinariness itself was strange.

But I try not to worry too much over Caddie's ways. I've got my life in order now, and that's enough. Nights, I sleep in the supply closet, one ear alert for intruders, the rest of me relaxed against my bed. I've had my love for long enough now that it feels permanent. I try not to think about what could take my sweet diner away.

CHAPTER SEVEN: CADDIE
■ ■
■

That summer, sweat made thick circles underneath our armpits. Only Selena's blouse stayed dry.

"How do you do it?" Gwen asked. Selena only smiled, lips full of mystery.

"Someday I'll show you. Not now." It was always "someday" when we asked, till one afternoon when the diner cleared out—something rare, something that made us feel reckless. Gwen winked at me, and I knew she was thinking of sneaking into the dessert case. We shared a sweet tooth, Gwen and I, so I winked back, but before we could make our move, Selena shimmied the two of us behind the counter. Bet and Bobby were cooing at Sean in the kitchen, but poked their heads through the order window to watch the show.

"I'm about to reveal one of the Seven Wonders of the World." Selena unbuttoned the top button on her blouse. Bobby whistled, but I had to turn my face. It was some kind of joke, sure, but when was the last time I'd seen another woman's open body? I thought then about something Jo had said to me, that I should leave Cartwheel and see the world. Or at least just visit Indy.

"There are bars there for girls like us," she said. But leaving wasn't something I could imagine. I knew how to hide here. What if, somewhere else, people could read my face? When I turned my attention back towards the Seventh Wonder, Bet and Bobby had come out from the kitchen, Sean in tow. Selena was still unbuttoning, Gwen, Bet, and Bobby were bursting, and even Sean's cries sounded suspiciously like giggles. Selena's fingers were halfway down her chest. I could see the little ribbon on the front of her pink, front-snap brassiere. Just when we all thought she'd lost it, she stopped messing with buttons and rummaged under first one armpit, then the other.

"Voilà!" Selena held out two damp pads of white cotton. "Falsies. They soak up sweat and wash out real easy." She turned them over to reveal a strip of Velcro. "Stays snug, and I stay cool. Any more questions?"

"Are you open for business, sir?"

Selena turned to face the customers who'd somehow slipped in without jingling the bell—two boys, both keeping their gazes fixed firmly on Bobby.

Bobby shrugged. "Sure. Why not?"

Selena stuffed the cotton wads back under her arms, wrestling a little with the Velcro, then buttoned up her blouse. "We're open as we'll ever be." While Bobby and Bet ducked back into the kitchen, she grabbed two menus and napkined sets of silverware, bustled over, and led the boys to a booth—one of Gwen's.

Gwen gave me a knowing glance and fell back on my shoulder in a mock swoon. We both knew why Selena was so generous.

Missionaries.

"Been a while since we had any," Selena mused when she rejoined us.

Gwen looked curious. "I thought the Mormons set them in every town."

"They rotate. New boys every couple of months. Girls on the odd occasion."

"Did we rotate ours too fast or something?"

"Better than that. There was a scandal."

Gwen wanted to know the story, but her eyes kept roaming to the missionaries' table. She was trying to make out their names, I could tell. They wore name tags, same way we did, only theirs were black and ours were bright blue. "Weird," Gwen said, squinting and interrupting Selena's gossip. "They've both got the same first name. E-something."

"Elder," Selena and I said, both at once.

"They always have it on their name tags, instead of their first names," Selena explained. "Elderwhosawhatsit. The girls are Sister."

"We should have something like that." Gwen's face was dreamy. "I could be Lady Gwen."

"How about Mother?" Selena suggested, but Gwen made a face.

"That sounds like cursing. Can I call them by their first names once I find out what they are?"

"Sure, I guess."

"I think I will. Elder sounds silly, and besides, they're younger than me. When are you going to finish your story?"

Selena rolled her eyes at me. "At your service, Gwennie. So where was I? Cartwheel's last two started some hijinks, so the big important fellas kicked them out and decided to wait a few years before sending in new troops. I guess this pair must be very upright and careful if they're supposed to make us forget all the scandal that went on."

"What happened?"

"Caddie, you want to tell it?"

"I don't remember. Was it in the papers?"

"All over. Must've been around the time you and Jo were so tight you forgot the world was turning."

"Caddie never reads the papers." Gwen's voice was smug.

"How would you know?" *Gwen was one to talk,* I thought. She rarely read faces even.

"That cigarette fire in the bathroom of the bus station—the headlines were telling that story for days, and you missed it."

Selena shook her head. "You two bicker like sisters. Sure you're not kin?"

My stomach plummeted. "Absolutely not."

"Who knows?" Gwen giggled. "Indiana's full of unexpected relations."

"I don't find that comforting."

"Lighten up, Caddie. Anyway, back to my story. See, Gwen, how there are two of them?" Selena's voice was very knowledgeable, like a school teacher explaining fancy math. She liked gossip, Selena. The stories themselves didn't seem to matter—happy or sad, sexy or boring. She liked the telling and watching people's faces during and after. Mostly it was fun to hear her spin out her tales, but once in a while it got odd, like when she'd relate some tragedy and not seem to notice how tragic it was. "The rule is, they have to stay in sight of each other. It's to keep them out of trouble, but the last pair stuck a little too tight, if you know what I mean. One day Gladys Lindt, the lady whose house they were staying in—she rented out the basement, I think it was. The way the papers described it, the room was moldy and run-down, as if she didn't care for her house at all. But it was a Victorian, you know that block on Illinois Avenue, over by Buck and Doe's gun shop, with all the falling down gingerbread houses that could be so pretty if someone would just take a concern for wood like people did back in the olden days. It's a pretty house, just a little on the sleepy side, sort of a cake that's not got yeast in it, but they say the room she housed those poor boys in was all moldy. Their shirts got greeny patches on them, and the walls—"

"What happened?" Gwen was itching to take their orders, jostling from one foot to the other.

"Oh. Anyhow, one day Gladys had some important tidbit to tell them and she just walked in without knocking. Caught them not just close but in a clinch, kissing each other and everything."

Gwen leaned over the counter, made a scrunched-up face, and pretended to stick her finger down her throat. "Hurl!" The way she said it made her voice come through her nose.

"Aw, c'mon. They were just boys. And everybody's different. Not saying it's right or wrong, just different." Selena shrugged. "Gwen, you can't be such a slug. Why don't you go on over and take their orders? They've been sitting there forever. They're probably hungry. Religious folks don't always eat snacks in between meals."

Gwen was still making gagging sounds. "What if those two are faggy? The one by the window is so cute. What if he's faggy and I just can't tell?"

"Whadya think, Caddie?" Selena turned to me. "How can you tell if a boy's got fagginess inside him?"

Before I could answer, Gwen sighed. "I guess I just have to see for myself." She pulled two cups from the shelf and reached for a pot of coffee, but I stopped her hand.

"They don't drink coffee."

"Decaf, then."

"Not decaf either."

"What's grease without coffee?" Gwen looked genuinely perplexed, but Selena saved her.

"This'll win 'em over," she said, holding out a carton of strawberry milk. "Go to it."

We watched her walk to the missionaries' table. It was so perfect, Gwen's walk. Sort of ambly, like she wanted to take her time thinking about where each sneakered foot should fall. She had little pom-pom socks poofing out of the back of each shoe and barrettes nestled in her golden hair—blue plastic ducks. Usually I enjoyed watching her in motion. She didn't try to be anything, she was just Gwen. But right then she put on a mask, a mask that stretched the length of her whole body, a sort of bodysuit that changed little things about her gestures. She didn't seem to be just Gwen, but someone Gwen wanted herself to appear to be. She'd changed to match them or please them or sniff them out. It was what she'd never been known for doing, Gwen, and I for one was sorry to see the change. Even if maybe everyone comes to hiding someday. Even if it's unusual to last as long as Gwen did, being natural. That was when my feelings for Gwen truly died. All that day I walked around with a heaviness, carrying the dead feeling like a still-born. I didn't release it till I was safe at home and could cry, letting Cat knead my belly.

Maybe I was just angry because of what Gwen said. Maybe I made her ugly ignorance into that suit, that long suit altering her pretty gestures, making her body stiff and cautious, her face prissy. Maybe I let the word *fag* blind me to how she was really still the very same, not a different girl but the one I'd loved—stupidly, without knowing what was inside her soul.

As we watched Gwen pour the pink milk into the chipped white cups, Selena shook her head. "She's so good at flirting, it's inhuman. She won't stay single for long."

By then Selena knew about Gwen's hasty divorce—Selena and the rest of Cartwheel. The town was alive that way. It inhaled gossip in gulps, exhaling in gusts that spread news from foyer to bus stop to farm. Even pets knew things in Cartwheel. It sometimes saddened me, the way the town had no secrets. I like a little mystery now and then, but except for my Jo, Cartwheel hadn't had one interesting thing happen inside its fence posts in so long. Too, the town's gossip hunger made my own secrets heavier.

"Caddie, I can't believe you don't remember." Selena poked me in the ribs. "How could you forget the biggest scandal Cartwheel's ever had?"

"I don't pay heed to gossip, Selena. You know that."

"Except fancy actors." Selena winked. She knew I liked flipping through ladies' magazines. Once she'd caught me gazing away at an actress, some new one, her hair golden like Gwen's but her face a little tough, a combination of Gwen and someone else, not Jo but coming close, boyish the way movie star girls weren't usually supposed to be. I was just staring at the picture, imagining a fantasy where I was visiting California for some reason and ran into her on the street. In my daydream I smiled at her, very Mona Lisa mysterious. She smiled back, and I knew she recognized our shared secret. When Selena came up behind me and laughed at my concentration, I had to hide what I was looking at. On the opposite page was a photo of an actor starring in some war movie, very famous and handsome I suppose, only I never cared to remember his name. He was geared up in fatigues, his muscles all shiny through his ripped-out shirt. I didn't like the picture mostly because there was a dead soldier draped along the rise of a hill behind him so how could he be sexy, there with some dead man for scenery? But I knew he was supposed to be so I tapped his nose on the slippery page and told her I was crushed out on him, to where I couldn't sleep. I remember she asked me a funny question—"Crushed out on which?"—and for a moment I thought she'd clued in that the girl was more interesting but then she finished her thought, "The actor or his picture?"

I didn't see a difference, really. They were both made only for gazing on. But I thought flesh and blood would do me better as an excuse so I said, "The actor, of course." She seemed not to care that I couldn't remember his name.

"You're funny, Caddie. You don't see anything going on around you. I wish I could live in my own little world like you." Selena's voice seemed to have an edge to it, though I couldn't be sure, since I couldn't see her face as she bent down to stack silverware beneath the register. "You really oughta find yourself a good man and start popping babies. You're wasted on work, you know? The kind of spaciness you have is perfect for mothering."

"What makes you think I want to have babies?"

"You're a girl, aren't you?"

I couldn't tell if she was teasing. "Just because I don't remember some silly scandal doesn't mean I'm spacy. Maybe I do pay attention but you don't pay enough attention to me to know I pay attention to you."

"I think you should get married soon."

"Maybe YOU should get married soon. Why do you get to hold off but I have to do the thing?" I hadn't meant for it to come out so negative. Selena turned around and looked at me funny.

"Maybe I will."

"Don't you need a boyfriend first?" I'd gone mean and so had she. We'd snapped. It happened with us sometimes. I hated it, hated how easy it was for things to get ugly when really I liked Selena and Selena liked me.

"I think you remember the scandal, Caddie."

My stomach burned, the way having an ulcer must feel. I remembered, all right. I'd been at work, busing a table. A customer had left behind a rumpled paper and the word *missionaries* in the headline lured me. I knew and liked both boys. Verne and Mert. *The Cartwheel Chronicle* didn't say what exactly they'd been caught doing, just that they'd "broken the rules of proper missionary conduct" and been sent back to Utah. I took the paper home. Even before I unlocked the kitchen door, I knew Jo was inside because the lock was twisted round to the left and I always turned it to the right. She was sitting at the kitchen table—unusual both because she got home later than I did and because she never just sat. Jo always had to have something to occupy her hands.

She had the paper spread out in front of her, but she wasn't reading, just gazing at the stove as if she might've left it on. I stood behind her, put my hands on her shoulders, and massaged her neck, but she didn't respond. Pretty soon I stopped, pulled up a chair, and sat across from her, waiting for her to tell me what I'd already guessed. When she spoke, though, it wasn't to tell me the story she'd heard about Verne and Mert. The story came later. What Jo said was, "I'm scared."

If I had it to do again, Jo, I'd push my chair back and go to you. I'd move a thousand miles away from Cartwheel, to one of the big cities you talked of, so we could live openly, so we could be with others, so we wouldn't have to hide. If I could do it again, your departure would have a *we* in it. But time passes. I heard the new tenants painted our old kitchen pink and white.

"Caddie, I think you don't want to confess the crush you had on Mert. What is it with you, that you think you have to be so pure? It happens all the time. People fall in love with someone but get a craving for a taste of someone else. I think you just feel stupid because it turned out Mert was no way interested. You were plain old the wrong species."

"Not species. Sex."

"Whatever. But how could you tell? Like Gwen said, fagginess is just something you have to wait and see about. It can creep along at any time." She ran a hand along the counter, checking for crumbs and sticky spots. "Not that I'm saying it's wrong or anything. I'm not trying to be a fat-mouthed bigot like Gladys Lindt. I'm just saying it's hard to see."

I felt so blue remembering Jo that I flat-out lied, angling for sympathy. "It stings about Mert. It stings to know I had feelings for someone else."

"Caddie, you've got to let go of Jo. You're stuck. It's getting stale." Selena didn't turn her head from watching Gwen, but I felt the curtains fall around us. We'd made privacy happen in a public space.

"It's hard, knowing there won't be another."

"There's always another. But you have to let go of the old one first." She was still watching Gwen, who could've profited by giving lessons in flirting with the pious. She was bent over their table, pointing to something on the menu. You could tell she liked boys by how she used her breasts, like they were separate from the rest of her body. "She's good, isn't she?" Selena smiled. "But you'd be fine at it, Caddie honey. You just have to let go of the shyness a little. What about one of those two? Gwen can't take both of 'em. Why don't you have a little patience, find out which one she picks, and go after the other? He'd be steady. They're family men, Mormons. They provide. Wife gets to stay at home."

Hurl. But I didn't say it.

"Or one of the morning rush factory men or Cory or that plumber who buys Danish on Saturday mornings."

"I thought you were interested in Cory."

"Naw." She smiled so big her teeth gleamed.

"You two always used to talk so private."

"I talk private to lots of fellas." It was true, she did. Selena had dates all the time. She met men in the weirdest places—truck stops, museums, once a Halloween haunted house. She'd go out with them once or twice and then dump them. Bet called it picky. I called it heartless, though not to Selena's face.

"Who's the latest lucky beau?"

"No use jinxing it with talk."

"What's his name, at least?"

She looked like she had to think about it. "Chrome."

"Chrome?" It wasn't a name I'd heard for a man before, but who knows what crazy things mothers will do to their infants? Gwen was the sort might've named a baby Chrome if she'd had the fire to think it up. That was when I decided Selena's date was real. Chrome was too clever a name for her to invent.

"I'm cozy, Caddie. But I'm wondering what you do for yourself, nights when stars shine and you wish someone would sing to you."

What was it Selena had said to Gwen? "Everybody's different. Not saying it's right or wrong, just different." What if I told her now? Would she say the same back to me or was she only easy on Verne and Mert because they were long gone and she'd never got close to them? If I told her, she might think I had a crush on her. There'd be no way to deny it without hurting her feelings. I couldn't say, "You're not pretty to me." It would scare her if I did like her, but it would insult her if I didn't. Worse, she might guess that I thought Gwen was lovely. I didn't think Selena would snake out on me, biting and hissing and warning the others off, but who knows what someone will do—someone who's friendly but not exactly a friend—when you show them inside the glen of your heart? I thought I trusted her, but I wasn't sure. She liked boys so much herself, was so much the flirt, so straight on the beeline. I knew she'd never understand what it felt like to love differently, to want something you could never have or just didn't know how to find.

Just then a wail pierced the quiet chatter. Gwen blanched and excused herself from the missionaries' table to run back into the kitchen and soothe Sean's howls. "Damnit," she muttered midflight. Selena and I both knew what she was thinking—Sean had ruined her rendezvous. I figured she'd tote the baby seat over to the boys' table—they were known for being family men, after all—but when she reemerged a few minutes later without Sean, Selena nudged me.

"She'll hide the baby as long as she's able."

I'd seen enough of Gwen's maternal workings to know it was true. Then a family of six tore in, all sandy from miniature golf, and business picked up. Soon it was time for me to head home. Selena never got my story, but once I was back in my apartment, Cat convinced me to keep quiet. Something in her purr said, *Keep your secrets here with me.* Because I didn't want the sleek surface of my tidy life—the plants winking at the sun on the sill, the doily on the sofa, the kitchen table Jo had made for me herself—disturbed, I wrote a promise to myself in milk on the back of my hand: "Keep silent, self. Stay Cozy."

The missionaries made news enough to keep my mind off things.

Our breakfast and lunch business picked up off the two boys alone, they were so hungry. Gentle but firm with their food, they never tore in, but somehow every bit vanished, down to the last drip of ketchup on their fries, the last slurp of sugary milk. They liked strawberry best, but went for chocolate too, vanilla-maple when we had it. When we ran out of flavored, they'd stir sugar into plain; sugar, and they drank it from coffee cups because that was what Gwen always brought them, and they always sat in Gwen's section. Once or twice the diner was full when they arrived. Too polite to turn away, they sat dutifully in Bet's area. They avoided me, I guess because they figured me for Gwen's rival and didn't want to riffle her, and of course they avoided Selena like a short skirt under a streetlight. "They think I'm a whore," she'd sigh.

Bobby would snort into his soda. "That's what you get for doing the striptease so keen."

But Selena didn't seem bothered by it. "I just want to know how they got our door open without jingling the bell. One of them's got a way with doors."

"Ever heard of a back door man?" Bobby grinned. "Maybe the Hardy boys have extra steady hands."

"Lord works in mysterious ways." I winked at Bobby. It always made me happy when he came out from the kitchen and spent his break time joshing.

"Isn't anyone around here pious?" Bet took some offense at wisecracks where God was concerned. It was a stone in her bosom that Roy wouldn't do church Sundays the way she wanted to. Bet was one for church, very hard on it, though the church was always changing. "God's God, no matter how he's housed. Keeps me on my toes to sing all the different songs and stand up at different moments." She liked variety, Bet, and not just on Sunday. You could see it in what she ate. Always the special, even when the taste wasn't one she favored or when it was stew, which we all knew was just whatever leftovers from the week before.

Bet was attentive to the missionaries, just like Gwen. *"So* skinny," she'd say, over and over, till Selena and I got tired of hearing it. Everyone beamed at them when, as far as we could see, all they'd done was take a liking to Gwen's service and Bobby's cooking and set up shop in a corner booth.

"Which one do you think is cuter?" Gwen would ask Bet. They'd spend hours tossing the question like a beach ball between them. Gwen finally decided that Elder Christiansen was cuter, but Elder Leavitt liked her better. "I just can't leave it alone," she'd giggle.

Bet would smirk. "Honey, you wait till you finally take him home. Then we'll see who can't leave it alone."

When Gwen laughed, she forgot to cover her mouth with her hand and let her teeth grin along with the rest of her. "His first name is LaMonte. LaMonte Leavitt. He said I could call him by his first name. And Elder Christiansen is Jared."

"Would somebody please serve this hash before it turns back into a cow?" Bobby poked his head through the cook's window and raised an eyebrow at Gwen, who scurried over to pick up her food. We all four watched her walk over to the missionaries' table, set their food down, and start in on the special service.

First she broke their rolls open for them.

Then she opened four foil butter packets and buttered the rolls inside and a thin layer on top.

Then she handed around the salt and pepper shakers.

"This is ridiculous," Bobby sighed, ducking his head back inside the window. It was the first time I'd ever thought about becoming a cook. I wasn't good at putting foods together—when I made dinner myself on a weekend evening I usually burned it or mixed all the wrong flavors together—but being a cook meant relating to food instead of people. When Gwen acted stupid or Bet acted high and mighty or one of the men tugged on my hair like my braids were reins, I could see the advantage in it. Maybe that was why Bobby seemed so cheerful. He could afford to be nice, since food never talked back.

"I think Gwen just picked one." Bet yammered while Selena and I made faces behind her back. "She's taking Elder Leavitt's order first. She's pouring his maple milk. Now she's turning to the other one but her face is plainer—"

"Touchdown," Bobby mumbled through the window.

"Quiet! Oh, Caddie. Now the tall one, what's his name? Christiansen— he's getting up to go to the bathroom. Gwen and Leavitt are talking. Oh! He's giving her something. A book. A Bible?"

"The Book of Mormon." Gwen showed us proudly after the missionaries left. "They give 'em away free to folks who have a concern for spiritual life and so forth. But look here." She opened the book to its inner cover.

Dear Gwen,

May this day be a day of beginnings. I know you are a very spiritual person. Inside are truths I would have you press to your bosom. Hopefully you will feed from this book as I feed from the food you set on the table practically every weekday morning and/ or afternoon. Best of all is the hash, and I know you don't cook it but to serve is also to live. I know you are a very spiritual person and I hope you keep this book to save our discussions by.

Yours in brotherly affection and servitude,

LaMonte Leavitt

Scrawled beneath his name was a phone number, nearly illegible. Selena pointed at it. "He gave you his phone number? Isn't that immoral?"

"He asked me to call him to schedule another discussion."

"What exactly do you plan to discuss?"

"They're religious discussions, Selena. They lead up to being baptized. You have to have a series of them before you convert."

"Wait a minute." Bobby had his head through the window again. "You're planning to become a Mormon?"

"I think she just wants to marry one," Selena said. "What do you think, Caddie?"

I walked over to the milk shake machine and started cleaning it. It always needed cleaning, but no one ever wanted to do it because it was such a huge pain to take the thing apart and put it back together again. When two families came tumbling in, I let Selena and Gwen take them on. I was absorbed and liked the easy feel of it. It was like being on a boat, though I'd never been, only dreamed of it. After I cleaned the shake machine, I cleaned the coffeemaker. Then, since no one was behind the counter but me, I pulled up the rubber mats, lugged them through the kitchen and out the back door, and stacked them on the concrete landing in back of the diner. I tugged fresh mats from the pile of clean ones in the storage room and arranged them on the floor. There was an art to placing the mats. They had to line up just right, no overlap or crevices. Otherwise someone might trip and take flight.

While I was kneeling, tugging one of the mats up to the wall just beneath the order window, I heard someone call my name. The sun was coming in through the window down at the far side of the counter. Sun and the mesh of the mats made grill patterns on my hands as I picked each one up and set it down in turn. The voice floating above me as I knelt reminded me of something, only something I knew about, not something I'd actually lived. Then the voice again—my name, softly spoken.

"Miss Ruby."

Jo liked to say my hair had red in it. Not just auburn streaks, like most brunettes have, but real red. Deep red. Scarlet. "Ruby-for-to-save-the-day," she'd call me. That was when we were in love, or at least I was and she seemed to be, and we knew not just the finer colors tangled in each other's hair, but the taste of each other's blood.

I looked up, and it was Jo.

Her dark hair falling across her eyes, her solid chin, her small, fine-boned face and narrow shoulders.

I stood up, brushing my hands off on my apron. "Miss Ruby," came the voice again. Then I knew I wasn't dreaming.

"What are you doing here?"

"It's a free country."

"Not really."

"I thought you'd be glad to see me."

"I'm not telling you to leave, am I?"

"Come out here where I can get a look at you."

"David, I have things to do." I busied myself tallying checks.

"C'mon, Caddie." He stood as if he knew me well enough to make me into what he wanted. Just then I felt as if I stepped back, away from my body, away from myself, and watched Miss Ruby walk around the register, out to the front of the counter to stand beside him. The diner had gotten busy. Selena stared, but Bet and Bobby were buried in the kitchen and Gwen didn't know who David was so she ignored our reunion. I tugged at my apron, smoothing the pleats around my waist.

David reached out and captured my hands in his. "I came back for you, Caddie."

I was still a little bit away from my body. I could hear him speak, and I could speak to him in return, but the part that did the hearing and speaking was different from the part that should've been feeling his hands. "I didn't ask you to come."

"Yes, you did." He smiled his shy smile and let his hair flop like a horse's forelock. "I heard you calling."

Calling, but not for you. "David, you took someone with, wherever it was you went."

"That's over."

My words came out very slowly, almost slurred. "She was a baby."

"She was a whore."

"A girl can't be a whore unless a grown man makes her."

"You bitch." He spoke softly, so that only I could hear.

My thoughts and my body came together then. I shivered so hard my teeth chattered. Arthur Parks was sitting nearby on a stool, trying not to stare. Why had it taken me so long to figure? "You're drunk, David. That's what. You're completely drunk. Get out of here, or I'll call Bobby and have him kick you out."

"Aw, girl." He was still holding my hands. Now he squeezed them but I shook him off. It was as if my body was stronger for its rest away from soul.

"Get out."

"She was a whore, Caddie."

"Good for her. Get out."

"I'm through with her. Gonna get me a nice girl like you. Dontcha wanna come with me, Caddie?" His voice was still a whisper, shivery. "I'll take you someplace warm. You come with me, stop working this job here. It's killing your hands, Caddie. Girl like you should have pretty hands." He reached for my wrists but I stepped behind the register.

Then I spoke very loudly, so that the customers who weren't already watching would start paying attention. "Bobby! Would you come out here a second?"

"I'm gone." And he was. After, I had to ask folks if the whole thing had really happened. I stayed shook up awhile, worrying he'd seek me out at home. Once, in the middle of the night, Cat jumped onto the bathroom sink and knocked over my fish-shaped china toothbrush holder. I heard the crash, all of it, as if each noise was broken down into a little song: the swoosh of Cat's leap, the slither of her tail slashing, the bump of the object's tumble off the counter, the slice of its fall through air, and then the crash. What I thought was *David*. I got up, put on my robe, and paced. Even after I found Cat sulking behind the shower curtain, I still wasn't sure, and I dressed and spent the night awake, wishing morning would break or my eyes would slide shut of their own accord.

David stopped in again from time to time, but I told the others to take him on and watch out for me. It was what we did for each other. It was ordinary. Selena had a man visit angry once. He was from some furniture store in Martinsville, drove clear out here to chide her in front of all the regulars. He must've been as drunk as David. Maybe worse, because what he said didn't make any sense. We still joke about it—how he accused Selena of hiding in the store after hours back when she'd worked in the mall. "I've been looking to track you down forever. You slept on the Barcolounger," he said. "You rolled around on the king-size sofa."

"Why would I do that?" she said, flicking her fingers at him from behind the counter.

"Selena, I don't know why you did what you did. I only know you need help."

"I'll show you help, all right." She called Bobby to come out of the kitchen. "Crazy. You are flat out crazy."

"Let me show you the door." Bobby's smile was as friendly as ever, but the man backed off. He stood still a moment, staring at Selena very hard.

"Fine. You win. You wanna feel up my furniture, you feel it up. Anytime, babe. Anytime. Just don't leave marks, you hear me? A man's gotta make a living." He turned quickly and left, slamming the door behind him.

Bobby put a hand on Selena's shoulder. "You OK?"

"Takes all kinds," she shrugged, and that was the end of it. But David— David was persistent. He kept coming back and back, but since he never hassled me again, never even talked to me, there wasn't much anyone could do. Marv asked me one morning after David left whether I wanted Marv and Helen to ask him, very politely, to keep away. I appreciated the thought and said so, but I also said no. Partly I worried that it would make him angrier, that he'd seek me out somewhere else if he couldn't see me here. I figured it was safer having him stop by the diner than the laundromat or grocery or, worse still, my apartment. Mostly, though, I stopped worrying what David might do or say to me; I stopped worrying because I could read him as easily as my own scribbled bills. Watching him eat his eggs and cheese, watching him douse his beans with hot sauce and stir sugar into his milk, I read his gestures and realized I'd been mistaken.

He was looking, all right. But it wasn't me he was looking for.

I realized there was someone else on David's list when he showed up for lunch at the same time as the Mormons. Usually David and the missionaries missed each other. David worked janitorial, night shift mostly, so he'd come in early in the morning when he got off work, making breakfast his late dinner. But once in a while he'd be off work and he'd sleep in. Then he'd come into the diner in the afternoon, twoish, for a huge meal he ate in gobbled snatches.

One day David showed up around noon, usually too late or too early for his personal clock. When he walked in, he bumped right into Elder Leavitt. Both boys were standing stiffly by the door the way they always did, waiting for one of us (Gwen really, it was always Gwen) to acknowledge them by name and formally seat them. They had to be led practically by the hand. The sign that announced "Please wait to be seated" was just another scripture. They took it literally. It was one thing about them that made the otherwise mostly pious and respectful townies snicker to themselves, how the boys obeyed the sign. No one else paid it any mind, which was how you could tell the regulars from the tourist types. That, and the way the tourists gawked at the place. "Isn't it cute?"

mothers would say to their daughters. Men called it "handsome" or "old-fashioned." But none of those words made sense to us, because the diner was our everyday.

David opened the door, jangling the bell heavily the way his body made sound happen, and walked smack into Elder Leavitt, the one Gwen liked. You could hear their elbows hit. David grabbed his arm, and LaMonte sucked in his breath loud enough that I caught it clear across the room.

Gwen scurried, but as she approached the men she slowed down. I hated that part. It was as if there was a heavy door in front of LaMonte. Whenever Gwen neared him, she stopped before the door and calmed down all her girlishness, smoothing her face and body and mind until they were very still and white, and then slowly opened the door and stepped into what must've been a very quiet, uninteresting room.

She nodded at David but didn't meet his eyes. "Someone will be with you in a minute, sir." The way she said "you" made it sound dirty. Gwen showed the missionaries to one of her tables. "Are you ready to order or do you Elders need a little time?"

I was hoping Gwen would finish up quick and come back to seat David. Not that I didn't need customers. Tips meant groceries, after all. But I didn't like serving David. Gwen and Selena had agreed to take him when he came in, so I waited. And waited. And waited, growing angrier and angrier as Gwen chatted away with LaMonte and Jared. Selena was on the phone, taking a complicated to-go order. From the scratches on her pad, it looked like the factory lunch call. She shook her head and mouthed "Sorry." I shrugged, grabbed a menu, and strode over to the door. "Good afternoon," I said, very businesslike. "I'll seat you, and someone will be with you in a minute to take your order."

I stuck David in Gwen's section, right behind the Elders so that Gwen wouldn't forget he was there. But as I turned to go, Arthur Parks stepped up to the table and cleared his throat. David realized before I did that Arthur had been sitting there. He must've gotten up to get the newspaper he was clutching to his chest. I liked Arthur, and though I knew he wouldn't make a fuss if I seated him elsewhere, still, it wouldn't be fair. Besides, David was already out of the booth. He didn't apologize, just glared at me.

Arthur tipped his hat. "Even Our Lord Jesus Christ made mistakes, Caddie." He smiled his decent smile.

David stifled a laugh. Once I'd seated him in my section, he smirked. "Trying to get rid of me, eh Caddie?"

"Wish I could."

"You must think I came back to town just for your pretty sake." I didn't reply, but my hands shook as I poured his coffee. "Maybe you'll be relieved to know it's not you I'm thinking of. There's someone else." His hands were shaking too. I could smell Budweiser, what all the townies drank. "Someone younger. But you know what?" His voice was getting louder with each syllable. I stepped away from the table. "I'm done with her. Done with her, because you know why?"

"Why, David?" Bobby had his head out the counter window. I gestured with my chin.

"Look here." He held out his palm—red marks, little scabs. "She bit me. Bit me! The little shit."

"Do you want to eat, or are you taking up table space just because?" Selena to the rescue. I flashed her a smile and let her take over. The counter was mostly empty, so I set about scrubbing hard at ground-in coffee stains.

My hands were in such a frenzy of motion that I didn't notice Jared's shy fingers on the counter till I nearly whisked him away. I could've. I had a solid thirty pounds on him for sure. But he tapped at the Formica like a woodpecker, persistent if not rhythmical, till I recognized his cuffs and turned around.

Jared's gestures were soft and tentative, as if he was holding fresh-baked bread. When he spoke, the strain in his voice reminded me of Bix McGuire, asking me to junior prom over a staticky telephone. "I'm not one to back away from helping a lady who needs help. That is to say, Caddie, if you'd like me to speak with that gentleman," lifting his pinkie in David's direction, "I'd be more than pleased."

What was it Jared offered me that I imagined taking up? Maybe it was what David had held nestled in the crook of his dirty palm. A house with a fence and a garden. A garage and a car that really ran. A wedding—me in white, my man in black, the two of us grey together before the eyes of an approving God. I'd long ago stopped reading my Bible. It sat gathering dust on my night table. Sometimes I used it as a coaster for hot tea. But I'd never stopped wanting a ring, something to bind me to another human being. Sleeping alone night after night, it was easy to forget why men would never suit me. And when a man came too close—

this close, close the way Jared stood close to me now—it was easy to blink twice, catch his face in a glance and think, *Maybe it wouldn't be so terrible.* Easy to think, *I could kiss him. I could do that. I could sleep curled against his chest.* The awful thing was, I could. I had. Maybe I would again. But the thing I loved so much would always be missing. It was the thing that escaped language. Jo and I had never discussed it. We hadn't needed to. It hung over us, a halo, and gave a glow to every gesture.

It could have been so easy. So easy, and yet, once I'd dived, so cold the water. I smiled at Jared. "No thanks," I said. From the corner of my eye I saw Gwen's jealousy float towards me, so I set to work again, scrubbing the stains on the counter. So many circles, so many saucers come and gone.

David stopped in a few times after that, but got himself in trouble not long after, DUI and resisting an officer. A few months later, I heard from this or that gossip that he'd moved to Cleveland where he had family. Cleveland. I had to smile when I thought of David shoveling snow, every word he spoke freezing before its meaning could come true.

■ ■ ■

Piety had come to Cartwheel in a big way. Lots of folks were church-goers around town, but only recreationally, the way they played soft-ball. Social. The missionaries changed that, at least temporarily. Piety took on a new pace. Not the sluggish drone of a sermon, but the whip-lick of a tennis match was what evolved out of the Mormons' corner. At first it was mostly Gwen talking them up, but soon young women (never the bulk of our customers) started stopping in, sometimes just for coffee and Marv's peanut butter cookies, sometimes for lunch or breakfast if the missionaries got there first. Talk of the Celestial Kingdom floated as freely about the diner as talk of the weather and factory gossip ever had. When the girls visited, they lured factory hands in, till sometimes the missionaries' booth was crowded with men, their faces serious, watch-ing those two skinny boys as if they held the secret to winning lotto tickets.

Gwen had it so bad that she got a talking-to from Helen. Usually Marv gave us our little lectures, so gentle we rarely realized we'd been chided. Helen was a different story. She'd never had to give me a lesson, but I knew from Selena (who got caught smoking in the kitchen) and Bobby (who got caught picking up a frozen burger off the floor and slapping it on the grill) that Helen came down hard. "Hard, but fair," Bobby said. So when Helen emerged from the back room one morning and caught Gwen resting her hip against the missionaries' booth, chatting away while another customer sat at a bare table looking at his watch and making tsk-tsk noises under his breath, we all knew Gwen was up for a warning.

What none of us figured was that it would take half the day. When Gwen came out two hours later, she looked shaken. Bet touched her shoulder gently to comfort her, but Gwen shook her head.

"I need to think," she said. Everyone assumed that Helen had said something terrible, threatened to fire her maybe, but Gwen went right back over to the missionaries' table the next morning, so it couldn't have been that. The incident sparked my curiosity more than most. I couldn't figure it. Finally, since if anything Helen's talk seemed to have pushed Gwen closer to the missionaries instead of further away, I came up with the idea that Helen had given Gwen a lecture on how to take a husband. I imagined Helen telling Gwen how wonderful Marv was, how she'd found and kept him. It was just like Helen to think what would work for her would work for us. One of her lessons must've been to keep Sean out of things, because soon after their talk Sean started spending time in Helen's office while Gwen flirted and waited tables intermittently.

The things Gwen told us about their religion made the Mormons' world sound like a fairy tale.

I had to admit, her tales of movie theaters and basketball courts inside the churches lured me. It seemed the Mormons represented heaven and earth and all the in-betweens with special rooms. Earth was blue and beige and looked like somebody's grandmother's parlor, but the heaven-type room had antique furniture and velour wallpaper, all in yellow and white and gold, with a great big glass chandelier.

"Do you want to go up to Indy someday and visit the Temple?" I asked.

I could see Gwen's feathers ruffle. "The Latter Day Saints ceremony is not a free show. Besides, Caddie, you couldn't even get into the Temple unless you'd converted too."

The secrecy of it all was such a draw that even I was curious. The wedding ceremony was the most fantastical of all. It sounded full of excuses for how things were anyway, excuses made over into something pretty. "The man steps through a veil and reaches his hand out and pulls his new wife with him. That means, when they're dead, he has the power to get her into heaven. I mean, the Celestial Kingdom. He knows her secret name, so he's the only one who can admit her." Gwen seemed to like this idea, but it freaked me out.

"I wouldn't want anyone else to have the power to give me heaven or hold me from it. What if he changed his mind when he got there? What if I died first?"

"He wouldn't change his mind. I mean, that would be really jerky if he did. I guess if you died first, you could just wait around. There's probably a room for that too. Like in a doctor's office, before you change into the paper gown."

I could just picture it—a huge room full of wives, waiting for their husbands to die so they could sit in more comfortable chairs. I imagined a receptionist behind a glass window calling names as they came up. "Maybelle Hinks!" Maybelle would trot up to the window. "Your husband's just been run over by a truck." Maybelle would cheer. The other ladies would run up and congratulate her. "We're waiting right now for him to speak." Maybelle would fan herself with a back issue of *Ladies' Day,* exhausted from the strain. "Hang on just a sec. He's opening his mouth! And he's saying—oh, Maybelle, dear, I'm so very sorry. He's decided he wants a brunette with him in the afterlife."

I didn't share my fantasy with Gwen.

Still, I watched her as she fluttered towards them, closer every day. "What happens after all the discussions?" I asked.

"You're a member and you attend church or Temple and live by LDS rules."

"Do the missionaries ever come back to check up?"

I could see she hadn't thought that far ahead. Worry flashed across her face like a bird speeding south. "Of course they do. Of course." But after that, Gwen put on the brakes. Suddenly she had reservations. Suddenly she needed extra time, longer discussions, more meetings and prayers.

"She's dragging it out," Selena observed. "She's finally realized that LaMonte's interest in her is only statistical."

I nodded, but I wasn't so sure—about LaMonte, anyway. There was something between them. You could see it simply because he was trying so hard not to let it show. Even I, with all my love-bitterness and reserve, with my old crush on Gwen still stinging in my bosom, even I had to admit that they were entertaining to watch, LaMonte aiming for serious and intense, Gwen coy and coaxing, trying to weasel a smile out of him, beaming big when she did.

The sad sideshow was Jared. He worked at tugging the conversation back where it belonged, guilting LaMonte into remembering what they'd come for. You could see they weren't too crazy about each other, LaMonte just tasting his freedom and wanting to savor it, Jared growing daily deeper into the strictest ways of the church. Once they'd settled into a booth, LaMonte would take off his jacket and loosen his tie. Jared would frown, button his jacket till only his white collar showed, and go off into the bathroom to slick back his hair.

"Can't they find better partners for each other?" Bobby asked Gwen.

"You don't get to choose your companion. That's God's will. But they change companions when they change stations, so they're only together a couple of months."

"You sure do know the rules by heart." Bobby tugged on a strand of Gwen's hair, but she flounced away from him.

"I don't let men touch my personal belongings."

"Your hair isn't a belonging, Gwen."

"It belongs to me, doesn't it? Besides, LaMonte wouldn't like it if he saw."

"Gwen, you've always liked my teasing before. Now you want me to alter my ways just to please some kid? That would be no, missy. I'll act as I always do, or why be friends?" Bobby was angry. It was strange, like hearing a familiar song played at twice its usual tempo.

"Fine and dandy. Maybe we're not friends then." Was I imagining things or did Gwen's skirts have teeth? It gave me grief, watching them fight and knowing why. Because I understood Gwen's snaps and her need to impress LaMonte. There was the baby crying at home, Tim walking out on her, her own childish helplessness. She was looking for a caretaker, pinning all her hopes on a Mormon boy.

What saddened me was how she didn't realize that the energy she put into LaMonte was energy she could've used to save herself.

Wasn't that how I lived from day to day? I had my crushes; I had my heart flutters and girlish fondle fantasies. But I knew I could swim to shore with my own two arms. I wondered what made me and Gwen so far from sisters, that way—what there was inside of me that she didn't have, the thing that let me be alone.

After Jo left me, happiness came in small doses, cubed like sugar, barely enough to be savored. I couldn't remember the kind of grand passion that had kept me awake nights, shivering beside her, touching her as she slept, touching myself because there was never enough time to do all that we imagined. I had come to accept that that person, Caddie, was dead, and that I'd never again feel anything—even grief—with such heightened senses. I felt lucky I didn't have a craving for beer, because it would've been easy to ask a bottle to substitute for the wild swings and dizzying drops. But instead I'd made myself, much as I could, come round to want calm, to crave emptiness inside, to want everything to be pale blue and green, serene and faded. To fear people who shook up their own worlds with feeling.

Cat was the only difference. Watching Cat, I could sometimes feel the highs and lows. She'd spurt through the door, dive for the sill, ruffle the curtains, patter out a fancy jig on the window, then hop down, prance across the rug, arch her back and leap clear in a circle, only to slow to a saunter, stretch out on the floor or amble over to the sofa and curve into a creamy sleep, purring like heat, her belly butter and her fur silk. When the mood struck, she'd start highway patrol again, resting atop a chair, waiting for me to round a corner so she could flash and attack my ankles or even my hair. It made sense to me, why I loved her. She mimicked Jo with her leaps and spirals, her stalkings, her wild frenzied sprints and slow rubber-band stretches. Her breathy sleep and her uncoilings came in spurts the way our calms and passions had. Her motions and measures made visible the very patterns of my old love. It was comforting to see this in another animal, to know what we'd felt was more than human, connected on some level to all that breathed.

I envied Gwen the way I envied Cat: all that feeling. I wanted to feel again, but I'd turned it off a second time now, first after Jo and now after Gwen. Sometimes at home I tried turning it on again, just for practice. In my mind I'd steal away, imagining her there, the one I could finally trust, the one who'd stay, who'd marry me, even if only in our very kitchen, a teapot and teaspoon for witnesses. She'd marry me, this one. But that was all I could imagine. Sex was dead for me. I could only see a ceremony, me and a faceless woman who'd wrap her hand around my hand, binding herself to me with a needle's prick the way, as girls, Melly and I had done in a blood-sister ceremony. We'd sworn love forever as Patrick read our vows.

I'd let myself think this way for ten minutes and then slap my fingers away from my own wrist. "Eat some pie, Caddie, if you're hungry," I'd say aloud, as Cat would slur through the door, curious about this voice, one she rarely heard. "Sip some tea. Stop dreaming."

It wasn't that it was hard to give up hoping Gwen would come around. It was watching her pin her hopes on someone else. I'd lost trust. I watched and watched and the days sped by, the diner grown busier because of the missionaries' bold promises.

They moved fast.

For those who showed interest, they'd return again and again, each discussion leading somewhere.

"Steps on a ladder," Bobby said, drizzling ketchup on fried eggs. We were on break together, talking it over. Everyone seemed charmed by LaMonte and Jared, even Bet and Roy. There was talk among the factory men of asking the mayor to declare Cartwheel a Mormon settlement.

"There'll be a mass baptism soon, that's for sure," I told Bobby.

"Maybe they should just declare the next rainstorm holy and save themselves the trouble of dealing with font water."

"Are we the only ones who aren't going to be saved?"

Bobby sopped his plate with a butter biscuit. "The whole thing's a scam. LaMonte and Jared are the biggest fools of all. The church makes them pay to come out here and win new names to add to its roster. I'd bet ninety percent of the folks who convert go back to their old gods a year later. But the LDS can keep their names on the rolls for as long as they'd like. That makes 'em look powerful, see? Like the religion's growing. Like they have lots of members."

"Hi, y'all." Tiffany sat down beside Bobby and stole one of his biscuits. "Caddie, tell Bobby to go away. I have a secret. Girls only."

I had to hide my disappointment. Bobby was good for talking to. He was smart and never made the moves on me.

"Sure thing, sis. I just hope it's not some story about the missionaries." He winked at me, bused his plate, and left.

"Why did he say that?" Tiffany nibbled a fingernail. "It's none of his business what religion I pray."

"What's your story?" It was pie day. Bobby and Marv had made four fresh. I was on my second piece, pecan this time. Tiffany watched me while I started the crust.

"If I even look at pie, I get fat."

"Don't inhale." I licked my fork.

Tiffany pouted. Her lips would've been pretty, but she painted them all wrong. She was a girl but should've dressed more like a boy. It would've suited her. Maybe she would've been attractive, that way, but I certainly wasn't going to tell her. "It's like this." She spread a napkin out on the table and drew lines across it with her longest fingernail: orangey-pink lacquer. "You know that rumor going around about the Mormons?"

"Which one?"

"About their wives."

"About them wanting some?"

When she giggled it was like a cat landing on its head. "About their having more than one."

"Whatever. I think my break is over."

"Can I have the rest of that pie?"

"It's yours."

"Ohhh." She rolled her eyes as the whipped cream met her tongue. "I can feel my hips expanding."

"Bye, Tiffany."

"Caddie! Hang on." She put one hand on my arm. Her grip was astonishingly tough, which confirmed it for me. It struck me sad then and still does now that there's no way of telling someone when they've got their signals all mixed up and confused. There ought to be words for that—common, so it'd be simple to say. While I was thinking this, she just held on, one hand glued to my arm, me with my face all philosophical, not entirely minding how she was touching me. "I have to finish my story."

"Fifteen seconds."

"OK. Jared says it's not true. He says they don't take more than one wife anymore, except maybe a few folks out in a tiny town somewhere in Utah. But they're exceptionals. So the coast is clear."

"What coast?"

"I mean, for marrying."

"Who's getting married?" Now it really was time for me to get back to work. Impatience tickled my nose like a sneeze.

"Jared asked about you." She let go of my arm and stood up. "That's all. He asked Gwen about you, and later he asked me. So have a nice day, Caddie! Have a very nice day." Tiffany ambled off. Her walk was like a factory line, all bits and pieces.

I didn't think much about what she'd said until the missionaries stopped by later for a snack. They sat in Gwen's section as usual, but I caught Jared gazing at me from over the cusp of his strawberry milk. It felt so unexpected, coming from Jared—the strict one, the one who hated LaMonte's fooling around—that I stared straight back. His cheeks flushed the color of his drink and he turned away. "Shit," I said to myself.

Helen surprised me with a hand on my back. She'd quietly come out from her office, a rare event, for a glass of soda and a lemon cookie. "Caddie, watch the profanity." Her words were sharp but her tone was kind. "Do you need to talk?"

"I'm just tired of everyone trying to marry me off." I hadn't meant to say what I was thinking, but once I had, it didn't seem too terrible. Any girl could feel that way, couldn't she?

Helen's expression changed. Her face was more like a pond than anything. You knew on first sight that there was something underneath its smoothness; the plain surface was pretty enough, but it was the tangled weeds beneath that kept you looking long past when your eyes should've shifted. It made her beautiful, what was beneath, but it made her different too. She didn't look like a farm girl. She looked like she belonged in a fancy city where everyone had secrets boxed away, not to be recovered, only wondered after. When her face changed, her voice did too, becoming tender.

"You miss Jo. He was the only one. If there's only one, no use looking elsewhere for second best."

"Exactly." It was true. I breathed a sigh of relief as she vanished into her office.

The missionaries took off that day after an hour. Once they'd left, Gwen went slow and stumpy, even surly. Tired of it, Selena and I decided to prod her.

From Selena, it came out teasing. "Any chance you'll return to earth in time for the rush?"

"Cool it, Selena."

"Gwen, we're not trying to hurt your feelings. We're just worried that you're letting your duties lapse."

"Caddie, who asked you? You think you're so perfect just because you don't need anybody else. Well, maybe I'm not so happy being alone. Maybe I have feelings and sometimes want to talk about them. Maybe I don't get off on mumbling to myself and walking around with my nose all snooty like I'm too good for factory boys to touch. Maybe I don't think I'm queen just because I had a boy who loved me once, a long ways back. A long ways ago, Caddie. Just because you had your Jo doesn't mean anyone else is going to come along. Just because you had—"

"Gwen, shut up." Selena stepped between us. I clenched my fingers tight together because my hand—not my heart or my head—wanted to hit her. It tingled and twitched of its own accord. Selena started scolding; when Gwen sassed back, I could see things getting uglier, spiraling out of control, so I just fled.

The ladies' was occupied, so I took over the men's.

The bathroom was tiny, a horse stall drenched in blue paint. Even the toilet paper was blue. The ladies' was all pink and had a potpourri holder and pictures of cute animals on the walls. I'd just assumed everyone had the same color before their eyes when they peed, but here I was, and I'd been wrong.

I turned the water on full blast, put the toilet seat down, and sobbed. I knew I could only cry a few minutes before someone banged on the door and wanted in, and I knew I needed to save my face, which goes blotchy and pimply when I cry. So I couldn't let loose, only release, like unbuttoning the top button of jeans that don't fit. It helped a bit, but not nearly enough. After a few minutes I made myself slow the tears down and blotted my face with water. I combed strands of hair down from my bun so they hung, wispy, into my eyes. I waited a little, smiling very hard into the mirror to rub the creases out of my cheeks. Then I opened the door, taking a big breath as I turned the knob.

I exhaled into Roy Birdy's face.

"Hi there, Caddie. Got yourself a new body, huh? Or just searching for a little variety?"

My laugh came out like a cough, husky. "Some old girl was taking a bath in the sink and I couldn't cross my legs much longer. Thought I'd borrow. Here's your door back."

When I returned to the counter, Gwen was bustling about, Selena was handling a take-out order, and there were three customers waiting by the door. I shepherded them to empty seats and picked up the food that had piled up at the order window.

"Did ya make like Columbus, Caddie? Off to visit India but got stuck in the New World?" Bobby's smile filled the window.

I made my teary voice nasal. "Had to borrow the men's for a sneeze."

"How's about doing your sneezing a little quicker next time? These mashed are nearly congealed."

"I'll warm 'em up."

"You do that, Caddie. And apologize to the nice lady for being late with her spuds."

"Sure thing." I stuck the plate into the oven and watched it through the glass, keeping my back to the customers so they wouldn't see whose food was being reheated. When the timer beeped, I took the potatoes out and searched for a sprig of parsley to decorate the plate. When my search came up bare, I had a sudden flash of creativity. In two minutes I'd transformed the dish from spuds to something special. Maybe it was crazy, but it felt so good to be creative, to make something, even something silly. I stared down at my masterpiece, remembering how I'd been in school. I was very creative back then. Caddie Crayon, they called me, partly because I used to eat Crayolas, but also because I drew pictures that were different from everybody else's. And I sewed—doll dresses and socks and tiny pillows. Sometimes I made things out of Play-Doh, cool things, not just the lumps other kids called mountains. Then I grew up and Pat died. Then I grew up more and met Jo and began spending all my creativity pleasing my love. It was like coloring or sewing, being lovers with that tough, raw girl. But now I never even thought to try my powers. The potatoes were the first art I'd done in so long.

Even if the customer didn't like them, I'd have a chance to win this week's pot. Bet, Bobby, Selena, and I all put a dollar in each week. On Fridays we'd go around in a circle and ask who'd done the weirdest, wickedest, or plain old dumbest thing on shift. I figured my potato story would win me four bucks fast.

I carried my creation to table seven, where I set it down in front of Marigold Spencer. Marigold was what we all called an old sweetie. She lived with her adopted sister, Vera Train, in a big rambly house on the south side of town. They'd lived there going on thirty-three years now. Vera worked in the elementary school as a secretary and Marigold was a retired dog sitter.

I explained the dish. "It's a potato volcano. The sides here are dark because they're covered in lava. The top is exploding with fire and so forth. Just peel the spinach leaves back—that's right. That's the lava. Now smoosh the ketchup and paprika in. There's plenty of marge and cream inside already."

Selena passed by carrying an empty tray and pinched me on the butt. "You win," she said. I smiled.

Marigold smiled too. She had on very thick glasses attached to a necklace-style chain that kept the glasses perched on her chest when she wasn't seeing with them. The chain had black beads and a few silver nubbles to match her hair. Her blouse was also a sort of silvery color and it made her blue eyes gleam. She peeled back a spinach leaf, pushed it neatly to the side of her plate, scooped out a bite of potato, and nibbled.

"Delicious. Bobby always outdoes himself." Then she scooped another bite and offered it to me.

Now, there's a rule about not eating in front of customers while you're on the job. If you're eating, you're on break. If you're working, you're not eating. But if someone offers you something, it's rude to turn your face. So I took the spoon, or tried to, but her hand stayed tight to the handle and so together we guided the food into my mouth.

It was strange, eating so intimate with a lady I didn't know. Her eyes got very close to mine as the food touched my lips. "Vera always asks after you, Caddie. Says you'll have to come visit again sometime, out to the house. Says she thinks you'd fancy some of our china animals. Cats and so forth."

I thought about Vera. The two of them were like one body. Folks said they could've been blood sisters—they'd even grown to look alike. "It'll be an ugly day when one of those two finds a beau," factory men were sometimes heard to say. "The old maid left behind'll wither up like a slug on salt."

I'd been to Marigold and Vera's once, when Jo and I were still together. They'd invited us as a couple. No one else at the diner had ever been inside that house.

"I'd love to visit again. Soon?"

Marigold was getting busy with the mashed. Her round face was filling up and she looked happy to be eating something someone had taken time with. Since she was in the middle of a bite, I asked a yes-or-no question. "Dessert?"

A big nod.

"Let me guess. Pecan pie?"

Another nod. She finished chewing and wiped her mouth on her napkin. Most of her lipstick came off in the wipe. "Soon, Caddie."

I winked. Then I went off to fix her pie. One thing I'm known for is remembering specials: Marigold's pie, Arthur's oatmeal, Mr. and Mrs.

Buckskin's omelettes. So I remembered it was coffee ice cream, not plain vanilla, and one chocolate cookie, crumbled. And I remembered to sign her check with a swirly heart over the *I*.

Bobby grinned while I scooped the ice cream. "Heard you won the pot already."

"It was easy, for a creative type such as me."

Marigold was almost done by the time I set her pie in front of her. I left her to good eating, but winked again as I walked away. Bet was busing the table beside Marigold's. "Heard you won the four this week."

I started to say, modestly, *Not yet,* when Gwen's voice tangled with my thoughts.

"I don't guess you'll ask me who I think should win."

Bet cleared her throat. I felt my face flush. When I was growing up, my mother always said not to talk about a birthday party with someone who wasn't invited. I felt sorry for Gwen, being left out of the game, but it was our tradition. It hadn't ever felt right to let her in.

I mentioned it to Bobby back in the kitchen. "Do we need to let Gwen chip in money and choose the winner?"

Bobby shrugged. "Up to you. She doesn't seem to care."

"I think she does."

Marigold waved her hand like she was hailing a cab. I alerted Bobby. "Travel at table seven." He wiped his hands on his apron, dimmed the grill, and walked out to meet Marigold with his arm crooked like a fancy gentleman. She grinned. Together they walked slowly to the door and then out into the lot, where he helped her into her car.

Gwen was pouting. Serving sloppy.

"Gwen, I'm sorry you feel left out. We just forgot, is all. Why don't you join in this week? Give Bet your money and you vote too."

"I've worked here all this time, Caddie, and you just today thought to invite me? I think not. I know when I'm not wanted." A new customer tried to pretend he wasn't staring. You could always tell the newbies because they hadn't learned not to act surprised when we had spats or dramas on company time. "Besides, what you're doing is wicked. I'm done with wickedness. I'm living a life the Lord can recommend. LaMonte says he's proud of how I'm doing now, so you can keep your gambling to yourself."

"Gwen, the weekly pot isn't gambling."

"If it's not gambling, what is it?" Her voice had changed since the missionaries showed up. It had a grown-up sound to it now: tired, worn thin. "Why don't you come to one of our discussions soon and hear for yourself?"

"I have my own beliefs, Gwen." But I felt curiosity fill me, rich as Marigold's pie. "If you want me to come, though, I guess I could make time."

She could still lure me. Her buck-toothed smile had bits of hair in it because her bun had come down and all that gold was hanging over her face. "Caddie, would you? I promise I'll stop being sad over the way you-all leave me out. Come and listen. I know you'll like it, what LaMonte and Jared have to say. It's very convincing."

The first thing I noticed when I walked into Gwen's apartment Friday after work was that the place no longer smelled like Sean. There weren't even any baby things scattered about. I figured she'd shoved the mess into the bedroom. "Is Sean sleeping?" I asked her. We'd settled down at the kitchen table to wait for the missionaries' knock.

"I need to ask you a favor." Her hand on mine across the table felt smooth as water. "Please, let's not talk about Sean tonight. I'm tired of talking about him. He's all I ever get to think about. I want my mind to be blank, so I can receive the spirit."

"If he starts crying—"

"He's with a sitter." She fumbled in the drawer behind her for a pack of cigarettes, then remembered the Mormons didn't smoke and hastily shoved it back in the drawer. "Just let's forget about Sean for once, OK, Caddie? I need to clear my head. Go along with me."

Right then the doorbell rang. As the missionaries settled in, I understood how they'd opened so many doors for themselves in Cartwheel. They weren't what people were used to, in a religion. They were so much like waitresses. They catered to the customer, though they served up stories instead of food and promised happily ever after instead of a happy tongue and a pleasant belly. It felt odd to me that Gwen would be sucked in, since she knew the trade.

They sat down across from us at the table, carefully adjusting their chairs so that they were neither close to each other, nor close to us. The conversation began in the middle and kept going in that direction. It was a circle. I wondered if that was another thing they offered: it had the same feel as the factory line.

I mostly stayed quiet, listening to Gwen's responses. She was as easy as a regular customer. You could see LaMonte and Jared liked it that they didn't have to push. They'd propose some religious theory or other, run through a few scriptures to prove it, and then ask Gwen if she had any questions. She always said no. Since they didn't ask me, I didn't say yes. At first I felt like I wasn't there, but then I felt like I was. I wasn't sure which was worse. The hardest thing was seeing Gwen so contained. She'd moved away from shy after working at the M&H a few months. Now she looked shy again, Gwen Girleen. It didn't suit her the way I'd once thought it did.

LaMonte liked it. Maybe Jared did too, but he kept his face and body statued. But LaMonte. He was trying to hide it, but his words and gestures were too excited. The sad thing was, I knew Gwen well enough to know that the girl he was falling for wasn't Gwen at all.

I knew because it had happened to me.

As they began winding down, after maybe an hour, Gwen tried to detain them by offering to fix us all snacks. The missionaries glanced at each other and said some silent thing I couldn't decipher. To save face for Gwen, I jumped in. "Don't you need to pick up Sean from the sitter's?"

Gwen's lips flew into a smile that didn't match her eyes. "I'm not taking care of the little one tonight." I felt a sharp pinch on my thigh, painful even through my cotton skirt. "I have all the time in the world where my soul is concerned."

"Thank you for the offer." Jared stood and LaMonte followed sluggishly. "But we have two more homes to visit tonight." As Gwen walked them to the door, LaMonte tapped the Cartwheel Brake and Tire calendar hanging beside the entry.

"Are you still planning to join the mass baptism on the sixteenth?"

"Absolutely."

Jared rummaged in his bag for a Book of Mormon, which he gave me for free when I confessed I didn't have one. Then they said their goodbyes. Gwen and I watched through the window as they buckled themselves into bike helmets and pedaled away.

I lay in bed that night, Cat pooled between my legs, counting names— all the folks in Cartwheel I'd heard express interest in changing to this fancy religion. I thought of LaMonte's words, "mass baptism." What if everyone converted except me? What if—as some folks were starting to joke—Cartwheel became known as Little Salt Lake? I tried to imagine myself feeling even more different from everyone than I already did but it was impossible. If the whole town changed over maybe that would be my sign to move, get a line job up in Indy. I'd never worked the line before, but it was something I'd always known I could do, if I had to.

■ ■ ■

Soon it seemed that all the folks who came into the M&H were carrying the Book of Mormon under their armpits. They'd sit down, glance at the menu, flip open to a page, and run their fingers left to right. Once in a rare while you'd see somebody running a finger right to left. If they were alone, while they ate they'd stare at other customers or one of us waitresses. It was very stare-y, the M&H. Not like some snooty restaurant where you weren't supposed to care about people's business. At the M&H it was OK to walk over to somebody's table, point to their food, and say, "What kind of dish is that?" Sometimes folks would start conversations with you from the table next door or across the room. If you definitely wanted to be left alone, you had to signal—hide your head behind a magazine or take a corner booth and turn your back.

Once a townie had finished flipping through the Book of Mormon, they'd leave the book lying very obvious and bold in the middle of the table. Then anyone who wanted to talk over Mormon things would feel free to jump in. It was the same with the paper, lotto cards, and racing tickets. Folks left things on their tables by way of talking, so there was always a stir in the air, like a breath someone's waiting to take.

Pretty soon everybody was speculating about the mass baptism. Who'd come to dunk and who'd come to gawk? Everyone planned on going but no one seemed certain whether they'd take the water or not. It worried LaMonte and Jared, you could tell. They wanted people to promise, but nearly everyone was dragging their feet. I figured they were waiting to see who else went under before they committed.

Bobby agreed. "Cartwheel folks operate in shifts, one after the other. Factory blood, right, Caddie? If Mr. Smith sees Mr. Jones bobbing like a rubber duck, he'll bob too, and then they'll dive. Problem is, they've gotta get the chain started. If one won't go, the others won't either."

"Maybe Gwen'll set the whole thing off."

"Maybe she will."

As the baptism approached, it took on the feel of one of Cartwheel High's basketball championships or the firemen's annual pancake supper. Everyone was talking around it, not about what was going to happen, but who they'd see, and what they'd eat after. None of us thought to take advantage till Tom Jensen suggested such to Marv. He was leaning on the counter, chatting with Marv through the order window. Tom wasn't going to be baptized. He said he'd seen hell in Nam, so he had to be going to heaven. "Know what, Opal?"

"Nope, Jensen. Don't know a damn thing."

"Ha. Funny man. But seriously now, know what, Opal? You-all oughta open Sunday and serve a unique menu come baptism day. Special hours, special dishes, everything special. If the Mormons are gonna make some profit off the thing, why can't you?"

The idea spread among us like the cold we shared every December. What we couldn't figure was what the theme of the specialty day should be. I was proud when my creative streak kicked in and I thought up something clever. "Let's make it all dunkable," I said. Bet looked at me like I was crazy, but Selena, Gwen, Marv, and Bobby picked up on it right away.

"Soup and crackers."

"Fried potato slices and honey."

"How about frying up some chicken nuggets and serving 'em with barbecue sauce?"

"Celery and peanut butter."

"No one will eat celery, Gwen."

"Little kids will."

"Maybe. How about lady fingers and chocolate pudding?"

Marv sighed. "Too bad I'm allergic to chocolate. Guess I'll give Sean my bite."

It shaped up very edible. All the foods were easy to make, mostly things we already had on the menu. It was the combinations that were special and the gesture: finger food, everything touchable. Bobby's eyes lit up just talking the menu over.

The only problem was, we all wanted to go to the baptism. So we decided we'd open that Sunday, the first Sunday open ever, from two till six. That gave us time enough to see the ceremony and still fall asleep at a decent hour.

On baptism day, I woke around six when Cat made a flying leap for the window and landed on my chest instead. Once I'm up, I'm up, so I went ahead and brought in the paper, set water on for tea, and fixed some cereal. While I was waiting for the teapot to boil, I flipped through *The Cartwheel Chronicle*, stopping on page five to read a full-page ad.

Names. Neat rows of tiny print.

At the top of the ad, in huge bold letters, "See the Celestial Kingdom!" Then in slightly smaller type, "Baptism for new LDS converts this Sunday (today) at the Cartwheel Community Center, 10 a.m. Come join us!" What followed in miniature print was a list of names, maybe twenty-five in all. I knew about half: Tiffany, Arthur Parks and his family, a few regulars, the owner of the Dairy Queen, the mayor's secretary. Marigold and Vera were the big surprise—it was hard to imagine them doing anything in a crowd. I thought of Marigold and Vera's rambly house, set away from town, beyond the farmer's market, even. Thinking of the two women brought to mind that visit with Jo, in what felt like another life. I remembered watching Marigold's hands on the curved china handle of their great yellow teapot, tiny olive age spots nestled just beneath her skin. When she poured, her hands trembled, but it wasn't me who thought to hold my cup up, close to the spout, and to steady Marigold's wrist with a gentle touch—soft, flirtatious.

Jo.

The list of names grew grey, then blurred like rain as I remembered. What would Jo have thought of this whole great drama? Certainly she'd have appreciated the missionaries taking over the community center pool: one of the few spots in town where east, west, and south siders mixed. The community center housed the town's only gym, which included the only indoor pool in Cartwheel and a couple of classrooms used for day care and kids' camps. Jo had worked out there—not swimming, which would've given away her secret body, but lifting, and pedaling frantically on one of those little bicycles that never go anywhere. We'd meet at the center on the odd occasion we had somewhere to be at night. It was only a fifteen-minute walk, through woods, from the diner. She'd wait for me in the windowed lobby, a damp towel around her neck, a bulky CUBS bag resting by her feet. She was always happy once she'd finished because every session was a test. She risked being recognized at the gym more than anywhere else. There'd been several close calls and she got a thrill out of narrating them, I could tell.

Would Jo have turned Mormon, leaving me behind? I tried to think of things she'd said about religion, belief or disbelief, but nothing came to me. It was another mystery, another way in which I'd never known her.

It seemed further and further away, our loving. And hiding—how many lies I'd told for her! Yet here I was, no better. Still lying, my own self, about who we'd been.

It made baptism make sense. Something to rid your soul of tangles.

Still, I knew it was a gesture I'd never be able to make with any honesty. My life was already so deep in mystery, my desires already so invisible. I didn't need any more silent ghosts demanding faith in what would never meet daylight. But I had to admit I was curious. I wanted to see their faces. When I was baptized there weren't any pictures. We didn't have a camera—no one we knew did—and since the church was a lean-to and the font a sink, there wouldn't have been much to commemorate. I can't begin to remember the slippery tug. "They stuck you under the water and your little dress near 'bout dragged you to heaven right then and there." It seemed silly to baptize someone when they couldn't even say yes or no to what was happening. The Mormons had some sense that way—they held off till a person could ask questions. But Gwen told me they sometimes baptized dead people, and that seemed worse than dunking kids.

I tried to fathom what it must've been like to be LaMonte or Jared, to believe you could connect another person to God. That was the part that fascinated me. Baptism was supposed to secure a place for you, like a plane ticket. What I wanted was to see the converts' faces the moment before they went under and the moment after. Really what I wanted was to be underwater, to watch the spirit enter, filling their lungs like tobacco, choking or stirring them, changing the tint of their skins and the range of their voices forever after. I figured they'd look puffier, what with thinking God had noticed them and all.

The community center was off Quarry Road, the street that bordered the woods behind the diner. The quickest way from my apartment was through the woods, so I put on a long skirt and a long-sleeved blouse to protect against scratches. As I reached for my keys, Cat began mewling. When I got to the door, she wrapped herself around my ankles and nibbled the hem of my skirt.

"You can't come, sweetie. Sometimes I wish you were a dog."

I walked without thinking much of anything. The whole town seemed shut down. Even stores usually open on Sundays had cardboard signs with Magic Marker letters saying "Closed for baptism" or "Shut down on account of God." The very weather seemed an accomplice: hot enough to make dunking pleasurable, the sky lush blue, the clouds fluffy.

I tried to remember the last time the town had come together for anything but couldn't. Up ahead, the diner glinted, a great glacier amidst so much stone. Most of Cartwheel was built out of limestone. The diner was different, metal and glass. When the sun struck, it glowed as if it was on fire.

I walked around the back of the building. Ordinarily the place was dead on a Sunday. Marv and Helen did a big cleanup on Saturday and made a point of staying away one day a week. But there was a shadow visible through the kitchen window. As my eyes adjusted, I saw the shape clearly, a bulky bear shape—Bobby. Of course it was Bobby, because today was the special post-baptism supper.

Dunking Day, it was.

He moved past the window and then wasn't there. He'd crossed the kitchen towards the freezer or maybe the spice rack; he was bent over the grill or adjusting the oven. The window was chest-height, so as I approached I ducked down. Even though he wasn't visible, I knew he might enter the silvery picture at any moment. What was it about his vanishing that made me want to surprise him? I snuck and snuck, my voice hanging in my throat to dry. I thought, *so this is how spying must feel, the jelly of the heart.* My soles snapped twigs. Stubbed cigarettes were dandelions dotting the lawn.

Then through the window above me the back of his head rose like a great pale sun. The bandanna around it was some faint color flecked with black. He wore one particular color every day of the week. What was Sunday? Pink? Yellow maybe? As I moved closer the color did too; it was yellow, but very faint, nothing like the sun. He was sitting in a chair facing the table in the center of the space behind the grill. Usually he didn't sit to work, but maybe he was doing some dull motion: shelling peas, icing cookies.

His back was so solidly towards me that I couldn't imagine him turning. Finally I just stood up, rubbing my waist where it ached from stooping. Bobby's head was bobbing. He'd hunch and sit up, hunch and sit up. It was mysterious, whatever he was doing. A laugh trickled out of me, because I realized that if I was in the kitchen, his motions would make perfect sense, wouldn't look so much like some odd new sit-down dance or a bear courting a fruit fly. My feet jostled the gravel beneath the window. Now I could see straight in. There was a sneaky, chocolate joy in watching someone. It made my legs tingle and the light at my back tickle my nape.

Up close, the thing he was doing looked like prayer.

It was prayer.

But there was no god in the diner. Bobby bent over a pan of brownies, ran his hands along the rim of the pan, sat up again, and inhaled deep breaths. Then he bent forward again and started over. Except you couldn't call it starting over because the whole cycle was one long smooth strand, unbroken, the way, when he chopped carrots or grated cheese, his wrists made waves. He was eating now, so smoothly and steadily that it looked as if he was breathing food. Bits of brownie disappeared in one long blurred gesture, his hands stretching like Cat leaping from sofa to sill. When the pan of brownies was empty, Bobby sat for a few moments, not moving at all. I stepped away from the window then because I could feel in the tension of things that he'd stand, and I was right.

With his back still towards me, he walked over to the refrigerator and took out a glass mixing bowl filled with cookie dough and a pitcher of chocolate milk. He turned to the dough first, smelling it, turning the bowl around in his hands. Then the silent communion of spooning, each bite vanishing with utmost grace, hands working first the center, then the sides of the dough mound in rhythmical swoops. As he ate, his body pulsed, the short, delicate contractions of a lover who thinks only of absorbing pleasure. I thought of the way Bobby ate lunch during his shift—gobbled bites, as if he fed himself only out of necessity. This was the real Bobby.

I wanted him to see me. I wanted to greet him. But the thing that made his gestures beautiful was his isolation, so I shied away. Time to walk on. I headed into the woods, taking the same scuffed path that led to Doe's grave.

I didn't walk the extra yards that would've brought me to her. Instead I turned right at the broad, flat stone someone had long ago painted with a sloppy yellow arrow and CCC, marking the path to the center. There'd been talk once of making this path a real trail, complete with logs bordering the sides, flat enough for bicycles. The idea made sense, since plenty of folks walked from my side of town to the center. The path saved time but stayed mostly unused because folks were too prissy or nervous to hike the woods by themselves. I've never been afraid to be anywhere alone. Jo didn't like that. Called me foolish. "You're asking for it," she said, which angered me mightily. Being alone wasn't asking for anything. It was about wanting nothing, nothing but myself and my own company. So I didn't much like all that talk of expanding the path, and I didn't like the talk of making a road through the woods that would intersect with Old Station right where the diner lived. For a while, when even the mayor was involved and it looked like it might happen, Marv and Helen were very excited by the thing. "Good for business," as they put it. But it never came about. Cartwheel was too poor to make changes and not big enough to care. That was what most townies liked about it—that it stayed mostly the same. They wanted it that way, which was how we made money serving the same breakfast special day after day.

I hadn't taken the path since I'd last met Jo at the center. An odd sort of remembering crept up on me while I walked. The tints of the leaves, the smell of sap, and the birds' call and response brought back memory. Had I really loved her or only loved the thrill she gave me, her body sleek as the letter *C,* curling over me, pinning me against any soft surface, pleasing me with watching her take pleasure as she did? If Jo had come back just then, a whole girl or hollow, either way I'd have turned on my heels against her, whoever she was, and walked over the sparse border of the scattered path into uncharted forest, heading for the heart of what passed for wilderness in Cartwheel. Not caring where I might come out.

Thinking this, feeling so tired of pleasure staying always out of reach, I didn't hear what crept up on me till the noise had breath for a bass. I didn't stop, didn't take flight, but kept on at a steady pace, thinking, *I am almost to the other side,* thinking, *if I run I might be followed.* Still it kept on, a queer sort of noise, and my curiosity overrode my caution. With the community center in shouting distance, I whirled around, half expecting a hunter.

Nothing.

Then through the bushes, on the edge of orange, the creature leapt, ember to flame. It looked like Cat, but Cat was at home, snoozing on the sofa or sipping cream. Then I could hear the creature but not see it. Then all I could hear were the cars outside the center.

I spotted Arthur Parks' Nova and several trucks I recognized from the diner. Cory Flint's battered pickup was backed into a space. The silver ladies silhouetted on his mud flaps glinted in the afternoon light. Beside it was a new green Mazda—an east-side car. One glance around the lot told me it wasn't the only one. The east side had come out to see the show.

The community center was a huge old limestone house. It reminded me of the mansions on the outskirts of Bloomington that I'd seen when

I drove through on a bus headed for the somewhere that turned out to be Cartwheel. I was surprised by how cramped the lobby felt. It was empty, the reception desk shrouded, except for a sign propped up on an easel: "Religious service today in pool" with a thick black arrow pointing towards a flight of stairs. I slipped down into the belly of the building till I reached a tiny landing that reeked of chlorine. Facing me were two dressing rooms, "Men" and "Women." I knew something of the interior of the men's room because Jo had described several of her trips inside to use the toilet like the plot of a full-length motion picture. There were no other doors. I could smell the pool, even hear it, but there was no way in. Frustrated, I started back up the stairs, almost bumping into Bet and Roy.

"Going the wrong way, aren't ya, Caddie?"

"Just trying to find the pool."

"Follow me. The dressing rooms wrap around the water. We have to go through to get to the pool."

We entered the damp air of the dimly lit, tiled room. Inside was a row of lockers and two sinks. A varnished wooden bench ran the length of the lockers. To the left was an open doorway leading to three toilet stalls, to the right was a foggy glass door. "This way," Bet said. "Be careful, because we'll have to walk through the showers." Muddy footprints guided us onto a sort of hazy field that became a pool as my eyes adjusted to the sudden light. Roy joined us; it took us all a moment to find LaMonte and Jared. Then I spotted them sharing the broad seat of the lifeguard stand while they filled out stacks of paperwork.

"Not your usual pool party, is it? But I wore my suit underneath just in case." Selena's skirt had been replaced by a thigh-length terry cloth jumpsuit that didn't make one bit of sound. The silence startled me.

LaMonte and Jared hopped down from the stand and motioned to the converts, who stood out in their white dresses and shirts. As they made their way towards the missionaries from the four corners of the room, the light from the windowed ceiling above the pool made their white clothing glitter brightly. As LaMonte and Jared huddled together, conferring over something, Jack and Sally Ryan approached from the corner closest to the diving board. The Ryans owned Cartwheel Construction, as well as much of the wooded land on the outskirts of town. There was talk of building condos, a movie theater, even a shopping mall. "Little Bloomington," the Ryans called their development, which made the folks at Cartwheel Community College practically wet their pants. It seemed everyone wanted some part of the 'Wheel for themselves. Bloomington was always the model. "Educated folks are what we're wishing to attract," Jack Ryan was quoted in the paper.

"I don't think he means high school graduates," Selena said when Bobby showed it to us. I didn't say anything. I wish I could say I'd finished high school, but when you have to leave a place, you have to leave it.

Whenever I saw the Ryans, I thought of Helen and Marv, because their trailer rested on a narrow strip of rented land—forest, really—that would someday be a Target or McDonalds or Kerasotes. It was beautiful, where they lived. I'd visited once, and Marv had taken me for a long walk out in the midst of it. He knew things about nature, Marv. I guess I've never really loved the natural world the way some do. What I like is people. I can get inside them and understand them quicker than they'd ever guess. I see through them. That was how I knew Jo's secret. The body beneath her body bled through. People, that's what, people and animals. I don't see the same lines between them that other folks do. Take Doe, for example. She was just another girl, fragile, ripped open like a girl I'd danced with at The Depot. The fear Doe felt when she smelled the hunter was the fear I felt when men watched me onstage. And Cat. She knows how I'm feeling. When I cry she tends to my tears. When she boggles the mouse toy hanging from the doorknob, her happiness isn't different from a person's happiness. And when the sun shines through the window and she lies beneath on the little quilt I folded up for her on the sill, when she arches her back and then stretches out into one great long sentence, she comes, the way Jo used to come when she'd stretch her body alongside the length of mine and kiss my nipples.

But trees and leaves. Moss and stones. Nature felt cold to me, a pretty, dead thing with no history, no way for me to tie it to myself. So when Marv asked me to stop, to look over the coat of a tall, skinny pine, I wasn't too impressed.

Then he asked me to put my hand on the tree's skin.

That was what he called it—the tree's skin.

"See if you can feel its heart."

I put my right hand on the tree, though my mind was on anything but how it might be feeling. Then I put my left hand on too, since Marv was watching me so intensely. I wanted him to think I took him seriously.

The tree's pulse took me completely by surprise.

Why hadn't I known before? Who'd kept it from me, the knowledge that trees also bled, that flowers breathed and reached for sunlight, stretching like Cat on the sill, like Jo beside the length of me? Why hadn't someone told me that moss has roots that drink, inhaling water from the porous earth the way Bobby inhaled milk: loving the slip and slide of it, craving, focusing only on that one thing?

The missionaries had the converts clustered about them. Everything was white. Marv and Helen joined us. They'd left Sean at home with a sitter "so Gwen won't worry." The six of us stood, shading our gaze from the deep glare that made the start of the ceremony sizzle like a flash-bulb. Just for a moment the light was so fierce—from the see-through roof but also from the windows along the pool's right wall—that the group became a mass, indistinguishable, and the light very bitter, not white any longer but a yellow that stung our eyes like mosquitos.

Then the Ryans broke away, followed by the McIntyres.

Then Missy Jackson.

Tiffany.

Arthur and Heather Parks.

Others I didn't know.

At first I didn't understand what was happening. It seemed part of the ceremony that groups of folks should travel, taking in different corners of the room. I let my imagination run horse-wild, concocting scenes where they all dove at once into the pool and swam, like those water ballet girls I'd seen once on TV. But then the Ryans split, and Jack went into the men's room and Sally into the women's. The others followed, dividing by sex and disappearing, leaving behind the light and the water and the missionaries' droning prayer.

As the sun got on with its shiny business, I could see who was left: Marigold and Vera, Ernie Copper, and Gwen.

The missionaries went right on praying.

"Why are they dividing up?" Bet nudged Roy.

"I guess they go into the dressing rooms and meditate."

"Maybe they didn't wear the right clothes," Selena mused.

I watched while LaMonte and Jared kept on, undaunted. Ernie looked eager; Gwen looked serene. Marigold and Vera were arm in arm, resting on each other, their matching lacy long dresses sagging at the hems.

Just then Sally Ryan hurried out of the women's room and over to a slatted chair by the kickboards, where she picked up a pair of flip-flops she'd left behind. As she walked quickly back towards the dressing room, Helen stopped her with a smile.

"What part of the ceremony are you on?"

Sally clapped the flip-flops together, applauding herself. "Jack and I decided we didn't want to participate, after all. We decided to head down to Lake Monroe for a nice afternoon outdoors."

"Too much God in the church for ya, Sal?" Marv grinned. "Or not enough?"

When Sally smiled, one eyebrow went up. She bent towards Marv. "Too much *something.*"

I went back to watching Gwen. LaMonte was doing a demonstration of sorts, showing the others how the ceremony would go. He'd chosen Gwen to demonstrate. She was having trouble keeping a smirk off her face, you could tell. As his hand met her back, she shifted from one foot to the other. I tried to read LaMonte's face, but it was as calm as the pool.

"That's a shame. A real shame." Marv was staring at the women's dressing room where Sally had disappeared with a swoosh.

"No surprise to me." Selena had her arms crossed over her chest. "Not even God can bring Cartwheel together."

I just watched and kept on watching. I didn't want to miss the moment when they all went under, meeting or losing what they came for.

Marigold and Vera had twined themselves together. They were both standing on the balls of their feet, gazing out at the pool like it was full of gold coins. Right then the missionaries led the group around to the other end of the pool, the kids' part where the water was low.

Gwen was first. Suddenly there was a funny little scuffle, LaMonte doing a skittery two-step in the water to put his hand on Gwen's back. I saw Jared give him a sudden, sharp look. Then LaMonte dunked Gwen, who came up shaking off the droplets like a shaggy pup.

Selena walked over to Gwen to help her towel down. I started to follow, then thought to stay and watch the sisters. First Jared did Ernie, who must've swallowed water because he sputtered a little, coughing till Jared thwacked him on the back. Roy, who worked near Ernie on the line, had his towel ready. Ernie used it on his face and hair, then dried between his toes. While Ernie was drying, the sisters separated for the first time, Vera to LaMonte and Marigold to Jared. They went down.

Right away when they came up they found each other and held hands once more. That was when light tore through the windows, setting their white dresses all on fire.

They stood in the midst of it, the fire, with the blue water beneath turned silver and their lace gold, rust, almost red in spots. The sun was slanted so that LaMonte and Jared looked simple, their shirts still the same blank color. Only the sisters caught. For a moment every color imaginable seemed to spark from their silver hair and sopping cloth. I walked around to the kids' side and helped them up the ramp. As they toweled off, they thanked me. Then Marigold bent to whisper, "Caddie, we're safe now."

"Safe?"

"We can be together." Vera's voice, clipped and matter-of-fact, but never harsh. "That's why we did it. I know her secret name, and she knows mine."

"If one of us goes first, the other will call her home." Marigold had finished rubbing at her hair and started in on her skirt, twisting the fabric in both hands, wringing it dry. When they'd finished, they walked off hand in hand, their dresses nipping their ankles. At the door to the dressing room, they both turned and waved good-bye.

Later that afternoon, after I'd spoken to Gwen, when I was walking again through the woods alone on my way to the Dunking Day dinner, watching and listening for the fire-creature I'd seen earlier, I thought about the sisters. Folks said they'd sacrificed everything—marriage, children—to hang on and take care of each other. And they weren't even blood relations. I thought again about how almost no one ever saw the inside of that house, but how they'd singled me out, me and Jo, to visit, eat with them, and listen while Vera played piano. I remembered Marigold leading the way up the winding staircase carefully, Jo and I side by side on the broad steps, and Vera following. I remembered the sisters showing us the second floor, with its sewing room and library and generous bath. They'd showed us each room in turn, saving their bedrooms—side by side—for last. They'd watched our faces. They'd watched the way our bodies crossed. Later, as we drove home, I asked Jo a question and she laughed.

"Of course."

"How can you be sure?"

"Try counting, Caddie."

"Counting what?"

"Beds."

"They have two bedrooms."

"But Vera's doesn't have a bed."

The baptism ceremony took less than an hour. After, Marv and Helen reminded us to be at the diner no later than two. All except Gwen, who'd asked to spend the rest of the day in "prayer and contemplation."

Selena searched through her purse for keys. "Caddie, I can drive you? Do you need to go home first or should I drop you off at the diner?"

"Actually, I'm in the mood to walk."

"Is it safe?"

"Don't worry about me. I want the time to think and be alone."

She said she understood. I think she did. "See ya in a bit," and she was off, her terry shorts clinging to her skinny legs.

I didn't feel like chatting with anyone. I'd had too much of other people already and was in for a long day's more. I'd just taken the first steps towards the women's room, thinking to maybe walk home before I went to the diner, when Gwen idled up, wet from the water, her yellow hair dun, plastered against her cheeks, spidery snakes. She'd wrapped herself in a bathrobe, pale pink velour with the usual flowers. She looked like a Girl Scout who'd just earned her swimming badge.

"Caddie, wait up." I let her tug me over to the kickboards. LaMonte and Jared were conferring beside the lifeguard stand. A family with several kids had just arrived for swimming lessons. "Caddie, I need to talk to you. Something amazing just happened."

"Don't tell me. You were blind, and now you can see again." Was it because I'd loved her once—lusted after her—that I couldn't be nice? I felt irritation rise within me, but Gwen seemed to miss the edge in my voice as she rushed to lay out her story.

"When LaMonte took me to the edge of the pool to baptize me, just before I went under," she looked over her shoulder, letting her voice drop to a whisper even though there was no one close enough to hear, "he asked if I believed in love at first sight and I said yes and then he asked me if I'd be his wife." She was one huge smile. The flowers on her robe looked like thorns.

I stayed grumpy, didn't let her tug a grin from me with her simple news. But I couldn't be flat-out mean, either, so it was "I'm sure you'll be very happy together" from Caddie to Gwen.

"Oh, I know we will." Like thorns. "But Caddie, that's not the thing—there's something more."

"Don't tell me you're pregnant again."

"Caddie!" Gwen looked genuinely shocked. "I don't believe in pre-marital sex. I mean—I mean, I did believe in it, but that was before I found out about the Celestial Kingdom. LaMonte loves and respects me too much to defile my body. Fornication is a sin, you know."

"So I've heard." It was hard to remember wanting to live with Gwen. But I could still get back to wanting to touch her, what with her soft body in all that plush velour. I hoped LaMonte had gentle hands. "Does he know that Sean was conceived out of wedlock?"

Gwen glanced around again. The family full of kids had multiplied into three. There were brightly colored balls everywhere and unexpected splashes. "Caddie, that's the thing." She kept her voice soft, softer. "That's what I need your advice on."

"Gwen, you need to tell him. You know Cartwheel. If you don't, some-body will. I'm sure if he really loves you, he'll forgive you. After all, when you got pregnant you weren't Mormon. You were following a different set of rules. It wasn't a sin in your eyes back then."

She tugged on the belt of her robe. Her hair had already begun to dry in the steamy heat, frizzing a little at the ends, sparking glitter on her cheeks. "LaMonte doesn't know about Sean."

"So explain it to him. Tell him you used to have different ideas about religion."

"I mean, he doesn't know about Sean at all."

It took a moment for the meaning of Gwen's words to register. "You mean he doesn't know Sean is Tim's?"

"He doesn't know Sean is mine."

At first I thought she was kidding. I even laughed. It came out sound-ing like a laugh, ha ha. That's never happened to me at any other time. Ha ha. But Gwen wasn't laughing, and pretty soon I wasn't either.

She explained. It went pretty deep, her lying, though she insisted it wasn't a lie, "Just something I never told him. I didn't do it on purpose. It just sort of happened. He knows I was married. I told him how Tim left me, and he was really sympathetic. But then he asked—then he asked if we'd gotten divorced. And I—then I did lie. I told him yes. I had to, Caddie. If I'd said no, he wouldn't have given me a second thought." It was true. LaMonte followed rules. Gwen wanted to, but always managed to break them. I wondered if these lies were the beginning of honesty, or the beginning of a long deception. "So then he asked, did we have any children. Only before I could answer, he started in on how, if you have children and are in a bad marriage, you should stay in. For the children's sake. How he doesn't believe in divorce where children are concerned." She looked down at her hands. Right after she stopped wearing her ring, there had been a thin line around her ring finger from where the band hid her skin from the sun. It had vanished long ago, but I always expected, still, to see it.

"So you said no children."

"I said no children."

"How the hell did you explain who Sean is?"

"LaMonte thinks I baby-sit him sometimes. When he comes to my apartment, it's only to talk religion. He has to come with his companion, and they stay in the kitchen. He and I aren't allowed to be alone even, and he never gossips. He doesn't know anything about me but what I say. Caddie, you can't tell, and you can't tell anyone this next thing, either. Not even Selena. Not even your kitten. Not anyone or anything, because it's too big a secret."

"Why are you telling me then, if it's so secret?"

Her face changed. It became a grown woman's face. It reminded me of my face in the mirror at nineteen, putting on makeup in The Depot dressing room, and six years later, facing myself in the bathroom glass the day after Jo left for good. The thing in Gwen's face that looked grown-up was the instinct to survive. But she wasn't as strong as me, I found myself thinking, evil as they say pride is, because she couldn't carry her secret burden on her solitary back.

"I made a deal with Helen. It was her suggestion. She gave me some money and I'm leaving Sean with her when LaMonte and I move to Utah."

"You sold your son?"

"Shhh!" Gwen scrunched her eyebrows at me. "Caddie, please. I didn't sell Sean. Helen adopted him."

"For money?" It was a mystery to me why anyone would have a baby, much less buy one.

"The money's just—it's just to help me get on my feet again. A loan, really."

I tried to think of the last time I'd seen Gwen with Sean and realized it'd been a long while. Everyone was so used to her neglectfulness, to other folks filling in the gaps, that no one had noticed when Helen took over. Not even me. "Do you still take Sean home with you?"

"Sometimes. Sometimes Helen and Marv keep him overnight. Caddie, please. Please don't judge me. Helen loves Sean. She's always wanted a baby. That's why she and Marv have been so unhappy. She told me— you promised to keep this secret, right? She told me they can't have children. All they have is us, us girls and Bobby and customers. But we always move on. She loves Sean and so does Marv and they're so good with him. Caddie, don't you see?" Her fingers were flitting over the belt of her robe, tugging it tighter and tighter. "Caddie, they love Sean more than I do."

It was true. There was no denying it. Helen practically bled her fingers to nurse him. Marv couldn't get enough of showing off before the grill. Sometimes he'd take his cook's cap and place it atop Sean's tiny head. The boy gurgled while Marv played peekaboo. But Gwen didn't love him. I knew that, I'd sensed it and then seen it for myself.

"I don't love him, Caddie. I never did."

"What if LaMonte wants kids?"

"I told him I can't. Can't have them. I'll take the pill in secret and burn the divorce papers if they come through."

"If they come through?"

Gwen put her hand over her mouth. "Oops." She grinned weakly. "I didn't want you to know that. It's not final, but it will be soon, it's just that I don't know where Tim is, so how can I—"

"Gwen. I can't believe this. You're not divorced, but you're getting remarried? You have a son, but you've sold him and told your fiancé that you're sterile?" I wanted to shake her. "Silly girl," I said, and then her face crumpled and I gave in and hugged her. Crushed her to me. The smooth rose scent of her robe clashed with the antiseptic scent of chlorine; her belly felt startling against my own. Jo was so slender, so much almost a boy. Gwen was all curvy. Her body felt like my own body. I pulled her towards me with one last, fierce embrace, then let go. "I won't tell," I said, "but you're on your own."

The look on her face made me feel I'd kicked a puppy, but what was there left for me to say?

Many, many years later, I woke from a nightmare, dreaming that Gwen was calling to me from some strange and sandy place. It looked like a cliff. There was a name etched into a rib of the stone. "Angel's Landing," the sign said. Gwen was stranded, and there was snow on the mountain, and she was alone, abandoned. "Caddie, take it back," she called across the miles. Somehow I was able to turn back time to that moment by the water, to her baptism, to our conversation and my turning a stone face on her lies, but also on her cry for help. "Caddie, take it back," and I tried, but when I opened my mouth to say, "Gwen, if you need me, call my name. We're still sisters," all that came out was water.

I thought of tracing her after that, but too many years had passed.

Chapter Eight: Jo
■ ■
■

I might've put down roots in Lima, Ohio. I had a job—pumping gas—and a girl named Anna. True, I never let Anna discover my secret body, but if she couldn't have stood it, I'd have found another town. Or another girl. The trick is watching the way she fixes her coffee. Thick with cream and sugar, flavors drizzled like marble, rubbing the spoon along her tongue, licking her lips after. Sensuousness shows clearly in everyday life, but most folks are blind to it. That was one of the tricks I taught the factory boys in Cartwheel. What to seek. Not a bikini-trim body, not eye makeup in volcano layers, but a way with objects, small animals, and the very air of any place she spends her time.

It took me over a year to admit that I missed Caddie. News travels slowly from brain to heart, and this wasn't news my heart wanted to hear. At first loneliness tapped softly, like a twig scratching a window, but before long I woke to a peal of private thunder. Anna slept on beside me, oblivious to the rattling behind my ribs. My heart resisted, but sound broke through, the insistent words of a lover whose voice had risen from the dead.

Caddie called to me. For a while, it meant new fantasies, remembering her body and gestures even while Anna slid through my hands. But when her voice took on the consistency of a litany, I began to worry. Was she in trouble? Was she begging me back, not for lust's silver sake but because she needed help?

Who am I kidding.

I'm no savior. I caught a bus bound for Cartwheel because I wanted to spread her legs and taste her. My ego thought it'd be easy, winning her back. My ego thought she was still pining away, missing me as I'd come round to realize I missed her. That whole bus ride long, I imagined myself in a cinema. Pictures flashed across the windows but instead of eating up the scenery, I imagined Caddie running to meet me, stripping herself of history as she ran. We'd meet pure, outside of old angers and past haunts. We'd meet, and I'd run my fingers through her hair and we'd be who we were when we first met. Full of surprises, each daring enough to risk chicken—that long drive for sky's sake into the trees.

As the wheels droned on, night covered the bus like a blanket. Soon snores studded the gasp and stutter of rubber on asphalt, soon I was the only lively passenger. As we neared Cartwheel, I played games to keep from sleeping because staying awake made me feel closer to Caddie. Still, once the bus pulled into Cartwheel's dusty station, I ambled into the men's bathroom like I had all the time in the world. Inside was a tiny stall, a urinal, and a narrow, spotty mirror lit by a single bulb. I stuffed my bags in the stall (never did get those boots or boxers back) and glanced in the mirror to spruce my spiky hair. At first the stubble on my chin looked like grit. Skimming one wet finger over the mirror, I checked to see if the surface was playing dirty tricks. But when I rubbed at my face, the tufted hair felt real.

Who's to say how far our jealous hearts can take us?

Changing into a man hadn't been enough. There was something still more I wanted.

How do cats see in the dark? How does it feel to let your belly brush the skin of a tree, what's visible from such a height?

How do you come down?

I'd dreamed it before, cold dreams I woke from in a patch of sweat. But I didn't believe it could happen, or at least not to me. When I saw shadows underneath my chin and knew my wish had worked its magic, when I felt fur prickle like unwashed flannel, I lit one last cigarette (there are things only humans can appreciate) and exhaled, covering my face with fine white film.

It takes heat for change to happen. Smoke for certain. Sometimes flame.

When the air cleared, I glanced around, grateful for the deserted room. Struggle and reach: I summoned change, I let lust happen, I welcomed the great leap out of skin. No one else saw what I saw, staring myself down, fascinated and horrified by what my wishing had brought me.

The door opened soon after. I took advantage of a stranger's hands to speed away, out of the station and into night's offerings.

At first the texture felt heavy and tight. Later I came to love my velveteen, my putty bones and keener senses. Into the brush. Trust. Rough sparks and the skittle of something waking above. My head in the nest. My tongue carousing the far reaches, my mouth around the egg.

I slipped away, to watch and wait. To test. To see about loving past the switch, to see if Caddie's bliss could withstand change.

It would've taken me forever to find her, but I had help. Hands that cupped me, carrying me to Caddie for the love of us both. The building was brick. The way to her heart was all uphill. Stairs and more stairs. At the top my savior dropped me off. I flicked my tail good-bye, then faced the door, unsure how to signal without human hands.

I called her name. She took me in. Then it was up to me to wait, up to her to open her body to an animal.

Chapter Nine: Caddie

■ ■
■

LaMonte finished his mission on a Friday. I remember because he celebrated at the diner and ordered fish sticks, which puzzled Bet.

"Catholics eat fish on Fridays."

"Maybe he just likes fish, Bet." I was in a terrible mood. I could see it coming. Sure enough, the next day, his first day of secular life after two years of service, LaMonte made his proposal to Gwen official.

It was to be a short engagement.

"All I could think was, 'I really need a cigarette.' But look here." Gwen held out her left hand.

Another band. Not a sun streak, this time.

On Monday LaMonte flew to St. George, Utah, to be with his family. Gwen explained to me that he hadn't seen them in two years. "That's one of the rules," she said, her face serious. None of us were sure how genuine Gwen's interest in either the Mormon Church or LaMonte was, but she'd made it clear there was no stopping her. A little over a week later, on her last day at the diner, LaMonte sent her a one-way ticket to St. George, which she flashed around like a hundred-dollar bill.

"Remember, Caddie, you promised. Say it again—your promise." We were in the storage closet. Gwen had dragged me in under the pretext of needing to refill the mustard.

"Gwen, you know I won't tell anyone. Not about Sean or Tim or Helen. But if something ever happens to Helen and Marv, what about Sean?"

"Helen and I have already thought of that. It's taken care of. There are papers. Things we've signed."

I shrugged. "I need to get back to my station."

"Caddie." She caught my hand as I reached for the door. "Haven't you ever had a secret?"

Something in the way she said it made me stop, one hand hovering over the knob. "Maybe. Maybe I have, Gwen."

"Was it a secret about love?"

"Maybe."

"Did you keep it to hurt other people or because it was the only way you could get what you wanted?"

"Gwen, there wasn't a child involved." I put my hand on the lock and started to turn it, but her kiss stopped me. It was warm, full of things I remembered from childhood: cocoa and quilts and sparrows. At first I held back, in spite of memory, but as her lips moved, first against and then in sync with mine, I remembered other things, things I'd forgotten. Gwen's lips made me go back to places I hadn't wanted to revisit, places I couldn't get enough of, till she and I were Jo and I in our old kitchen. When I pulled Gwen's face to my chest, into the dirty, waitress smell of me, it was Jo I told to stay; more memory, me breaking through the ice Jo had left covering my skin like a clingy film. Gwen's kiss went deeper and deeper and she ground her body against mine, striking me lit like a match, so that when she stepped away from me half teasingly, who could blame me for reaching for her—half an open embrace, half a fencer's lunge.

"I know who you are," she said. Then she opened the door into the kitchen and walked out.

I didn't say good-bye when she left that day for good. I hung back, and if the others stared a little at my shyness, Gwen acted like she didn't care. I didn't say good-bye because I couldn't face her and because, for me, she was already long gone.

Helen drove her to the airport. I had to act surprised when Helen pulled into the diner's lot hours later with Sean in his baby seat in the back of the car. Mostly I think I did a good job—of acting surprised, I mean. But the Oscar went to Helen, who explained that Gwen had left Sean with her and Marv "just for the Leavitts' honeymoon."

I knew better, of course. Days turned to weeks, and folks kept asking after Gwen's childlessness. "It's sure some lengthy frolic, it is," Laddie Farris kept saying. He missed her, I could tell, though he wouldn't say it. I felt sorry for him—his wife had died in the Westville factory fire six years earlier and he'd been slogging around town like a hound dog ever since. Gwen had perked him up, the way she'd perked me up, the way she'd kept a lot more folks awake, men and women both, than she probably realized.

But Helen was happy.

Really happy, in a way none of us had ever seen her. Always before, she'd been grey to everyone else's colors, the one who blended in, the girl we forgot to mention when we counted four. Now our grey lady was a great rainbow blur of motion—carrying, burping, feeding that baby like he was an ambulance needing a clear path on the highway.

Folks commented on it, how good she was, so maybe I didn't give the locals enough credit when I said I knew and they didn't. It was in the air, Gwen's abandonment. There was pity mixed in with the pleasure customers took in tickling and soothing the child.

I waited for the day the news would break.

Finally, over a month after Gwen's departure, Helen called us all into a little huddle before the diner opened. First she told us to steady ourselves for a bit of a startle, then gave us the story. "Gwen's husband LaMonte wants to build a house in St. George. Gwen asked if Marv and I would take Sean for a longer time, till she's ready in their new house for a tiny baby."

What was it in Helen's voice that let us all know Gwen was never coming back—not for Sean or anyone? Selena reached for my hand and held it; Bet and Bobby exchanged glances. Marv broke the silence, his voice decisive, which was something new. "Maybe it's for the best, seeing how she cared for the child."

Nods all around.

Even though I nodded too, my heart knew sorry. She was our girleen, Gwen, and she was gone. I'd never told her what I felt, never even told her about Jo. Although she'd guessed, I didn't know how or when. Was it early on? Was I that obvious to everyone? Now I couldn't learn. Worse, now I knew for sure that time was passing, right under our noses, things changing that couldn't be undone. There was something melancholy about it, so when Marv and Helen started searching for a new girl, we waitresses and Bobby weren't as cordial as we should've been.

It did help to see Sean happy.

I never liked that baby—skanky—but maybe he was cranky and ugly because his mother wished him so. Helen and Marv were born to parenting, that was the irony. "Never could have kids of our own," Marv would murmur, tickling Sean's forehead or turning his tiny baseball cap wrong-way round. He'd still spend his break gossiping with factory men, usually the Marrieds, but he'd bring Sean with him, propped on his hip the way he held sacks of flour. He was gleeful with the child. Sean took to him, giving him coos and gurgles and finally—a day Marv celebrated with free ice cream all around—"Da."

It sounded sort of Irish. Folks still said he had Tim's face, but now it came out a compliment. "Those sharp blue eyes," they'd say, "that thick, tousled black hair."

"He'll be a charmer." Selena winked at Marv. "Must've got it from his adopted father."

A few weeks after Helen's announcement, I stopped by her office to let her know a sales rep was waiting up front, his sample case all bulky by his side, eating pie like there was no tomorrow. When the door opened, I couldn't believe the change in the decor.

No more numbers.

Stippled color and razzle in long lines, instead. Ducks and castles. Umbrellas and dinosaurs. Unicorns and apples. Everything was shape, gloss, texture, to catch and keep a young one's eye. At the center of the room was a huge bassinet made of nubby white wicker, its belly striped black, its innards lined with thick white flannel. Impossible not to comment on, since it was shaped like a cow.

Helen looked at me expectantly. What I really wanted to know was how she'd gotten it to fit through the doorway. "Interesting," I said. Then I flat-out lied. "Beautiful. Just beautiful."

Mostly it was big and stupid looking. But Sean slept like cream floating to the surface. "We got the idea from our china. My mother's." She said the words carefully; talking about her family must've been difficult. I leaned into her. She smelled of baby formula and talc. "It's so elegant, Caddie. Limoges. It included its own little sugar bowl and creamer—the usual kind, a sort of rectangular cup. But Mother," Helen laughed, "Mother liked layering jokes on top of anything fancy and refined. So when she'd serve tea—and she served an English prince once, back long ago when she and Father were first married and still wealthy and lived in Wales—she'd serve it in those delicate, fragile cups with slim silver teaspoons and a tiny sugar bowl filled with lumps and then she'd plop down a cow creamer instead of the other. Guests always laughed. Even the prince laughed, that's what she said. So I thought it might be amusing to have Bobby make us up a bassinet with a hollow back. I particularly wanted a Beltie because Marv took a liking to the breed long ago."

"When did your mother pass on?" I wanted to say *die* because that's what bodies do. They don't pass or kick anything, when they go. But for other folks' sake, I changed my words to match their worlds.

Maybe with Helen that wasn't the right thing to do, because her face blanched, the way almonds do when you treat them for candy. White on a face is actually ugly, and Helen looked ugly then. Usually she was beautiful. Her beauty was the kind you had to take for granted after a while, or you'd stay distracted all the time. The easiest way to describe her was to say her beauty was the opposite of Gwen's. Where Gwen showed softness, curves, and circles, Helen showed sleek lines and angles. She was tall, taller than Marv, and thin, and her black hair fell to her shoulders, very straight and shiny. It was going grey now, in streaks, but the grey wasn't yellow, as some hair goes. She had high cheekbones, her nose was thin and sharp, and her eyes were gentle and huge, like a horse's.

Marv resembled her the way Marrieds come to look like each other. He was tall too and had the same pale skin, dark hair, thick wet-looking lashes. But there was more flesh to him; you could see he ate his own cooking. Helen looked hungry for something all the time. Since she'd taken Sean, she hadn't gotten any fatter, but the hungry look was fading fast. Surrounded by the hollow cow and all those baby baubles, she seemed calmer, her usual nervous energy focused on one thing very intently. Then Sean started crying and she jumped up from her chair.

"Caddie? Did you come knocking for something particular or were you just stopping by to see Sean?"

"There's a man outside, wants you for something." I felt sorry because she got a panicked look, the way she always did when strangers stopped by the diner. She was a homebody, Helen. Marv too. They didn't do well with public tasks like advertising and hiring. Selena, Bet, Bobby, and I always had to help. Much as we didn't like to think about replacing Gwen, we all finally conferred and decided to take a load off their minds. Do a little searching on our own.

Selena found Peg.

Or remembered her.

It wasn't that she was unmemorable. I'd never paid enough attention to her to really see her face. One day Selena stopped scrubbing the counter mid-swipe.

"Caddie, take a look at that young one there. Tell me if you recognize her face."

Bleached skin, green eyes, red hair. Very thin, her arms like summer twigs. Sixteen, seventeen at most. She was eating a plate of hash like she hadn't eaten in a season.

"Can't say I do."

"What if," Selena took the plate of cookies out of my hands and set it on the counter, "I said another name? Like David."

I would've dropped those cookies, so it was a good thing. "Peg."

She was the girl he'd taken, the one too young for him to be touching, the one we all knew he was touching to make up for me. I've made mistakes in my life, and then I've sinned. One of my sins was not shoving David away from that little girl, or at least giving her a good talking-to.

Not that she would've listened.

I hadn't at sixteen.

Maybe she was like me and had something worse than David to run from.

"Peg." As I stared, her attention drifted till her eyes met mine. We held steady till I turned away, gone Judas, and hushed Selena's curiosity. "I don't want to think about it. I'm glad she's back, and I'm glad David's in Cleveland. But I don't need to be making friends with her and neither do you."

What was it in her that I saw? She'd been a beggar before and she was a beggar now. One of the motherless ones on the lam from some man— father, uncle, brother, son, or the usual stranger. One of the motherless ones who recognized me, knew I'd escaped, wanted to know how. For a time in my life, when I was younger, I gave out helpful hints like I was Heloise. But there comes a day when you have to cut your past out of your soul, trimming the edges carefully. I'd done the cutting. No room left in my heart for more taking care.

After all, no one was about to take care of me.

So I turned away, thinking my refusal would make Peg want to take her lunch break at Dairy Queen. Was I really surprised when she ate not just lunch, but breakfast, at the diner the next day? She began haunting the place, and I remembered what I'd let myself forget: persistence is everything to ghost girls. It's all they know, to do the same thing every day at the same time.

"Caddie, she wants to talk to you. Take pity," Selena said, after Peg sat in the same seat and ate the same hash for lunch a fourth day running, all the while staring me down.

"Let her sit in my section, if she's so hot on being my best friend."

"Meanie." Selena said it seriously. I heard it so. The sting spread across my face and onto my throat like a burn. I didn't want to fight. I just wanted that ghost to vanish and her spot to fill with some factory boy in yellow boots and a careless smile.

Boys were easy. Easy to please, easy to leave behind.

The day Peg sat in my section, I felt the whole diner go still. Word had gotten around, or maybe the townies had a better memory than I did. Only they got the story wrong, making us rivals. Two girls and a man means a wicked triangle. It never occurs to anyone that the two girls might find something in common.

Sixteen. That was my guess for her age. I flipped my order book to a blank page. Instead of writing "12" for her table number, I wrote "16," then had to scratch it out.

"What'll it be?" I didn't even ask what she wanted to drink or if she took cream with her coffee. I just poured, paying attention to the way the liquid filled the cup.

"English muffin."

"Buttered or dry?"

"Buttered. With jelly, please."

"Jelly's on the table already. Look here."

"Oh."

"Anything else?"

"Strawberry milk."

"You should eat more. Thick food. Eggs and bacon and cakes." I took the menu from her hands. "You're too thin."

"Caddie."

That was all it took. I slipped into the booth beside her and watched while she got her voice back. She talked about the weather, but I knew from how she saw the sky that she had buried stories, and she knew from how I took an interest in temperature that I'd be one to listen. It took a long while, her description of the sky, so long that Selena, who was keeping an eye out, had to take over my tables for a stretch. But I wasn't thinking about time, I was thinking about trips and why we take them. Whether they choose us or we choose them. When she finished, I put my arm around her, the way a sister would, but also with a little bit of something else, imperceptible to the eye.

The way she leaned into my arm, making it a friendly pillow but also with a little bit of something else? I knew she was asking me what I'd learned could be. But she was sixteen, and she'd only just gotten her voice back.

I dropped my words to a whisper, the way she'd told me her sky story, so the nice couple behind us couldn't hear. "I can't give you your body back, but I might be able to get you a job. One question first: how old are you?"

"Nineteen." Somehow I knew she wasn't lying. It made sense that she'd look different than who she was.

Marv and Helen were both glad we'd found new help without much trouble.

Selena and Bet agreed that I should train Peg.

The only thing Peg balked at was couples. "I can't serve couples where the girl looks glazed." I tried explaining that you can't pick and choose—it was probably illegal—but Peg was stubborn, right from the start. It was hard working with someone so fierce, but her stubbornness reminded me of another girl.

"You remind me of someone."

"I remind you of yourself."

"That's not what I said." But she was like me in her stubbornness, and in her gestures too. And one more thing, the thing we sensed but wouldn't say.

"I'll serve women alone, but not women whose men have taped their mouths."

I watched her with women—the way she bent over them, her eyes meeting theirs, giving their words her full attention. They'd gone so long invisible, those day care workers, secretaries, mothers, and telephone operators, and got so involved in attention, so lulled by it, that they ordered four-course meals.

"I'll take fries. Make that fried potatoes. No—which do you recommend? Really? Slaw, then. Slaw. That's a start, a fine start, don't you think? Now, if you were me—but you're way too young to know what it feels like to be going grey—if you were me, which of these soups would you choose?"

It was my job to please the ladies. It felt a little tingly to see a mirror. In that manner, Peg was different from Gwen, but in other ways, training her was like discovering Gwen all over again. Peg played the sweetie ("Weetie," the factory boys called her and she'd blush like Gwen, pale skin turned paper), the one who made charming mistakes and grinned awkwardly. But there was a difference, and it changed the whole shape of things behind the counter.

Peg was keen.

Now, Gwen wasn't stupid. In fact, I sometimes wondered if she wasn't smarter than the rest of us put together. She'd found herself a solid future, someone who'd support her till her dying days. She'd got rid of what burdened her without penalty and she'd found a way to avoid having any more kids. I remembered the day I'd first asked her what she saw in LaMonte.

"He'll never leave me. They take marriage seriously. He'll never leave, and I won't have to work. I can just sit home and watch the soaps." She tugged on my sleeve. "You should think it over, Caddie. Jared's single, you know."

But if Gwen was smart, she wasn't clever. There was naiveté to her knowing. Naiveté and selfishness. Peg's intelligence was hard won, a little harsh. There was risk in it. She seemed to know things there was no reason for her to know. It wouldn't have been so bad, Peg's keenness, and her only nineteen, but sometimes in the midst of all that intelligence she'd fade away. It was as if the things her brain carried were so heavy they sunk her under the river of the everyday.

Plash. The waters parted and Peg went under. What was left was a shell. Pale pink lips that pursed and pouted, dimpled cheeks, a narrow chin, a high forehead scattered with stray red bangs that matched her flapper cut, her rebel sense suited to another decade. But Peg was a tough girl. Any prettiness she had was accidental. When Bet asked her where she got the bob, she sighed, as if the answer wasn't worth her breath. "Hacking shears." You could see that it was true. If it looked chic, in a tousled way, it was by chance. Peg was cursed that way. She did all she could to numb her beauty, but it stayed and stayed, a gentleness her work boots and dirty jeans and scars couldn't mask.

Jo would've liked Peg. Peg was me and Jo both, layered, one over the other. "Kiki," Jo had said they called girls like that in Indy, girls who didn't fit into either slot. The way folks read Peg told you what they wanted to see. Women saw her as their younger, tomboy selves and gave her beauty tips—Mary Kay ladies always brought Peg free samples. Families saw her as the child she was and joked about setting their kids to labor. Men and boys were sadly predictable. They flirted, winking her up. At first she'd turn away, her cheeks scarlet. Later she learned to tease to earn her tips.

"Get used to it," Selena told her when Peg complained.

I took pity. "Selena's right, but it's not so bad after a while. Just don't ever forget you're faking it and you'll be fine."

"I won't forget." As she said it, I took her arm and squeezed it. I told her through touch what was there to recall.

It wasn't bad for customers, being left alone with Peg's shell. She never brought buttered toast to the dieter who'd ordered dry. She never forgot the hot sauce or straw or water without ice. It wasn't a hardship for customers to have half a girl; probably none of them knew the difference.

Helen and Marv didn't seem to notice either, and Bet liked Peg's shell. She got soaked, Bet, with the bit about the hacking shears. She didn't like quips, didn't like clever. She didn't like to riffle the water. Peg and Bet chafed at each other, Peg wanting always to break through to true things, to hold up what was ugly and take a look. It was always, with Peg, like she'd once tugged her own innards out and knew exactly the worst thing a human creature could see. What Bet didn't realize was that Peg must've seen her own heart also. That was what I liked, Selena and Bobby too. When Peg dived under, burying herself inside her body like her body was water, we missed her. We weren't content with the shell, but wanted the breathing soul, anger and all, so we could see fire spark in her red hair, which was otherwise pumpkin-orange.

Besides, it was creepy when she'd disappear. The first few times it happened, I didn't understand. Once we were in my apartment, which made it worse because for a moment I was actually frightened the way I'd be if I'd let a stranger into my house and the stranger turned crazy.

For a while, I thought crazy might be what she was.

We were in my apartment trying to find something fine for Peg to wear to work. Jeans weren't allowed; it had to be skirts or nice pants, though the nice pants part was long forgotten, since Selena, Bet, and I were all for frills. Peg had revived the nice pants rule by wearing a fancy, soft pair of dark blue pants, very loose and wavy, "high fashion," Bet called them, because Peg wore them with a baggy white shirt and looked like one of those models strutting her stuff, all lost in her big clothes, fabric swinging, elegant and soft and full of motion.

Everyone was impressed with those pants, me included. Then one day while I was showing Peg how to clean the milk shake machine, I had a revelation about where she got them.

"Are those men's pajamas?" It just slipped out. Peg scrunched up her face like she was deciding how to feel, then started laughing.

"I was wondering when someone would notice."

"Do you have anything else to wear? Not that those aren't nice, and all, just—" She'd worn them five days in a row. When she shook her head, I told her where I lived. "Come over after work. I'll let you borrow something of mine. It'll be too big for you, but we can pin it up."

I didn't expect to feel temptation.

She was only nineteen. Almost twenty.

But what's nineteen when someone's full of herself already, not in an ego way, but in an I've-faced-my-own-mirror sort of fashion? I let her rummage through the clothes in my bedroom closet. The way she touched things told me she understood the secret lives of objects. She could feel or glance at a thing and know what it would make her over into. The things she chose to wear were all designed to add age, but also cover over what sometimes slipped through her veiny skin: fat scars.

Me, I like scars. I was trying to tell her so, in a soft way, not ever direct, when temptation happened, its petals an aureole glistening bright as her skin. She was holding a dress we thought we could cut down, a blue one, pretty with her green eyes and red hair. "Like sky," she said when she found it, tucked way in back because it didn't fit now that my belly was rounder than before.

No Jo bed vigor to keep me fit.

It had been a while. Yet all of a sudden there it was again, passion, and all wrong this time once more, because she was too young, someone I'd taken under my wing, not a grown girl. Peg wasn't someone I could feed from, but someone I was expected to give to, so she could start up on her own—grown. I was the nest she was to fly from. Who wants to make love to brittle twigs, bits of fluff, spider's webbing?

Temptation started with wanting to take the dress from her hands and drop it on the floor, to be done for once with work worries and time. Then she'd find my hands on her shoulders, ready to start what already felt unfinished. There was something in the air between us, not like the one-sided current I'd felt from Gwen but like what had been between me and Jo. When I thought of Peg as body, her age flashed before me. The number nineteen formed a sturdy plate of glass, a windshield really, because by then the room was in motion, at least for me, or she was, she was speeding past, not ready for me but not waiting either. It was so hard then to know she was moving towards a time when she would be what I needed, and me, what she wanted, but to know also that to stop a girl's body in motion is to stop change and lose the thing that would be. If I touched her, she'd never become the one I could imagine loving. I had to stand back, honoring glass, the glass that forms automatically around girls of that age yet shatters so easily, sometimes with something as simple as a sigh.

I turned my face away from hers for the few seconds it took to wash wanting out of my eyes. Then I turned back, Caddie Solo, to show her the seams that we could take in to fit the dress to her unfinished body.

"Sky," she said, holding skirt's blue up to the window to see if it matched. "Could we sew clouds across the bodice or on the sleeves?" She described what she'd envisioned—white cotton, several circles joined to make one puffy shape, stitched to the cloth till they nearly rained.

"Clever Peg. Clouds." I took the dress from her hands and examined the hem. "I could take this up, so it doesn't hit you at the ankles. Tuck it where it'll meet below your knees."

She wasn't even facing away from me or gazing out the window when she disappeared. If she'd been sky watching I could've fathomed where she'd gone. I might've figured her for a sky lover, cautioned her with the story of my brother. But her eyes were on mine, seeing me, tending to who I was. Then her gaze shifted; then she was gone.

I tried to bring her back. "When it's dark," I said, "you can see the stars make stories." But Peg wasn't listening. Her face was there, but it was stalled, the way a film can be paused on-screen, motion turned photograph. When she snapped into her body again a moment later, she didn't seem to notice that her soul had vanished and returned.

I didn't tell her what had happened because I was so frightened. Superstition welled up, ladders and black cats and pins in wax, all panic and magic. I thought, *She's a witch,* and after she was gone I checked the apartment to make sure she hadn't messed with Cat: Cat, my familiar.

■■■

The next day at work Peg was as chipper as ever. We spent our break together sewing clouds for the blue skirt of the dress I'd outgrown. I felt ashamed of the ugly things I'd thought, ashamed both of wanting her and thinking her a witch. That week and the next I tried to make it up to her by helping out in little ways—busing her tables, speeding her orders through to Bobby when I could. So when Jim O'Donnell came in and sat in Peg's section, I readied the horseradish sauce: what he always asked for on fried ham. Sure enough, Peg wandered over to the counter where I was pouring coffee for Tiffany and asked me where to find the jar.

As I handed her the sauce, Tiffany asked Peg some ordinary "How are you doing?" question. Peg reached across the counter and said "Fine" to Tiffany, who smiled and went back to her fries. Then suddenly Peg's nodding face was frozen. She wasn't Peg any longer. She stood there a moment, filling space with her shell. Then time snapped back into happening. Peg began whistling the tune she'd whistled that morning on the stoop, Jim got his sauce, and it seemed I was the only one who realized someone had lost seconds of her life.

I stopped being scared then, seeing it happen so public. I wanted to know why, but also where. Was it pleasant, the place she'd found for hiding?

The next day I timed one of my breaks to overlap with Selena's. We were both standing out back nursing cigarettes when the nerve to ask her about our Pegatha startled me like a tornado siren. "Have you noticed a way Peg has?"

"Girl has numerous ways about her."

"Something odd."

"Caddie, you like watching new girls, don't you?"

Shiver. Nothing so cold as thinking I was caught. But she went on, not meaning what I'd worried. "It seems to me they might take you too much for a mother. Do you always have to be criticizing their every move?"

Was that what Gwen had thought, how it had looked? "I didn't mean to be critical. I'm afraid there's some grief she's hiding."

"What is it she does that makes you think she's hiding?" Selena ground her cigarette lazily under her heel.

"Sometimes, when someone's talking, her face falls in on itself like a cake and she's gone. Not Peg any longer. Just Peg's shadow."

Selena tucked a stray hair back into the loose nest piled on top of her head. When her hair was fixed, she sighed, drawing all the breath out of her body. "I know the thing you mean. The dreaming, I call it."

"You've seen it happen?"

She opened the door and gestured me in. "Shoo, girl," she said. Only when we were in the kitchen putting our aprons back on did she answer. With her back towards me and her piled-up hair bobbing slightly, she said, "Not on Peg." She gestured for me to tug the strings around her waist and tighten, showing off her narrow middle. That was when I noticed that she'd gotten thinner.

"On who, then?" Curiosity made my hands clumsy.

"Remember your first year at the diner? How nervous you were?"

"I'd never worked tables before."

"You changed with Jo, and you've since changed more. You're here all the time now. But you used to vanish, same as what you described."

That night I dreamed about the diner.

In my dream, everything silver or blue about the place was turned to red. We served red food only and wore red and all had red hair, like Peg. When a customer came in, the bell jangled like real life, but we did a little dance to warn them off. If they stayed, their flesh changed after eating a few bites: to plastic, metal, cloth. They became part of the diner, though their thoughts stayed theirs.

I wondered where Peg went.

It seemed logical to ask her. "Peg," I practiced saying when I was home alone, "sometimes you look frozen. Do you know when and why it happens?" I worried over it till it almost made me sick. Finally I decided to ask Selena for help, since she seemed to understand.

Time to visit the Yellow Horse.

"She's too young," I said, when Selena first suggested it. That got a huge laugh out of her, her mouth so wide she spit on me a little.

"No one's ever too young to drink in this town, Caddie. The Baptists preach hell for fornication, but they like their beer warm and their girls green. Besides, kids these days have a whole system worked out for getting into buildings where they shouldn't be." I didn't question how she knew, but took her up on her offer to ask Peg if she could meet us at the Yellow Horse. That night Selena and I were both a little late. We had to scan the place three times before Selena finally discovered her. "Look there."

Peg was all a grown-up queenie. Makeup on her, and my blue sky dress, her bra stuffed, clunky boat feet poking out the toes of a borrowed pair of Selena's heels. At least she looked better than the girls who dressed that way because they took it seriously. The men stared from above their beer cans, looking for the lady they'd prod over to a pool table for lessons she'd have to pretend to need. "Hold the cue this way. That's right, a little firmer. Like a handshake. You ever shake hands, missy? I'm gonna stand in back of you, line your hips up against this table. I don't expect you to understand at first. These things take time."

That night no men approached us. I think it was Peg, sending signals out in neon: *stay away.* Her expression and voice covered all three of us, floor, roof, and walls, our own small shed. Inside we were girls together, not quite friendly with each other, because Selena and I wanted something from her, but not predators either. We all three knew we were there to do some opening. There had to be darkness and privacy, other people's noise a cover, so we sat upstairs, the way Jo and I used to, the way Selena and Bet and I had when we'd talked over Gwen like she was just some problem.

Selena was already through her first beer. Peg was sipping like it was tea. I stayed sober. My mouth felt raw. When I drank my soda, it tasted like licorice, so I knew soon I'd kiss or be kissed. Peg was watching me. It was silly, how we pretended not to care. *Caddie,* I reminded myself, *you're here to learn her history.* Once she realized we were curious more than caring, would she vanish inside her floofy dress? The stuffing in her right breast was saggy, too lopsided even for reality. When Selena turned away to signal for another beer, I reached across the table and gave a poke.

Peg stared at me. "How could you tell?"

"Too perky."

"Girls. Let's drink to the Horse and its cute little furniture." Selena leaned over, pressing her cheek against the surface of the table. "Rough," she said, looking down at all the initials etched into the varnish. "Everyone and their dog is on here."

"Got a knife?" Peg poked me. I sighed inside. Jo had given me a Swiss army knife for my birthday years back, but I'd tossed it into Lake Ellis after she disappeared.

"You'll get one with your burger." And she did. Once she'd cut the thing in fours, very precise, Peg wiped the blade on a napkin. Then she handed the knife to me and said solemnly, "Tell your story, Caddie."

Selena turned her face away, bored probably. I paused, knife poised over the surface of the wood. First *J* and *O*—predictable—then *SEPH* to make my old man's name.

Where my hand trembled was on the *I*, but I did it.

For a moment it stared up at us like another sort of eye, wide-awake, daring me to finish what I'd taken on. But then I crossed my fine, upstanding letter. I carved *C* and *A* and double *D*—predictable as Peg's burger. *JOSEPH + CADDIE,* instead of Jo-Jo-JOSEPHINE.

But I never finished my own name. Selena stopped my hand, squeezing it so hard it stung even after she left off. There were tears in her eyes, smudging her mascara. "Stop, Caddie. It hurts." My turn to stare.

I felt so tired I could hardly sit up straight. Why did Selena have to cling to my memory? It seemed so selfish. Couldn't she busy herself with her own beau? Was I supposed to leave off ever mentioning my lover just because Selena still harbored an old jealous crush? Maybe Peg noticed my anger flicker, light on water, because she rubbed her calf against mine under the table. She could split herself in two when the occasion called. While she was secretly stroking my stockinged skin, she squinched her nose up and made her voice stern. "Selena's right, Caddie. No carving tonight. That's not why we came. Speaking of which, why *did* we come? Your interest in me caught fire awful sudden."

Selena daubed her smoky eyes with a napkin. "Caddie, I try to forget and just be ordinary, but sometimes it doesn't happen." She massaged the hand she'd clutched so hard. "Sorry."

"Accepted." I smiled, not so much to let her know I meant it, but because Peg's bare foot had climbed my knee.

"Enough." Peg gave one last toe-tickle, then told my leg good-bye. "Tell me why I'm here."

I had to laugh. Jo would've liked Peg best at that moment. "Pegatha, we invited you because we want to get to know you better."

"We want you to share your history with us, the way friends do," Selena said.

"I don't have history." Peg snarfed her last burger quarter. Her front was drizzled with mustard and bits of lettuce.

"Everyone has history, Peg."

"I erased it." She slurped the last few drops of beer. "I knew you'd come looking." She turned her mug upside down. "All gone."

"No one can erase their history. That's why it's called history. For what's happened," I added, "not what will."

"All gone." She slid out of the booth and stood up. "C'mon, Caddie, Selena. It's past your bedtime."

Selena walked downstairs first, cautiously because of heels and three beers. Peg followed me. After a step or two I felt a hand brush my back. When I turned around, mouth watering, she was waiting. Her kiss was brisk, past my lips to circle round my tongue. Then she gave me a tiny shove and I turned back again, just in time to smile big at a factory boy with saucer eyes, talking into his beer. We made our way to the parking lot, where I took Selena's keys and slid into the driver's seat. I had to drop Peg off first, then Selena. She let me drive her truck home after making me promise to drive back to her house Sunday afternoon. It felt funny to park in my lot. I'd never owned a car myself and rarely borrowed. I understood the lure of it, how it could make people feel important, like they had places to be. But I had only to glance at the sky to remember Nancy, and the craving stopped.

When I got upstairs, Cat was pacing by the door and the phone was ringing.

"I just wanted to say—"

"It's OK that you kissed me." Cat bit my ankle. I had to curl my lips to keep from yapping.

"Kiss?"

"Peg, I liked it. You kiss fancy." Later I reached down to soothe my wounded ankle and found that Cat had actually drawn blood. But right then I wasn't thinking about teeth but tongues. I wasn't thinking about Cat's ruffled fur but Peg's soft skin.

"Kiss?" she said again. "You're a great jokester, Caddie. Funny girl."

"Why did you call me, Peg?" My stomach dropped like a grain elevator.

"I forgot to pay. I owe you money. I'll give it to you Tuesday." She hung up on *Tuesday*. That was all, except for my tears: crying to think I'd made up something that felt so real.

Tuesday at the diner, I started off avoiding Peg, thinking she might be angry. But roundabout ten, during my first break, she joined me on the stoop to smoke and watch the sky change from blue to blue. We were sitting side by side, not talking. My body was rigid because I'd already wired myself into not wanting, only to have her follow me outside. But I needed my smoke and I liked watching sky, and as I puffed and peered, I relaxed, so much so that when her fingers began toying with the hem of my skirt, I didn't flinch, even as they traveled. Now, there are two kinds of travel—desperate and exciting. Mostly I knew about the first kind. Peg did too, I could tell. So it seemed extra special that she wanted to map out the second, finer kind along my upper thighs.

It was a day for surprises. That afternoon, my legs still tingling, I got a letter in the mail, very unexpected. At first I thought it was from Gwen because the postmark was from Nevada—near to Utah, wasn't it? But the envelope was so fancy—blue and gold trim, my name printed in

swirly calligraphy in thick black pen—that it didn't recall Gwen's careless ways.

"Open it, Caddie," Peg said, even before the door had stopped jingling behind the mailman's back. Curiosity made her pale skin splotchy.
"Who's it from? You have to show."

I had a nasty thought then. Peg's ways were so changeable; I couldn't
help wishing for something to make her jealous. If she thought I had a
beau, would she divvy out her attention on a better basis? It was just a
thought—a fleeting scheme—but maybe there is a God, a mean one.
Maybe the letter was meant for penance.

I slit the envelope with a knife, thinking I might want to save it. I
would've been afraid of bad news, but the outside was too cheerful for
anything grim. I was still wondering if maybe it was from Gwen. Had
LaMonte addressed it? Of course, tucked away was the thought that Jo
had taken to practicing fancy letter writing and written me a note explaining all the reasons she'd had to leave. I wanted most to hear from
Jo, but there was fear in that also, since a handful of eager faces were
crowded round and might snatch the letter away from my trembling
hands. Where would I be then if she'd said something to give away our
lives?

Not Gwen, not Jo, but another J, one I wouldn't have guessed in a
thousand years. "It's from Jared Christiansen."

"What's he say?" Bet and Bobby asked.

I read slowly. The insides were all in calligraphy too. The letters were
pretty but hard to make out. "He has a question, only not really a question. Bet, what's this word?" Bet read a lot. Harlequin and such, but also
the paper every day. Every single day. I couldn't fathom wanting to know
that much about the ugliness in life.

Bet squinted, forming words from squiggles. "Oh, Caddie." She took a
big breath. "I'm so happy for you!" Tears and gulps of air.

"Why the hell is she crying?" Peg mumbled under her breath. Bet
heard her and glared. "Let me see it." Peg snatched the letter, feisty, and
began to read. "'Dear Callie,...' Caddie, he got your name wrong! That's
two Ls, not two Ds."

"Keep reading. We're all waiting with our bellies falling out," Bobby
chuckled.

"'Dear Callie,'" Peg continued, "'I'm writing to you from the beautiful
state of Nevada. Have you ever been to Nevada, Caddie?' Oh, he did
use Ds. The circle part is just tiny, that's all. 'I've lived here since I was

two. When I first saw you, you seemed very pious. Although we did not persuade you of the significance of accepting the LDS faith, I truly believe you will soon be salved.' No, saved. 'Soon be saved. My offer should come as no surprise, since a good woman knows that her soul shines forth to a good man like a bell in a temple that rings across a busy town.' That's a mixed metaphor. We learned that in school. He said, 'shines' when he was talking about—"

"Finish the letter, Peg," Bet snarled.

"'A busy town. I would like to take you as my wife, till death do us part, to have and to obey.' He sure picked the best parts of the ceremony, didn't he? Sorry, Bet. 'To obey. Please reply in the enclosed envelope. A CTR ring will arrive shortly through registered mail. With all respect, your loving fiancé, Jared Christiansen.' Wow, Caddie." Peg sounded hurt. "You never told me that you two messed around."

"You never said anything to me either," Selena added.

"Why keep secrets from us, Caddie?" Bobby frowned, but then his face cleared. "Congratulations. It's been a long time since Jo. You sure deserve a decent fellow."

"Why CTR?" Peg's voice still held hurt. "I thought your middle name was Sue."

"It's not an initial ring, Peg. CTR stands for Choose The Right." Bet patted Peg's shoulder like a mother. "Caddie, I'm so happy for you." She sniffled into a paper towel, her mascara smudging under her eyes. "Will you have the wedding here, so we can all be in it?"

"Whensaweddik?" I don't know who said it, but it rang like a bell across a busy town. "Whensaweddik," over and over, till I was dizzy with the drone of it and couldn't hear my own voice protesting.

"I never spoke to Jared Christiansen. I can't even remember what he looks like." No one was listening. They were too busy. They had a wedding to plan. "I don't know him. He doesn't know me. This is crazy." I heard the word "veil" float by. "Aisle." "Give her away."

"Everybody. Hey, everybody! I'm not getting married. Got that? I'm not even getting engaged. I won't open that package. I'll send it back right off. So you can all stop gossiping about something that's never going to happen."

People don't always act like themselves. That's a rule. Maybe people aren't ever themselves anyway, only how they act, and what it all adds up to. Right then I didn't know them—my friends—and they didn't know me. It made me feel alone in a room full of people, as if they'd turned to trees and it was winter and I was lost in a forest somewhere, without even a trail of crumbs to guide me home. *Stop being trees,* I wanted to shout. *Pry your ears open with toothpicks if you can't hear.* But it was no use. After a time I went back into the kitchen and sat next to Sean, who was cooing in the high chair Marv had rigged up.

"How's the dude growing, Marv?"

Marv had his back towards me, prodding a frozen slab of chicken. "Caddie, it's funny you should ask. Just last night, he spoke a true new word. Never were two people happier to have a voice to listen to."

"What did he say?"

Marv turned, wiping his hands on his apron. His face was rosy from the oily heat. "You'll never guess."

"Hamburger."

"No, but you're close."

"Milk? Juice?"

"Nothing to eat or drink."

"I give up." Usually I left Sean to the hands of people who liked the mushy feel and baby smell and random kicks of him, but just then I wanted Marv to know how happy I was that this baby they'd taken on was turning out to be normal after all. That Sean was doing the ordinary, dull things babies will do. So to show I was interested, I picked him up. I held him to my chest, even. It wasn't as bad as it could've been. There was warmth, holding something living, and his face lit up like the neon cross next door. Then he drooled on my shoulder. I tried not to be prissy, what with Marv grinning away at his son like Sean had won the lottery. Instead I pretended to scratch my shoulder, flicking the spit away with the side of my hand. "What did he say?"

Marv turned the chicken, then came over and brushed his hand lightly across the top of Sean's hairy head. The baby's eyes were trusting, like a cow's. "That's my boy. Aren't you a clever one? He said 'diner.' Diner. Isn't that smart?"

"Seems like a fine way to start off on language." I wasn't sure what else to say. Diner. At least he was interested in where he was. Maybe he'd grow up to like buildings—construction or landscaping. Or architecture, if he made it through high school and went clear to some college.

"What's the ruckus out there?" Marv took Sean from my arms and set him back in his chair, then went out to investigate. "Folks," he said to the gaggle of aprons clustered around Jared's letter, "recess is over. Selena, the chicken's done for table four."

All the rest of that day I kept my mouth shut. I remembered how angry Jo used to get when the Marrieds did their whensaweddik song over and over in her ears. "Worse than the sound of the conveyor when it's not oiled properly." Wearing her out, wearing us down. This wasn't any different, just another verse of the same old standard. But I couldn't do a damn thing about it if no one would listen.

Towards the end of my shift the doorbell jangled and a man in a blue uniform swooshed in, straight up to the counter, and asked after my name.

"Sign here." I took the pen from his hands but froze when I saw the size of the package.

Jared's ring.

Isn't it funny how sluggish folks can startle each other into speed? Suddenly I was surrounded, Jared's ring made flesh, with the package man himself the diamond, heading the band made up of Bet, Bobby, Peg, Selena, and a few curious customers thrown in for good measure.

I held the tip of the pen over the paper. And it was a clock or the pen or the ring of watchers or the rowing motions of my hesitant fingers or the ring itself, audible through its brown wrapping, tick-tick-ticking away the time I had left, telling me I couldn't wait for Jo forever, reminding me that I'd failed with Gwen. My hair was still the same reddish-black Jo had revelled in, but that tick-tick-ticking came in colors, grey and white. Was it Cat I'd let fool me into thinking time stood still? Had I let her night company lull me into believing I'd always have something warm to keep me sleeping well? For so long I'd let myself hope, a secret even from myself, that Jo-Jo-Josephine would open the door to the diner someday with a perfectly simple explanation. We'd be a couple again, lying to everyone but happy ourselves at home. Hope had let me put off looking—really looking. Like searching for the bars Jo had told me about, full of girls like us, fancy Caddies in dresses with dangly bracelets, smirky Jos playing darts or shooting pool and watching their Caddies cluster, lining their lips in the lingering light thrown off the dance floor where women danced in twos or threes, parts of their bodies fitting together perfectly, as if God made them so, as if there was a heaven. As if God weren't just another corporation.

I knew what CTR really stood for: Caddie The Rock. "Send it back." The pen in his hands again; the box untouched by mine. It was the only way to say no.

Again the jangle of the door, the package man vanishing. Around me the band dissipated, stones turning back to faces, faces turning into words. "Why?" over and over, as if they couldn't guess. As if it wasn't obvious.

"I don't know him. I don't love him, and I like living alone."

"It was that last bit was your mistake." Peg and I talked it over later. She alone apologized, explaining she hadn't realized I didn't know the man, much less love him. "I thought you must've just kept the story hidden."

"It would be too ordinary a thing, loving a man like Jared, for me to care to keep it hidden."

"That's true." Then a smile. "At least we came out of it with a party."

I was glad about the party. Right after the package man jangled away and everyone's glee died down, Peg got practical. "If we can't celebrate Caddie's wedding, can we celebrate something else?"

"Not much going on to celebrate." Bet was still crushed that she couldn't be a bridesmaid.

"What about anniversaries? Bet and Roy, Helen and Marv—when did your weddings happen?" Peg had taken to kissing up, trying to look interested in Bet things.

"Five five." Bet held out both hands, like cupping a drink of water. "So we've missed it and it's too far forward to plan ahead."

Peg frowned. "We missed my birthday too. I'm twenty now, did I mention?"

I tried not to smirk.

Marv had been standing close to the order window, trying to get Bobby's attention for a good long while. When Peg turned to him, he shook his head. "Sorry, kid. Our wedding came on top of a funeral. Helen's father passed on the same evening. Not something we care to celebrate often."

Maybe Selena lied because Peg's face went so shadowy when Marv spoke. Maybe she lied because she likes attention, or maybe she lied out of plain old confusion. When she told us all that her birthday was coming up, we knew better: we'd celebrated her birthday before in late summer. I remember because one year Bet, Selena, and I went down to Lake Monroe and had a picnic and a raucous swim. We doused and dunked each other like kids, staying out all afternoon and into evening. I got a terrible sunburn and Selena caught cold from sitting in a wet suit after, but it was worth it for the fun we had.

Bet and I looked at each other, trying to decide what to say. Bet smiled at Peg, almost genuine. "Let's have a celebration for Selena's day." I seconded the motion. Bobby chimed in with a cake and Marv donated money for beer. He also said he'd let us use the diner after hours.

It started shaping up right away. Bet, Peg, Marv, Helen, Bobby, and I were all in on it. We made Selena promise to pretend to be surprised.

"Is there anyone from outside you want invited?" Bet winked at her. We all knew she was thinking of Selena's dates, the ones she went out with once and then discarded.

"You know there's no one but you girls." Selena winked back. "But I have one request. Would you decorate the diner? Fancy it up a little, special?"

Since I'm a sour cook, I volunteered to spruce up the place. Marv and Helen agreed to help. Bet and Bobby got food duty, and Peg said she'd make up little invitations. But to my surprise, Selena had another idea in store for Caddie.

"Marv and Helen can handle the diner on their own. Caddie, I want you to help me with a dress, since you're clever with needles and colors. You can come over and rummage through my closet with me. We'll pick out something to alter, spice up one of my old skirts."

Everyone calmed down after they found something else to celebrate, and I was awfully happy not to be getting married to some man I didn't know. I had a part to play in this new party, an important one. "Assistant to the Rustle," Peg called me, since I was in charge of Selena's sounds.

Still, there was static in the air whenever I walked into a room. My being single made everybody nervous. They couldn't understand how I stood it. What they'd cooked up to ease themselves of worry was the idea that I simply couldn't get another man. I had poor luck, some said; I didn't try hard enough, said others. All agreed it was too bad I was so shy and tucked-away at home all the time. Selena was single too, but Selena flirted, taking attention when she could get it, giving back when it tickled her to tease. She was looking and went out on dates nearly every weekend. She'd describe her Saturday nights in great detail. None of the men she met ever made it past the first date, and we never got to meet them, but no one minded that. To be single but looking like Selena was normal, different from liking living solo, which was what folks were starting to see about me. When Jared's offer came, easy and unexpected, no one could grasp why I might choose to stay in Cartwheel without a man, without a ring, not searching but staying home a lot and liking laughing with the women at work. The Marrieds couldn't figure out

how to talk to me. I felt lucky, mostly, that their teasing stayed gentle
and the word *queer* never came up. That was the protection my hair
and dresses gave me. I was just shy, folks said. Just an old maid, alone
with her cat and her doilies and her lady friends.

I wondered how much Peg knew.

When a single lady walked in and seated herself in Bet or Selena's
section, they'd pour coffee without looking at her cup and hand her a
menu while they checked the window for the weather. They didn't scrawl
smiley faces on her check or wink when she asked for hot sauce. They
didn't drawl "Cream?" when they asked after the state of her coffee.
Maybe they didn't offer cream at all, thinking, *she'll take it black.* But
Peg—Peg asked questions that weren't on the menu and talked about
things that weren't Marv's specials. She'd pour coffee, then pick up the
cup and hand it to the lady. "Here you go," she'd say. She did it to see
their eyes, whatever color. She did it to check what else they might be
hungry for. I felt sorry because I knew it might be a long while before
Peg's Jo came along, to release her from those who'd never give back
the right kind of attention.

On Saturday, the day before I was going to meet Selena at her house
to talk dress-up, Peg spent her break sitting at a corner table, cutting and
pasting things on sturdy paper. "Invitations," she told anyone who asked
without looking up from her scissors. She took it so serious, her face a
lake of concentration, that before her break was up I got curious and
had to wander over to check out her craft.

What I saw made me laugh.

Bet would get her wedding, all right.

The wording was a scrawly imitation of Jared Christiansen's calligraphy:

You are invited to be in a Ceremony for Selena.
She will be Married next Sunday at 4 p.m.
The Groom will be chosen by a Random Drawing.
Unless a piece of Furniture is chosen.
Dress is Casual and come Hungry.
Presents are Fine but You don't have to.

"What made you think of the wedding bit? I thought this was going to
be a birthday party."

"Selena suggested it. Said it would be a good joke on everyone and I
said OK."

"You're a good writer. I wish I could think up ideas and put them on paper. I can't even spell or figure out commas."

"It's nothing. I'm just closer to school than you are. When I'm your age, I won't remember anything either." She looked down at the paper. "Sorry, Caddie. That came out wrong. I didn't mean that you're old, just that—"

"I know what you meant. School stuff fades, it's true."

"Caddie? Don't tell anyone, but I'm thinking of going back. Finishing senior year. I'd be a couple years older than everyone else but I wouldn't care. I just don't know where I'd live or how I'd eat if I didn't work full time."

"Would your sister kick you out?"

"Are you kidding? If I don't pay rent on time, I sleep outside. If I don't buy groceries for me, I eat crap from people's garbage. It's true, Caddie. Caddie, don't look at me like that. I hate when you get wide-eyed. Don't tell me you never ate garbage or slept on someone's steps."

I got quiet.

"I can tell, Caddie. You have it in your face. So don't go high-and-mighty on me."

I thought of the deer in the tree's hollow shell. How some stories are ugly because someone's tried so hard to make them clean.

"I wish you'd tell me your history, Ruby. You're the only one. I wouldn't ask Bet or Selena. Or Helen or the guys. Just you."

On my way to Selena's the next afternoon, my mind was full of Peg's words. Was I wrong not to trust? But when Selena met me at the door, the question faded. I'd never been to her house before and I gasped as I stepped into the front room.

It was a tiny house, the sort common to Cartwheel. The door opened onto a narrow living room. A door on the left led to the closet-sized kitchen, a door on the right to a bedroom with a bath beyond it. The doll's house suited Selena. In it she looked grand, her sparkly jewelry and poofy skirts filling the small space with glitter and music.

But even Selena was dwarfed by her collectibles. The walls were covered with pictures—small children with big eyes smiling out of seashell frames, teddy bears with hearts on their bellies, telling the world how much Selena was and would be loved. Opposite an overstuffed plaid sofa were shelves filled with miniatures, neatly organized: stuffed animals, cloth dolls, porcelain dolls, tea cups, ceramic houses. The sofa was hidden beneath mounds of pillows, and the floor beneath three or four rugs piled each on each. The top rug was black and red to match the mural on the wall facing the entrance, a skyline, New York maybe, maybe imaginary, the buildings lit and sparkly against a blue night sky. Before I'd even put down my purse, she'd offered me a piece of candy from a glass bowl shaped like a watermelon filled with miniature choco- late bars, candy corn, rock candy, and gummy bears. I chose a piece of rock candy, a big one that dangled from its drippy string. Selena was pleased. As she set the bowl back on the wooden table next to the door, which also held a clock, keys, gloves, and a thimble collection, she explained that she'd made the rock candy herself just that morning. "It's my hobby, making candy. But don't tell Marv and Helen, or they'll have me back in the kitchen, slaving over a stove all day instead of out on the floor, where there's jokes and chatter."

I understood. I'm such a lousy cook that no one would want me to oversee recipes, but there'd been talk, when I first got hired, about having me help Bobby with routine kitchen things: chopping and dic- ing, wrapping and dishing. That idea happened a couple of times, till I nearly took off a finger grating cheese. After that I was back on the floor, where for some reason I'm not half so gawky, though still maybe worse than some.

"This is beautiful," I said, pointing to the mural but meaning every- thing. It made me embarrassed, really. When I'd had Selena over to my place, she must've thought I was just dull. My walls were bare, no knick- knacks or even rugs, just the sofa Jo and I had bought together, the table she'd made for me, and a whole bunch of cat toys. Still, much as I was amazed by Selena's house, much as it made me think I should put up a picture or two, I knew I never would. I liked white space too much. I needed things to be simple so I could think and feel, otherwise my mind got tangled on the objects it saw.

"Welcome to my cozy abode." She popped a candy corn. "Would you like something to drink? Are you sure? Then come on into the bed- room, so I can show you the dress I had in mind."

The bedroom was a lot like the living room, except that it had a bed instead of a sofa. Every inch was covered and there was another mural on the wall, this one of a castle, very complicated, with lots of towers and doors and bridges. Selena had to open the closet door very slowly, it was so heavy with pictures. There was a pastel Eiffel Tower, a photo of the White House, a charcoal drawing of a cabin surrounded by trees, and a photograph, very faded, of an Egyptian pyramid. "Where did you get these?" I asked as she rummaged among the hangers.

"Old flames." Her voice was muffled. I could barely see her body, she had so many dresses and hats and belts and shoes piled up inside the door. I wondered if she ever got lost in her own closet. It looked like the sort of place where you'd never find anything except by accident. "Here it is." She emerged holding a long snaky thing wrapped in a dry cleaning bag.

A wedding dress.

Not only did I laugh, but I threw my head back till my hair tickled my spine. "So Peg wasn't kidding when she said you told her to write invitations to a wedding. What a great idea, Selena. Bet can have her wish, and we can auction you off to the highest bidder." When my eyes were done laughing and they met Selena's expression, I knew our friendship was having a test. Her mouth was frozen in a fake smile, like a prom queen who's been stood up but still has to wave from the top of the float. The dress sagged in her arms. She held it like a body, and it was her tenderness for it, for the fabric and mossy lace and beaded trim, that let me know this wasn't a joke.

"I'm sorry, Selena. I thought—"

"Caddie." She sat down on the bed, cradling the dress like it was a baby. When she motioned me to sit beside her, I parted the sea of stuffed animals and pillows. Then I put my arm around her because her face was still cold. "I bought this dress a long time ago. I'm not ever going to have a chance to wear it."

"Selena, that's not true. You never know who might—"

"No, Caddie. Trust me, I'm not the marrying type. And I'm not sad over it either. More like Bet. I want a party, I want to wear white, I want people to tell me I look lovely. So I thought we could plan a wedding. No groom, just me in my dress and you-all the audience."

"That makes sense." It did. What she wanted from the ceremony, a groom couldn't give her. "I'll help you fit it. But first you have to try it on."

She stripped down right there in front of me. I focused on the mural. The castle was more complicated than any building had a right to be. There was a moat and towers and little V-shaped windows. It was made of dark grey stone and the door was made of wood with iron Xs on it. I liked looking at it in daylight, but couldn't imagine sleeping with its shadow hovering. "Do you sleep with the light on?"

"Not ever. I know the house by heart."

I sometimes leave the bathroom door ajar and the light on, so there's enough to see the door and window. Where the outs are. It isn't that I worry about specific things—burglars, fire—but that I never trust a room not to shift with the hours.

When the dress was on, I wondered why she'd asked me to come. It fit perfectly. The material clung to her body. There was so much of it that she made her own little community. Once she was zipped (I had to help), she could barely walk. I looked at her, astonished, because she kept turning into different things: a river, iced over; an unfinished story. I understood about wanting to dress up. I like a new dress myself, the way different skirts bell or skim and the feel of a new cuff or collar against bare skin. Maybe the heavy feeling inside me was jealousy. If Jo and I had gotten married, if we'd taken the law into our own hands, would she be waiting home for me now, practicing songs on her guitar, building the chairs she'd promised to go with the table? Would signing her name, seeing me in white, standing up in front of other Marrieds have been anchor enough for her to stay?

Jo. It was starting to be hard to be sad enough to remember her face. The feel of her hands, her warm breath on my breast, her soft hair and cold thighs—body I could remember. But her face was drifting, had been since I'd fallen for Gwen.

"I'll never marry either," I said to Selena, knowing it was a promise.

"You wanted it once, didn't you? With Jo."

"With Jo."

"But not anyone else."

"Not anymore with Jo either. If he came back, I wouldn't trust a piece of paper."

"What stays, Caddie?" I turned my back as she changed into an everyday skirt and blouse set. After, she placed the gown beside me on the bed. I helped her smooth it and slid it back into its plastic sleeve. We worked together till it lay flat, as if it had a very, very skinny body in it. When we were through, we stood up to look at it from a different angle. I didn't answer her question but asked another. "Should I tell the others it's a bride's day party?" She nodded, and then that was its name. Bride's Day. Because it wasn't a wedding, really. Not tying two things together, but setting one free.

CHAPTER TEN: PEG

■ ■
■

Have you ever been someone's girl so hard you've forgotten yourself?

I'm Peg.

Margaret Katherine Satie.

But so much of me was sometimes or all the time David's that I forgot the way to me and became his missy Kandi.

Before, there was the way air slid beneath my dress when no one was near to disturb my breathing. There was the way my bones sounded in an empty house. There was the way my feet made music for the empty furniture to dance to. When I was Peg I used to sing. The words were always in a foreign language, the language of a country that hasn't been invented.

There's a story I'll tell to someone someday. Not to my children (no children), not to a man, but maybe to a woman who understands what it means to change too fast, so that your body becomes part of something else. Something animal. The story has a title, "Vanishing Lessons." There's a girl in it without a voice.

I want to say the story starts with Roger, but I keep pushing the beginning further back. Last time I told it (to myself, of course), it started before I did. Real Mom and Daddy met in a QuikStop in Beatrice, Nebraska. Maybe it should start there, with Daddy's truck and Real Mom's red hair. Or maybe it should start with their first serious argument—in a QuikStop in Beatrice, Nebraska. Ten minutes after they met.

■■■

My first clue was my broken heart.

When I moved too fast, it had to race to keep up. My job cleaning cages at the animal shelter started wearing me down, in a different way than before. The cages were suddenly too heavy to lift and walking dogs left me out of breath. My heart mostly wanted to sleep. The littlest motion set it pounding past meaning.

That was the first clue. The second was hunger. Me, I'm a skinny one. Don't eat much. That's just how it feels to be me. But suddenly one day my belly's clawing. It doesn't go away and soon I'm scarfing strong. And growing—weird, but for a while there I had breasts. Which wouldn't have been so bad, except that they hurt, my new breasts. One day I was running to catch the bus and had to hold them with my hands to stop the bouncing because it was killing me. That was when I realized they weren't big because they'd grown but because they were swollen. Still I didn't clue in, just went on about my days. Even when I started crying and feeling bluer than ordinary, it didn't register. Only when I threw up one morning, and then the next—only then did I think what mystery all those clues might solve.

Not my body any longer.

I felt stolen from myself. I felt taken over.

But disasters give back when they take away. I didn't ask for her company. David made her come. Once she had me, gripped by the innards, I saw South in the stars. I'd found my way out of Cartwheel. Away from running. Away from Roger.

South. Where sun doesn't fight frost but rules the day.

I made David take me with.

We drove till heat melted the windows of his truck, till the trees grew scales and sparrows turned into lizards, slimy on bottom, little legs tucked underneath like pocket knives. When I saw sunburn starting on my arm just from sticking my hand out the window, I knew I'd shaken Cartwheel off at last.

Only thing was, I wanted a one-way ticket. A baby's two ways. Takes you backward in the end. So I knew as soon as we got South, which was where I wanted to be, I'd need to get rid of it. I figured I could undo the thing myself, even though David made it happen. That's why when we reached Florida, I made a practice of sitting. For a whole month, every morning and every evening, I sat and wished her gone. I wished her gone without remorse, because I didn't want her. Told her to go back where she came from, so that she could start her work again, become another girl's ticket, keep the cycle flowing.

She never listened. Stubborn, right from the start. Just kept growing, no matter how much I chided or shouted. Got to where I felt so frantic I couldn't sleep or eat properly. David didn't notice, said his job tired him out too much to talk. He picked tomatoes, oranges, sometimes straw-berries. Strawberries were the worst. He liked oranges best, but even that job wore him out. He came home and only wanted to sleep.

I worked the 1:00 p.m. to 9:00 shift at a grocery, stocking shelves. But my real job was getting rid.

I wanted my body back.

I wanted to feel emptiness again, to fill myself with thoughts and mu-sic. I hated sensing her floating inside me, holding onto the cave of my body for dear life. Eating the food I used to feed myself. I wanted noth-ing to do with her, I wanted her gone, I wanted my house back.

Got to where I started thinking things not so pretty.

Got to where I wanted her gone so bad I wanted her dead.

I felt so spacy anyway. One day when I was throwing up and dizzy, I stayed home from the grocery. David was off picking strawberries. I found myself thinking about objects and how to climb up inside myself, tear her away from where she was hiding. Tried my fingers for starters, but that did nothing, so I paced the house, looking at everything long or thin or sharp, wondering what it would take to drive her out.

Wire. A coat hanger, twisted into a triangle to hold shirts' shoulders taut. I took it from the rack and undid the coiled knot that held the shape together. Made it long, a radio antenna, then went back into the kitchen and took a beer from the refrigerator. Drank it down like water. I rarely drink anything but milk and juice so it made my head spin, in a good sort of way. Then in the bathroom I swallowed aspirin and sat down on the lid of the toilet, tucking my skirt up around my waist.

An antenna to nowhere.

Radio Peg.

Have you ever wanted something badly enough to bleed for it? I wanted my body back, wanted to feel Peg again, skin sure, feet for walking away. I reached up, found what felt to wire like a girl, and flecked her out.

When David came home, I was dead.

At least that's how he tells it. I was lying face down on the tiles, blood running down my legs like a river bucking its swollen banks. He picked me up, searched for my heart, found me still breathing. Got an ambu-lance to take me to the hospital, which was why I woke up to white everything. I thought I'd died and finagled my way to heaven. David explained it by saying I was in a coma; the doctor said it wasn't coma but shock and what comes after.

I say they're both wrong.

I was visiting my country.

When I was Peg I used to eat at the diner, 7:00 a.m., before starting my shift at Woolworth's. I always sat at the same table, in Caddie's section, because Caddie listened every day to my order—coffee, strawberry milk, and a buttered English—as if it might someday change. She never once pressured me to try anything new, but left open the possibility. And then she left me. No refills to disturb my almost sleeping slump.

Except I wasn't sleeping.

That slump signaled travel, not tired bones. My eyes weren't glazed but focused beyond the sticky tables. My ears were tuned to another station.

Radio Peg.

Dottie at Woolworth's complained on the hour about where she was. Sometimes it was Hosiery, sometimes Household, sometimes Cartwheel, or Indiana, or the Heartland of America. She never got beyond hating the Midwest, because that would mean hating the whole country, which would make her unpatriotic. So Dottie pretty much stuck her hatred to local scenery. Talked a lot about leaving for some big city: New York, Chicago, Los Angeles. Thing is, when I asked her what she'd do once she was there, she didn't have a clue. Not one. Just said she knew she'd like it better, that people would be decent there. Not like here.

But here is where we are.

I don't say that out loud.

If anyone ever asks what I'll do once I get where I want to be, I'll tell them I've been already. When I vanish, floating up to the ceiling, I visit a country where cats can speak. There's tall grass, ladybugs, and a sky so blue its clouds look orange. The ladybugs sit on my arm, sliding their wings apart like scissors. When they fly away, I wave at them, and they swoop back.

No one ever asks.

But I've been there.

And sometimes there is where I am.

When the hospital released me, my legs shook so that they had to wheel me to the truck, a blanket over my knees. David had to hold my hand as I took the stairs to our apartment. I rested on every landing, even though he kept pushing me, repeating my name, Kandi, in his impatient way. Inside, I sat stiff on a corner of the sofa while he fumbled with coffee in the kitchen. Scorched the pot—David doesn't cook—but in the mug it was warm and the steam tickled my chin till it felt pink and prickly. I turned the mug round and round in my hands while David settled into his chair across from the sofa. I waited for him to turn on the TV.

Then I realized that I was the television.

I dropped the mug.

The coffee slid down my legs. I watched David's face to see what he'd do.

"You'll have a visitor this afternoon," he said and left, taking his CAT cap with him.

I was sleeping for real that afternoon when the door shook and it was David again with Jordan Cardiff, the Baptist minister David listens to on Sundays. Jordan had a Bible with him, its red leather bookmark sticking out like a tongue. He sat in David's chair. I almost warned him not to, but David put a finger to his lips and I stayed quiet. Jordan sat as if the chair was his. He spread his legs wide, let the Bible dangle between his knees. He didn't open it but quoted some passages from memory, then made David and me join hands while he said the Our Father. David and Jordan closed their eyes. I watched the Bible's red tongue pant like a dog's.

"Your husband has a question for you."

Husband? I felt for a ring. No ring. David put a finger to his lips and I waved at him, my fingers stuck together, my hand barely moving, like a queen waving at pedestrians. David didn't wave back but sat on the far other end of the sofa, leaving one whole cushion between us. Which would've made sense if we'd had a cat to fill the space.

"I want a cat."

Jordan and David looked at each other. The whites of Jordan's eyes were yellowish.

"Your husband has a question for you." Jordan motioned to David, who leaned his face close to mine, till I could see the little hair stubs scattered across his upper lip. He took my left hand and put his fingers to my wrist, as if feeling for a pulse. Made a circle, then twelve tiny scratches with the longish nail on his pinky.

Time.

And me a ticking clock.

He asked me what I planned to do all day, now that I'd never be somebody's mother.

Really he was mad that I wouldn't be his.

Neither would Caddie. It was some other kind of loving. I watched them kiss through the window of the diner, a complicated dance. She'd take a cigarette break, sit out on the front steps and wait for him to call her over to his pickup. He never got out of his truck and she never entered. She'd stand outside the door to the driver's seat and he'd pull her head to his. If he thought no one was looking, he'd tug her up by the armpits till she went tiptoe, pressing her chest towards his mouth. I always wondered what would happen if he forgot to roll down the window. Would they notice they were touching glass instead of lips?

Somehow I knew one day it would be me instead of Caddie. Only I wouldn't stand outside but climb right in. Then I wouldn't be Peg anymore, but whoever he named me. It would be fate, and he would drive South slowly. I could watch the changing colors of the trees.

One day, while I was finishing my breakfast, I saw her walk up to the window and stop about a foot away—too far for kissing, close enough for talk. I wanted to know what it was all about, so I spooned more jelly onto my English and shimmied out the door. Then I went around the side of the diner and spied.

I couldn't hear much, but I could see everything. His face was red and his fists were bold. She turned away almost as soon as I got there, back into the diner. He opened the door, put one foot on the ground, then stopped like he was stuck. It looked uncomfortable, but he stayed like that for maybe five minutes. Not sure, because I've never owned a watch.

Time.

I had my knapsack with me. Had my wallet in it with pictures of my dead Real Mom, my alive Fake Mom, my Dad, and my dead dog Biscuit. I had last week's pay, half of it anyhow, my other pair of shoes, and cotton socks for changing into after lunch when my feet got sweaty. I had my lunch—peanut butter and apple jelly on rye bread (rye because it was on sale), a can of pop (I like it warm), and a box of raisins. I had a library book for reading while I ate and my notebook and two pens for writing deep thoughts. I had all those things, and I had half a breakfast, so when I saw that he was truly stuck I walked over to his pickup and opened the door on the passenger's side. Slid onto the vinyl cushion and finished my muffin before stretching out a hand. Then I introduced myself, very ladylike, just like Fake Mom taught me.

"Hello. I'm Peg."

He settled himself into the driver's seat and shut the door. He started the engine. He backed the truck onto the road. "Say it. Say your name."

"It's Peg."

At the stoplight he stared at me. Our gaze met like in the movies, only I couldn't look for very long because the sun was dense and hurt my eyes.

"Your name is Kandi." He put one hand on my knee, not gently but with force behind it. "Nobody in this truck named Peg. No Peg, nowhere." His thumb was pressing the outside of my knee and his pinky found a soft spot on the inside. I couldn't lift my leg. "Say it. Say there's nobody in this truck named Peg."

My mouth was in my knees, and my knees were bloody.

"Spell it." The light changed. He shifted gears. As the truck stirred into motion, he pushed on my knee till I heard a crackle. There was heat, and something round skittered in front of my eyes, like lightning but without the rain. "Spell your name."

I started with *C*.

"Not *C*. You don't spell *Kandi* with a *C*. It's a girl's name, dammit. Spell it how a girl would spell it."

I started with *K* and worked my way back. Somehow I knew it ended with *I*.

Except that wasn't how it happened.

Jordan Cardiff is a made-up name.

What happened was David wadded up his jacket like a pillow. There was a little moss, not much, and it started drizzling halfway through, or what I figured to be halfway. Not sure, because I've never owned a watch. When he was finished he fell asleep across my body. From an airplane flying low we would've looked like a crucifixion. I thought about running away, but wasn't sure how asleep he was or where he'd put my clothes. I moved a little, just to see if he'd slide off. He made a snoring sound, only angrier than snores. I moved a little more and he rolled some off my body, so I kept inching till he was all the way off. I stood up quietly to look for my clothes, but he woke up and grabbed my ankles and my legs froze.

Except that wasn't how it happened.

I didn't use a coat hanger, but a knitting needle. That's the honest truth. Other stuff I lied about, but that's real, and you can ask the doctors.

After that first time, I tried working up the nerve to ask Caddie. I thought maybe if I kept on as always, sitting in her section, ordering the same thing every morning, she'd figure out it was a sign. She'd understand that I'd gotten stuck, that I couldn't move forward from the day David touched me. I kept thinking she'd ask questions like "Shouldn't you enjoy a wide variety of foods from the four food groups?" But she never asked, just brought out coffee, strawberry milk, and a buttered English, then bustled about or went behind the counter to gossip.

Meanwhile, I had this She inside me that was David's too. I'd sit and watch Caddie, wondering whether she'd ever done what I did. Wondering if she had something growing inside her also. If that was why they'd fought.

She knew what love was.

She knew when to walk away.

But there were stones beneath the moss. But his jacket had a zipper, and the metal teeth scratched ridges along my back. But he said nothing happens if you only do it once.

One time. I told him only him. He said I was an animal. I said the grass grows thigh-high in my secret country. I said I spoke to cats and cats spoke back. He said crazy, he said slit.

But the first time wasn't David.

We were in the woods, back of our house, and it was nearly midnight and I opened my mouth to cry but he shut it with his fingers, knitting my lips together like a broken seam. I couldn't see what he did but the feel was this—first hot but no pain, then stinging, like a wasp, then prickly like when I cut myself shaving, then jagged pain like a knife. It was the jagged pain that stayed and stayed, so long I thought I'd faint, and wanted to, pain worse than any knife because it wasn't coming from outside to rip at the surface but from inside to push out, so there was no moment when the weapon was pulled back, even only to thrust forward again, and it was my brother, my own brother, the one who'd pulled the pears down when I was scared to climb, the one who'd picked up our bloody dog Biscuit when she was hit by the Johnsons' car, Roger, Rog for short, Rog who was inside me, bringing pain forward through my belly and out my back because that was what was worst of all, the way the pain (like a knife, but thudding the way only something blunt could ever do) seemed to be moving so fast and hard that I could only imagine his prick working its way through bone till it reached the other side of me, breaking my body in two, like in the movies when the bad guys have arrows gored through their heads, one end out each ear. Pain shot through me, and when he stopped at first I didn't notice because my body picked the rhythm up, like a commercial you can't stop singing in your head, so that the thud-thud-thudding he made when he rose up on his hands like push-ups and pushed further back and further stayed with me, my insides beating themselves like a drum even after he'd run back to the house again and I'd curled myself into a little ball, which was where Fake Mom found me next morning when she came out to feed Myra and Eleanor.

I said Rog.

She said get cleaned up.

She said take the day off from work. She said boys would be boys. She said Roger sometimes did these things but he was really good at heart. Not like your father, that goddamn bastard. But when she brought me toast later and juice and coffee I spit it all up just looking and couldn't eat for two whole days and then the first time I saw Roger, after I was finally up and walking, I spit up my breakfast again and Fake Mom had to scold me and tell me to stop being such a baby because boys would be boys and if I wanted to get married someday (and you do want to get married, don't you, you stupid whore) I'd have to get accustomed. But then later she took me aside in the pantry and said if I didn't bleed that month to tell her because then I was in trouble. So when I didn't bleed I cut myself on the inside of my thighs and dabbed my pants and showed her and she said I was good and I sure was because I bled anyway the next week, this time from the right parts, and he didn't do it again, only stuck his hand up my dress a few times, but once when we were alone he tried pushing me around and that time I was so tired I kicked him to stop and he bent double and I ran to the laundry and locked it from inside.

That was why I said, "Take me with you."

South. Where sun doesn't fight frost but rules the day.

What happened was, after two months and no bleeding, I decided to tell someone. Decided it would be either David or Caddie, whoever found me first. So at 7:43, two minutes before David usually pulled into the lot, I went outside and sat on the steps of the M&H. Played with my hair, braiding it down the back, tying it around itself in a poof on top, nibbling the stringy ends, then letting it all down loose and running my fingers through.

I heard the truck pull in and the diner door open at the same time.

Caddie came out on the steps and put her hands on my shoulders. Smiled, asked me how was the English. "Too much butter?"

"Not enough." David's truck pulled to a stop. I waited for him to say my new name.

But he didn't see me. He only saw Caddie. Caddie saw two people, and I saw two people, but David saw one. I never thought I'd have the chance to speak to him but Caddie made a face and went back inside before he could even wave a hand and that's when I knocked on the door of his truck. Passenger's side. His face said *you again* before I even told him I was pregnant.

Take me with you.

"Who's the father?"

I told him only him. He said I was an animal but he was scared too, I could smell it coming off his skin. He fiddled with the radio dial. Unrolled his window another quarter inch. I said take me with you South or I'll tell the town. I said take me with you, it's yours, only you, and he said I was a slut and a whore and then looked me over, breast to bone, like he was watching a movie and then said midnight, no, make it two, be there or be square. He said bring as much money as you can get from your pap's pocket. Bring your ma's diamond if you can tease it off her finger. I said will there be a wedding and he laughed. You can have a gumball ring and we'll fuck hard for your honeymoon. He said something else too but spit at the same time so I missed it.

■■■

After all that white I stopped speaking. Sometimes he said I was dead anyway so he could do whatever. Sometimes the way he touched me made me dead, only there was always another country and the tall grass and the cat to take on a woodsy journey. In that place people fall in love with anything that strikes their fancy. The cat loves me and the dead baby never comes back but stays buried like an orange rock.

She knew what love was.

She knew when to walk away.

That's the honest truth. Other stuff I lied about, but that's real, and you can ask the doctors.

He wanted me to bury it but I said what's left to bury? It's all bled out and then he hit me.

The first time was in the car. The third time was only almost, in the grocery store, but by then the cat owned me and I stopped his hand.

Stories in the tall grass. Buildings that bend and speak like mothers. Rivers that feed as many people as they want to. A map on every tree, sketched in pencil so it only tickles where bark is most sensitive. And always the cat and the ladybug. Swooping its wings to wave.

South was nothing special. South was just North, only hotter, and people who talked with extra syllables. Sometimes I dreamed about Caddie. Thought maybe if I could find her again I could ask her why. She knew how to save herself. I figured she'd understand about the other country.

Time.

Not sure, because I've never owned a watch, but I figured if I sat long enough, some bus would come and take me North again. I packed my knapsack and took some of David's money and Ma's ring and snuck down the stairs so Mrs. Ellman wouldn't see me leaving in case David came home early and asked where I was. Then I walked the whole stretch to the Greyhound station. The man behind the counter said 2:12 p.m., so I asked him if he'd tell me when the time came but he said he was too busy to be bothered waking up passengers and that there was a clock over the door. So I sat across from the clock and watched the metal hands carve air. The ticking was just loud enough to make me jumpy. The hands didn't move every minute, but saved up their energy, jerking from five to ten to fifteen like a grasshopper from blade to blade.

At 2:14 p.m. I set off backward, thinner and older than before.

To find Caddie.

She pays attention, she sees me. So good to me sometimes I think I love her. But I'm not sure. When I get too close to her, when I try to show her what I feel, I vanish. Sometimes when I come back she stares, as if I've said or done something ugly or wrong.

What I want is to kiss her. To kiss her, different from David, different from Roger. Different from the other one, the girl I have now, whose ways are what I understand. I want to kiss her, not hold her down but let her travel, not take her apart but put her pieces back together. Whole. I could give to her, I could carry, but when I get close to Caddie, I feel so much I go.

Hard to stop once you start. Soon you can't control it. It just happens. That's why I call it my country. Because even though I made it up, now it owns me.

Better vanishing than traveling with David again. He came back to Cartwheel to cart me off. First he bothered Caddie and then he came for Kandi. But I shook him off. I stood up for myself.

I bit him.

I also told him I'd been kissing girls. He freaked. Fled back to Cleveland. Still, I lock the doors at night and don't answer the ringer. I want to leave someday soon, maybe for Chicago or New York City. Leave Kandi behind, vanish somewhere he'll never find me.

Carrie says she'll go with me.

I met her on the street. We passed each other, strangers who both turned back around to check out something sweet. She dances at the Blue Tango. She's silky but tough. Sometimes angry. What we do together is ugly but at least I don't have to worry about vanishing. Like when I love someone.

Like with Caddie.

Carrie's hands tear at my thighs and the bruises feel comforting. The scratches, the little flicks of blood feel like the thing I know best how to do—holding my breath as long as possible, surviving what I think I can't. It's sexy, how she goes for my throat. It's sex, I know it is. Some people think sex is different, but this is what it is for me—to push myself past what I can endure, to come out knowing I can take anything.

Sometimes, before I go, she kisses me. The tenderness is like cream in black coffee. I stand back in my mind's eye and watch it swirl around till the taste is all one thing again.

At the diner, when they ask after the bruises, I tell them I'm clumsy. It's not a lie, so I don't mind when they believe me.

When it hurts most is when I say I'll never leave.

When it feels OK I think it might be over.

Her hair is long, black with red in it. Like Caddie's, but she dyes it so it looks bloodstained.

Her smile is wide like Caddie's, but she purses her lips tight and her eyes squinch, so she looks mad instead of happy. Mostly she's angry. She says she knows Roger and David. She says she's known them, only they had different names.

What's in a name?

■ ■ ■

Carrie doesn't have a bed. She won't sleep on one, ever. When we fuck, we use the floor. For a long time she told me it was money, that she'd sold her mattress, but when I found a decent one in a dumpster she wouldn't let me drag it out.

When we fuck she scrapes my arm till I'm bleeding and I go.

I still drink strawberry milk. I like sweet things in my mouth, to drown out the taste of blood.

Days, I sling hash and pour OJ. It's not so different from Woolworth's or home. Nights, I sleep with Carrie or my sister Deirdre and her three kids. Fake Mom tries to tug me back but I just tell her I don't believe in daughters.

Out in the tall grass there's music, a song I recognize but can't name. I don't know where it comes from but it keeps growing louder. One day I'll radio out and stay for good. There's strands of crabgrass for whistling with and warm earth to keep my toes company. I'll stay and wait for the song to start from the beginning. I'll memorize the words and sing it to her: the one I was before, shriveled now, the one I feed, keeping just enough alive to remember her by.

I haven't told Carrie.

She'd want to touch her too, and then what would be left that's only mine?

When I serve customers, I lie. I tell them they're whole. Poor fools. They have no idea.

CHAPTER ELEVEN: CADDIE
■ ■
■

The excitement built up all week, till even the customers started noticing how goofy we were. "What's the private joke, girls?" Jim O'Donnell asked when he caught me and Peg giggling behind the register. We'd bought a copy of *Bride* magazine and were comparing dresses. "Planning for the big day?"

Peg poked me and pointed to a sexy one, a curvy girl with curly hair, her dress all slit and coiled and fancy. "Pretty," she said, and I burst out laughing.

"That's right," I said to Jim once I had a handle on my laughter. "A friend of ours is getting married just this Sunday."

"Big day in a girl's life." He handed me a five. "That's how different men and women are anyhow. Worst thing a man can imagine, some girl getting hungry for a diamond ring." I counted change into his open palm. As he left, he tipped his Hoosiers cap at Peg. "You be sure not to let Caddie wrestle you down over that bouquet. I know how you girls get. Scratching like cats to have your run down the aisle."

Peg and I watched Jim shut the diner door. Rule was, we had to wait for the bell to stop jingling before we set in. When its high note went still, our mouths flew like sparrows.

"Wanna scratch?" Peg said, holding out her hand.

I made my best meow.

She didn't move her hand.

I lifted it to my lips. I kissed it.

"Flowers." She was smiling. "I mean, we forgot the bouquet."

When Sunday rolled around, we gathered in the diner an hour before Selena was set to arrive, impressing each other mightily with our Bride's Day talents.

"See what a wedding we put on? You should've accepted Jared's proposal." Bet grinned. She seemed sarcastic at first, till I clued in that she was simply hopeful.

"If I ever need help planning a ceremony, I'll ask you first."

"I'd do the cake for free, honeypie." Bobby tugged on my sleeve. "Nice and fancy, with a little lady and gentleman up top. Pink and blue flowers all down the sides."

"I'd make the bouquet," Peg smiled, all fake innocence. "But you'd have to tell me what kinds of flowers to use, Caddie. Black-eyed Susans? Pansies?" I stepped on her toes—gently, but she stopped after that.

"What kind of cake did you do for Selena?" Changing the subject seemed like a good idea. Bobby ducked into the kitchen and came out carrying a big white cake box on a tray. It shifted the dimensions of the room, it was that huge. He told us he'd made the box special, out of two regular boxes. "Like a double-wide."

Marv scratched his jaw. "D'ja ever hear tell of the Trojan Horse?"

"Sounds obscene." Bet wrinkled her nose.

"Not at all. Something I learned in school. A group of soldiers built a big wooden horse and gave it to some other soldiers like a present. Only they hid themselves inside, so once the horse got behind the walls of the city, they all jumped out and beat the pants off their enemies."

"What's hiding inside your cake, Bobby?" Bet looked puzzled.

"I don't remember learning that in school," Helen said, sort of to herself.

"Mrs. Covach. Sixth grade."

"Did you two go to the same elementary?" I thought they'd grown up in separate towns, but it'd been so long since they'd told their coming-together story, maybe I'd got the details vague.

Helen walked behind the counter, rummaged for a box of tissues, and handed one to Marv. "Blow, honey. You're stuffed up. Rest your throat. Don't talk."

"I still want to know what's inside the cake." Bet looked sour when she pouted. Her eyes had yellow in them, which made her face resemble a lemon.

Bobby grinned. "It's the outside that matters. And the taste. The taste is special."

"Chocolate." Peg and I together, hopeful.

"Not so easy."

"Vanilla."

"Not so plain. Think Selena. What would suit her?"

That was a hard one; you had to hand it to Bobby. We all guessed at once. "Pudding!" "Lime." "Carrot." "Mint?" "Not banana, I hope." "Apple?" "Coffee!"

Bobby's eyes were big with laughter. "Nope. Keep trying."

Peg finally got it. "Something noisy. Something that crunches, but has lots of smooth layers too. Peanut butter?"

"A+ for Peg. You got the flavor and the thought."

Peanut butter cake. Crunchy and silky, both. We couldn't wait for Selena to arrive and do her twirly steps and sing or whatever. That made it feel like a real wedding for sure, wanting the thing to be through so we could finally eat.

Still, none of us were quite ready for the lady who slid through the door. One minute we were all laughing and begging Bobby to take the cake out of the box. The next minute our mouths were open, goofy-looking because she'd so surprised us—a body we never quite knew she had, all wrapped up like a present, and who was going to open it after, we each wondered?

I know I did.

It's hard to see a woman—any woman, not just the few who mimic models—and not flat-out stare. What is it makes this true? I've never understood. It's just a need to look again.

I was seeing Selena in white, so fancy. But I was remembering Jo.

She had a mole on her right shoulder. I named it after a planet.

The first time we touched was when I understood my own body. It was like she gave it to me, who I was.

Selena reminded me just then. For all her frilly poof, she had a look that told us she was herself unto herself. It was tough, suited to a bride without a groom.

Peg handed Selena the bouquet. It was different. Peg and I had searched half the stores in Cartwheel.

Glass flowers.

Something a bride would never throw.

Selena ran her fingers along the stems. "No thorns."

I put the music on and helped her ready her veil. We lined the aisle, giving her our full attention like a gift. But she surprised us: she wouldn't march. Instead she sat down beside me on a stool.

"Count down," she said. "One, two, three—" She pushed against the counter and set her stool spinning. We all watched her twirl and listened—taffeta swooshed, lace crinkled, silk sighed. She spun for a very long while, playing her dress like an instrument. I almost expected her to blast off and burst through the ceiling like a rocket. When she wound down and finally stopped, she was flushed, breathing a little heavily.

"Let's eat," she said.

That was the end of the ceremony and the start of the party.

Bobby tugged off the cake box and we gasped at the shape, a minia-ture version of the M&H, all the doors and windows in the right place. The whole cake was frosted white with tiny round silver candies dotted across to give the sugar a silvery gleam. On top were silver candles.

Selena grinned to burst her dress. "It's perfect," touching the tiny door. "It looks just right."

Someone snapped a photo. When the diner was new again, the photo reappeared, blown up big behind the counter—Selena bent over the cake, glowing, her face framed by the stiff white neckline of the fussy dress. It was a good shot, but couldn't do justice to what happened when her hot breath ruffled the cake. We were all startled by the strength of the rush, like someone whose lungs had something to say.

Bobby had bought trick candles, the kind to flicker but never die. "She'll have to douse them with water to stop the fire," he chuckled when he told us. We'd all laughed too, imagining Selena sputtering over tiny flames.

The candles flickered, all right. They shone bright gold before her breath hit, then, basking, broke into an orange the shade of Peg's hair. The colors changed as the flames twisted, ebbed, and went out.

And stayed out.

Selena beamed. "That means my wish came true."

"I don't get it," Bobby said later, reading the box again. "I got cheated. They're supposed to stay lit, no matter how hard you blow."

"Selena has a way with objects," Peg said. "The candles would work on me or Caddie, so try again when our day comes." Peg pinched my waist as she said "our day."

After we'd feasted on cake, there was singing. Bet took over Gwen's place and made us sit very still while she did "Evergreen," missing some of the high notes but getting the quiver in her voice just right. "I've been practicing to use it at a wedding," she confided. "Roy said use it or lose it, so I decided I'd share."

"That was fab, Bet." Peg had one hand on the radio dial. "Now can I put on some dancing sounds?"

Through the window of booth five, which was bare because Lolita McCabe's son Jeeter had splattered strawberry ice cream all along the blinds, I could see a night sky that looked to be having its own celebra-tion. Maybe the full moon was what got us swaying, all unexpected, to the ballad Peg switched on. For once, we could understand the lyrics to one of Peg's choices. I said so to Bobby, and he smiled, offering me his arm. "Dance?"

Marv and Helen were already up. Helen's arms were open and then Marv was gone. Bobby and I didn't fold into each other; instead we rested our arms lightly on each other's shoulders, giggling like teenagers. "Remember that bunch of high school kids showed up here the morning after prom?"

"All jumping up every five minutes to call their parents." They'd surprised us by beating us to the stoop of the diner. From a distance they looked like a big quilt, hung over the front door to dry. Up close, texture was what came to matter—the girls in cheap nubby lace and frothy polyester, the boys in starchy stand-up shirts, their daddy's shoes stinging their bulky boy feet. They joshed with us, and none of us were so far away from those years that we couldn't enter into their giddiness.

One of the boys, the shyest-seeming, had a big pink lipstick blotch on his cheek. His girl clung to his arm and he ruffled her feathery hair, but when I took their orders, his eyes stayed focused on mine for too long, and I sensed he was like me.

After that, the scratchy sound of tulle from their corner just sounded sad, barbed wire.

"Did you go to the prom, Caddie?" Bobby tilted his head to meet my eyes.

"Junior. I didn't finish school."

"That's right, I knew that. I went by myself and stayed in the corner with the punch and cookies. Best date I ever had."

The song was winding down. The last "ohhh baby" and "love" broke through the guitar. Then the DJ bopped in with tomorrow's weather. After that it was a fast one, raucous the way Peg liked. "It's the Bloody Marys!" she shouted, grabbing my sleeve. "Caddie, it's my turn. Dance with me while Bobby fixes the ice cream."

Do other people ever realize that the planet they're on is round, rolling like a ball in the middle of billions of miles of blackness? Jo and I sometimes used to lie on our backs in the middle of Boyles Field after her Sunday softball practice and watch the sky. She'd remind me that it wasn't sky moving, but us. The dizziness would start deep down, and sometimes a hunger for her that was about looking over the edge, knowing life drops off like any cliff. We'd lie so for an hour, maybe more. As the park darkened, we'd slide closer together.

I think I knew that she was planning to leave.

Dancing with Peg wasn't so far from sky gazing at Boyles Field. We weren't even touching because the song was fast, but Peg made not touching about how close we could come. Our arms sometimes brushed, and my hair rode her shoulder for a second. Bobby was back in the kitchen, getting busy with the sweet stuff, Marv and Helen were talking very earnestly with Bet about the cookies and pies Bet had offered to bake. "Too bad we don't have an audience," Peg grinned, but I was glad. I felt silly throwing my arms up in the air, waving them around like I was inspecting the ceiling. I felt even sillier shaking my hips, feeling my breasts bounce, the whole weight of me awakening into motion. I felt silly all right, but secretly I liked it—the wildness of moving parts I usually held still. There was a bump and grind to Peg when she shimmied. I let myself imitate her and brush past her the way she brushed past me when she turned in a circle.

The song went on and on. Then another. No one else was paying attention. We might've been alone in my apartment, it had that much privacy to it. I shouldn't have felt such surprise when Peg touched my shoulder mid-wiggle and whispered, "Caddie, I like you."

"What's the name of this band?"

"Did you hear what I said?"

I took advantage of a guitar solo to jitter around her.

"Caddie, do you want me to repeat what I said a little louder?"

I stopped dancing.

"It was really a question. Do you or don't you? I need to know."

It was nine, my favorite time of night because the dense blue-black of the sky was my best-ever color. It looked alive, the sky. I understood why my brother fell in love with it and I understood why he made her female.

"Caddie?"

I looked at Peg's face and felt my stomach drop. Her eyes and mouth were pain, not Pegatha. I hadn't realized till then that she was curdling inside over me. For a moment I'm ashamed of, it gave me a flicker of power. Then that energy drained away and I felt sadness fill the hole. Putting one hand on her shoulder after looking around to make sure the others were still occupied, I whispered, "Peglet. You're very young."

"I'm not so young that I don't know who you are."

"Will you tell?"

"Caddie, I would never. But, I mean, do you want to?"

"Want and can are different things."

"Tell me about both."

"Want, yes. But can, no."

"Take some time to think it over, Ruby. I'll ask you again later."

"It would be wrong, Pegatha."

"It wouldn't feel so."

"To my head it would."

"Not your body."

"No." I looked down. "Not wrong for my body."

Peg turned and said, "Helen!"

Everything opened up then. I thought she'd tell and my world would rupture.

But Helen and Marv chimed in at once and talk turned to Sean's baby-brilliance. Then Bobby practically cantered out of the kitchen to tell us the ice cream was ready and we should come eat.

As we walked into the kitchen, I moseyed over to Peg and started to say *sorry*—or was it *someday?* But she brushed my hand off.

The kitchen was full of little cups. Not seven, or eight for Sean, but maybe twenty-five. In each cup was a tiny round of ice cream atop a lady finger with a skinny squirt of butterscotch sauce drizzled in a crescent.

It was so beautiful, a mosaic made out of taste.

"Eat up. I don't want to toss a single bite."

"I don't think I can," Helen said, holding one hand against her stomach. But somehow the cups all disappeared.

That was when we realized someone was missing.

The crescent moon shone down through the kitchen window, its sideways smile the exact shape of Bobby's butterscotch swirls. Maybe sugar made us drunk. We counted heads but it was Peg who finally got it. "Stupids! It's Selena who's missing."

Bet checked the front room while Bobby checked the stoop. Helen and Marv glanced into the office, but I thought I knew where she was. I slipped into the storeroom quietly and shut the door behind me.

It was the real ceremony. And she needed a witness.

Ten minutes later, we emerged into the kitchen.

"Honeymoon?" Bobby laughed when he saw the two of us. Selena's dress hung funny and there was dust on the hem. The lace at the neckline was stretched slightly. Her spiky white heels were grey at the tips.

"Hard dragging a hundred pounds of silk into the ladies' room." Everyone laughed, and Bobby pulled out the tub of ice cream, box of lady fingers, and can of sauce to fix fresh treats for the newlywed.

We were all hungry again and knew that once she'd eaten, together we'd finish off the tub and the box and even the can. We knew eating would turn messy and silly, that we'd dip lady fingers into the sauce and pretend they were cigars, that we'd feed each other bits and smirk at our partner's pleasure, that we'd sugar ourselves up till we were high, and still gape for more. It was to be a night when hunger was satisfied.

But first we watched Selena eat.

Why hadn't I noticed it before? When she ate, she held the cup in her left palm and her hand ate too, feeling out texture, filling her skin with the shape of the new.

I've never told anyone her secret.

For a time after Bride's Day I was tempted—not a bad thing, since temptation suits me. I wore it like the thin gold necklace Jo gave me, the one that broke prophetically two weeks before she left, on the day she gave notice at the factory. But if temptation's pretty as any gold bauble, it's twice as breakable. Mine broke when I realized how fragile Selena's heart must be.

Shunning live things.

Once I'd witnessed Selena's ten minutes in heaven, I felt more grateful for Cat than ever; that was good. But there was bad also. Now I knew I could never tell Selena my Josephine-history. If men repulsed her, and men and women together, how could I expect her to sympathize with my special hunger? Weeks passed, then months, and I let go of the opportunity. I let myself forget. It seemed necessary.

Cat consoled me.

For so long I'd thought of her as sleek; sleek she was, but slippery too. One evening we were cuddling together underneath a blanket on the sofa, me resting tired soles, Cat coiled around me, purring like a box of clocks and loving me the way I'd come to want. Then I got up to answer the teapot and catch a smoke. When I slipped back beneath the blanket, a cup of chamomile cooling on the floor at my feet, she'd slid out from under the covers and hidden somewhere. I called but didn't think much of it when she didn't answer. Cats are funny that way. They like affection on their own terms. It seemed normal that she'd vanish for a time, under the tub's gnarled legs or behind the curtains on the kitchen sill.

But she never reappeared. By the third day I was worried. She'd disappeared for a day before, enjoying the solitude of a shelf, the fertile darkness of a plant pot, the cozy confines of the space between the sofa and the wall. This was different. There were no sounds of her, subtle, no rustles or clunks that reassured me even if I couldn't trace her.

That evening after work I rested a bit, fixed a sandwich, paid some bills. I'd planned to climb into bed with a magazine and a cup of tea around eight, but when eight rolled around, I realized I was out of hose. So I set about washing my nylons and night things in the kitchen sink, making a volcano of soapy water, enjoying the warmth and slide of the slick material. I missed Cat badly, knowing how much she enjoyed chasing soap bubbles, running to catch them as they flew from my hands. When the knock came, my arms were full of soap, an iridescent baby. I carried the floating thing with me as I walked to the door.

It didn't occur to me to be afraid, though maybe it should've: eight-thirty, and the face through the peephole blurry on the landing. It was a firm voice answered my "Who is it?" At first I didn't recognize the voice, but with the name came clarity. I let Peg in.

She swiped a cookie from a plate full of Bobby's irregulars. "How come there's kitty litter but no cat?"

I explained that Cat was hiding, teasing me with her absence.

"Maybe it's a test."

"How so?"

"Maybe she wants to see if you love her enough to seek her out, no matter where she is."

"I try and try." Choking up.

Peg whistled, goofy. I wished she'd stop and be serious. "I just had a question that was too deep for the phone and couldn't wait till morning. Am I interrupting anything?"

"Ask your question, Peg."

"I can't yet. It's going to take me a little while." We both paced around. I showed her some things and she gossiped about diner regulars. All the while she was already asking her question with her body and I was saying *yes, yes, yes* with mine. Why then was I surprised when I sat on the floor, back resting against the sofa, a pile of photos stacked beside me, and instead of sitting down she straddled me, her face wicked? Peg was different from Jo. I hate to say it, but at first she was better, not because she was young but because she wasn't trying to still me with every stroke. She used her hands to open me, not smooth me over. Her tongue didn't choose its syllables carefully, but flickered, fire, as if it had no choice but to burn. When a body rubs against your body, it can't move backward or the tiny scales on your skin will chafe. Peg moved forward, hard too, as if the only way she could be sure of anything was to take my body with her. I'd never been somebody's beacon. As darkness came down, I saw my own light projected in front of us, a beam to guide us home.

In that same light I watched her erase things I'd thought I could never forget from the surface of my skin.

I want to say I did the same for her. But it wasn't possible, that was what should've clued me in. She nibbled my earlobe and the harshest words Jo ever spoke vanished. She licked my shoulders and Gwen's flowery dresses faded, replaced by stars I could bear to see. But when I stroked Peg's back with silky nails, nothing happened to the story someone had written there. It stayed and stayed, indelible.

Sometimes something happens between two people that makes you doubt what's real and what's just dreams. When she stood over me, all brave, and I looked up at her face like the first human looking up at the sun, it should've been something else. We should've become part of each other's bodies. She showed me where the wire went in, but when I bent to kiss the raised pink skin, to heal her scars as best I could, she brushed me away and started rubbing salt.

On her wounds. On mine.

Maybe what she really wanted was for me to write my name inside her body, so that if ever she got lost or stolen, I could prove I'd known her with that fierce tattoo. But if she asked a question, I didn't hear it. She was suddenly gone, some ghost filling out her flesh, lending strength. It happened all of a sudden, and yet, looking back, there were signals first. I missed them because I wasn't expecting any of it—not sex with Peg and not Peg's idea of sex. When she pressed my arms back on the couch with one hand it was coy at first; at first I laughed. Jo and I used to play that game. But when I pressed forward, she pressed down harder, till where I was was where I had to be.

My back buckled. I tried not to think about this creature, Pegnolonger, pinning me down. I could only watch her other hand fumble for something, as if what she'd lost, what someone had stolen, might be hidden beneath my skirt.

I can't swim. David tried to teach me once, on a picnic out at Lake Monroe. He made me walk onto the dock with him "to get a better view of the boats" and then pushed me off. Being with Peg was like that day—one minute admiring the view, the next going under, thrashing, water caving in on top of me in a great rush. Then somehow I shoved her off and stood, shaking out the folds of my rumpled skirt. When I'd caught my breath, I stumbled to the window. Two fingers to slit the blinds and the view was mine, all mine, my eyes focusing on the lamp across the way. Water everywhere. The lamp was far away, yet it looked as if I could touch it. I ran my finger along the window, wanting that light against my palm, wanting the scald of it to burn through bone. When I turned back around, Peg was Peg again, putting on her jelly shoes. They were yellow, breaking down at the heels.

We looked at each other.

I could've told Peg she'd gone away, could've told her how violence erupted from beneath her skin. But I couldn't speak it aloud. It was just another secret and still is. Maybe someday she'll try it again, not on me but on someone blunt. Maybe someday she'll wake up in the middle of pressing someone flat and unleash remembrance of whatever happened, but right then we just looked at each other, me not knowing what Peg knew, if she remembered anything of what had happened at all or if she was just ashamed about her shabby shoes.

"Back home, my best friend Janie and I kiss that way all the time. I just forgot you were Caddie, for a minute. It wasn't supposed to be anything."

"We're close friends, right? So you can kiss me." I was still trying to get my breath back. The words were dry in my mouth, like leaves.

She looked relieved, rubbed her eyes. "I feel sleepy."

"You sort of dozed off there after that kiss." I've always said I couldn't be a mother—a mother daily gives her soul away. Yet all that I could do, right then, was take care of Peg, however much she'd hurt me.

"I feel like I took a nap. I'm sorry. It wasn't you, though, Caddie." She giggled. Her voice sounded more her own. "It's not like kissing you put me to sleep or anything. What time does the last bus run past your stop?"

"Nine-forty-three."

"I still have time."

The stop was across the street. I could see it from my window if I craned my neck. Peg drank a glass of water while I bundled myself into a sweater, then followed her downstairs. We stood together, not talking, till the bus pulled up in a cloud of exhaust. I watched while she climbed on, but turned my back as she paid her fare. I didn't want to wave good-bye.

I warred a long time after inside myself, whether to tell Peg or not. When someone accidentally uses you to understand their own violent history, when you own what someone doesn't know about themselves, what they need to know, and knowing hurts, what do you do? "Tell her," I'd say to myself, but the time was never right, and I never did. It's something I'm not peaceful with, how I keep it hidden, her secret that's now mine as well.

I locked the door behind me with the dead bolt, sat down on the sofa, and tried to piece together what had just happened. It wasn't making any sense. I pinched my own palm every time I said to myself, "Peg held me down." I felt dirty for imagining this ugly thing true. I was making it up or it had been a joke, a joke, and I'd thought I had a sense of humor. "How dare you think of sweet Pegatha that way?" I was hitting myself, my right hand hitting my own left arm.

I wanted to cry, but tears wouldn't come. I was too angry at myself to feel release. What was confusing was that it wasn't Peg's fault. It was a ghost, whoever it was who'd held her down. Whoever he was had held me down too. The room stank of his ghost, and my body stung, little prickles.

I paced about, wishing for Cat, needing her then as I hadn't before. Needing a cigarette. I found the pack I'd hidden and took the box of matches from underneath the sink. Then I stepped out on the landing to light up, craving the feel of smoke, something tingly to wash away the razor-prickles.

But my cigarette wasn't what was meant to burn. A long fall below, nestled in grass, was my flame-colored baby. She looked so peaceful sleeping, or eyeing some slow night crawler. I almost didn't want to disturb her. But I tiptoed towards the stairs, my eagerness to hold her winning out over my pleasure in watching her easy posture.

Cat's stubborn, like me. As my feet met grass, her shaggy rest turned into a streak of fiery motion. Cat skedaddled an escape worthy of Houdini, maybe who she was in some past decade. I knew I had to chase after, but I was so tired. Angry too—where had Cat been while Peg was fumbling me? I was glad to know she was safe but wished she'd greeted me before taking her leave. Didn't I feed her crunchy bits, the expensive kind, shaped like fishies? Hadn't I bought her a bed, white material that looked like insulation but tingled her fur, a round cave of a cat hotel? I loved her, but cats never do hold to love. I'm more of a dog myself that way. I cling, I follow what I know once I find it. Cat fled, reminding me that she belonged to a different species.

I ran upstairs, flicked off my slippers, and tied my work sneakers in a clumsy hurry. Grabbing my keys, I locked the door behind me. Then it was all rush-rush: the stairs two at a time, the flight into night full of poorly lit sidewalks.

I could see her tail twitching through the occasional glow of whatever light night offered. If I'd been smarter, I would've been more cautious, held my hand out, a fat bite of salmon scenting the path. Instead the more I ran, the more she did. She'd wait till I could see the streaks of red in her coat before she fled. As we moved farther and farther away from the apartment, I worried more and more about losing sight of her and never finding her again. Her shape vanished, reappeared, vanished again. Street lamps, illuminated windows, and headlights helped a little, but it wasn't till we hit the start of Third that I felt grateful for neon for the first time ever. The clock perched over the entry to Rick's Gas glared pink and aqua: 10:13. The cars on my left had slowed to a trickle; still, I was half afraid to watch her, in case her paws wavered and she stepped towards the spinning wheels. She kept on, regal along the crick-cracks of the sidewalk she'd mistaken for a red carpet. Cat was so much like the bubble-baby I'd created earlier from suds. She was all there and then she fizzled, leaving a sweet scent behind.

Big Boy's missile-like forefinger glinted, his smile's overeager tilt demonic in the dim light. *Had I lost her,* I wondered, thinking of Cat. *Had I lost her,* I wondered, thinking of Peg. There are stories they don't teach you in high school history: a man stabbing, stealing a woman's body, the woman's soul ballooning like a cartoon character's voice. The story of his face, returning every time she kisses someone new, the story of how she passes on his ghost, its violence a virus. There should be a test to check. Go to the clinic, hold out your arm, let them prick you. Let them read your cells to see if you're infected—under the microscope, malice that swims in the blood of everyone you touch.

Peg didn't remember, not only what had happened with Mr. Everyday, but what had just happened between us. I slogged on, calling Cat's simple name, heavy with the weight of this new ghost. Beneath my skirt, my cunt still prickled. Now an ache was starting up, a rough, raw stinging, and I ran, my feet pounding pavement, hoping the jolts would quiet sensation.   ‾

I wondered how much a cat could know of a town. Maybe her past owners had lived on the other side of Cartwheel and she was trying to get back to who she was. I felt the sky like velvet on my neck and thought about soft darkness. It made me wonder how her other family had treated her. I'd taken in a stray. I could never know her history. But it had a magnetism for her, surely; surely that was why she'd fled.

Had they sewn a bed for her, its lining dark as the sky now, with catnip stars? I wished for a sure star as I stood at the crossroads. I could keep on along Third, hoping she'd followed a straight line, or I could turn left or right onto Old Station, hoping I'd guessed her path correctly. Some Knowing tugged at my sleeve and I turned. Was it only habit, my feet accustomed to turning left here on my way to work? But I thought I heard not a yowl but a purr, thought I saw not a tail but a Cheshire smile. I knew I smelled cedar, from the chips I used in her pillow to scare off fleas.

As I stumbled past the Dairy Queen, its arcade games flashing their lights in the darkened windows of the shut-down shop, it was that scent that grew stronger, tugging me towards her but also overpowering me, as if she'd grown so large that her cedar scent filled the town, her fur the only thing anyone could smell, her bright eyes' glare the only thing visible for miles, flickering, blocking out even the thick dark sky.

Her red, red eyes.

They glowed and pulsed, the cedar scent fluttering into something else. Ash. I wanted her back but the thing she'd turned into was splitting Old Station open. She'd grown giant, Cat, her eyes huge, all-seeing, blinding me. Her scent was suffocating. Her claws had turned to tiny prickles that fell from a blistering sky. Had she become something so horrible because I'd lost her? If I found her, would she be whole or singed or hollow? The closer I got to the M&H, the more Cat became something else, her supple body lit from within, and long—a glowing silver cylinder.

The diner was on fire.

CHAPTER TWELVE: HELEN
■ ■
■

How much I wanted you, down by Green River, while the vast sky frowned disapproval and someone's radio sang "sweetbird sweetheart" and up above real birds fleeing, as if it were autumn, as if summer weren't still stretched ahead. You bent— and I can see it sometimes now, when you bend to scrape grease from underneath the grill—to skip a stone across the skirt of the lake, and I could see through your thin shirt the muscles of your shoulder blades, winged, and I wanted to rub my face against your back and bite through skin till my tongue grazed ribs and I reached your heart. When you turned to face me, all aglory because you'd rippled something in a staggering circle, startling the beauty of the surface, altering something's rest, I had to suck in my stomach, tight, till I could feel it in the lips between my legs. Wanting felt like pain. I had to hold back an embrace.

Not then. That wasn't when it happened. We were still ordinary. But that was summers ago, and in another county. When our hair was different, and our names.

"Don't ever tell," you said, and I promised. I wrote the words on my wrists with a knife, "Don't tell," and the secret felt like a child between us. But then they died, and there was no one to stop us. With no one to remind us of who we were, our secret faded into the smooth surface of the everyday and we just went on, for all the world another childless, happy couple.

If I could tell anyone, it would be Caddie. She keeps her own secret, you can hear it when she breaks dishes: shhh. Pottery speaks, and when I see her readying an accident I listen in. But there's always someone laughing or burping, pushing air away with their clamor, and I always miss the story beneath the clatter, so I don't know who she really is.

When mother died, I was halfway sorry. She was a tart little mother, like summer preserves—bits of gold in a jar, sweetness and wax. When her heart finally stuttered to a stop, there were three of us gathered round, waiting for the apocalypse—a choked sigh, rapid gasps and blurtles, fluttered grasping, finally peace and the hereafter. Before she stopped breathing she made us promise to be good to one another, keep the house safe and tidy, change the sheets, bleach the laundry. *Put family first, keep family ties unbroken.*

Oh mother, we did. We did.

But not then. We went so far but no farther for the longest time, and it was like falling asleep and waking to the clock's alarm, angry at the buzz for ending something so pleasant. I grew to wanting you so badly I couldn't stay dry, couldn't leave the house for the scum between my legs and my tongue lolling in my mouth. Not then, but the night he died, you lit candles on the newel, carried me upstairs, and tossed me like laundry on their quilt. Six months after mother, he couldn't breathe any longer. The doctor said smoker's lung, but I knew it was her name caught in his chest, *Rebecca Claire,* her name the one he'd picked from a list, without seeing her face or hearing her voice or tasting anything more than those singsong syllables, *Rebecca Claire,* the name that became *wife lover mother,* a name to murmur or roar or spit, finally a name to stick in his throat like a bird bone, like the words he choked on in his deathbed, *sorry sorry,* blood-red and black as his lungs bubbled up his throat, as he reached for us, one on either side, rattling our buttons with his fingers' last curls.

The first night we were truly alone, you unrolled the curtains in their bedroom, and we slept side by side on that creaky four-poster. There was a spider inching its way along the wall. Its web was delicate, cautious. I loved you more than ever because you let it live.

It was like wanting salt on some plain dish. It was like wanting sunglasses when the heat's high. Wanting you inside me. You bent over me, hasty, and it hurt when you went in and I bit my lip to bear it but then the hurting stopped and there was just sort of nothing, like when someone puts their hand on your arm very softly. Then the surprise happened. My belly felt warm first, but also something else, low and soft, library whispers, then quicker and deeper and I recognized pleasure and the warm spread, perfect water for a bath. I gave a yelp and you looked at me, panicky. You thought I was scared, but it was you who got scared. That first time I held myself back just so I could watch you finally see, so I could watch your eyes finally find me beautiful. I laughed loud and long, something hot inside me, syrupy, and I told you, and you said my true, old name. Still I wanted you, closer, and you asked me did

I know you and breathed out, swoosh, in my face and I inhaled all that air of yours and made it mine. After that it was like candy or those chips they say you can't eat just one.

Always before boys bored me. You were the first one to feel special. It was me against a whole bunch of other girls, like the Miss Livestock contest at the September fair. Except maybe it was more like the horse judging, because I had to jump hoops and gallop faster. I never thought it'd be me who won, but it was, even with my jutting jaw and cow eyes that Mother said meant I'd never be beautiful. You wanted me. You picked me on your own, and I picked you back. We were fifteen.

Fifteen minutes in between.

I don't believe the things other people believe about love. When I fell for the first time, it was love for always. The folks around us saw we were tight, but they never imagined. They'd miss a circus if it camped on their front lawns. Still, we were cautious. We kissed the way Aunt Mattie used butter, dabs and drizzles, never slathered like church cake frosting. We were sly and we held back, back, back, till they'd died and it was time to be moving on anyway, nothing suspicious, nothing out of the ordinary for us two to leave town together at just turned twenty-one, to sell the farm and search for a settling place after the folks passed on.

We traded in the farm for a new car and a wad of crumpled cash. Tucked each other in the front seat, handed back and forth a map. The wheels spun off the Baxter's gravel for the last time. As the dust stormed around us, we kissed deep and frivolous. You said (almost a shout, over the bawdy noise wheels make when they spin out), "They'll never find us."

Truth was, there weren't many Baxters alive to look. But you were careful, and it rubbed off, and now it's permanent, caution, a cold we can't shake.

Somewhere between where we started and where we finally settled, somewhere along that ribbon of streaky highway, we tossed our names out the window like a Dear John letter, ink facing into the wind, and took new ones, christening ourselves with freedom's kisses and the wind's spittle. *Genivere and Dray Baxter* vanished, ghosts. In their place, two sweet-faced newlyweds, *Helen and Marvin Opal*. We chose that milky-white stone to remind us of snow on the farm, the way it clouded the fields, covered the river and frozen earth. While the wind was breezing past, stolen music, tickling our ribs and ears, while the car windows were bleeding wind and the radio rhyming, telephone poles speeding past and a damaged forest, while we took turns driving, we promised till death do us part and kissed on it, throaty kisses till the car swerved over the double yellow and danger thrilled us both, till we had to pull over and finish what we'd started.

Never a single soul's doubt. We held each other to our speeding hopes. It's been our holding on that's kept the diner together, made it flourish, money coming in steady even as the country skids to a halt, as presidents preen and parade, decades of dour men with greasy hands, decades of factory doors swinging shut, slowly opening only to shut again.

Entering in was so easy. They like married couples in Cartwheel. They like to see a man and a woman together in the ordinary way. They saw love in our eyes and didn't ask questions. When they opened their doors to us, they didn't check lineage—our clear white skin, green eyes, handsome features were pedigree enough.

The diner was your idea. We'd been driving four days when we hit the tornado weather Indiana is famous for, the sky gone green, trees thrashing, fear scenting the air, animals scattering across the highway in their fleeting haste, and you and I driving aimlessly, pointing to meaningless names on a map—Spencer, Elliotsville, Bedford, Nashville, Bloomington, Greenwood. We figured one of those tiny towns would take us in, but how to choose which door to knock on, how to know which narrow haven would best welcome our battered Ford, our too similar faces, our aspirations? We drove without noticing danger till it sent the car careening off the road. We slid to a halt just inches from the concrete sidewalk of a Woolworth's glassed front. The store was taped tight, closed against the weather. We huddled in front, arms wound around each other, praying to mother and father and, when they ignored our calls, to various dead or dying relatives until they took pity and the stern storm stopped.

It was an omen. "We're stopped," you said, and I understood, as always, without another word of explanation. Not that the car was dead but that the map's invisible ink had come clear under the sky's garish green, an X for Cartwheel, home of at least a dozen churches. We started walking west.

The diner squatted between a bank and a Baptist hideout on a weedy lot, its once-shiny silver cylinder draped in dust and muck, windows snarling with broken glass, innards stripped skeletal. Above the wreck

loomed a cheap roadside philosopher's motto: "DI E HERE," the sign's
N as thrillingly absent as a first-grader's tooth.

"I can cook."

We both could; it was a Baxter talent. You unrolled the pouch with
money in it. We counted, there in the receding green of the storm, and
decided what seemed proper. We slept in the car that night. When
Woolworth's opened, even before breakfast coffee, we strode in, camped
out in front of the pay phone, and made an offer to a creaky voice on the
telephone.

He was glad to have it off his hands. As the M&H Diner rose from the
rubble, as our grand scheme metamorphosed into something actual,
those ruddy-cheeked townsfolk folded around us. They wanted us. We
were young and energetic; we professed belief, wore our skin white,
and talked about the money our awkward cylinder would bring the
shuttered town. And it did. Still does. We keep a line of pretty girls, and
the factory men drag in their damaged heels. Best show in town. The
food's nothing compared to the daily drama. Twenty-one years of open.

When I dream about you, when I let myself, it's Dray I dream of, never
Marv. Not Opal, iced over. When I dream, it's not lovemaking that's
happening, but what comes first or maybe after: birth.

I swear I remember. You slid out first and I followed, not because it
wasn't warm enough where I was (the little house, rose-colored and
mother-scented), but because I couldn't stay without you. Even then I
knew that we were meant to be together.

I remember discovering that I was born a girl.

Different from you in that way, but not that way alone. Our differences leave spaces where we fit together like a puzzle. Folks say marriage is opposites coming together—stars coupling with loam—but really it erases. Pink pencil rubber. That's what we want, and how we fit in
at Cartwheel socials. The pact we made long ago still stands: *be one
together.* One birth, one name, one body. Married folks guard their simi-
larity like a ruby ring in a potato cellar, liking red best when it's close to
darkness.

"Helen," you say. The name sounds unfamiliar, even twenty-one years
later. *Gen,* I want to say, but I want even more to hold onto you, so I stay
quiet. "Helen." It's a wonder I hear you, you whisper so soft. Which
ones are ghosts—*Dray and Genivere* or *Marv and Helen?*

When Gwen birthed Sean, all four got jealous.

The one thing we could never have, the only difference between us and other married people. Much as sex brings our bodies closer, only before birth were we truly one. We can't undo the journey. A child unites mother and father forever, ceaselessly replaying their fateful coupling in its features, a living cinema. We wanted to wake up to a free show every day, a child whose every breath would remind us of the perfect togetherness no couple can really have.

In my dreams, our child was born very beautiful, but imprinted with letters like inky paper. Across its face was the letter *I*.

When Gwen gave birth to Sean, we knew for certain she'd abandon him. Up to us to take him in. We saved him. At home alone, we play games, we speak a special language. Sean is our son, blood of our bodies. We lie to him and to ourselves. We coddle him, careful never to let him want, never to let him feel desire. Every need is met before he can think to feel it. He won't want, our son, but neither will he know where he comes from.

Why should he care about beginnings?

Only the middle matters. There's no past and no future, ever. Time's waist is its best feature.

I like to think we love him the more for what we can't see in his body. There's no sex in him, since he isn't ours and never will be. Never the breathing replica of our coupling. Instead his innocence glints out at us like the blue light at the center of our opal rings, the more mysterious for its fickle flickering. Our love for him is purer because his face doesn't reflect our history. We see in him nothing but Sean and love him for who he is, himself, in isolation.

I never think of Gwen when I scratch his chin. You never think of Tim when you tickle his belly. They gave up their rights to his body and so the echoes of their faces have vanished from his, leaving only the pure essence of the boy: the clean soul of Sean's spirit.

Cartwheel's a fine town for raising children. But we promised ourselves never to stay in one place too long. Now it's up to us to cart ourselves away, to escape detection, to move on, carrying our bright boy with us like a beacon to someplace safe, someplace no one would think to look. To start up a new livelihood and raise our son as if he really were.

We were making love when I thought of fire.

You brought me there, raising my body above us, higher and higher, until my fingers brushed sky and my face found sun. The glare was dazzling. I headed for heat like a lemming to surf. The way my skin tingled when light burst across my chin and cheeks, even inside my open mouth, was like absorbing you, atom by atom, incorporating you. The light became you.

I sat bolt upright, shaking as much with discovery as pleasure. One word—fire—and you knew the plan.

Fireflies shimmer, leaving shards of lantern as they tear circles in crisp night air. I remember mother teaching us how to make our own lanterns—glass jars, though you said it was cruel to keep anything living locked up. I remember wanting to fly—our pell-mell drive west was the closest I'd ever come. I just wanted to recreate vanishing—the way we shed our names, our old identities, invisible until we chose to be seen. Cartwheel has come to feel like a glass lantern.

I set us free by setting it alight.

Flames are tongues. They gossip, and the rumors they spread come round to truth. I wanted to see red tongues describe our spitfire passion, the heat we'd found and would find again. I didn't set about it stupidly. I know something of the world, I know something of money. Maybe more than you do because you've always left it up to me, as if the green paper we need to live on is too ordinary for your hands. You left it up to me, so sixteen years ago I set out to furnish us with insurance deep and wide enough to dig a tunnel.

Finally the time came to drop down through.

I set out on foot one evening when most of Cartwheel was in bed or in front of the TV. The night reminded me of another, the same blue dusk and threat of fire. Awhile back, the Greyhound station nearly burned down when someone tossed a lit cigarette into the men's room trash. When I caught the news on the radio, I dragged you off the sofa to see it. I knew you'd love the light show as much as I did. It was a good thing too, because your eyes are keener than mine. You spotted the living creature among so many shadows, a great orange cat with golden eyes. You risked singe and smoke to snatch it by its ashy scruff. I wanted to keep it to coo at, but you said someone lonelier than we should take it in. Do you remember sneaking over to Caddie's place, climbing her stairs like a thief? You left the kit there on the mat and we watched from a spot across the way to make sure she took it in.

Disasters give back when they take away.

I carried kerosene, matches, and crumpled paper in a grocery sack so if anyone stopped me, they'd think I was carting provisions for the diner.

I carried fire starters, but also Sean. I bundled him well and jostled him on my hip. He was so new, I wanted him to learn the beauty of escape. I wanted his baby memory to hold our history. And it was Sean who saved me, saved us. His cries alerted the hobo fumbling in darkness with the diner's back lock. Whoever it was disappeared in a rustle, fear speeding their steps. Following their flight I waited for the skid of tires, a getaway sounding the all clear for my bonfire.

After that, the match.

What I hadn't expected was the beauty.

I stood, heartbroken by the sight of something larger than our dreams, more glorious than anything except your body that first time and your body this morning, wrinkles and snarled hairs. It was the one thing could ever rival those flickering newel candles. I couldn't take my eyes away. I'd have burned to death, set alight by the sparks my skirt wooed, if Sean's blanket hadn't caught, waking us both. The only moment of fear I had was flapping out that tiny spark.

We woke the next morning to the phone, not our stern alarm. For a moment I forgot what I'd done and couldn't think why the telephone was ringing. There was a moment of panic, the kind we both feel too often, of thinking, *We've been found out.*

But it was only the chief of police, calling to say our diner had burned down. I made my voice go ragged, but the second I hung up, I turned to you.

"Dray," I said. Your eyes lit. "Dray, the check is in the mail."

How we laughed then!

That's why we say it to each other instead of love, since it means the same thing. The check is in the mail. When it arrives, love, lover, we'll fly again ourselves, chance like wings, once more shedding our names as we go. We'll kiss, unrolling the windows, leaving behind the possibility of pursuit. I'll cut and dye my hair, gain enough weight to make me look new. You'll grow a beard, shave your head, buy tinted contacts and stack-heeled shoes. A new life for us both.

What's in a name?

We're lucky. The cops believe our story. They always do. We're magic that way. It's the Baxter in our blood, times two. True storytellers, good enough that we can lie big as a barn and still garner enough trust that folks will give us, say, their firstborn child.

But trust needs luck. And luck is all about timing: too many ticks to a clock and your fortune's run.

It takes heat for change to happen. Fire brought us back our passion. They'll never find us.

CHAPTER THIRTEEN: CADDIE
■ ■
■

The first big change was the decor.

Hearts.

Not pink, though, and no cupids or ribbons—Selena had too much sense for that. Knew factory boys would balk at eating in a boudoir. No, the insides were still mostly silver with a little red thrown in for good measure. The floor was red and white, a checkered pattern, but a racy red, more like a fast car than a bleeding heart. The new place was sexy, but still family-oriented, with the checkered trim, white curtains, and homey customer chatter. The booths were slick red vinyl, the table tops smooth white with curly silver squiggles dug into the laminated surface and silver chrome down the sides. The walls were chrome and white too, and the outside shone silver, much as it had before. The place gleamed, silver and white, so the hearts on the menu, the heart-shaped clock above the counter, and the heart-shaped sign that blared its neon message twenty-four, seven up above the place all stood out special.

The sign lured them in, townies and tourists alike.

The words were fashioned out of bold red neon, tucked inside a luscious valentine: "Diner, My Love." It made advertising simple. Folks came to know the heart-shaped logo meant quick, tasty dishes, mostly homestyle but with the occasional experiment thrown in. Some of the experiments flopped—Cartwheel didn't trust fancy foreign dishes like stir-fry and enchiladas—but Selena never told Bobby to tone it down.

"He's an artist. Burgers get boring after a while. I like to keep my staff happy and letting you-all show a little imagination is the best way to do it."

Imagination was the key, all right. The new diner didn't spring up instantly. When the M&H burned, the fire made the front page of *The Cartwheel Chronicle,* next to Cartwheel High's Lady Wheelies' championship win over the Martinsville Lady Mustangs. The caption focused on Marv and Helen: "Local Couple Retires After Fire Fades Future." But the story went deeper, in keeping with the diner's tradition of housing mysteries.

It was Selena's idea to rebuild. A little over a week after the diner burned down, she called an emergency M&H staff meeting at the Big Boy. Peg and I were the first to arrive.

Peg smiled when she saw me. Together we waited by the register. "Selena said it was special, what was happening."

"I'm not sure special's the word for it, Peg. Marv and Helen are leaving town and taking the insurance money to pay for Sean's education."

"So the diner's finito. Honestly, Caddie, I don't see why you're so upset."

"We'll have to get new jobs. We'll be separated and have to start over."

"But that's what work is. People come and go. You always want to hold on to things, Caddie, have you noticed?"

Maxine approached us and pulled two menus from the rack. "Hiya, girls. Sorry about the tragedy. Remember what I said to ya, Caddie. Just ask, is all." She showed us to a booth.

Peg slid across from me and scanned the menu. "They have more things here than we did at the M&H. Why don't you work here? That was what Maxine meant, wasn't it?"

"I want to work with you and Selena and Bet and Bobby." It came out a whine. "You-all are what I have."

"No, we're not." Peg unrolled her napkin and folded it on her lap. "We'll come and go too. You can't hang onto anyone except Caddie."

"That's an ugly thought, Peg. Seems to me you might want to do some thinking about what makes people family."

"Seems to me you want something you can't have." She stretched a hand across the table. "Caddie, be honest. Are you angry at me?"

Would it always be so complicated with Peg? There was a cloud over the two of us, even while we'd been working together. A cloud, as if passion had accumulated drop by drop but instead of binding us, it floated overhead waiting to douse us, cold and clammy. I'd never understood, and still don't, why it was that Jo, who I sometimes didn't even like, could hold me to her. "Not angry," I paused. "Stuck, maybe."

"Who's angry? Tell the whole story." It was Bet. She'd snuck up on us in her quiet way. Bobby followed and slipped into the booth beside me.

"Looks like we're waiting for Selena," I said. "Peg here doesn't seem much for talking about ways to keep the family together."

"I didn't say I wouldn't talk it over. I just said change is natural." She kicked me under the table and my lashes prickled, remembering how she'd stroked my calf.

Maxine brought drinks for five and three more menus. "I counted four. But I figured there'd be a fifth one coming." As she vanished, I heard a newspapery rustle. Selena's skirts were crinkling sharp, their crisp edges chafing, setting off sparks. Her smile sent sparks off from the corners too, white-hot.

"There's change afoot, all right," Bobby said, grinning like he hadn't since Bride's Day. "Looks like Selena has another scheme."

All four of us watched while Selena settled into a chair pulled up at the edge of the booth. "You're welcome to scootch beside me, hon," Bobby offered, but she pulled her skirts under her and smiled coyly.

"Can't wrinkle."

We waited for her to unfold the plan.

Instead she flipped open the menu, scanning with her pinkie. "What looks good?" After settling on pancakes with blueberry syrup, she stood up, ran both hands along the table, then knelt down underneath and began rapping on the supporting leg. When she sat again, all tousled, her eyes had a glint that reminded me of Jo's when she saw me after a long day at the factory. "I want my tables to be made of what's sturdy. Not this flimsy cardboard stuff. I want my tables to be ready, because customers are going to weigh them down with Bobby's cooking."

That was how we knew she'd decided to rebuild.

Peg knocked over her water, very Pegatha-clumsy, and Bet sniffled into a homemade hankie while Bobby and I grabbed hands and waltzed together as best two seat-bound folks can do. But the disco ball failed to materialize, and the confetti, because practical Caddie had to spoil it all by pausing to ponder. "How will we get the money?"

If you've ever seen a cake sink in an oven, its top caving in to become its center, you've seen the kind of fall that sank our faces.

Selena has a practical streak, like me, but she keeps it hidden, tucked into the lining of her petticoats. She whipped a schoolkid's notebook out of her purse, which had tiny buildings appliquéd along the sides and a lock that burped when it opened and shut, and set it down on the table. As Selena paged through the notebook, I noticed that she no longer had long nails. They were still done in a French manicure, pink enamel with white at the tips, but short. It made her seem more businesslike. I knew she was serious.

The page she opened for us to peruse was full of numbers, and I thought of the walls of Helen's closet. I tried not to look—numbers make me nervous—but Bet's got an eye for what they mean, and she scanned it for all of us.

When she'd finished, she glanced at Selena quizzically. "Sounds fine. All the calculations make sense to me. That's about what I'd estimate too. The only problem, hon, is that we don't have the lump sum to start," pointing to a huge number etched in the upper left-hand corner.

"Scoot." Selena shoved me and Bobby over, sliding into the booth beside us. "Bend your ears close. I don't want anyone else to hear." The Big Boy was mostly deserted, except for Fred Elkins and Sonia O'Donnell, who looked to be on the lam from their spouses and weren't eager to be listened to either. "I've got a secret that's made for your ears only." When Selena said secret, it didn't surprise me. There have to be secrets built into the foundation, or a building won't stand. "You probably already know that Marv and Helen had the place insured." She waited for the word's echo to die down. *Insurance* was a word that meant *magic* to us. We'd mostly never had it, mostly knew we never would. "They want the money to set up house elsewhere and to school Sean. But the other night I pressed. I said, 'If you won't rebuild, at least let us do the job.' I asked if they'd help out somehow. Helen got to thinking."

"Tell us the end of the story now," Bet chided.

"Land," Selena said, describing the scabby stretch the diner sat on, smooshed between the bank and the church, lots of lazy woods out back. "They agreed to let us have it. Said they'd sell it to all five of us to split, with the agreement we rebuild, for a dollar total. The money's just a formality, of course."

"Wait a minute." My head hurt already. "You told them we'd rebuild the diner?"

"Yup. They want the diner to keep going."

"Why don't they do it?" Peg's question was on all our lips.

"Helen says she's tired. Said, 'I'm forty-three and just started raising my first child. I can't begin the business all over again.'"

"Can they afford to give us land? Maybe they should sell it for real," Bet tore at the corners of her napkin, "for Sean's sake."

"They'll do OK. They showed me." Selena lowered her voice. "They showed me the money. It's a lot. They'll work hard, where they're going, and they already have some savings, so a donation to us won't finish them off."

I felt sad, thinking about the way I'd ignored Helen for so long, thinking how I'd never taken Marv up on his offers to confide in him. Their
hearts had been hidden from me, and it was too late now to know them.
But I wasn't sad about the diner. What I wanted was to keep on. A
family. What we were, what we might be.

"Land isn't enough." Peg's voice was heavy with scorn and impatience, but when Bobby rolled his eyes, I mouthed, "She's a child," and
his face behaved. "Where will we get the money to rebuild?"

Maxine ambled over to take our orders. "Hiya, folks. Heard about the
M&H. Mighty shame. Wish it'd been Big Boy instead. What'll it be?
Special's ham biscuits, side of Jell-O or slaw." When she'd taken our
orders, she bent over the table conspiratorially. "The night manager's
making to snatch two of you up. Help at the M&H has a rep for fast and
friendly. She'll be in at three—her name's Lydia—so you should come
back and see about hiring. You especially, Caddie." She winked at me
and I winked back.

"I wouldn't be caught dead serving at Big Boy," Bet whispered after
Maxine was out of earshot. "I've heard the kitchen is...unhygienic."

"You won't have to work here. Not here, not anywhere but my new
diner. *Our* new diner."

"So you're planning to hire all of us?" Even Peg's lashes looked
skeptical.

"That's right. Here's the plan. I'm to run the numbers end of things. To
manage, the way Helen used to, since I'm handy with calculations.
Bobby, you're cooking, no surprise there, but with Marv gone, you're in
charge of the kitchen too. Figured you could try some of those fancy
recipes you're always dreaming about. Bet, you'll take over Bobby's
kitchen spot as second in command. Caddie and Peg, you're to wait
tables, bus, and manage the register, same as always. For now it'll be
only two girls serving, because the new place will be lots smaller. But as
soon as business takes off, we'll hire a third waitress. How does that
sound to everyone?"

"You still haven't answered my question," Peg said. "How will we
find money enough to build and set up?"

Selena pointed to a set of calculations. "See here? This is the loan I've
already asked for, down at First Cartwheel. And this," pointing to another sum, "is what I'll chip in myself."

"How did you get *that?*" Peg's question was tacky, but Bet, Bobby, and
I weren't too appalled to listen in.

"Sold my house."

"No." I choked on my own surprise. "Not your house. You love your house, Selena." But she stopped me with a look, and explained very calmly that she'd been meaning to sell for a while now.

"It reminds me too much of Ma. It's time I moved on, made a fresh life for myself."

"Where will you stay?" Bet asked.

"I'm going to build a back bedroom onto the diner and move right in. No separation between work and pleasure." She leaned across the table and fondled the salt and pepper shakers. "Suits me just fine."

"Selena, it isn't fair for you to use your savings," I said. "We should all chip in too."

"You don't have money to give, Caddie. None of you do—you're barely making it now, what with no more diner paychecks."

"That's a fact. I'm living on beans and canned peaches," Bobby frowned. Peg and I nodded. Still, what Selena had said stung. We all four wanted to join. Wanted it to start equal and go on.

I thought back to the first paycheck I ever earned. What I remember is crazy, because it couldn't have happened. But it's my memory so I've kept it, along with other crazy thoughts and a few believables. What I remember of the check is that it glowed, like those silly shoelaces kids wear. After I slit the envelope, I walked over to the grocery, where I wandered around stroking soup cans and chocolate bars, feeling safe because I knew I'd eat.

I'd moved up since then. Waitressing was better than stripping, even if sometimes customers treated me the same. But the kind of money Selena was waving—I'd never have that. I'd never have a house or a car or be able to build something and hire other people on.

"Listen." Selena reached her hand across the table to touch ours, each in turn. "I've been planning all my life to have something—one thing— that I really wanted. The right thing never happened, so I stayed put, keeping Ma's house well oiled just in case. Now it's time. This is what I want. You'll have to trust me on it."

I fingered her notebook. "What if it goes under? You'll lose everything, while we've risked nothing."

"Caddie, don't you know me by now? I don't believe the things other people do about money. I don't think it grows like mold if you keep it in a jar. This is what I want. Join me or not."

There was no question that we'd all four join in.

That night my apartment was haunted. I heard Cat's whispery voice and felt her nails nip my ankles. It was as if the part of me that had loved her had broken loose, become a similar creature. There in the dark, staring up at the ceiling on my bed, I couldn't see Cat, but I could feel her golden eyes look through me and hear her purr tickle my ears. All night the sound echoed and kept on, till the apartment was full of it: a soft vibration, low and smooth, slippery as change.

After the burning night, after losing Cat and finding her, losing her again, watching my whole world go up in flames, the circumstances a crazy mystery, maybe ugly, after the long chase and the loss of the creature, I dragged myself home to find my old lover sitting calmly on the stoop, sucking a cigarette.

She blew smoke over her shoulder. All she said was "Hello." Then she stood up as I unlocked the door as if she knew I'd take her in.

Without one minute's scolding.

What was I to think of a Caddie who would?

Stroke her hair, I mean.

Take her in.

After all that time spent as Caddie Solo—all that time living with a girl I barely knew, a girl (me, Caddie) I had to learn to know slowly, the way you sneak up on a cat when it's escaped your hold—after all that time and me finally settled, mostly cozy, who was this other to come along and undo me?

I made her wait two weeks before I let on that I was hungry. When I finally gave in, she pounced. Her nails scritch-scratched my thighs, she climbed me, the scent of cream hung like a cloud as I went under and it was good, the feeling, glorious even, her motions like the part of a dream you never remember, only carry into the next day's gestures. I carried that first night with me a long while: the look on her face, the feeling of falling.

I want to say it was easy, after that.

Easy to let her split me open. But the easing into everything was full of awkward starts and stops, the way Gwen waited tables when she first began. We never talk about the things I could've done. We never talk about how she left, or where she stayed. I don't want to know who she's been, and she doesn't really want to tell me. What's unspoken, of course, is that she tested me.

I passed.

Am I sorry?

■■■

Funny to think none of us picked up on the next mystery that day at the Big Boy. No one raised their brows when Selena mentioned that Marv and Helen hadn't returned her calls. Not one of us stopped to wonder why the couple hadn't joined us. It seemed easiest to assume that they were busy or blue, absorbed in their own losses, that they walled themselves in, shutting off communication. They were gentle people—fragile—and when gentle people vanish, no one much notices. It's what gentle people do, to protect themselves from the bustle and frisk of everyday commerce, though more often it's spiritual, like Peg, the body left behind.

But when Selena called and called with questions about rebuilding, when Peg and I called and called to see about hugging good-bye, when Bet and Bobby called and called to see if they needed help with Sean, well, we began to wonder. Peg and I took it on ourselves to hightail it over, borrowing Selena's truck to reach the outskirts of town.

Selena didn't offer to come. "I don't want to know if something's happened to that trailer."

"I'm sure they're fine," I said, my voice sugary.

Selena brushed all my sweetness off. "Caddie, how can you be sure? They probably aren't. Wake up, girl. This is the real world."

That stung, but maybe I needed to hear it. "Pegatha, am I too dreamy?" We were heading past Bread Lake—so many leaves, it felt like we were swimming. "Do I make up the world or am I in it?"

"We all do it."

"Do what?"

"Make up our worlds. There isn't a real one, really."

I liked it when Peg got deep. She could do it too. "You should go to college, missy. You have so much in the brain department."

"Nah. I've seen those kids over in Bloomington, and they're not any better off for the education. They make up their worlds, same as us. They just make more money at it." We pulled onto the gravel road that led to Marv and Helen's curvy driveway. "How'd they get this spot of land, anyway? Seems like it'd be pricy."

"Too far from anything to be pricy yet. Just wait, though. The Ryans will make it a shopping mall, I bet the first pot on it." We wound around a couple curves, sun falling through the windshield like hail, then pulled up beside the oak that shaded the trailer. It was such a tree, it could've been a monument to trees. Thick and tall, with great leafy branches that turned green to orange to red to yellow to gold to mahogany to silver through the seasons. It reminded me of a tree house Pat and I had hung out in. It belonged to our neighbors, the Moons. Mr. Moon had built a woodsy room climbing-height high and we used to sit up there with Melly, singing silly kid songs about sex and poop. Pat didn't sing quite so much as me and Melly. He was already into sky and just sat staring, whispering under his breath. Melly and I used to hold hands. Now I wonder if that was a sign. But all little girls held hands back then. We brushed each other's hair and hugged and said "love" and cried when the bell rang at school and we had to do good-byes.

"It doesn't look like anybody's home."

"Maybe they're sleeping."

"At two in the afternoon?"

"That's always when I get tired."

"That's because you work long morning hours. They're not working now, this is like vacation. Why should they be tired?" Peg hopped out of the cab of the truck before I'd come to a full stop. I followed a minute later and caught up with her as she approached the door of the trailer.

"Peg, if they were here, we'd see their truck."

"Maybe Marv is watching Sean in the bedroom while Helen runs to Foodville for more diapers."

Peg knocked. And nothing happened. Then she knocked again, and then I did. Then we shouted, which was fun, actually—I'd forgotten how it felt to let go of my voice. Being with Peg always brought up what I'd forgotten. I felt happy then, just at that moment. Peg was staying Peg, no sign of vanishing. She was warm to me but not rough. The Tree of Trees shaded us from the Indiana sun and I could smell moss and see strips of Pat's sky through leafy cover. I wanted to tell her, give her a green Valentine then and there, so I stepped behind her as she peered through the front window. "Peg," touching her shoulders very lightly, "I just wanted to say—"

"Shit!" Peg jumped off the concrete blocks she'd used to raise herself window-height. "Shit, Ruby, look at that." I let my Valentine fade and stepped up to the window. Inside the narrow living room and kitchenette was nothing. All of Marv and Helen's things were peeled away. It was like looking down at a chocolate wrapper, crumpled and empty, but not remembering when you ate the candy.

It didn't take a Bloomington education to realize what had happened.

Peg rummaged through a pile of junk for a brick. "Should we break in?"

"We can't vandalize their home."

"Just one window. C'mon, Caddie," she grabbed my arm, "they could be inside. They could be hurt."

"The trailer's empty, Peg. They've left town."

She looked startled. "Is that what you think?" She set the brick down and climbed onto the blocks. "We don't know anything, except what we can see. Someone might've broken in and stolen stuff. Or maybe they've been packing and right now they're resting."

It struck me funny, how much she wanted to smooth the situation over. Usually Peg was the first to be cynical, but now we'd switched places.

But I was curious. There was a chance Peg was right. Maybe something had happened; maybe someone had broken in. Maybe they were even now trapped in the bedroom, tied up like in the movies, wishing, all desperate, for help. "You win. But no bricks. Let's find a gentler way."

It turned out to be embarrassingly easy. The window was open. One boost from me and Peg slid through. "Be careful," I said, both glad that I was too plump to slide through myself and ashamed of being glad. "Run right over to the door and unlock it so I can help you." Peg being Peg, she didn't run, but took her nosy time till I got nervous and called her name.

"Come in," she said, unlatching the door. The air inside was musty and still, suspicious of human breath.

What I saw was nothing. Not one scrap or shard of anything Marv and Helen had possessed.

We paced around, glancing every so often at the door to the bedroom, never coming close enough to touch. Finally Peg stopped and stood still. "Enough chicken. We have to look. They might be inside and need help."

"Absolutely," I said. Neither one of us moved. "Absolutely right," I said again. We stood imagining, listening to each other's breath, till a bird squawked outside and we both jumped.

"This is silly," Peg said. "We're brave girls. We're brave," and saying so, she proved it, pushing open the door with her hands, her body as far from hands as a body can be.

Why did we savor suspense? If they'd truly been wounded, the silly seconds we spent pacing and joshing would've mattered. We'd have blown our girl-cop rescue with bad timing. Maybe we wanted to insert Marv and Helen in some sitcom drama the better to remember them by, maybe to swallow the bitterness staining our throats. When Gwen abandoned Sean, it was in increments. Somehow that was easier to understand.

Sean's fearful cries had taught me something. Babies cry at strangers' faces because trust is learned, not what we're born with. I was starting to wonder about trust—why I had it, and for what sorts of people. Their bedroom held no bed, no chest of drawers. The pictures of the diner— before and after shots, and a Fourth of July employee photo for every year—were stripped from the wall, which had faded beneath, leaving phantom photo frames on peeling paper. The room was bare but, like the living room and kitchen, not specially clean. They hadn't dusted or wiped or washed, just carted stuff away.

"Looks like someone was in a hurry," Peg frowned, running a finger along the grimy door frame. After exploring the bedroom, it wasn't hard to open the bathroom or the storage closet.

Nothing but years' worth of smudges.

"You'd think they would've left a forwarding address."

"Maybe they were kidnapped," Peg suggested. It was a suggestion she made again later that day when we returned to Selena's. After listening to our story, Selena called Bet and Bobby and, at my request, Marigold and Vera. Crowded in Selena's front room, they sipped coffee, ate candies, and listened attentively as Peg and I told our tale.

It reassured me to have Marigold and Vera join in, though I knew that the other M&H-ers were puzzled by my request. All except Peg. When Marigold and Vera ambled up Selena's walk, we were sitting on the stoop and Peg grabbed my arm.

"I want that someday," she said quietly. Then I knew why I'd asked them.

Once everyone was settled inside, Peg told our tale, very dramatic, with me joining in for accuracy's sake.

"Good gravy," Bobby said when we'd finished.

Vera shook her head. "I'd started to suspect as much."

"Suspect what?" Bobby looked from Marigold to Vera. He always got them mixed up. I could tell it grated on Vera's nerves.

"It seems obvious, doesn't it? They've skipped town."

"Isn't that jumping to a pretty serious conclusion?" Selena asked.

Bet nodded. "Just because their things are gone doesn't mean they've left town. They'd tell us if they had plans to travel."

"Then why didn't they?" Vera sounded angry. "I'm telling you, I don't like it. The fire was suspicious to start with. We know they had insurance up the wazoo—"

"Vera!" Bet looked shocked. "What a thing to imply."

"But it wants consideration." Peg's words quieted all of us. I felt sadness fill my stomach, numbing the hunger of a missed lunch. Would they? Could they? What would it mean?

"Maybe they've just gone away for a few days and moved their stuff in with some friend or relation out of town. Maybe the stress broke them, and they needed to vanish for a time." Bobby's lap was full of chocolate wrappers, a miniature ocean of silver paper. As he spoke, he popped another chocolate, then twisted the wrapper till it tore in two.

We talked for hours, but the conversation didn't progress much. It seemed folks had already decided what to believe. My musing questions and speculations had no place here. Everything was black or white, yes or no, Vera or Bet, Peg or Bobby. Everyone agreed on one thing, though—we didn't want the police probing too deep into Marv and Helen's affairs. We even shook on it.

"They're good people," Vera added. "I'm not saying otherwise. Even if the worst were true, I'd still trust them with most anything."

"They're fine parents to Sean."

"Not just fine parents, Bet. They saved him. Gwen abandoned the boy. Let's call it what it was." Bobby's lips formed a serious line.

"No one's pure good through and through. Bits of bad float to the top, like these marshmallows here." Peg pointed to her cocoa. "That doesn't mean the rest isn't sweet and dark."

"Maybe they had some desperate need for it." Marigold rubbed her temples. "The money, I mean. We don't know why they did it, assuming they even did. Maybe there was a good reason, something necessary but hidden."

"They could've trusted us enough to say."

"Bobby, secrets don't usually feel easy."

It was true, what Peg said. I was glad she didn't glance at me when she said it. The conversation wound down after that, with Marigold and Vera leaving first.

"One thing's for sure." Selena passed round the candy dish for the last time. "This means we can't wait for them. We've got the deed to the land. We need to get started." She smiled and kept smiling even after Peg spilled cocoa on a pale grey pillow.

That was how I knew she meant to go through with it.

■■■

Marv and Helen stayed gone. Over a month after the fire, a letter arrived in Selena's mailbox, postmarked from a town in Wyoming we couldn't find on any map: "Gone searching for a new start. Sorry no time for good-bye. Sean teething. Hope the new place takes off. Love to all, always, M&H&S." It was food for controversy, all right. Selena shared it round at the next new diner meeting. After everyone had read it, with all of us watching, she ripped the postcard sheer in half, and passed both halves to me.

I understood and set the two halves together and ripped down the middle. Peg went next, tearing twice for good measure. Bet shredded. And Bobby flushed.

It stays a mystery, the fire. The police chief claims they're still working on it—"case active," he says, but it seems to me he mostly sips coffee and issues parking violations. So we all figure Marv and Helen are safe, wherever it is they've got to. I for one don't miss Sean, though Bobby and Bet positively pined away for a month or two. I miss Marv and Helen, of course, but once they left town, our memories melted. It became hard to remember which one of them had said or done any particular thing BF (Before the Fire). We tried sending a Christmas card addressed to "Marv and Helen Opal, c/o Post Office, Sibling, WY," but it came back "Return to Sender Address Unknown," with that funny inked-in picture of a finger. Bobby turned detective then and tried tracking them down, calling city directories and so forth. But they'd clear disappeared and have stayed so since. It was sad, but we got over it.

"Nothing to be done. They know where we are," as Selena put it.

We all have it better in the new place. The customers are mostly the same, with some newbies thrown in. We still specialize in good cheap food fast, wide-open smiles on the waitresses, stained shirts and torn denims on most customers, and gossip floating table to table. We each have the same number of tables, pretty much. Tips and salary come out mostly the same too. It was easy, once business blossomed, to hire another girl. Selena thought of Trini, whose husband Jesús visited the diner on his rare days off.

"He's an old friend of my mother's," she explained. "They farmed for the same boss."

Bet got funny at first, I'm sad to say—poking her nose, acting snobby. But Selena set her right by pointing out that if she didn't want to work for a Mexican boss, she could always bus tables at Big Boy.

Bet shut up after that.

Trini complements Peg and me perfectly. With Bet shifted to cooking duty and Selena managing money, we needed someone reliable and calm to balance out Peg's storms and my moodiness. Trini's steady, like Bet but so much less boring. Now that her shyness is wearing off, she lets her artist self shine through. It's Trini who draws the cards we slip into laminated covers to advertise daily specials. It's Trini who rearranges the dessert case behind the counter so that color and light spark appetites. And it's Trini who made our new name tags—big bright pins, with our names coiled in fancy embroidery on felt.

At first Bet steamed about Trini's frail English, but Trini learned so much quicker than anyone could've asked her that soon Bet had to cool down about that too. Trini's even got the rest of us speaking bits of Spanish. At first she wouldn't. "I need to practice English," she said, but Selena persuaded her.

"I need to practice Spanish," Selena responded, gesturing toward the small group of men in a back booth who always smiled when Trini spoke their language. Bet and I felt a little stupid. We'd never realized how many of our customers spoke Spanish. Some of the shy quarry workers and farm help who'd sat silent over breakfast years running now perk up when Trini takes their orders.

I've always craved to learn another language. It seems learning isn't so much about finding new ways of saying old things, but discovering how many new things there are to say. When Trini learned the full story of Marv and Helen's disappearance, she laughed. *"No se vaya, que ya viene la marimba,"* she said. "Your Marv and Helen, they left in such haste, now they must miss the music."

The new place suits all of us. Selena of the noisy fashions lets us wear any old thing we want, so long as we tie bright red aprons across it. I like the freedom, and so do Peg and Trini. Bet grumbled at first about what's the world coming to, but cheered when she realized she could wear the blue windsuit Roy bought her for Christmas. "I sure don't do aerobic exercises in it," she said. We all laughed at the thought of Bet shaking her booty. Trini mostly wears dresses. I do too, of course, because girl things have always suited me, and because I only own one pair of pants. Peg wears jeans, though, so there's more variety. The atmosphere's livelier too. We take turns choosing music. I tune strictly to the country station, Bet listens to oldies, Bobby always chooses top forty, and Trini, public radio, but Peg sometimes has us listen to frisky stuff—punk, she calls it.

Bet grumbles, but I like the pulsations.

"Dance with me, Ruby?" Peg sometimes offers, and I sometimes take her up. The whole diner shakes when it's Peg's turn to pick music. The lyrics are so nonsensical they give you hope. Anyone could write a song like that, even me, and so I started thinking about it and now I make up songs in my spare time, to go with the guitar music playing again when I get home.

Once in a while the new place gets raucous. When Tiffany shows up for her fries and ketchup, Bobby sometimes takes a break from sizzle and spit to twirl her around the narrow space between the counter stools and booths. They whirl, expert as fancy TV ice skaters, showing off the moves they've learned at Arthur Murray.

"Bobby, you'll make a fine husband someday," Bet always says, and Bobby blushes clear up to the edge of that day's bandanna. It's specially nice to see Bobby so happy. I'd always thought of Bobby as Marv's secondhand man, but he was so much more. He made greasy diner cooking into an art and still does. Sometimes I sneak in back on break just to watch him go to it. No more dull days of chopping carrots hours on end, no more endless rounds of flipping burgers with only the fry basket to break boredom. He moves like one of those NBA fancies, all big and bulky but still graceful, flitting from one end of the kitchen to the other, sometimes tossing Bet an apple, a potato, or a jar of vanilla, sage, or basil. Bobby is always high on the scent of spices. He'll bend over his stew and breathe deep. Once I caught him dripping tears. He wiped them away when he saw me, but there was no shame in it. "It's my special ingredient," he said. "Salt. The best-tasting kind there is."

It's his religion, cooking. We have to drag him out of the diner, day's end. Mornings, he's at it again—filling puff pastries with iced squiggles, squirting molasses into biscuit batter, grating cheese till the strands hang fine as hair onto popovers lighter than the paper towels we use to sop up spills. Usually the fanciest of the pastries are gone by the time we arrive—Bobby's belly grows with his glee. His fat self shakes and it's beautiful to see all that body so happy, his skin so ripe with things he's made himself. It's true, I suppose, what Bet said, about him making a good husband. But he's so busy with food, it doesn't seem likely to happen. Still, once in a while one of the girls from The Nail Wheel stops by, her hands a cinema, each nail decorated with a tiny sticker—stars, flowers, flags. She sits close to the order window, close enough to watch Bobby working. She watches, the diva, and sighs, and says (just loud enough she hopes he'll hear), "I like a man with graceful hands."

And it's Bobby's food (Bet isn't half as creative, although her plain tastes are favored by those who can't fathom fancy) that draws crowds. The new place is always brimming, clear to the top, like our customers' coffee. More and more regulars are serious eaters. Bobby's way with dough, spices, and fancy fillings makes it so.

But it's still a cozy, basic place to come to. None of us want to see the diner taken over by east siders who'd snub their noses at the factory boys' dirty fingernails, who'd call coveralls "quaint" and laugh at homey conversations. I've heard tales. Once the community center was for working folks. Now it's full of stay-at-home wives whose husbands work white-collar jobs in Indy, ladies who do aerobics so they can drink cocktails at night in sequined dresses.

We don't want them taking over. We want our good food to go to plain people and our hospitality to stay on this side of the tracks. So Selena keeps things playful, tickling customers' throats with laughter, leaving their bellies jelly-shaky, hungry after. Once in a while she'll decorate some part of the diner—the stools, say, or the coffeemaker— with surprising tidbits to lure the eye. Once we all showed up to work only to find that the counter had cardboard hand- and footprints pasted up and down the sides of it.

"Why?" Peg asked once, but Selena only smiled. It keeps us on guard, never knowing what to expect. The diner feels alive, the very air tingly. Best of all, it keeps the east siders mostly away.

"Too weird for 'em," Bobby suggested.

"Tacky," Peg tried.

I think it's something else—too much family in us. They don't want to feel part of our community, only stand back and observe. It's one thing to drop by the DQ and buy a shake. They can gawk in the parking lot at preteens in pickups and toothless old men sucking cones and sharing Skoal. But it's another thing altogether to be part of the fun and games, to have folks mosey over to your table, poke your food with their fingers, and ask after your kids' middle names.

So it stays casual, the diner. It stays nosy. Folks still come to gossip and spat and show off. They just eat better while they're here. It stays simple, the way it's always been.

Some things feel so similar that if I close my eyes, I might move back in time. I try to hold tight to one calendar page, saying the prettiest names over and over to stop time: *Tuesday. January.* But it's all still a carousel. Bit by bit the very air is changing temperature. It's heating up, and sometimes now you can spot folks fanning themselves with folded newspapers or napkins. Even crisp dollar bills.

It's not just the temperature. It's Selena of the shifting skirts, Selena of the house museum, Selena boss lady, Selena who lives in a studio out back, Selena the brain behind Diner, My Love's great takeover—Selena's changing. It shows in the smallest gestures—the flick of a wrist, the flex of a palm. When she works the register or does the day's tallies, she piles the money up in stacks on a special table in the kitchen, far away from the flickering lights of the grill.

It's in the way she touches each and every bill.

Rubbing their surfaces with the side of her palm, flattening creases, folding crimps backward so they'll lie flat. Keeping her fingers busy with how numbers feel. I walked in on her once in the office, caught her pressing a specially tattered bill to her face, letting it drift across one cheek, inhaling, pressing her tongue to taste the felty surface of a fifty, her nostrils flaring slightly, her lips widening, a slow flush starting at the base of her throat.

No one else seems to notice. I tried talking to Bet and Bobby about it one afternoon when Selena was busy out back, conferring with the dairy man whose shipments were always late. "Doesn't it seem perverse to you?"

Bet frowned. "Caddie, everyone loves money."

"Hell, if you put a fifty in my palm, I'd kiss it too." Bobby laughed, but it didn't strike me funny. Only Peg understands why it bothers me.

Peg understands a lot of things.

There's still something between us. After all that ugliness, I still feel Peg's gravity. We joke around while we work. To all the world we're friends as ever. Sometimes our hands meet, not quite by accident. Then the spark's so fierce I worry customers can see it. Not that I'd be stupid enough to let her go for my skirt again, to risk more violation and vanishing. But we take walks, Sundays when we're off, when I'm sick to death of the TV's droning voices, accents of blood and money. Sundays it's trees I want, trees no one owns in particular, trees with their own lives, independent of us, that keep on growing whether our hearts break or mend.

I'd told Peg all about Doe's funeral, but she'd never seen the site. One Sunday we decided to pay our respects. At three o'clock we met and just set out—without even a hello—into the woods, as if creeping up on the dead girl might bring her back. It wasn't morbid or anything, it was just wanting to touch the earth to make sure it still lay smooth and flat, that no animal had torn through to ruin what we'd rested. Peg wore shorts. I had on a short skirt without stockings. We sat on the mossy stretch to the left of the grave without speaking. Somehow Peg got the idea of reciting all our people's names—the dead loves, the villains, the never forgotten.

I was smoking. I keep trying to quit but can't. It's like having a watch around your wrist and taking it off—you know you've forgotten something and can't rest till you remember. I exhaled wide. Maybe this is vain, but a tiny part of me wanted to think I looked like a movie star, there in my short skirt with a pretty girl beside me, sighing for love, exhaling a cloud of ash that covered us with a rancid scent, the scent of love gone wrong. "Jo's the only one who matters."

Peg went next. While she spoke, I looked at the hair on her legs. She didn't shave, and her legs were covered with fine, almost invisible red-gold hairs. His name was all she said, and all she needed to say. I noticed new things. How the freckles across the bridge of her nose looked blended together but were really always separate stars. How her eyelashes were the same color as the hairs on her legs. How the scar beside her ear traveled just a little, onto her cheek. How it never seemed to start or stop but faded into her skin.

"Look," Peg said, pointing to a tangle at the base of a tree. "A bird's nest." She picked it up and set it in my lap.

Nowadays she's busy elsewhere, Peg. I see her around town, in Foodville or Woolworth's, shopping with her roomie, one of the dancers from the Blue Tango. Carrie, her name is, and she has long, reddish-black hair and Irish eyes and looks a bit like me. When Peg first introduced us, I held out my hand and Carrie squeezed too hard. It hurt, how she gripped me. My hand stung after, and Carrie's face was smirky, as if the hurting was how she liked to say hello.

It's what Peg's used to. All she knows.

When I come home from walking, with Peg or solo, someone's always waiting. She calls to me, "Caddie Sue," and I come, because she's finally realized we have the same middle name.

Folks in Cartwheel all have their own versions of why Jo returned, why she'd left in the first place, where she'd been, and why I opened my door. Some say another woman for Jo, some say it must've been another man for me. Some say marriage or money, religion or children. Some say Jo was bored, had and has a roving eye. Whatever they think, they get no food for gossip from us. We agreed on that, promised to stay tight-lipped so we wouldn't slip, spilling secrets deeper than the ones they thought we had.

We could be pretty interesting if we wanted to be.

I know I could.

The new diner's not sweet and neither are we.

It went up in four months, our great silver sweetie. We made sure it opened on Valentine's Day, and served an all-red menu—for love, but also for lust, jealousy, betrayal.

Jo worked on the building the whole time.

She likes climbing—a natural. Can claw her way to the top of any skeleton and balance perfectly, even when the whole structure's shaky. Says climbing reminds her of something—climbing and working with wood. When the diner was done, she got hired on for another building, a new apartment complex on the margins of town. She worked there till I heard from Bet that the factory was hiring again. Jo went back so she could hang out with Roy and her old buds.

I can tell she's glad to be back on the line. Construction depressed her. "The big dogs are taking over," she'd say, disgusted by the rich folks buying up the land all around Cartwheel—farms and forests and restless, gritty fields—to build condos, complete with fake ponds and miniature bridges. It's sad to see, so we don't drive to the town outskirts for R&R anymore.

We still drive to Bloomington every so often. The college boys murmur when we sit behind them in the pizza parlor: "White trash," and their girls giggle, shiny teeth flashing, long pink nails greaseless, flat bellies taut. We just eat, ignoring them, laughing inside because their taunts could be much worse. Then we drive out to the lake, where we first showed each other pieces of who we might become.

Sometimes when she snores, my pillow shivers. I wake up and go into the kitchen to remember how I spent my evenings when it was Cat and not Jo, when I was Caddie Solo. Some nights after we touch each other, I stay awake, pinching myself, stretching my eyelids away from sleep, so I can remember how I breathe, differently from the way she does: deeper, slower.

My heart is stronger.

I think I know.

I think I comprehend the mystery, and so we go on, craving and hiding, and I go on wondering if honesty comes with loving, slow, or has to come of a sudden, a break you decide on in advance. I go on wondering about trust. And the land around Cartwheel keeps getting bought out, our part of town getting smaller and smaller, closing in on itself, crowding together, moving in from farms on the outskirts to rickety apartments like mine. Working the factory line six to two, two to ten, or ten to six. Stopping by the diner for a bite, dog-tired, after. Smiling when someone sure-handed pours the coffee, easy, into a white ceramic cup with a heart-shaped handle.

I work breakfast still, into early afternoon. Lunches are different. That's the thing I added to the new place, my own creation. Every weekday at noon, I take Selena's truck and drive to the factory. The seat beside me holds a bulky cardboard box. Inside are thirty brown paper sacks, each filled with one of Bobby's sandwiches, two of Bet's cookies or bars, a plastic side of slaw or beans, and Bobby's stroke of genius—a thick hash brown or turnover kept crisp in wax paper.

When they buzz me into the factory break room, the lunch crowd cheers for me. At first it made me feel silly, but there was the pull to be close to Jo. It's still there, no matter how much I'd like to shake it. She looks at me, smiling as if we have more than one secret, but as I hand round the bags she stands away. The men like it: not only the lunches, but the drama. They laugh silently at Jo, eyeing me from beside the pop machine. They watch the way my hair swings as I bend to take each sack out of the box. They watch the folds of my dress nibble my knees, the very fabric of my life impatient for Jo-Jo-Josephine, impatient for night and the magnet, the moment of the taking off. Taking in.

Taking her on.

It's still a charge. If we stayed together for what we each have of forever, it would always be like looking into the night sky and seeing stars for the first time. Once in a while I think of Pat, loving blue because it took him beyond the range of ordinary emotions. I understand his passion. The men know some of what I feel—maybe everyone understands desire's language—and turn their faces when there's one bag left. Jo steps up, hungry, but I don't kiss her while the men don't watch. They unwrap their sandwiches, pry open the plastic tops of slaw or beans, bite into the greasy treats wrapped in waxed paper (the practical ones eat that first, while it's hot), or nibble their way around the edges of Bet's desserts, savoring the nuts or chips glistening in the center of the chewy dough. They keep their tongues busy with flavor and their mouths full of selection, but they're listening, hoping for a clue to what binds me, even after Jo abandoned me.

Jo's return sparked a series of reconciliations among folks in Cartwheel who believed we were content. Some of the couplings were very beautiful, glinty the way a promise should be. But some masked betrayals. Some were lies, and others stable. Some happened in secret; I wouldn't know about those. I only know there were too many to celebrate.

Ours was secret and public both. Everyone knows we're back together, but no one knows I've gone cold inside again.

Not even Jo.

She doesn't know what I lost, how deep the scars. When she kneads me, I see colors. Sometimes I scream but there's still a part of me she hasn't touched. I hold back. There's something I haven't shown her yet—the shadow. The part of me I discovered while she was gone.

The part that can get along without her.

We never speak of it. It's only there in our touch, the way we kiss, and the glimpse I catch when she undresses—fur on her belly, a thin line guiding me like a map.

I haven't forgiven her. Not yet. Where forgiveness should bloom is a thin layer of anger, ice over kindness, kindness hard to the touch.

Frozen earth.

I'm thinking of leaving.

Jo likes to tell stories after sex, when we've rubbed the cricks out of each other's necks and kissed each other's mouths clean. She tells stories about people who love buildings and brothers, trees and animals. Fire. Then she runs her hands through the length of my hair. I feel tender towards her; I come round to understanding. She wants me to stand still so she can really run.

Tender, but disobedient. There will be wrecks, because the clock won't stop. Not for me, not for Jo, not for anyone. The hood will crumble, the forest will step forward, the engine will smoke and sputter, and the glass between you and blue freedom will break.

"Caddie," Jo says softly, the refrain of a song I only remember when it's sung, "don't you cut this." Flooding her hands with my hair, she repeats, "Don't you change."

I don't have the heart to tell her it's too late.

When Jo rolls my sleepy body over and nuzzles my belly, I feel she knows fire better than ever before. What happened changed her. Her hands prickle, little ashes, and her tongue becomes embers that leave a crimson flush on my throat and chest. Who might I be? There's an idea I have that I guard like my history, a secret I learned I don't know where. The country Peg vanishes to is close to my own.

How would I appear to Jo from there? I might find myself a man, wrists thickened with power. I might find myself a floaty ghost, following her from above the trees. I keep my eyes open, alert to things that sway. The trick is timing.

Her eyes are golden.

They used to be grey.

When I was in school, back when I thought teachers could actually give you something you could save and use, I did so well on all my tests that I was Caddie Star Pupil. There was a chart on the wall with our names printed longways. After each name, a row of stars for outstanding work. My strip was the longest. When I danced at The Depot, I wore stars on my breasts. Little pasties. Things come back around, just not the way you expect them. Jo's back, but she has that look in her eyes sometimes, the way Cat used to look at some live thing she'd trapped, paws a cage, tongue flickering. Enjoying most the decision to let it live or bleed it dry.

But the game feels old and over.

There's a difference between now and how we were back in the beginning. Back then, every day she woke and, first thing, decided whether to keep me. It was a battle between us, me charming her uphill and down, Jo testing me, always wanting what she couldn't have. Now it's me watching and wondering, unsure of whether, unsure of how long.

Some of what used to be easy is gone.

Before, it was simple not to touch her.

But after thinking through how and what with Gwen, after remaking myself, after making that switch, I want more from her than her body will give. Her eyes flutter open, asking for me. Her lips part slowly, but when I reach for her, she pulls away.

I don't want to travel alone to the places she sends me. I want her with me, I want us both to see the scenery. I want to taste what she tells me when she says I make her wet.

I want to know her.

But you can't force someone open, even under the guise of loving or equality. I'd be no better than a rapist then.

In my heart there's a request, written in silver pencil. *Let me touch you.* Josephine, are you listening? *You also hunger.* In my heart there's a request, written in silver pencil. *Tell the world who you are.* If I were still Caddie Solo, sooner or later it would come around to this: from a place of safety, surrounded by the things I'd need to flee, I'd shout her name, and shout my knowledge with it. I'd unpin my blouse, revealing a heart that beat for *her her her,* and never pin it back again. I'd find a city or island or country where I might teach my heart as I pleased and never be punished for it. Oh, inside I'm a reckless one. But I live with *him him him,* and so I cage my impulses, watch them wither.

I don't know if I have the nerve to draw the line in bed between us, in Passion Fruit lipstick, wavery because the sheets won't allow me to sketch it straight. The color might bleed through to the mattress below, a mis-carriage of the sort only two women could have. What would sweet Pat's sky say to my dilemma? But it's a question only I can ask and only Jo can answer. More than a wedding, I want my freedom, so I prepare myself to pop the question, practicing the words while staring at my own eyes in the bathroom mirror: *Won't you give the world a glimpse of who we are?*

Where will I go if she says no? Where will we go if she says yes? We have no country, no city, no street of safety. For now I stay quiet, listen-ing to the weather, wringing my hands, serving coffee and the $1.99 special to the regulars. I let their chatter wash over me, I watch Peg vanish and reappear, Bobby lose himself in his own cooking, Selena count. I wonder what sort of person Sean's becoming, and what Gwen will make of herself. I imagine Marv and Helen driving, following highway numbers on paper till their truck sails over a cliff. I imagine their tires turning to fiery wings and I watch the clock, wondering what it will take for me to want freedom more than love, imagining a place—some dazzling city in the past or future they never teach in history—where people have both.

EPILOGUE: SEAN
■ ■
■

The heat. The heat from Mazie's back and shoulders. She's facing away from me, curled towards the wall, her hair flung over the pillow, sloppy so I know it's Mazie. Six inches separate us, six inches at least. But I feel steam and then smoke rise from her skin. I feel the flush of her shoulders' new color. I smell singed hair and ash-soiled sheets.

Usually when this happens, I try to wake her. "C'mon, Mazie," I say. "Wake up. We're burning. We're going up in smoke."

Sometimes she won't wake no matter what I say. When I try shaking her, she just slips deeper into sleep, vanishing somewhere I think I'll never find her. But sometimes she responds, rolling over, so I think I've got her. She props herself up on one elbow, sort of smirky, and winks. She says, "Yes, sweetie?" in a smoky, B-movie-sexy kind of voice. "I know it. We're *hot.*" Then she laughs and laughs, and no matter how much I try to talk sense into her, she won't listen, leave, or see hellfire.

Tonight I'm awake, not dreaming, and she's alert, I can tell by the way she runs her fingers along the sheets, pretending to play, practicing even at four in the morning. She plays piano, and she's good, so good she makes a living at it. Her fingers never stop. They burn up the keys in coffee bars and the sheets on nights like this, when neither one of us can sleep for wondering what the other is thinking.

She rolls over. "Sweetie," she says, her voice sticky, "What's wrong?"

When she asks me the same question the next morning at breakfast, I do what I did the night before. I look her over like a painter, like someone in love, taking in all the little things, the mole on her left cheek, her straggly eyebrows, the lines at the corners of her mouth. She likes it when I look at her, I can tell, and also she's told me. "Sexy," she says, "sexy to be noticed." I use sexiness to evade the question. It always works. I feel bad, but not as bad as if I'd tried to tell Mazie some grand story.

We share an apartment that used to be just mine. We have electric heat. Even when winter does her worst, we keep it low. Mazie's warm-blooded. Definitely a mammal. And she has a plodding walk—that's a charmer. Her fingers fly but her feet sort of drag. It's the contrast that lures me—hands like wings, all speed and efficiency and drive, feet like stones, pebbles, gravelly, slowing her down the way rough roads slur breakneck drivers.

She's breakneck, all right. That's what I need. A woman who isn't afraid of anything, but whose body promises to keep her grounded.

Our apartment's the first floor of a shotgun house with two doors. I'm not taking any chances. And don't tell anyone, don't spread this around, but the windows are unlocked. Burglary's nothing compared to fire.

We've been together since my sophomore year in college, five years. She's starting to talk about babies. A baby, rather. She just wants one. Just. One. She says I don't have to do much work. She'll carry it, she'll stay home, she'll do the busy, boring stuff. I can have the fun part. But a baby. How can I tell her I know, if we had a baby, that the baby would burn? I'm not sure how; maybe it would burn inside her, the rose of her stomach glowing like some alien thing till her skin crackled and her face pained up and her belly split. Maybe the baby would be born all right, fingers and toes all accounted for, but then catch smoke suddenly, like cotton curtains, melting to ash, something charred, something Mazie would have to pick up, carry out with yesterday's trash or bury out back next to the run-over cat and the bird the cat killed a few weeks before it died.

But I just say I don't like children. I just say I don't like helplessness, don't like being responsible for anyone beside Mazie and me. She likes that because when I say it, I rub the back of her neck, tug on the scruff a little, like she's a kitten. She arches and sort of purrs. Mazie's so much to me. If I don't tell her something that might make her leave, who can blame me?

The piece that's missing has to do with fire.

Once I tried asking Aunt Gwen about my dreams. We were having dinner in the Avenues last year during my Christmas visit, just us two, and we both got tipsy. I don't know how she does it, Gwen; she's got a taste for almost every vice the Mormon church prohibits. Maybe when she's at home in St. George she's on better behavior, but when she visits my folks she really lets go. I used to joke about it with Mazie, but my jokes made Mazie sad.

"Lousy marriage," she said. I knew she was thinking of her own parents, years of ugliness leading to divorce. So I don't talk much with

Mazie about Aunt Gwen. They don't get along anyway—Gwen thinks Mazie isn't good enough for me, I can tell, but who is she to talk? She married LaMonte.

Gwen's a mystery. She can be so prissy. Then the wildness inside her shows through and I smile. We get along so well it feels like forever. I sometimes forget that Mom didn't even introduce us till I was fifteen.

"My sister and I needed space for a time," was all Mom said when I asked why this terrific aunt appeared out of nowhere. I wanted more info, but I knew not to press her. There are questions Mom answers and questions she won't.

We hit it off right away, Gwen and I. Now I see her twice a year when I visit my parents. She makes the six-hour drive from St. George to Salt Lake and sometimes she and Mom don't even talk. Sometimes it's all about visiting with me.

The closeness I feel with Gwen was what let me ask her about my dreams. There we were at dinner, Gwen peeking around to be sure no one she knew would spot her ordering red wine and espresso, me drizzling Italian over my salad, not thinking much about whether she'd like my question or not, just curious, and tired of setting fire to my own skin. "Gwen," I said, "every night, practically, I have this dream." I spread the dressing around with my fork till every leaf, carrot, radish, and crouton was covered evenly. "It's always the same." Then I described it: I'm an infant, just a bundle in a blanket, and someone's carrying me, someone I know intimately. She's walking quickly. Everything is fine, everything is dandy, till whoosh! Whoever it is starts sprinting. I'm jostled against her hip, slipping down, nearly falling. Till then my eyes are closed—I'm a baby, sleepy in that baby sort of way—but when I open them, everything is the wrong color. The sky is violet, and the building we're running past is orange, almost. Red streaks jump out at me like the hands of strangers with blue sparks for lollipops, and as we round the corner of the building, the fire catches the edge of my flannel blanket.

Then things slow down, like an instant replay on ESPN. I watch it spread, first low like Mazie's whispers, then fast like the legs of whoever's carrying me. I cry out, but she doesn't notice the sound I'm making. Only when the flame is singeing my hair does she stop, startled, and beat the fire out with her sleeves. That's where the dream ends, with black cloth covering me, wiping everything away, danger and breath both.

Whoever carried me saw the flames like a painting and listened to the crinkling, collapsing structure like an opera.

When I finished my story, I glanced up at Gwen's face.

"Have you told your folks?"

When I said no, she looked relieved. I watched her struggle with whether to tell whatever she thought she knew, but then her anxiety smoothed out and she turned into Sister Leavitt, very proper.

I knew then that I'd lost her. I knew she'd never tell.

The life Gwen's living is all wrong for her. I say this again and again to Mom and Dad and even Mazie, but they just shrug. "People make choices," Mom or Dad says. "I wouldn't feel sorry, sweetie." And Mazie, "She can leave if she wants out, can't she?" They don't seem to understand. It's not that I pity her, it's that I can't figure her out, and I want to. I can't shake the feeling that the key to Gwen unlocks more than just her history.

I don't like mystery. I like knowing. I try to let Mazie know everything, except about the flames nipping her own skin in my fiery night terrors.

Mazie burns. Maybe if I told her about my dreams, I'd stop the hallucinations and our life together would be normal, nights full of sleep, mornings full of toast, newspaper headlines. Not this dazzling neon, not this perpetual secret misunderstanding. Would I miss the radiance? But she'd burn anyway—even without my craziness, Mazie'd burn like oil.

The dreams started right before my senior year at IU. Before then I barely remembered my dreams. Feeling haunted was new to me. After a few months it got so bad I saw a counselor. I was doing everything I could to keep the dreams away. For a while I woke myself up with an alarm every hour, thinking it'd keep me from dozing deep enough to dream. But it made me nuts, not ever sleeping. I got so tired I fell asleep in broad daylight driving down Kirkwood, almost hit a jaywalker. It was serious. So I went over to Student Health and asked to see a therapist. They were going to make me wait a month, but when I said "arson," they set up an appointment right away. It was pretty useless. The fellow rambled on about theories of dream analysis, Freud mostly, and tried to tell me I was scared of sex or in love with my mother or gay. Hardly. What no one seems to get, except maybe Gwen, is that the dream isn't a metaphor for anything.

The dream is real.

It's four in the morning. Mazie's burning. I wish it were coffee I smelled, I wish I were dreaming. But her skin. I'm awake and my girlfriend's skin is blooming rose, so bright she's in danger of stopping traffic or bursting whole. I don't say "dying." It's a word I won't speak around Mazie. If we had children, I'd have no problems talking sex, no problems teaching them how to make life livelier. But death? The soiled skin, the crumpled expression, the finality—it's death I couldn't describe. My children would grow up knowing every word for "fuck" in the English language, but thinking—I mean honestly believing—they'd live forever.

When a body burns, I bet you smell it first, and the smell makes you think of water. Bodies of water. Oceanic. I bet you smell salt, and then you see the face dissolving in orange soot, a light so terrible that for days after, you sit in the dark. Sometimes in summer I'll be walking and the sun will strike metal or someone's mirrored shades. I'll catch a glimpse, just a glimpse, of unapproachable light. I stop dead—Mazie was the one who pointed this out to me—I stop dead on the street or sidewalk or steps and close my eyes till the light fades and I say my own name again.

"Sean," Mazie says. "Sean." Because her voice is full of sleep, wet and steamy, I smile.

"I'm here," I say, though really I'm somewhere else. She curls into me and I cover her with my whole body. When we make love, I wash over her, dampening flushed skin. I wet her body with my tongue, every inch, so nothing's left flammable. She thinks that lust makes me so hungry for her. I wish it were true. But I know the difference between ecstasy and fear. When we're inside each other, I see, out of the corner of my eyes, a great wall of fire rising out of sheets of grey metal heading towards me, towards us, because right then Mazie and I are one, one body, and the fire's spreading. If it were only me burning, I could stand it. I could learn to sleep. But it eats her skin too, and so it has to stop.

"Sean," Mazie says again. She never snores but speaks my name like a mantra. I bend to listen, resting my face on her chest, my eyes shut tight against the smoke. "I'm burning up," she says, or maybe I do. It's nearly morning. The light coming in through the curtains is different from the light in my midnight dreams, pale and unhurried. The alarm is my secret signal. *Time to forget,* the clock sings. All day long I do my best, erasing fire, erasing flames from my consciousness. All day long I pretend I'm not afraid to burn.

When I first met Mazie, she was in love with someone else. She lived off campus in a huge, rambly house out on Bloomington's west side. Her three roomies, all male, were musicians too. I somehow got asked to one of their parties. It wasn't the sort of thing I was usually invited to. Everyone was in vintage clothing, drinking microbrews, talking very earnestly about postmodern architecture, Sonny Rollins, and sodomy laws. I tried striking up a conversation with an anemic-looking girl in a striped lycra top, but she laughed at me when I asked her whether Steve Reich was art or music. I slunk outside to smoke and kill time until my ride was ready to leave.

Right off I noticed a dark-haired woman about my age with less piercings, makeup, and tattoos than the rest of her clique. I could actually see her skin, which I've always found attractive in a woman. "I'm sure he's bi," she was saying. "I can tell by the way he looks at me."

"But Mazie, the *shoes!*" one of the others said, and they all nodded their heads. One touched Mazie's cheek, not quite tenderly. I wanted to watch, but it seemed private, erotic, and I turned away. I got absorbed in my cigarette then—I was trying to quit using a Zen-like attention to the feel of each smoke—and didn't notice as the girls filed back into the house. When I realized I was alone, I burped. Then I stubbed out my cigarette and turned to go back inside.

"Gross." It was the dark-haired woman, sounding like some prissy Jane Austen character. "You don't have to act like such a slob."

"I didn't see you," I said defensively. "It was just a burp." It took me a few seconds to realize she was kidding.

"You're slow," she said.

"True." I kept thinking about the girl stroking her cheek. While I was standing there thinking this over, Mazie introduced herself and asked my name. Then she took me by the shoulders and marched me inside.

"Let's see what he wants," she said. I had no idea what she was talking about, but it felt good to have someone pay attention to me. The girls were clustered around inside the kitchen and filed after us, like ducks. I couldn't believe it; I'd never had a woman try to seduce me before. Everything sexual up to then had had a scratchy quality to it, like listening to the radio with the dial a fraction off. Mazie shepherded me through clumps of people eating chips and touching one another's faces till we reached a screened-in porch off the side of the house.

"Eric," Mazie said to a young, erudite-looking man, who barely halted his conversation. "Eric, make up your mind." One of the women behind us giggled till another shushed her. I realized then that Mazie was absolutely drunk. "What'll it be—boys, girls, or both?"

The minute Mazie finished her question, Eric strode over to her, tore her from me, and hugged her till she disappeared. One by one the women joined in till the porch was a giant heap of humped bodies, speaking to each other in some language I knew I'd never understand.

I can't remember how I got home that night. I only know I had a hangover the next morning, even though I hadn't slept with anyone or drunk anything but tiny sips of Mazie's beer. I saw Eric around campus from time to time and felt thankful that he never seemed to recognize me. After a while I forgot all about Mazie. Then New Year's rolled around, and I found myself alone again on the 31st. I was sick of girlfriends who dumped me days before major holidays, still reeling from the usual family scenes I'd encountered in my annual trip home. So I decided the best thing to do was to hide in my apartment. Around eight o'clock I ventured out to stock up on candy bars and rent a video. In line before me, practically the only customer, was Mazie, tapping her foot impatiently while one bored cashier replaced another. When I said "Hello," she glared at me like I was harassing her. "We met at Jon's party," I added quickly.

Mazie frowned. "I don't remember you." Then she shook a finger at me. "You must be Jon's ex."

"I'm straight."

"I am *so* sorry."

"No, I'm sorry. I didn't mean—"

"Which party was it?"

"It had a Love Boat theme, but no one was dressed up or anything. It was the one where you and Eric got together."

Mazie was still looking me over, but her eyes weren't quite so hostile. "Eric's gay."

"That's what you were trying to figure out. He hugged you. There was a whole bunch of girls and you had me by the shoulders." Her look was hostile again. "Never mind," I said and pulled a *National Enquirer* off the rack. While the cashier rang her up, I busied myself reading about some starlet's illegitimate baby's cosmetic surgery. But once Mazie had her things stashed in a grey plastic bag, she stood looking lost while the cashier ran my things over the electric scanner. When I had my stuff, I smiled at her, and she frowned back. We walked to the parking lot together. It was starting to snow.

After that we hung out once in a while, but nothing ever seemed to happen. Then one night I was hanging out in her room and it got late and the weather went downhill and it just seemed to make more sense to stay than to go. When we kissed for the first time, I stopped being scared. The next morning when we stumbled into the kitchen, all three of her roomies were sitting around the rickety table, big smiles on their faces.

Things moved fast. I thought then that it was because I'd never been so in love before, but I know now that's just how things are with me and Mazie. She's even more intense than I am, if that's possible. The air rubs us raw and the wind salts our eyes. The good thing is that her intensity sort of crosses mine out, and vice versa. We can be calm together, calm enough to slog through ordinary things that were tough before. All except my dreams. All except the slow burn and the fiery mystery.

When we first started sleeping together, there was no smoke in sight. We'd fuck or make love or have sex, depending on our moods, and everything would get frenzied or soft and then slowly return to normal. There was a wildness to it, the good kind, the kind they describe in books where the characters seem to be out of control but are really only moving towards the most ordinary kind of love and togetherness. Our passion felt like something outside us, but it always came from inside, and we knew it. We felt safe enough to pretend we were dangerous. Then, over a year after we first got together, something happened to split me apart—just me, not Mazie. Not even an event. Just a feeling of something finishing or maybe starting. That's when I began dreaming, deep dreams full of smoke.

I've been surrounded by sizzling ash ever since.

The dreams started after a little road trip we took the summer before our senior year. We'd both stayed in Bloomington, me working at the greeting card company where I work full-time now, Mazie giving piano lessons here and there but mostly living off student loans so she could practice five, six hours a day. She'd fall into bed exhausted. For a time she was too tired to do much more than kiss. Then her fingers settled into their calluses and she came back again, whole.

Midsummer she decided she needed two days off. "Let's get away this weekend," she suggested over dinner. It was easy enough for me to say yes. I was making enough money for a weekend jaunt, and my leisure time, unlike Mazie's, was leisurely. So that Saturday we got up extra early and joshed around the kitchen making silly sandwiches—PBJ, marshmallow, cinnamon-sugar—packing baggies full of raisins, nuts, and chocolate chips. We loaded the snacks and some soda into a cooler, tossed two days' worth of clothes into backpacks (neither one of us owned a suitcase) and drove down Walnut out of Bloomington. Mazie waved as we passed the golf course; we cheered as we hit 37.

We'd agreed in advance not to bring maps. Mazie has a keen sense of direction, and between the two of us we'd driven to Chicago, Ann Arbor, Madison, Cleveland, Louisville, and Champagne-Urbana: three conferences, one wedding, two road trips. So we knew the highways. Although we weren't sure where we wanted to go this time, we figured it should be someplace hopping. "Chicago," Mazie suggested in the kitchen. That seemed cool, but once we were actually in the car, the sandwiches seemed all wrong for a sophisticated trip to an urban center. "I'm not dressed for it," Mazie said, changing her mind. "Why don't we just toodle around Indiana some, see if any small towns have cute bed and breakfasts or weird museums?"

I liked the idea. I'm not much for pretentiousness, having spent my childhood and adolescence hanging around in my folks' four-star French restaurant. It made me jaded. When I left Salt Lake City for Bloomington, I resolved never to wear black jeans or use more than three utensils to eat my food. Mazie, on the other hand, aspires to elegance. She grew up solidly middle-class, and now she's fascinated by both extreme wealth and the kind of poverty I'm afraid she sometimes finds picturesque. What she hates is the in-between: the neat checkered curtains, ROUND TUIT pot holders, and cautious polyester loungewear she grew up with. If we weren't going to bum around Chicago, she seemed to think, we should aim for the outer reaches of the Midwest—the Cowboy Junkies' version of trailer parks, the Simpsons' version of pubs and RVs. I was fine with the idea of slumming, so long—though I didn't say this to Mazie—as we kept our hilarity private. No one wants to be parodied. I'd learned this from Aunt Gwen.

The year I turned sixteen, Gwen gave me a tour of the church back in St. George, where LaMonte worked as a secretary. They had videos describing "Mormon Family Values" and "Life Everlasting," a tiny model of the Temple made out of sugar cubes and blown-up photos of the rooms made to represent the various post-death geographies a Mormon could traverse. While she was chauffeuring me around, her face aglow with the lushness of everything, eager for me to be impressed, and, indeed, impressing me, a boy and girl came in through one of the side doors. They looked to be only two or three years older than me, and somehow I could tell that they were lovers. They were also decidedly not Mormon. The girl's breasts were visible through her thin shirt, and the boy wore nylon running shorts. No one paid them much mind as they breezed into the showroom—Mormons rely heavily on recruitment, after all, so gentiles are more than welcome to fly into the web—but I was fascinated by their casual sensuality. The girl was drawn immediately to the sugary replica. While she stared at it, I imagined taking the glass lid off the polished case, and feeding her bits of the model temple. Her tongue would slide over each sugary bite. When it was over (her boyfriend miraculously vanished for the occasion), she'd kiss me, and use her tongue, the way I'd seen the bus boy do with the hostess behind the dumpster at La Terrace.

But instead of parting her dark red lips for my slippery fingers, the girl snickered as her boyfriend whistled. "C'mere!" She ambled over to where he was standing, glancing down at one of the huge, glossy photos of the temple room meant to represent the Celestial Kingdom.

"*That's* their idea of heaven?" The girl's whisper traveled like her scent: laundry detergent.

"Can you imagine? Ethan Allen furniture, fake baroque chandeliers, and wall-to-wall carpeting. My god."

"I bet hell is a queer nightclub," the girl giggled. Beside me, I felt Gwen's blush rise off her cheeks like steam from a teacup. She took me by the shoulders and hurried me out of the room. After she'd sped me through the corridor, through the lobby, and outside onto the plaza, she covered her mouth with her hands and stood very still. For a second I thought she was going to vomit or, less embarrassing, curse. But instead her body shook and I realized she was laughing.

"It's too true, Sean," she said. Her cheeks grew even rounder when she laughed. "It's too true."

I was stuck then, my hand already raised to comfort her. So I slapped my thigh instead—ha, ha. This was when I first began to realize that there were two sides to Gwen: the proper Mormon wife she became alongside LaMonte, and the giggly, irreverent kid she showed me, my folks, and maybe her non-Mormon lady friends.

I didn't want Mazie and me to replay that scene, traipsing into some cheesy gift shop, waving our hunger for each other like a banner, flashing our collegiate intellectualism like a shiny sword. I figured if we hit some small town and found it amusing, fine, but we should at least keep our amusement to ourselves. Of course I was thinking of me, not Mazie. It's always struck me, her earnestness. She's not a do-gooder, but she has it in her to be, which is better.

Twenty minutes out of Martinsville we turned off the highway and just drove, letting ourselves wander the way the wheels wanted. The roads grew less and less tended, gravel even. We passed field after farm after field till a stop light loomed out of the nothingness of corn and scrub and spotty trees. Beside the stop light was a big wooden sign with gold lettering. "YOU ARE ENTERING CARTWHEEL, INDIANA" the sign said. "VOTED MOST LIVEABLE COMMUNITY."

"How many people constitute a community? I mean, is it like a city or a town or what?"

"I've never heard of Cartwheel, so it's probably tiny. Maybe the size of Elletsville or Spencer."

Mazie sucked on the end of her ponytail. "Take a left at the next stop. I want to see where that road up there is headed."

The left took us down what must've been the main drag. Then a short drive till "YOU ARE LEAVING CARTWHEEL, INDIANA. VOTED MOST LIVEABLE COMMUNITY. " Beyond the sign, a dark stretch of trees closed in. "Too bad," Mazie said. "I was hoping to sleep in Cartwheel tonight."

"We could go back and find a hotel."

"I'm not sure there was one."

We drove on a little further, not talking, just humming to the Nashville pop that was all we'd found on the radio since leaving Bloomington. When we reached a driveway, Mazie gestured for me to turn around. "We're almost out of gas," she observed. I felt silly for not noticing sooner. We hadn't passed a gas station in Cartwheel, so I wasn't sure if I should turn around.

"Should we try to make it to the next town?"

"We'll run out. Let's turn around, stop somewhere, and ask where the nearest station is." We drove back to Cartwheel. When we hit the main drag, Mazie gestured towards a diner I didn't remember passing. "That place is hopping. Pull in and ask. If we keep on, we'll hit bottom." I turned sharply into the parking lot. The tires squealed and I felt sheepish. Once I got the car parked, I realized why Mazie had picked the place. It's a standing argument between Mazie and me. She likes kitsch. Her old apartment was full of Elvis ashtrays, pink flamingos, and art deco cups in strange pastels. She likes to think it's about being an artiste. I think it's nostalgia for her failed attempt as a fag hag. She's always trying to get me to see the humor in camp, but I can't, the same way I can't see the beauty in music that's all uphill. But I bit my tongue and she knew it, because she turned to me before she opened her door and kissed me, hard the way I like, right where my throat becomes my left shoulder. It went on some, the kiss, and I kept my eyes open, looking up at the sign hanging over the diner.

A gaudy neon heart.

"I'm hungry. Let's grab something to eat while we're here."

Mazie's kiss must've lulled me into a stupor, because I nodded. I knew right off I'd hate the place, not just because of the silly, sentimental decor, but because the food was bound to be bland, greasy, and ordinary. I have a taste for good food and cook very well. It's a serious skill. Dad says I learned from growing up in the kitchen of La Terrace. He tells stories about how, when I was an infant, he used to prop me up on the counter and let me watch when he broke in a new chef. I like the story and don't have the heart to tell him I know the restaurant didn't open until I was five. My parents can be so clueless sometimes. They haven't realized, still, that I see through the lies they tell me about their history. Seems to me there are two possibilities. They were Mormon, but they're ashamed to admit they were ever a part of the church they're now so scornful of, or they were poor, and they're ashamed to admit they ever struggled. Maybe both—Mormon and poor, like Gwen. But even though I speculate, I don't ever push. It's their business. I figure when they're ready to tell me, they will.

The sign read "Diner, My Love." Inside it was all hearts. I'd been thinking to hate it, to gag at the smell of burgers fried in weeks of chicken fat, to stumble when I saw piles of greasy fries and ham biscuits mingling irreverently with Jell-O on cracked plates. But the moment we stepped inside, my wariness vanished.

"Two for lunch?" A waitress in a yellow dress approached us, holding out menus like garden flowers. I felt my throat freeze. Mazie was silent too, and we both took tiny steps through the sunlight puddling the checkered floor. When we slid into the booth, the waitress smiled at us both, but her gaze lingered on me, as if she wanted to ask a question. Sometimes now I think about going back, asking her what she wanted to ask me. But right then I couldn't make questions out of anything I was feeling, could only stare at her, my lips gummy and heavy. She filled her dress like a pillow. I could smell flour and coffee rising up from her skin. Her eyes were smart, and her face was wrinkling, tiny creases like secrets just beginning, the way grey was just beginning to streak her reddish-black hair. She was a good waitress, serious, but funny on her off hours, you could tell by the way she walked. I imagined that when she kissed whomever she loved, she used her whole body, its thickness a promise. I remember the music playing because she did a two-step when she left our table, not fast but stately, as if she were old already and liked being old, liked her dignity. She filled the place up. I felt swallowed but in a good way. I wanted to touch her apron or tug on her sleeves.

Mazie was smitten too. I know because she's my lover and I can read her. There was desire written in the slump of her shoulders and it felt funny, watching Mazie fall for someone else, knowing she was seeing the same startling lust in me. Suddenly love was confusing and transient, but I didn't care, I just stayed put, wishing for another bouquet, wishing for that scent of flour and coffee and maybe cream. Mazie and I just sat, not speaking, till I realized desire was everywhere. The rest of the diner was in love also, and we smiled at each other and held hands across the table.

We hadn't even opened our menus by the time she came back, so we ordered blindly—grilled cheese, I think. We ate blindly too, and ordered more and kept eating, both of us, not speaking, just watching our waitress bring plate after plate. We drank coffee till our fingers tingled, till we couldn't hold our cups steady, but still we held up empties just to watch her pour—sturdy arms muscular and soft at once.

We stayed till the diner closed. Mazie and I watched our waitress walk down the road alone. While she walked, she ran her fingers through her hair, a thick messy mop cut just above her ears. The gesture was little-girlish, but her walk was jaunty. At the corner she stopped and shaded her eyes. Then we'd stared too long for politeness' sake, so we hopped into the car, navigated the crooked driveway, found Cartwheel's only gas station, and drove back to Bloomington. No more talk of bed and breakfasts, weird museums, or traveling to Chi-town.

That night the fire dreams started.

ABOUT THE AUTHOR

■ ■
■

Carol Guess wrote *Seeing Dell* (Cleis, 1996), a novel of remarkable clarity and lyricism about a woman taxi driver living in the Midwest. She is also the author of two unpublished novels, *Island a Strata* and *Retrieval*, and a poetry collection, *Femme's Dictionary*. Her poetry and short fiction appear regularly in literary journals. She earned a BA from Columbia University (New York) and an MA and MFA from Indiana University (Bloomington). Currently at work on her fifth novel, she lives in Bellingham, Washington, where she teaches creative writing at Western Washington University.

SELECTED TITLES FROM AWARD-WINNING CALYX BOOKS

NONFICTION

Natalie on the Street by Ann Nietzke. A day-by-day account of the author's relationship with an elderly homeless woman who lived on the streets of Nietzke's central Los Angeles neighborhood. *PEN West Finalist.*
ISBN 0-934971-41-2, $14.95, paper; ISBN 0-934971-42-0, $24.95, cloth.

The Violet Shyness of Their Eyes: Notes from Nepal by Barbara J. Scot. A moving account of a western woman's transformative sojourn in Nepal as she reaches mid-life. *PNBA Book Award.*
ISBN 0-934971-35-8, $15.95, paper; ISBN 0-934971-36-6, $24.95, cloth.

In China with Harpo and Karl by Sibyl James. Essays revealing a feminist poet's experiences while teaching in Shanghai, China.
ISBN 0-934971-15-3, $9.95, paper; ISBN 0-934971-16-1, $17.95, cloth.

FICTION

Second Sight by Rickey Gard Diamond. A chilling portrait of one family's complicated and violent interactions, this debut novel details the friendship of two women entwined in their relationship with a violent man.
ISBN 0-934971-55-2, $14.95, paper; ISBN 0-934971-56-0, $28.95, cloth.

Four Figures in Time by Patricia Grossman. Tracks the lives of four characters in a New York City art school. It's full of astute observations on modern life as the rarefied world of making art meets the mundane world of making ends meet.
ISBN 0-934971-47-1, $13.95, paper; ISBN 0-934971-48-X, $25.95, cloth.

The Adventures of Mona Pinsky by Harriet Ziskin. In this fantastical novel, a 65-year-old Jewish woman, facing alienation and ridicule, comes of age and ultimately is reborn on a heroine's journey.
ISBN 0-934971-43-9, $12.95, paper; ISBN 0-934971-44-7, $24.95, cloth.

Killing Color by Charlotte Watson Sherman. These compelling, mythical short stories by a gifted storyteller explore the African-American experience. *Washington Governor's Award.*
ISBN 0-934971-17-X, $9.95, paper; ISBN 0-934971-18-8, $19.95, cloth.

Mrs. Vargas and the Dead Naturalist by Kathleen Alcalá. Fourteen stories set in Mexico and the Southwestern U.S., written in the tradition of magical realism.
ISBN 0-934971-25-0, $9.95, paper; ISBN 0-934971-26-9, $19.95, cloth.

Ginseng and Other Tales from Manila by Marianne Villanueva. Poignant short stories set in the Philippines. *Manila Critic's Circle National Literary Award Nominee.*
ISBN 0-934971-19-6, $9.95, paper; ISBN 0-934971-20-X, $19.95, cloth.

POETRY

Details of Flesh by Cortney Davis. In this frank exploration of caregiving in its many guises, Davis reveals the necessary and intimate distance between patient and caregiver in an unflinching examination of pain and grief.
ISBN 0-934971-57-9, $11.95, paper; ISBN 0-934971-58-7, $23.95, cloth.

Another Spring, Darkness: Selected Poems of Anuradha Mahapatra translated by Carolyne Wright et.al. The first English translation of poetry by this working-class woman from West Bengal. "These are burning poems, giving off a spell of light." —Linda Hogan
ISBN 0-934971-51-X, $12.95 paper; ISBN 0-934971-52-8, $23.95, cloth.

The Country of Women by Sandra Kohler. A collection of poetry that explores woman's experience as sexual being, as mother, as artist. Kohler finds art in the mundane, the sacred, and the profane.
ISBN 0-934971-45-5, $11.95, paper; ISBN 0-934971-46-3, $21.95, cloth.

Light in the Crevice Never Seen by Haunani-Kay Trask. This first book of poetry by an indigenous Hawaiian to be published in North America is about a Native woman's love for her land, and the inconsolable grief and rage that come from its destruction.
ISBN 0-934971-37-4, $11.95, paper; ISBN 0-934971-38-2, $21.95, cloth.

Open Heart by Judith Mickel Sornberger. An elegant collection of poetry rooted in a woman's relationships with family, ancestors, and the world.
ISBN 0-934971-31-5, $9.95, paper; ISBN 0-934971-32-3, $19.95, cloth.

Raising the Tents by Frances Payne Adler. A personal and political volume of poetry, documenting a Jewish woman's discovery of her voice.
ISBN 0-934971-33-1, $9.95, paper; ISBN 0-934971-34-X, $19.95, cloth.

Black Candle: Poems about Women from India, Pakistan, and Bangladesh by Chitra Divakaruni. Lyrical and honest poems that chronicle significant moments in the lives of South Asian women. *Gerbode Award*.
ISBN 0-934971-23-4, $9.95, paper; ISBN 0-934971-24-2, $19.95 cloth.

Indian Singing by Gail Tremblay. A brilliant work of hope by a Native American poet. Fall 1998. Revised edition.
ISBN 0-934971-64-1, $11.95, paper; ISBN 0-934971-65-X, $23.95, cloth.

Idleness Is the Root of All Love by Christa Reinig, translated by Ilze Mueller. These poems by the prize-winning German poet accompany two older lesbians through a year together in love and struggle.
ISBN 0-934971-21-8, $10, paper; ISBN 0-934971-22-6, $18.95, cloth.

ANTHOLOGIES

A Line of Cutting Women edited by Beverly McFarland, et al. The best prose from 22 years of *CALYX Journal*—a long line of acclaimed women share their visions, cut into the silence and cut out a space in the literary canon. Available Fall 1998.
ISBN 0-934971-62-5, $14.95, paper; ISBN 0-934971-63-3, $28.95, cloth.

Present Tense: Writing and Art by Young Women edited by Micki Reaman, et al. This anthology showcases the art and literature of 46 contributors (ages 14 to 33), providing a fascinating glimpse into the future generation of feminist writing and art. This is a literature not merely read, but spoken, performed, sung, and slammed.
ISBN 0-934971-53-6, $14.95, paper; ISBN 0-934971-54-4, $26.95, cloth.

The Forbidden Stitch: An Asian American Women's Anthology edited by Shirley Geok-lin Lim, et al. The first Asian American women's anthology, this collection explores the multiplicity of experiences and concerns Asian American women face. *American Book Award.*
ISBN 0-934971-04-8, $16.95, paper; ISBN 0-934971-10-2, $32.00, cloth.

Women and Aging, An Anthology by Women edited by Jo Alexander, et al. The only anthology that addresses ageism from a feminist perspective. A rich collection of older women's voices.
ISBN 0-934971-00-5, $15.95, paper; ISBN 0-934971-07-2, $28.95, cloth.

CALYX International Anthology edited by Barbara Baldwin and Margarita Donnelly. This stunning dual-language anthology of translated work by women from twenty countries spans centuries and the world. It features poetry by 1996 Nobel Laureate Wislawa Szymborska (translated by Grazyna Drabik and Sharon Olds) and the first color reprints of Frida Kahlo's art work published in the U.S.
ISBN 0-934971-59-5, $12.00, paper.

Florilegia: A Retrospective of CALYX, A Journal of Art and Literature by Women, 1976–86 edited by the CALYX Editorial Collective. This selection of fine literary and artistic work from *CALYX Journal*'s first decade includes 96 contributors: Paula Gunn Allen, Julia Alvarez, Ellen Bass, Olga Broumas, Frida Kahlo, Barbara Kingsolver, Betty LaDuke, Elizabeth Layton, Ursula K. LeGuin, Ada Medina, Sharon Olds, Margaret Randall, Eleanor Wilner, and more.
ISBN 0-934971-06-4, $12.00, paper; ISBN 0-934971-09-9, $24.95, cloth.

CALYX Books are available to the trade from Consortium and other major distributors and jobbers.

Individuals may order direct from CALYX Books, P.O. Box B, Corvallis, OR 97339. Send check or money order in U.S. currency; add $3.00 postage for first book, $1.00 each additional book. Credit card orders only: FAX to 541-753-0515 or call toll-free 1-888-FEM BOOK

CALYX, A JOURNAL OF ART AND LITERATURE BY WOMEN

CALYX, A Journal of Art and Literature by Women, has showcased the work of over two thousand women artists and writers since 1976. Committed to providing a forum for *all* women's voices, *CALYX* presents diverse styles, images, issues, and themes which women writers and artists are exploring.

CALYX holds a special place in my heart. Some of my very first published words—two poems—were published in CALYX years ago. I've never forgotten the thrill of turning those beautifully illustrated pages and seeing my name, my earnest words, printed there alongside those of some of my literary heroines. It made me feel as if I belonged to the important company of women.
— Barbara Kingsolver

The work you do brings dignity, intelligence, and a sense of wholeness to the world. I am only one of many who bows respectfully—to all of you and to your work. —Barry Lopez

Published in June and November; three issues per volume.

CALYX Journal is available to the trade from Ingram Periodicals and other major distributors.

CALYX Journal is available at your local bookstore or direct from:
CALYX, Inc., P.O. Box B, Corvallis, OR 97339

CALYX Books and CALYX Journal
CALYX is committed to producing books of
literary, social, and feminist integrity.

CALYX, Inc., is a nonprofit organization with a 501(C)(3) status.
All donations are tax deductible.